Selected Works of
BA JIN

THE FAMILY
AUTUMN IN SPRING

FOREIGN LANGUAGES PRESS   BEIJING

First Edition   1988

Translated by
Sidney Shapiro
and
Wang Mingjie

Illustrations by
Liu Danzhai
and
Huang Yinghao

ISBN 7-119-00574-X
ISBN 0-8351-1319-1

Published by the Foreign Languages Press
24 Baiwanzhuang Road, Beijing, China

Printed by the Foreign Languages Printing House
19 West Chegongzhuang Road, Beijing, China

Distributed by China International Book Trading Corporation
(Guoji Shudian), P.O. Box 399, Beijing, China

Printed in the People's Republic of China

CONTENTS

In Shanghai (1940)

In Shanghai (1947)

FOREWORD

I began writing novels in spring 1927, when a friend of mine and I were living in lodgings in the Latin quarter in Paris. In an essay entitled "Reminiscences," written later, I described the room:

It was a small room. The window was open all day. Below it was a quiet street with only a few people. At the corner of the street was a small café and from my window I could see people walking in through its wide open glass door. But I never heard any noise of drunkenness or gambling. Directly opposite me was an old, high building, which obstructed not only my view but also the rays of the sun, thus making my small room, already filled with the smell of gas and onion, look even more gloomy and depressing.

In the same essay I wrote about my life at the time:

My life was very simple and monotonous. Every morning, I went for a walk in the Luxembourg Park. In the evening, I went to night school for my French lessons. During the day, I stayed at home and let the old and shabby books eat away my youth, books which nobody would bother to read. Very often, after some unbearably quiet moments, the air suddenly began trembling. So, too, the street and even my room. The rumbling sound reverberated in my ears and I completely forgot where I was. Everything around me seemed to be undergoing great changes. Gradually, however, the sound died away. Experience told me that a heavily loaded lorry had gone past on the cobbled street below. Soon, silence resumed its reign. Slowly I stood up, walked to the window and leaned out to look at the seemingly wounded street. I looked at the small café, which was also very quiet, and I could see a few people drinking and humming a tune or two. An unbearable feeling of loneliness once again overwhelmed me.

After eleven o'clock, my friend Wei and I came out of the night school and we walked on the quiet street, which was drenched with rain. With my eyes set on the almond-coloured sky and the two tombstone-like towers of Notre Dame, I could feel the inextinguishable flames again burning in my heart. One evening, I was walking by myself on the path beside the Panthéon and came to the bronze statue of Rousseau.   Unintentionally, I stretched out my arm and stroked the icy stone base as if I were stroking someone very dear to me.   I looked up at the giant who was holding a straw hat and a book in his hand, the thinker whom Tolstoy called "the conscience of the whole eighteenth-century world."   For a good while, I stood there, all my miseries forgotten until the heavy foot-steps of the policeman made me realize all of a sudden what kind of world I was living in.

Every night, I got back to the lodging-house, tired.   After a short rest, I lighted the gas stove and made tea.   Then the bells of Notre Dame began ringing out their mournful notes, which knocked heavily at my heart.

In circumstances like these, memories of my past again came back to torture me.   I thought of my life in Shanghai, my friends in their battles.   I thought of my past loves and hates, joys and sorrows, hopes and struggles, pains suffered and sympathies received.   As I thought of all my past, I felt a severe pain in my heart, as if it had been cut through by a sharp knife.   The inextinguishable flames began to burn fiercely again.

Then it happened.

In order to alleviate the pain in my young and lonely heart, I began writing about the few things I had gleaned from life.   Every night, listening to the chimes of Notre Dame, I wrote in my exercise book something which read like parts of a novel.   Within three months, I completed the first four chapters of *Destruction*.*

So, even I myself had never expected that I would turn out to be a writer.   I went on writing for the next thirty years and whiled away, at my desk, the best time of my life.   Many a time, I have said that I would "give up art" and "put an end to my writing career."   But I have not been able to do so.

My major works were all written in the twenty years from 1927 to 1946.   In the long period before Liberation (1949), my life as a writer was painful.   I have confessed before: "When I am burning with passion, my heart is about to explode and I don't know where to place it; I feel that I must write.   I am not an artist, and writing is only part of my life, which, like my works, is full of contradictions.   The conflicts between love and hate, thought and action, reason and emotion — these combine to weave a net enwrapping my whole life and all my works.   My life, as well as my works, is a painful struggle.

---

* Ba Jin's first novel. — *Trans.*

Every novel of mine carries my cry in my pursuit of light. . . .
At the same time, the picture of extreme pain and suffering is
like a whip lashing me from behind." Inevitably, I could only
pick up my pen and write. I wrote to my heart's content,
throwing all caution to the winds.

Time marches on. Read in the present new age, my works
appear to have so little force; they are so colourless.

Even so, I have made selections from my past writings to
represent the fruits of several decades of my literary endeavour.
What gives me courage in reprinting these old pieces is my firm
belief in writing, which is still very much with me. In 1935,
I wrote:

> I will never lose hope. There may be different styles and
> emphases in my works, but the basic thinking which prompts their
> creation is the same. Ever since I started writing, I have never
> stopped attacking my enemies. And who are they? All the out-
> moded, old ideas, all the absurd systems which have been obstruct-
> ing the path of social progress and man's development, all the forces
> which seek to destroy love — these are my enemies. . . .

My works, I hope, will bear witness to my words above. I
have been writing for over fifty years. I have been searching,
all my long life. I am nearing eighty now, but I am still searching. During the ten calamitous years of the "cultural revolution" (1966-76), I was forced to give up writing for a long
time. But now my pen is finally back in my hand. In my heart,
the fire is still burning. In my mind, is still the same old voice
which continually urges me, "Keep writing, keep writing." I
feel inside me emotions rising and falling like mighty waves,
waiting for a free outlet. So deep is my love for my country
and my people!

I want to write. I will continue to write. Let that fire burn
me out, fiercely. When only the ashes of my body are left
behind, even then, I know my love and my hate will never
disappear.

Ba Jin
Shanghai, February 1981

THE FAMILY

(1931)

Translated by
SIDNEY SHAPIRO

I

The wind was blowing hard; snowflakes, floating like cotton fluff from a ripped quilt, drifted down aimlessly. Layers of white were building up at the foot of the walls on both sides of the streets, providing broad borders for their dark muddy centres.

Pedestrians and sedan-chair porters struggled against the wind and snow, but to no avail. They looked weary, and the snowfall was becoming heavier. Snow filled the sky, falling everywhere — on umbrellas, on the sedan-chairs, on the reed capes of the chair carriers, on the faces of the pedestrians.

The wind buffeted the umbrellas in all directions; it blew one or two out of their owners' hands. Howling mournfully, the wind joined with the sound of footsteps in the snow to form a strange, irritating music. This snowstorm will rule the world a long, long time, it seemed to warn the people on the streets, the bright warm sun of spring will never return. . . .

It was nearly evening, but the street lamps had not yet been lit. Everything was gradually disappearing into a pall of grey. Water and mud filled the streets. The air was icy cold. Only one thought sustained the people struggling through these dismal surroundings — they would soon be back in the warmth and brightness of their homes.

"Walk faster, Juehui, or we'll be late for dinner," said a youth of eighteen. He carried an umbrella in one hand and held up the skirt of his cotton-padded gown with the other. His round face was red with cold as he turned around to speak to his brother; a pair of gold-rimmed spectacles rested on the bridge of his nose.

Juehui, the boy walking behind him, although the same size

and wearing the same kind of clothes, was a bit younger. His face was thinner, his eyes were very bright.

"No, we won't," Juehui replied. "We're almost there." But he quickened his pace, mud splashing the legs of his trousers.

The two brothers soon entered a quieter street. Here the oil lamps had been lit, and their dull gleam, casting pale shadows of the lamp posts on the snow, looked particularly lonely in the frigid windy atmosphere. Few persons were abroad, and these walked quickly, leaving their footprints in the snow and silently vanishing. The deep imprints rested exhausted, without even a thought of moving, until new feet pressed down upon them. Then they uttered low sighs and were transformed into queer shapes; on the interminably long, white-mantled street the regular patterns of footprints became only large and small dark shapeless holes.

A row of residential compounds, with large solid wood gates painted black, stood motionless in the icy gale. Pairs of eternally mute stone lions crouched outside their entrances — one on each side. Opened gates gave the appearance of the mouths of fantastic beasts. Within were dark caverns; what was inside them, no one could see.

Each of these residences had a long history; some had changed owners several times. Each had its secrets. When the black veneer peeled off the big gates, they were painted again. But no matter what changes took place, the secrets were kept. No outsider was ever permitted to know them.

In the middle of this street, before the gates of an especially large compound, the two brothers halted. They scuffed their leather shoes on the flagstones, shook the snow from their clothing, and let their robes fall straight. Holding their umbrellas, they strode in, the sound of their footsteps being quickly swallowed up in the dark cavern of the long entrance-way. Silence again descended on the street.

The outside of this compound resembled the others in that a pair of crouching stone lions flanked its entrance and two big red paper lanterns hung from the eaves of its gate. What

Gate of the house of the Gao family.

made the place distinctive was the pair of large rectangular stone vats placed before the gate.

On the walls on either side of the entrance, hung vertically, were red veneered plaques inscribed with black ideographs. Reading from top to bottom, first the right board then the left, the wishful motto was set forth: *Benevolent rulers, happy family; long life, good harvests.*

2

Although the wind had died down completely, the air was still as cold as before. Night came, but did not bring darkness. The sky remained grey, the ground was paved with snow. In the large snow-covered courtyard, pots of golden plum blossoms were ranged on either side of a raised stone-flagged path. Coated with frosty white, the branches were like lovely jade.

Advancing along this path, Juemin, the elder of the two brothers, had just reached the steps of the one-storey wing on the left side of the courtyard, and was about to cross the threshold, when a girl's voice called:

"Second Young Master, Third Young Master, you've come back just in time. Dinner has just started. Hurry. We have guests."

The speaker was the bondmaid Mingfeng, a girl of sixteen. She wore her hair in a long single braid down her back. Her trim young figure was encased in a padded jacket of blue cloth. When she smiled, dimples appeared in the firm healthy flesh of her oval face. She regarded the brothers innocently with bright sparkling eyes, quite free of any timidity or shyness.

Standing behind Juemin, Juehui smiled at her.

"Right. We'll get rid of these umbrellas and be there directly," Juemin retorted. Without giving her another glance, he entered the door.

"Mingfeng, who are the guests?" Juehui called from the steps.

"Mrs. Zhang and Miss Qin. Hurry up." Mingfeng turned and went into the main building.

Juehui smiled after her retreating figure until the door closed behind her. Then he entered his own room, bumping into his brother, who was coming out.

"What were you and Mingfeng talking about that kept you so long?" Juemin demanded. "Get a move on! The food will be all gone if you delay much longer."

"I'll go with you now. I don't have to change my clothes. They're not very wet." Juehui tossed his umbrella on the floor.

"Sloppy! Why can't you do things right? The old saying is certainly true — It's easier to move a mountain than change a man's character!" Though he spoke critically, Juemin still wore a pleasant expression. He picked up the dripping umbrella, opened it and carefully placed it on the floor again.

"What can I do?" said Juehui, watching with a grin. "That's the way I am. But I thought you were in a hurry. You're the one who's holding us up."

"You've got a sharp tongue. Nobody can out-talk you!" Juemin walked out as if in a great huff.

Juehui knew his brother as well as Juemin knew him, so he wasn't alarmed. Smiling, he followed behind Juemin, his mind filled with the pretty bondmaid. But his thoughts of her vanished at the scene which met his eye as he entered the main building.

Seated around a square table were six people. On the side farthest from the door — the seats of honour — sat his step-mother Madam Zhou and his aunt — his father's sister — Mrs. Zhang. On the left sat his cousin Qin — Mrs. Zhang's daughter — and Ruijue, wife of his eldest brother Juexin. On the near side sat Juexin and their young sister Shuhua. The two seats on the right side were vacant.

Juehui and his brother bowed to Mrs. Zhang and greeted Qin, then slipped into the two empty seats. A maid quickly served them bowls of rice.

"Why are you so late today?" Madam Zhou, holding her

rice bowl, asked them kindly. "If your aunt hadn't come for a visit we would have finished eating long ago."

"We had no classes this afternoon, but Mr. Zhu wanted us to rehearse our play," Juemin replied. "That's what took us so long."

"It must be cold outside after that heavy snowfall," said Mrs. Zhang, half concerned, half for the sake of politeness. "Did you take sedan-chairs home?"

"No, we walked. We never take sedan-chairs!" said Juehui quickly.

"Juehui would never let it be said that he rode in a sedan-chair. He's a humanitarian," Juexin explained with a mocking grin.

Everyone laughed. Angry and embarrassed, Juehui kept his head down, concentrating on his food.

"It's not actually very cold outside, and the wind has stopped," Juemin replied courteously to his aunt. "We chatted as we walked, in fact we felt quite comfortable."

"When is your school going to put on that play you mentioned?" Qin asked him. She was a few months younger than Juemin. Qin was considered the most beautiful of all the girl relatives of the Gao family, and the most vivacious. She had entered a girls' school at an early age, and was now a third-year student in the provincial Normal School for Girls.

"Probably when the next spring term begins. There's only a little more than a week of this term left. When does your winter vacation start?"

"We started last week. They say the school is short of money, that's why we were let off early this year." Qin had already finished eating and put down her bowl.

"All the provincial educational funds are being used for military purposes. Every school is in the same fix. The only difference with us is that our principal is bound by contracts with our foreign teachers. They get their salaries whether we hold classes or not. We cut our losses by holding class, so to speak.... I hear our principal has some connection with the governor, so our money is not so tight."

Juemin also put his bowl down. Mingfeng handed him a damp face-cloth.

"As long as you can go to school, what's the difference?" Juexin said.

"What's the name of their school? I've forgotten," Mrs. Zhang asked Qin.

"Mama has a terrible memory," Qin said pleasantly. "They're in the Foreign Languages School. You've already asked several times."

"You're quite right, Qin. I'm getting old; my memory's failing me," Mrs. Zhang smiled. "I won a trick at mahjong today and forgot to take it."

By now everyone had finished eating and had wiped their faces with the damp face-cloths. "Let's go into the next room," Madam Zhou proposed, pushing back her chair and rising. The others also stood up, and all walked out together.

In the rear of the group, Juemin said to Qin in a low voice, "After next summer vacation our school is going to accept girl students."

Qin glowed with pleasure. She fixed her large limpid eyes on him as if he had given her the best possible news.

"Really?" she asked, a trifle doubtfully. She was afraid Juemin might be teasing her.

"'Really.' Have I ever lied to you?" Juemin looked at his younger brother, standing beside him. "If you don't believe me, you can ask Juehui."

"It's not that I don't believe you, it's just that this good news came too suddenly," Qin replied with an excited laugh.

"It's true all right. But whether the plan can be put through or not is another question," said Juehui. "Sichuan has entirely too many feudal moralists, and their influence is very strong. They're sure to oppose this thing. Boys and girls in the same school? That's something they never thought of in their wildest dreams!" Juehui grew heated.

"It doesn't matter about them. As long as our principal sticks to his guns, we can do it," Juemin retorted, thinking to comfort Qin. "Our principal says if no girls have the courage to register, he'll get his wife to put her name down!"

"I'm going to be the first to apply!" Qin said firmly.

"Qin, why don't you come in here?" Mrs. Zhang called from the next room. "Why are you still standing there by the door?"

"Ask your mother if you can come to our room," Juemin urged Qin quietly. "I'll tell you the whole story in detail."

Qin nodded, then walked over to her mother and said a few words in her ear. Mrs. Zhang laughed. "Very well, but don't be too long."

As the girl and the two brothers were leaving the main building, Qin could hear the clicking of the ivory pieces on the wooden table. She knew that her mother was good for at least four games of mahjong.

3

"This term we finished reading *Treasure Island*. Next term we're going to do Tolstoy's *Resurrection*," Juemin said to Qin with a pleased smile as they walked down the steps. "Our Chinese literature teacher is going to be the man who wrote that article, 'Cannibal Confucian Morality' in the *New Youth* magazine! Isn't that wonderful?"

"You're really lucky," cried Qin, her face flushing with admiration. "We always get old-fashioned scholars for our 'lit' teachers, the kind whose favourite texts are books like *Selected Ancient Chinese Essays*. As for English, we've been on *Chambers' English Reader* for the past few years and now I hear we'll be switching to *Tales from Shakespeare* — always the same dull old antiques! . . . I'd give anything if your school would lift its ban on girl students right now and let me transfer."

"What's wrong with *Chambers' English Reader?*" Juehui queried sarcastically. "It's already been translated into Chinese under the title of *Smiles from the Poets!*"

Qin gave him a severe glance. "You're always joking. We're talking seriously."

"All right, I'll shut up," said Juehui with a grin. "You two go ahead and talk." He slowed down to let Juemin and Qin enter the wing first, while he paused in the doorway and gazed around the courtyard.

Lights were burning brightly in both the left and right sections of the main building as well as in the wing opposite the one in which the two brothers lived. Mahjong tiles clicked in the left section of the main building. All sides of the courtyard were alive with voices. How beautiful the snow-covered garden was, how pure! Juehui wanted to shout for joy, to laugh loud and clear. He flung his arms wide, greeting the broad vistas before him. He felt free, unrestrained.

He remembered how the Old Sea Dog whose role he played in their school's dramatization of *Treasure Island* pounded the table at the inn and roared for rum. The gusto of it all surged up within him. Throwing back his head he shouted:

"Mingfeng, bring three cups of tea!"

There was a call of acknowledgement, and a few minutes later the girl emerged from the left section of the main building with the tea.

"Why only two cups? I distinctly asked for three!" Juehui was still shouting and Mingfeng, as she came up to him, was startled. Her hands trembled, spilling some of the tea.

"I've only got two hands," she said, smiling.

"Clever, aren't you? You could have brought a tray." Juehui laughed. "All right, take these in to Miss Qin and Second Young Master." He pressed back against the left side of the doorway to let her go by.

After a moment, hearing her returning footsteps, Juehui planted his legs wide in the doorway and stood facing the court-yard. She came up quietly behind him and, after a pause, said:

"Third Young Master, let me pass." Her voice was not very loud.

Either Juehui didn't hear, or he pretended not to; in any event he continued to stand where he was.

"Mingfeng . . . Mingfeng!" It was the voice of Madam Zhou, Juehui's stepmother, calling from the main building.

"Let me go; Madam Zhou wants me," Mingfeng pleaded. "She'll scold me if I'm late."

"What if she does?" Juehui turned and smiled. "Just tell her I asked you to do something for me."

"She won't believe me. If I make her angry, she'll give me the devil after the guests leave." The girl's voice was low, audible only to Juehui.

The voice of another girl, Juehui's sister Shuhua, came ringing across the courtyard. "Mingfeng, Madam wants you to put tobacco in the water-pipes!"

Juehui stepped aside and Mingfeng hurried past.

Shuhua came out of the main building. "Where have you been?" she demanded of Mingfeng. "Why don't you answer when you're called?"

"I brought some tea for Third Young Master," Mingfeng answered, hanging her head. Her voice was emotionless.

"Bringing tea shouldn't take all that time! You're not a mute. Why didn't you answer when I called you?" Shuhua was only fourteen, but she had already learned how to scold the bondmaids, just like her elders, and she did it very naturally. "Now get in there. If Madam Zhou knew you deliberately refused to answer, she'd tell you a thing or two."

Shuhua turned and went back into the house. Mingfeng quietly followed her.

Juehui had heard every syllable of this exchange, and the words cut him like the blows of a whip. His face burned with shame. It was he who had brought this on Mingfeng. His sister's attitude sickened him. He had wanted to come forward and defend Mingfeng, but something had held him back. He had stood silently in the dark, watching, as though it had nothing to do with him.

Alone in the courtyard, he could still see Mingfeng's lovely face. It was subservient, uncomplaining. Like the sea, it accepted everything, swallowed everything, without a sound.

From his room, another feminine voice reached his ear, and he pictured another girl. Her face was also beautiful, but it reflected very different kinds of emotion. Resistance, ardour, determination, refusal to submit to the least injustice. The expressions on the two faces were manifestations of two different ways of life, of two different fates. Somehow, even though the latter girl enjoyed a much greater abundance of happiness and gaiety, more of his sympathy and affection lay with the former.

The face of the first girl again loomed large in his mind, drawing him with its docile, beseeching expression. He wanted to comfort her, to offer her some kind of consolation. But what could he give her? Her fate was predetermined when she came into the world. Many other girls in her circumstances had suffered the same fate. Of course, she couldn't be any exception. Juehui wanted to cry out against the unfairness of this fate, to fight it, to change it. Suddenly, a strange thought came to him. After a moment, a faint laugh escaped him.

"It could never be. That sort of thing just can't be done," he said half-aloud.

Ah, if it only could, he mused. But when he thought of the consequences that might ensue, his courage left him. It's only a dream, he said to himself with a wry smile, only a dream.

Dream or no, the idea fascinated him and he was reluctant to abandon it. Suppose she had Qin's social status? he wondered.

There'd be no question about it! he told himself positively. For the moment it seemed to him that she really was a girl like Qin and that his relationship with her was quite ordinary.

Then he laughed, laughed at himself. Preposterous! ... Anyhow, who says I love her? She's just fun to be with.

Gradually Mingfeng's submissive face was replaced in

Juehui's mind by the stubborn, ardent visage of the other girl. But soon this too faded.

"Can a man remain at home while the Huns are still undefeated?" Although he didn't usually care for that hoary aphorism, it now seemed to contain a miraculous solution to all his problems. He boldly shouted it aloud. His "Huns" were not foreign invaders, nor was he intending to take up sword and spear to slay them on a battlefield. What the cry meant to him was that a real man ought to cast off family ties; he should go out into the world and perform great deeds. As to what kind of deeds these should be, he had only the vaguest notion. Juehui strode into the room with the heroic quotation still on his lips.

"He's gone crazy again!" Juemin, standing beside his desk, had looked round at the sound of Juehui's voice, then laughed and addressed this remark to Qin, who was seated in a cane armchair.

Qin glanced at Juehui. "Don't you know he's a great hero?" she asked with an amused smile.

"More likely than not, he's the Old Sea Dog. The Old Sea Dog was also a great hero!" Juemin said, laughing. Qin laughed too.

"Anyhow, the Old Sea Dog was a lot better than Dr. Liversey," Juehui retorted warmly, somewhat angered by their laughter. "Dr. Liversey was only one of the gentry."

"Now what in the world do you mean by that?" Juemin queried, half surprised, half in jest. "Aren't you also going to be one of the gentry?"

"No, I'm not!" Juehui cried hotly. "Just because our grandfather and father are members of the gentry, does that mean we, also, have to become gentry?" He clamped his lips together and waited for his brother to reply.

Juemin had only been joking at first, but now, seeing that Juehui was really angry, he tried to find words to calm him. For the moment, however, he could think of nothing appropriate, and could only stare at Juehui in stupefaction. Qin, seated off to one side, was observing the two brothers, but she did not speak.

"I've had enough of this kind of life!" Juehui could contain himself no longer. "Why does Juexin sigh all day long?   Isn't it because he can't stand being one of the gentry, because he can't stand the oppressive atmosphere of this gentry household? You know it is. . . . We've got four generations under one roof, only one generation less than the 'ideal' family, but never a day goes by without open quarrels and secret wrangles. They're all trying to grab a bit more of the family proper- ty. . . ."

Juehui was almost choking with rage.   He had a lot more to say but he couldn't get the words out. What was infuriating him, in fact, was not his eldest brother's fate, but that of the girl whose expression was so docile.   He felt he was being cut off from her by an invisible high wall, and this wall was his gentry family.   It prevented him from attaining the object of his desire; therefore he hated it.

Juemin looked at his brother's red face and flashing eyes. He came up and grasped Juehui's hand, then patted him on the shoulder.

"I shouldn't have teased you," he said in an agitated voice. "You're right. Your unhappiness is my unhappiness. . . . We two will always stand side by side. . . ." He still didn't know about the girl in Juehui's heart.

Juehui, quickly mollified, mutely nodded his head.

Qin stood up and walked over to them.   She addressed Juehui in a voice that trembled. "I shouldn't have laughed at you either.   I want to stick together with both of you, always. I have to fight too.   My condition is even worse than yours."

They looked at her.   There was a melancholy light in her lovely eyes; her usual vivaciousness was gone.   A troubled ex- pression bespoke her inner struggle.   The boys had never seen her like this before, but they knew at once what was disturb- ing her.   She had spoken correctly — her condition was much worse than theirs.   They were touched by this melancholy, so

rare in her. They were ready to sacrifice themselves completely, if only it would bring this girl's wishes to an earlier fulfilment. This was just an idle hope, for there was nothing specific
they could do, but they felt it was their duty to help her.

The boys immediately forgot their own problems and thought
only of Qin.

"Don't worry," Juemin assured her, "we'll figure something
out for you. I'm a firm believer in 'where there's a will,
there's a way.' Remember when we first wanted to go to a
public school? Ye-ye[1] was dead set against it. But in the
end we won out."

Qin steadied herself with one hand on the desk. She gazed
at them as if out of a dream.

"Juemin is right. Don't worry about a thing," Juehui earnestly beseeched Qin. "Just concentrate on reviewing your lessons.
Put in a lot of time on English. As long as you can pass the
Foreign Languages School entrance exams, solving the other
problems won't be so hard."

With deft fingers, Qin adjusted her hair. She smiled, but
there was a note of concern in her voice. "I hope so. There's
no question about Mama; she's sure to let me transfer. But
I'm afraid my grandmother won't agree, and there's bound to
be a lot of talk among our relatives. Take your family — except for you two, everyone else will probably be opposed."

"What have they got to do with you? Going to school is
your own affair. Besides, you're not a member of our family!"
Juehui was a little surprised that Qin should have mentioned
his family. Although Qin's mother was a daughter of the
Venerable Master Gao, when she married she came under the
jurisdiction of her husband's family, according to custom, and
she no longer had any say in the affairs of her original home.

"You don't know what Mama had to put up with when I
entered the provincial Normal School for Girls. Our relatives
said — A big girl like her, out on the street every day; what

---

[1] Grandfather.

will people think! What well-brought-up young lady would ever act like that? . . . Mama is very old-fashioned. She's more enlightened than most of them, but she has her limits. She's willing to take the brunt on her shoulders, no matter how our relatives sneer, because she loves me. Not that she thinks it right for me to go to school — it wasn't easy for her to let me do even that. Now I'm going to ask to enter a boys' school, to sit in the same classroom with male students! Can you think of one of our relatives who would dare approve of such a thing!"

The more she talked the more excited Qin became. She was standing very straight, her shining eyes fixed on Juemin's face, as if seeking the answer from him.

"Our Big Brother wouldn't oppose it," Juemin remarked.

"If Juexin were the only one, what use would it be?" said Qin. "Aunt Zhou will be against it, and it will only give Aunt Wang and Aunt Shen more to gossip about."

"Let them talk!" Juehui interjected. "They've nothing to do but stuff themselves all day. Naturally, they're full of gossip. Even if you never did anything wrong, they'd invent something to criticize. Since they're going to sneer anyhow, let them."

"Qin, there's something in what he says. Make up your mind," Juemin encouraged.

"I'm deciding right now." Qin's face suddenly grew radiant, and her usual vivacity and firmness flooded back. "I know that a high price must be paid for any reform to be put through, that many sacrifices must be made. I'm ready to be the victim."

"If you're determined as all that, you're suer to succeed," said Juemin soothingly.

Smiling, Qin said with her old stubbornness, "Whether I succeed or not doesn't matter very much. But I'm going to make the try." The brothers gazed at her admiringly.

In the next room, the clock struck nine.

Qin smoothed her hair. "I must be going. Those four games of mahjong are probably over by now." She walked towards the door, then turned to say, smiling, "Come and see us when you have time. I'm home all day with nothing to do."

"We will," the brothers replied in unison. They walked with her to the door and watched until she disappeared into the main building. It was cold outside in the courtyard, but there was considerable warmth in the hearts of both brothers as they returned to their room.

"Qin is certainly a brave girl," said Juemin. He lapsed into a reverie, then again burst out: "Even a vivacious girl like Qin has problems. That's something I would never have believed."

"Everyone has his troubles. I've got mine too," said Juehui. He abruptly broke off, as if he had revealed something he had not intended to.

"You have troubles?" Juemin asked, surprised. "What's wrong?"

Juehui blushed. "Nothing. I was only kidding."

Juemin looked at him suspiciously.

"Mrs. Zhang's sedan-chair!" the clear, crisp voice of Mingfeng was calling outside.

"Mrs. Zhang's sedan-chair!" echoed the hoarse tones of Yuan Cheng, a middle-aged male servant. A few minutes later, the inner compound gates swung open and two men came into the courtyard carrying a sedan-chair. They set it down beside the steps of the main building.

On the street, the watchman's gong resounded deep and mournful — once, twice. It was ten o'clock.

4

The night died, and with it the glow of the electric lights died too. Darkness ruled the big compound. The dismal cry the electric lamps uttered as they expired still quivered in the air. Although the sound was low, it penetrated everywhere; even the corners of the rooms seemed to echo with soft weeping. The time for happiness had passed. Now was the hour of tragic tears.

Lying in their beds, stripped of the masks they had worn all day, people took stock of themselves. They opened their hearts and examined their innermost secrets, peering into the recesses of their souls. Stricken with remorse and anger, they wept over the waste, the losses, the bitterness of the day gone by. Of course there were a few pleased individuals among them, but these were already wrapped in satisfied slumber. The rest were disappointed, miserable creatures in unwarm beds, tearfully bemoaning their fate.

Whether in the brightness of day or the darkness of night the world always has these two different aspects for these two different kinds of people.

In the female servants' room a wick floating in an earthen cup of oil sputtered feebly and grew dim, deepening the darkness of the humble quarters. Two women were snoring lustily on wooden beds on the right side of the room. On the left were two other beds, one occupied by Mama Huang, an elderly servant whose hair was streaked with grey, the other by the sixteen-year-old bondmaid, Mingfeng. The girl was sitting up, gazing dully at the lamp wick.

After working hard all day, now that the madams and misses of the household had retired and she had temporarily recovered her freedom, Mingfeng might, quite reasonably, have gone to sleep early. But lately, these hours of freedom had become especially dear to her; she treasured every minute of them. Thinking, remembering, she felt very much at peace. No one disturbed her. The noisy commands, the scoldings that were dinned in her ears from morning till night, were finally stilled.

During the day, wearing her mask like everyone else, she rushed around busily, a pleasant smile on her face. Now, in these precious hours of freedom, she could take the mask off; she could unlock her mind and spread out its secrets for her heart to see.

I've been here for seven years. That was the first thought.
It had been constantly tormenting her of late. Seven years was
a long time! She often marvelled that they should have gone
by so uneventfully. She had wept many tears in that period,
received many a curse and many a blow. But these had become commonplace, mere frills to her dull existence. Unavoid-
able things which, while she didn't relish them, had to be en-
dured. All that happened in the world was decreed by an
omnipotent being; it was her fate to be where she was and what
she was. This was her own simple belief, and it coincided
with what others told her.

But something else was now stirring in her heart. Though
she was not yet aware of it, it was beginning to waken, bringing
her hope.

More than seven years I've been here. It's soon going to be
eight! She was swept with a wave of revulsion for the emptiness of her life. Like other girls in her position, she began to
bemoan her fate. When the Eldest Young Miss was still alive
she often talked to me about a home of one's own. Who knows
where my final home will be.

Ahead Mingfeng could see only a dreary wilderness, without
a trace of light anywhere. The familiar face of the Eldest Young
Miss again floated before her. . . . If only she were still alive,
there would be someone who cared for me. She helped me
understand many things, she taught me to read and write. Now
she's dead. The good don't live very long! . . . Tears filled
Mingfeng's eyes.

How much longer must I go on like this? she asked herself
tragically. She remembered a snowy day seven years ago. A
fierce-looking woman had led her from the side of her father,
bereft over the loss of his wife, and brought her to this wealthy
household. From then on orders, exhausting toil, tears, curses
and blows became the principal elements of her existence. A
life of dullness, of drab, unvarying monotony.

Like other girls her age, she had dreamed beautiful dreams,
but they all passed quickly, blotted out by reality. She had

dreamed of lovely baubles, of beautiful clothes, of delicious food, of warm bedding, of all the things the young ladies she waited on possessed. She even prayed that these wonderful objects might soon be hers. But the days continued to flit by, bearing her pain with them. Nothing new ever came her way, not even a new hope.

Fate, everything is decided by fate. When she was beaten and cursed she used these words to console herself. Suppose I had been fated to be a young lady too? Mingfeng luxuriated in fanciful imagination: She wore pretty clothing; she had parents who loved and cherished her; she was admired by handsome young gentlemen. One of them came and took her away to his home, and there they lived together happily ever after.

How silly. Of course it could never happen! She scolded herself with a smile. I'll never have a home like that! Her smile faded and her face fell. She knew very well what would happen to her. When she reached the proper age, Madam would say to her, "You've worked here long enough." And she would be placed in a sedan-chair and carried to the home of a man Madam had chosen, a man Mingfeng had never seen. He might be thirty or forty years old. Thereafter she'd toil in his house, work for him, bear him children. Or perhaps after a few weeks she'd come back to serve the same wealthy family, the only difference being that now she would not be scolded and beaten so frequently, and would receive a small wage which she would have to turn over to her husband. Isn't that what happened to Madam Shen's maid, Xi'er?

How terrible! That kind of a home is no home at all! ... Mingfeng shivered. She remembered when Xi'er returned after her marriage, her long single braid done up in a bun on the back of her head. Mingfeng often saw her alone in the garden, furtively weeping. Sometimes Xi'er told of the brutality of her husband. All this gave Mingfeng a frightening premonition of what her own destiny would be.

Darkness, only darkness! I'd be better off dead like the

Eldest Young Miss! Mingfeng thought bitterly. The gloom of the room closed in on her as the wick again dwindled. She could hear the snores of her companions. Listlessly she rose and adjusted the wick. The room brightened and her heart felt a bit lighter. She looked at the stout Sister Zhang, sleeping buried in bed clothes; only a tangled mop of hair and half a fat face were visible. The woman emitted queer regular little snores that sounded like yelps. Emerging half muffled from beneath the thick comforters they were particularly frightening. Her massive body a great lump on the bed, the stout maid slept very deeply; she never stirred.

Like a pig, thought Mingfeng with a wry smile. But her heart was heavy. She was still surrounded by darkness, darkness filled with evil grinning faces. The faces came closer. Some of them grew angry, opened their mouths, shouted at her. Frightened, she covered her eyes with her hands and sank down on the bed again in a sitting position.

Outside, the wind began to howl. It shook the window frames, causing the paper pasted over the wooden lattice-work to cry out dismally. Icy air seeped in through the paper and the room became cold. The lamp flame flickered. A chill crept up Mingfeng's sleeves to her body. With a shiver, she removed her hands from her eyes and gazed around.

I'd better go to sleep, she thought dully, opening the buttons of her padded jacket. She slipped it off. Two mounds of firm young flesh pressed out against her undershirt.

I'm growing up, Mingfeng sighed. But who knows what kind of a home I'll have. . . . Then the face of a smiling young man appeared before her. She recognized him and her heart burst into flower. Warmed by a thread of hope, she prayed that he would stretch forth his hand. Perhaps he could rescue her from her present life. But then the face gradually floated away into the sky, higher and higher until it vanished. And her dream-filled eyes found themselves looking only at the dirty ceiling.

A cold gust swept across her exposed breast, wrenching her

back to reality. She rubbed her eyes and sighed. Only a
dream! After a final lingering glance around the room, she
gathered her courage and removed her warm cotton-padded
trousers.   Piling them and the padded jacket on top of the
bedding, with a quick motion she plunged beneath the covers.

She had nothing. The phrase the Eldest Young Miss had
always used in talking of woman's lot revolved in her brain —
"wretched fate."

It cut her heart like a whip, and she began to weep beneath
the bedding, softly, so as not to disturb the others. The lamp
flame dimmed. Outside, the high wind howled mournfully.

5

On the snow-covered street, the clash of the watchman's gong
sounded with deep solemnity through the quiet night. Rever-
berating in the icy air, it rolled past the sedan carriers' footfalls
in the snow.

The men carrying the sedan-chairs walked very slowly, as if
fearful that if they overtook the gong sound they would lose
this solemn friend. But after travelling two more blocks, the
gong turned off, leaving only its fading regretful sound to linger
in the ears of the sedan porters and their passengers.

Middle-aged servant Zhang Sheng led the way with a lantern,
his head hunched between his shoulders against the cold. From
time to time his sharp cough broke the rather frightening stillness.

The chair porters shouldered their heavy loads silently, walking more freely now, with large strides. It was bitterly cold
and the icy snow stung the bare flesh of their straw-sandaled
feet. But they were accustomed to this and they knew the
road ahead was not long. They would soon reach their destination. Then they could while away their time beside the
opium lamp or at the card table. Walking quietly, with even

footfalls, they occasionally shifted the carrying pole of the sedan-chair from one shoulder to the other, or blew hot breath on one of their hands. Exertion sent warm blood coursing through their bodies. They began to perspire, the sweat on their backs soaking through their tattered old padded jackets.

Qin's mother, Mrs. Zhang, sat in the leading sedan-chair. Although she had only just turned forty, she already showed signs of age. A few games of mahjong had exhausted her. Her mind was numb. At times the wind swept open the curtain of her sedan-chair, but she was unaware of it.

Qin, on the other hand, was very alert and excited. She was thinking of what was soon to happen, the first important event of her life. She could almost see it before her, adorable, dazzling. She wanted to grasp it, but she knew the moment she stretched out her hand, people would hinder her. Although not sure she could succeed, she was determined to try. Yet, in spite of having made up her mind, she still was a little worried that she would fail, and she was rather afraid. These complicated thoughts made her alternately happy and gloomy. Wrapped in her problems, Qin was oblivious to her surroundings. She came back to herself only when the sedan-chairs passed through the gates of her family compound and were set down in front of the main hall.

As usual, Qin first accompanied Mrs. Zhang to her room and watched the maid change her mother's clothes. Qin herself hung the clothing in the closet.

"I don't know why I'm so tired today." Mrs. Zhang sighed. She had put on a fur-lined silk jacket and sat wearily in a cane chair beside the bed.

"You played too long today, Ma," Qin said with a smile. She sat down on a chair diagonally opposite. "Mahjong takes too much out of people, and you played twelve games."

"You always scold me for playing mahjong, but what else is there for a woman of my age to do?" Mrs. Zhang laughed. "Sit around all day reciting Buddhist scriptures, like your grandmother? I just couldn't do it."

"I'm not saying you shouldn't play, I only mean you shouldn't play too long."

"I know," said Mrs. Zhang pleasantly. She observed the maid, standing half asleep on her feet beside the clothes closet. "Go to bed, Sister Li. I don't need you any more," she instructed.

After the maid had gone, Mrs. Zhang turned again to her daughter. "What were you saying? Oh, yes, that I shouldn't play too much mahjong. I know that. But somehow I seem to get tired even when I don't do anything tiring. A life with nothing to do is boring if it lasts too long. People who live too long are a nuisance, anyhow." Mrs. Zhang closed her eyes and folded her arms across her chest. She seemed to doze.

Except for the ticking of the clock, the room was very still.

Evidently Qin would have no opportunity to discuss that important matter with her mother tonight. She stood up, thinking she had better waken her mother and put her to bed so that she wouldn't catch a chill.

But as Qin rose, her mother opened her eyes and said, "Qin, dear, give me some tea."

The girl took a teapot from a low-burning charcoal brazier, poured out a cup and placed it on a stool beside her mother.

"Here's your tea, Ma," she said. She stood awkwardly. She felt her chance to speak had come, but she couldn't get the words out.

"You're tired too, Qin. Go to sleep."

Qin hesitated. Finally she screwed up her courage. "Ma," she began. Her voice trembled a bit with excitement.

"What is it?"

"Ma," Qin said again. Head down, she toyed with the edge of her jacket. She spoke slowly. "Juemin says next year their school will be accepting girl students. I'd like to take the entrance exam."

"What are you saying? Girl students in a boys' school? You want to go there?" Mrs. Zhang couldn't believe her ears.

"Yes," Qin replied timidly. She explained, "There's nothing

wrong with it. Beijing University already has three girl students. Co-ed schools have been started in Nanjing and Shanghai."

"What is the world coming to? It isn't enough to have schools for girls, now they want to have co-ed schools too!" Mrs. Zhang sighed. "When I was a girl, I never dreamed there'd be such things!"

These words struck Qin like a gourd ladleful of cold water. Chilled and dazed, she stood in silence. But she refused to give up hope. Slowly, her courage returned. She said:

"Ma, times have changed. After all, it's more than twenty years since you were my age; something new comes into the world every day. Girls are human beings the same as boys. Why shouldn't they study in the same classroom?"

Mrs. Zhang interrupted with a laugh: "I won't try to argue the merits of the case; I'd never be able to out-talk you. I'm sure you can find lots of reasons in those new books of yours to use against me. You probably think I'm a reactionary old mossback."

Qin laughed too, then she pleaded, "Let me go, Ma. You usually trust me. You've never refused me anything!"

Mrs. Zhang weakened a little. "And I've taken a good deal of abuse for that very reason," she sighed. "But I'm not afraid of gossip, and I do trust you. No matter what it's been, I've always done what you wanted. . . . But this thing is too special. Your grandmother will be the first to oppose. Surely you don't want me to fall out with her because of this? And of course all our relatives will be sure to talk."

"Didn't you just say you're not afraid of gossip?" Qin retorted. "Grandma is in a nunnery. At most she visits us once a month, and then only stays two or three days. The last few months she hasn't come home at all. Besides, who cares what she says? Since she usually doesn't concern herself with family affairs, you can decide — like the time you let me enter the girls' normal school. Our relatives won't have any reason to oppose. If they want to gossip, we'll just ignore them."

After a silence, Mrs. Zhang said in a deflated voice, "I used to be brave, but I'm old now. I don't want to be the butt of any more idle chatter by our relatives. I want to live in peace another few years, without any trouble. You know I've been a devoted mother to you. Your father died when you were very young, leaving me with the full burden of bringing you up. I never bound your feet like other young girls. I let you study with your cousins' private tutor at your grandfather Gao's house. Later, in spite of everything, I sent you to a girls' school. Your cousin Shuzhen has tiny bound feet, and she can barely read. Even your cousin Shuhua had very little schooling! On the whole, you must admit I've treated you pretty well."

Mrs. Zhang was too weary to go on. But when she saw that Qin was on the point of tears, her heart went out to the girl and she said kindly:

"Go to sleep, Qin dear. It's late. We can talk again about what will happen next autumn some other time. I'll do my best for you."

With a murmur of assent, the disappointed Qin walked out, crossed the small hall and went to her own room. Although downcast, she did not blame her mother, in fact she was grateful for her mother's affection.

Qin's room was dreary, as if devoid of all hope. Even her dead father's picture, hanging on the wall, seemed to be weeping. Qin felt her eyes grow damp. She took off her skirt and laid it on the bed, then walked over to the desk, turned up the wick of the pewter lamp and sat down. Picking up a *New Youth* magazine, she idly thumbed through a few pages. The following words caught her eye:

"...I believe that before all else I am a human being, just as much as you are — or at least that I should try to become one.... I can't be satisfied with what most people say.... I must think things out for myself, and try to get clear about them...."

Lines from Ibsen's play *A Doll's House.* . . .

To her they were a revelation, and her eyes grew bright. She saw clearly that her desire was not hopeless, that it all depended on her own efforts. In other words, there was still hope, and the fulfilment of that hope rested with her, not with others.

With this realization, her despair melted away, and she cheerfully picked up her pen and wrote this letter to Qianru, one of the girls in her class:

> Today, my cousins told me that the Foreign Languages School has decided to accept girl students commencing next autumn. I am determined to take the entrance exam. What about you? Would you like to go with me? I hope you're willing to take the plunge. We have to fight, no matter what the cost, to open a road for sisters who come after us.
>
> Please come and see me if you have time. I have a lot to tell you. My mother will be glad to see you, too.
>
> Qin

Qin read through the finished letter, wrote in the date, then painstakingly added punctuation marks, which had only recently come into vogue. Her mother despised letters written in colloquial. She said they were ". . . much longer than the classical style, and unbearably vulgar!" But Qin liked them, and she studied the colloquial letters in the "To the Editor" column of *New Youth* as a means of improving her own style.

6

To Juemin and Juehui, Juexin was "Big Brother." Though born of the same mother and living in the same house, his position was entirely different from theirs. In the large Gao family, he was the eldest son of an eldest son, and for that reason his destiny was fixed from the moment he came into the world.

Handsome and intelligent, he was his father's favourite. His private tutor also spoke highly of him. People predicted that he would do big things, and his parents considered themselves fortunate to be blessed with such a son.

Brought up with loving care, after studying with a private tutor for a number of years, Juexin entered middle school. One of the school's best students, he graduated four years later at the top of his class. He was very interested in physics and chemistry and hoped to go on to a university in Shanghai or Beijing, or perhaps study abroad, in Germany. His mind was full of beautiful dreams. At that time he was the envy of his classmates.

In his fourth year at middle school, he lost his mother. His father later married again, this time to a younger woman who had been his mother's cousin. Juexin was aware of his loss, for he knew full well that nothing could replace the love of a mother. But her death left no irreparable wound in his heart; he was able to console himself with rosy dreams of his future. Moreover, he had someone who understood him and could comfort him — his pretty cousin Mei, "mei" for "plum blossom."

But then, one day, his dreams were shattered, cruelly and bitterly shattered. The evening he returned home carrying his diploma, the plaudits of his teachers and friends still ringing in his ears, his father called him into his room and said:

"Now that you've graduated, I want to arrange your marriage. Your grandfather is looking forward to having a great-grandson, and I, too, would like to be able to hold a grandson in my arms. You're old enough to be married; I won't feel easy until I fulfil my obligation to find you a wife. Although I didn't accumulate much money in my years away from home as an official, still I've put by enough for us to get along on. My health isn't what it used to be; I'm thinking of spending my time at home and having you help me run the household affairs. All the more reason you'll be needing a wife. I've already arranged a match with the Li family. The thirteenth of next month is a good day. We'll announce the engagement then. You can be married within the year. . . ."

The blow was too sudden. Although he understood everything his father said, somehow the meaning didn't fully register.

Juexin only nodded his head. He didn't dare look his father in the eye, although the old man was gazing at him kindly.

Juexin did not utter a word of protest, nor did such a thought ever occur to him. He merely nodded to indicate his compliance with his father's wishes. But after he returned to his own room, and shut the door, he threw himself down on his bed, covered his head with the quilt and wept. He wept for his broken dreams.

He had heard something about a match with a daughter of the Li family. But he had never been permitted to learn the whole story, and so he hadn't placed much credence in it. A number of gentlemen with unmarried daughters, impressed by his good looks and his success in his studies, had become interested in him; there was a steady stream of matchmakers to his family's door. His father weeded out the applicants until only two remained under consideration. It was difficult for Mr. Gao to make a choice; both of the persons serving as matchmakers were of equal prestige and importance. Finally, he decided to resort to divination. He wrote each of the girls' names on a slip of red paper, rolled the slips up into balls, then, after praying for guidance before the family ancestral tablets, picked one.

Thus the match with the Li family was decided. But it was only now that Juexin was informed of the result.

Yes, he had dreamed of romance. The one in his heart was the girl who understood him and who could comfort him — his cousin Mei. At one time he was sure she would be his future mate, and he had congratulated himself that this would be so, since in his family marriage between cousins was quite common.

He was deeply in love with Mei, but now his father had chosen another, a girl he had never seen, and said that he must marry within the year. What's more, his hopes of continuing his studies had burst like a bubble. It was a terrible shock to Juexin. His future was finished, his beautiful dreams shattered.

He cried his disappointment and bitterness. But the door was closed and Juexin's head was beneath the bedding. No one knew. He did not fight back, he never thought of resisting. He only bemoaned his fate. But he accepted it. He complied with his father's will without a trace of resentment. But in his heart he wept for himself, wept for the girl he adored — Mei, his "plum blossom."

The day of his engagement he was teased and pulled about like a puppet, while at the same time being shown off as a treasure of rare worth. He was neither happy nor sad. Whatever people told him to do, he did, as if these acts were duties which he was obliged to perform. In the evening, when the comedy had ended and the guests had departed, Juexin was exhausted. He went to bed and slept soundly.

After the engagement, he drifted aimlessly from day to day. He stacked his books neatly in the bookcase and didn't look at them again. He played mahjong, went to the opera, drank, and went about making the necessary preparations for his marriage, in accordance with his father's instructions. Juexin thought very little. He calmly awaited the advent of his bride.

In less than six months, she arrived. To celebrate the marriage, Juexin's father and grandfather had a stage specially built for the performance of theatricals in the compound.

The marriage ceremony turned out to be not as simple as Juexin had anticipated. He too, in effect, became an actor, and he had to perform for three days before he was able to obtain his bride. Again he was manipulated like a puppet, again he was displayed as a treasure of rare worth. He was neither happy nor sad — he was only tired, though roused a bit by the general excitement.

This time, however, after his performance was over and the guests departed, he was not able to forget everything and sleep. Because lying in bed beside him was a strange girl. He still had to continue playing a role.

Juexin was married. His grandfather had obtained a grand-daughter-in-law, his father had obtained a daughter-in-law, and others had enjoyed a brief period of merry-making. The marriage was by no means a total loss for Juexin either. He had been joined in wedlock with a tender, sympathetic girl, just as pretty as the one he adored. He was satisfied. For a time he revelled in pleasures he had not believed possible, for a time he forgot his beautiful dreams, forgot the other girl, forgot his lost future. He was sated, he was intoxicated, intoxicated with the tenderness and love of the girl who was his bride. Constantly smiling, he hung about her room all day. People envied him his happiness, and he considered himself very lucky.

Thus one month passed.

One evening his father called him into his room and said:

"Now that you're married you should be earning your own living, or people will talk. I've raised you to manhood and found you a wife. I think we can say that I've fulfilled my duties as a father. From now on you must take care of yourself. We have enough money to send you to a university, downriver, to study, but in the first place you already have a wife; secondly the family property has not yet been shared out among me and my brothers, and I am in charge of the accounts. It would look like favouritism if I advanced money from the family funds for your university education. Besides, your grandfather might not agree. So I've found you a position in the West Sichuan Mercantile Corporation. The salary's not very large, but it will give you and your wife a little spending money. Moreover, if you do your work diligently, you're sure to advance. You start tomorrow. I'll take you down myself. Our family owns some shares in the company and several of the directors are my friends. They'll look after you."

Juexin's father spoke in an even voice, as if discussing something quite commonplace. Juexin listened, and assented. He didn't say whether he was willing or unwilling. There was only one thought in his mind — "Everything is finished." Though he had many words in his heart, he spoke not a one.

The following day after the midday meal his father told him

something of how a man going out in the world should behave, and Juexin made careful mental notes. Sedan-chairs brought him and his father to the door of the West Sichuan Mercantile Corporation. Entering, he first met Manager Huang, a man of about forty with a moustache and a stooped back; Chen, the accountant, who had a face like an old woman; Wang, the tall, emaciated bill-collector; and two or three other ordinary-looking members of the office staff. The manager asked him a few questions; he answered simply, as if by rote. Although they all addressed him very politely, he could tell from their actions and the way they spoke that they were not the same as he. It occurred to him with some surprise that he had seldom met people of this sort before.

His father departed, leaving Juexin behind. He felt frightened and lonely, a castaway on a desert island. He was not given any work. He just sat in the manager's office and listened to the manager discuss things with various people. After two full hours of this, the manager suddenly noticed him again and said courteously, "There's nothing for you to do today, Brother. Please come back tomorrow."

Like a pardoned prisoner, Juexin happily called a sedan-chair and gave his address. He kept urging the carriers to walk faster. It seemed to him that in all the world there was no place more wonderful than the Gao family compound.

On arriving home, he first reported to his grandfather, who gave him some instructions. Then he went to see his father, who gave him some more instructions. Finally, he returned to his own apartment. Only here, with his wife questioning him solicitously and at great length, did he find peace and relaxation.

The next day after breakfast he again went to the corporation and did not return home until five in the afternoon. That day he was given his own office. Under the guidance of the manager and his colleagues, he commenced to work.

Thus, this nineteen-year-old youth took his first big step into the world of business. Gradually, he grew accustomed to his environment and learned a new way of life. Gradually, he forgot all the knowledge he had acquired in his four years of middle school. He began to feel at home in his work. The first time he received his salary of thirty dollars, he was torn between joy and sorrow. It was the first time he had ever earned any money, yet the pay was also the first fruits of the sale of his career. But as the months went by, the regular instalments of thirty dollars no longer aroused in him any special emotions.

Life was bearable, without happiness, without grief. Although he saw the same faces every day, heard the same uninteresting talk, did the same dull work, all was peaceful and secure. None of the family came to bother him at home; he and his wife were permitted to live quietly.

Less than six months later, another big change occurred in his life. An epidemic struck his father down; all the tears of Juexin and his brothers and sisters were unable to save him. After his father died, the family burdens were placed on Juexin's shoulders. In addition to looking after his stepmother, he also became responsible for his two younger sisters and his two young student brothers. Juexin was then only twenty years of age.

Sorrowfully, he wept for his departed father. He had not thought that fate could be so tragic. But gradually his grief dissipated. After his father was buried, Juexin virtually forgot him. Not only did he forget his father, he forgot everything that had passed, he forgot his own springtime. Calmly he placed the family burdens on his own young shoulders.

For the first few months they didn't seem very heavy; he was not conscious of any strain. But in a very short time, many arrows, tangible and intangible, began flying in his direction. Some he was able to dodge, but several struck home. He discovered something new, he began to see another side of life in a gentry household. Beneath the surface of peace and affection, hatred and strife were lurking; he also had become a target of attack. Although his surroundings made him forget his springtime, the fires of youth still burned in his heart. He grew angry, he struggled, because he considered himself to be in the right. But his struggles only brought him more troubles and more enemies.

The Gao family was divided into four households. Originally Juexin's grandfather had five sons, but the second son had died many years ago. Uncle Keming and his Third Household were on fairly good terms with the First Household, which Juexin now headed. But the Fourth and Fifth Households were very unfriendly to Juexin; the wives of both secretly waged a relentless battle against him and his First Household, and spread countless rumours about him.

Struggling didn't do the least bit of good, and he was exhausted. What's the use of this endless strife? he wondered. Those women would never change and he couldn't make them give in. Why waste energy looking for trouble? Juexin evolved a new way of managing affairs — or perhaps it would be better to say of managing the family. He ended his battle with the women. He pretended to go along with their wishes whenever he could. Treating them with deference, he joined them in mahjong, he helped them with their shopping. . . . In brief, he sacrificed a portion of his time to win his way into their good graces. All he wanted was peace and quiet.

Not long after, the elder of his two young sisters died of tuberculosis. Although he mourned for her, his heart felt somewhat eased, for her death lightened his burden considerably.

Some time later, his first child was born — a boy. Juexin felt an immense gratitude towards his wife. The coming of this son into the world brought him great happiness. He himself was a man without hope; he would never have the chance to fulfil his beautiful dreams. His only function in life was to bear a load on his shoulders, to maintain the family his father had left behind. But now he had a son, his own flesh and blood. He would raise the child lovingly, and see in him the realization of the career he had lost. The boy was part of him and the boy's happiness would be his own. Juexin found consolation in this thought. He felt that his sacrifices were not in vain.

Two years later, in 1919, the May Fourth Movement began. Fiery, bitter newspaper articles awakened in Juexin memories of his youth. Like his two younger brothers, he avidly read the Beijing dispatches carried in the local press, and news of the big strike in Shanghai on June third which followed. When the local paper reprinted articles from the *New Youth* and *Weekly Review* magazines, he hurried to the only bookstore in town that was selling these journals, and bought the latest issue of the first, and two or three issues of the second. Their words were like sparks, setting off a conflagration in the brothers' hearts. Aroused by the fresh approach and the ardent phrases, the brothers found themselves in complete agreement with the writers' sentiments.

Thereafter, they bought up all the progressive magazines they could lay their hands on, including back numbers. Every night they took turns at reading aloud. Not even letters to the editor escaped their notice, and they had many lively discussions. The younger boys were more radical than Juexin in their approach. When they attacked the "compliant bow" philosophy of the conservative professor Liu Bannong, Juexin confessed he rather liked Tolstoy's "policy of non-resistance." Actually he had read none of Tolstoy's writings on the subject, but had only seen it mentioned in *The Story of Ivan the Fool*.

Indeed, Juexin found the "compliant bow" philosophy and the "policy of non-resistance" most useful. It was thanks to them that he was able to reconcile, with no difficulty at all, the theories expressed in *New Youth* with the realities of his big family. They were a solace to him, permitting him to believe in the new theories while still conforming to the old feudal concepts. He saw no inconsistency.

Juexin became a man with a split personality. In the old society, in the midst of his old-fashioned family, he was a spineless, supine Young Master; in the company of his brothers, he was a youth of the new order.

Naturally, this way of life was something the younger boys could not understand. They berated Juexin for it frequently, and he placidly accepted their criticism. But he continued to read new books and periodicals, and continued to live in the same old-fashioned manner.

He watched his first son learning to crawl, then to walk, then to speak a few simple words. The child was adorable, intelligent, and Juexin lavished nearly all his affection on him. "He's going to do all the things I couldn't," thought Juexin. He refused to hire a wet-nurse, insisting that his wife suckle the child herself. Fortunately, she had enough milk. Such goings-on were virtually unprecedented in a wealthy family, and they led to a great deal of gossip. But Juexin bore it all, convinced that he was acting in the child's best interests.

Every night, after his wife and child had retired, he would sit beside them, feasting his eyes on the baby sleeping in its mother's arms. Looking at the child's face, he was able to forget about himself completely. Juexin couldn't resist planting a kiss on the baby's satiny cheek. He softly breathed words of thanks and hope and love, rather vague words, but they gushed naturally from his lips like water from a fountain.

Juexin didn't know that his parents had loved him with the same fervour when he was an infant. They too had breathed words of thanks and hope and love.

7

On Sunday, Juexin went as usual to the West Sichuan Mercantile Corporation. In that office there were no Sundays off.

He had no sooner sat down and taken a few sips of tea, than Juemin and Juehui also arrived. They visited him at the office almost every Sunday. As had become their custom, they brought with them several new periodicals.

The company Juexin worked for, besides renting out shops in the arcade which it owned, ran a small power plant which supplied electricity — for a price — to its tenants and other neighbouring shopkeepers. The arcade was very large, and housed all kinds of enterprises, including the manager's office of the West Sichuan Mercantile Corporation. Near the rear door of the arcade, in the left corner, was a bookstore specializing in new publications. Because of its proximity, the bookstore became very well known to the three brothers.

"Only a few issues of *New Tide* came this time. This was the only one they had left, and I grabbed it. A few minutes later and it would have been gone. We might have had to wait ages before getting to see a copy!" Juehui lay back in a reclining cane chair beside the window of Juexin's office, reverently holding a magazine with a white cover lettered in red. His face was wreathed in smiles.

"I left word with the bookseller — come what may, he must keep a copy for us of everything new that comes in," said Juexin, looking up from his account book.

"Leaving word isn't enough," Juehui explained excitedly. "There are too many people wanting them, mostly subscribers, too. The bookstore only gets three bundles at a time. In less than two days they're all gone." He turned to an editorial and began reading it with interest.

"More will be coming in. Didn't the bookseller say they're on the way? These three packages came special delivery." Juemin, who had just sat down, now got up again, walked over to the desk and picked up a copy of *Young China*. He seated himself beside the wall to the right. His chair was one of a row of three, with two tea tables in between. Juemin chose the chair nearest the window; between him and the window stood Juexin's swivel chair.

None of the brothers spoke. Except for the sharp clicking of Juexin's abacus counters, all was still. The warm rays of the winter sun, filtered by the pale blue curtains, slanted into the room as only blurry shadows. Leather shoes, ringing smartly on the cement walk outside, rose above the other noise in the arcade. They were coming closer. Mounting the stone steps, they went through the company's door. A moment later the door curtain of Juexin's office moved and a tall thin young man entered. The three brothers looked up, and Juexin hailed him with a smile:

"Ah, Jianyun."

After greeting each of the brothers, Chen Jianyun picked up a copy of the local paper and sat down beside Juemin. He glanced through the provincial news, then placed the paper on the tea table and asked:

"When does your school start its winter vacation?"

"Classes are over already. Exams begin next week," Juemin replied briefly, in a rather cool voice. He resumed his reading of *Young China*.

"I hear that the Students' Federation is putting on some plays in the Wanchun Theatre today to raise money for a free school for poor people," Jianyun persisted.

Juemin raised his head slightly. "That may be. I haven't paid much attention," he retorted in the same cold way. "It's not necessarily the Students' Federation. More likely it's two or three schools doing the show together."

Indeed, Juemin seldom took part in student activities. He attended class each day, and when class was over he returned home. The only reason he was going to play Dr. Liversey in the school dramatization of *Treasure Island* during the coming Spring Festival was because his English teacher had chosen him for the role.

"Aren't you fellows going? They say they're doing Hu Shi's *When a Girl Marries* and Ibsen's *A Doll's House*. They ought to be pretty good."

"It's too far. Anyhow we're getting ready for exams. Got no time to think about plays," replied Juemin. This time he didn't even raise his head.

"I'd like to go. Those are two good plays," Juexin interjected, still manipulating his abacus. "Unfortunately, I haven't the time."

"It's too late even if you did. They've already started," laughed Juehui. He closed the magazine he had been reading and placed it on his knees.

Jianyun silently buried his head in a newspaper he took from one of the tea tables and leafed through it listlessly.

"Are you still tutoring the Wang family children? Why is it we haven't seen you for so long?" Juexin asked in a friendly voice. He had finished his accounts and had noticed Jianyun's awkward manner. "Is your health any better?"

"I had a bad cold for several days. That's why I haven't come around. I'm all right now. Yes, I'm still tutoring at the Wang's, and I still often run into Miss Qin."

Whether addressing her directly or talking about her with others, Jianyun always referred to Qin as "Miss Qin." Distantly related to the Gao family, he was Juexin's junior by a few months, and called him "Big Brother" just as the younger boys did. His parents had both died when he was a child and he was brought up by his father's brother. After graduating from middle school, he was unable to afford going on to a university. The only work he could find was a small tutoring job, teaching English and mathematics to the Wang children. The Wangs were relatives of Qin's mother, Mrs. Zhang, and both families lived in the same compound. Jianyun therefore met Qin frequently.

"You're pale, and much thinner. You've always been delicate. You ought to take better care of yourself," said Juexin sympathetically.

"You're quite right, Big Brother," Jianyun replied, moved by his solicitude. "I know that very well."

"Then why do you always look so downcast?"

Jianyun smiled, in an obviously forced manner. "Many people have asked me that. I don't know why myself. Maybe it's because I'm so frail, or because I lost my parents at an early age." Jianyun's voice trembled as if he were about to weep, but there were no tears in his eyes.

"If you're frail you ought to exercise. Just moping won't do any good," Juemin raised his head and said harshly. Before the words had all left his mouth, footsteps were heard outside and a feminine voice called:

"Cousin Juexin!"

"It's Miss Qin." A touch of brightness stole across Jianyun's face. His low voice sounded happy.

"Please come in," Juexin called with pleasure, rising to his feet.

The door curtain was swept aside and Qin entered, followed by her mother and their male servant Zhang Sheng. Having seen them to their destination, Zhang Sheng immediately went out.

Qin was dressed in a pale blue silk padded jacket and a dark blue skirt. There was a faint dusting of powder on her cheeks; a strand of hair curving down beside each ear flattered the oval configuration of her face. Beneath the neat bangs on her forehead long eyebrows arched over large eyes set on either side of a well-formed nose. Those eyes were exceptionally bright and penetrating; they shone with a warmth that not only added a glow to her enthusiastic vivacious face, but seemed to light up a room the moment she came into it. She magnetized the attention of everyone in Juexin's office as she and her mother smilingly greeted them all.

Juemin and Jianyun quickly offered their chairs to the two ladies, they themselves taking other seats further away from the window. Juexin ordered tea.

"We hear that the Xinfaxiang Department Store has some new dress material. I wonder whether they have anything nice we can buy," said Mrs. Zhang after a few minutes of general conversation.

"They have quite a variety now, mostly silks. I've seen them," Juexin replied promptly.

"Would you mind going with me some time?"

"Not at all. I'll be glad to. How about now?" asked Juexin cheerfully.

Mrs. Zhang was very pleased. "If you're not too busy, that would be fine." She rose and looked at Qin inquiringly.

"I'll wait for you here, Ma," Qin said with a smile. She also stood up and walked over to the desk. Juexin had already risen.

Juexin held aside the door curtain for her. "I'll be back soon," Mrs. Zhang said as she crossed the threshold. Juexin followed her.

"What are you reading?" asked Qin, observing the magazine in Juehui's hand.

Juehui looked at her. "*New Tide* — a new publication," he answered in a satisfied tone. He was clutching the magazine lovingly with both hands.

Qin laughed. "Don't hold it like that. I'm not going to take it from you."

Juemin laughed too. "I have a new issue of *Young China* here, Sister Qin. Would you like to see it?"

Juehui hastily sat up and offered his magazine to the girl. "Take it, take it. I don't want you saying I hoard new magazines!"

Qin shook her head. "After you've all finished reading it, I'll take it home and go through it at my leisure."

Lying back in his reclining cane chair, Juehui resumed his reading. A moment later he asked gaily, "Have you succeeded, Sister Qin? You're so happy today. Did your mother consent?"

"Not yet. I don't know what I'm so happy about. But it doesn't matter whether Ma agrees or not. I can make my own decisions. I'm a person, the same as the rest of you." She seated herself in Juexin's swivel chair, and idly leafed through the account book on his desk.

"Well said. Bravo," cried Juemin. "Spoken like a true New Woman!"

"Don't mock me," smiled Qin. Then her face fell and she

said in a different tone of voice, "I have some special news for you. Your aunt Mrs. Qian has come back."

That was special news indeed. Everyone's mood changed instantly.

"What about Cousin Mei? Has she come back too?" Juehui sat up and asked anxiously.

"Yes. Mei's husband died a year after their marriage. She's a widow now. Her mother-in-law didn't treat her well, so she went back to her mother. Now they've come together to Chengdu."

"How do you know all these details?" asked Juemin, gazing round-eyed at Qin through his gold-rimmed spectacles.

"She came to the house to see me yesterday," replied Qin slowly.

"She came to your house? Is she still the same?" asked Juemin.

"She looks a little haggard, but not too thin. Maybe a little thinner than before. It's only in those limpid eyes of hers that you see she's been through a lot. But I didn't dare ask her too much. I was afraid to stir up old memories. The only things she talked about were the county town she had been living in — the people there, what it was like — and a little about herself. But she never mentioned Juexin or the Gao family."

Qin's voice had become very sad. Then in a different tone, she suddenly asked Juemin, "How does Big Brother feel about her?"

"He seems to have long since forgotten her. I've never heard him mention her name. He's very satisfied with Sister-in-law," Juemin retorted frankly.

Qin shook her head slightly. She said in a rather pained voice, "But Mei probably hasn't forgotten him so easily. I can tell from her eyes that she still thinks of him. . . . Ma says I shouldn't tell Big Brother that Mei is here."

"It wouldn't matter. Anyhow Mei and her mother won't come to our house, so she and Juexin aren't likely to meet. Big

Brother's forgotten the whole affair. Everything changes after a few years. What's there to worry about?" said Juehui.

"I agree it's better not to tell him," said Juemin. "If he's forgotten there's no sense in reminding him again. And who can guarantee that he's really forgotten her?"

"That's right," Qin nodded. "It's better not to let him know."

Seated in a corner, Jianyun shrunk back, struggle and unhappiness reflected on his face. His lips moved several times as if he wanted to speak, but no sound emerged. His eyes were riveted on Qin as he listened to her talk. The girl didn't look in his direction. At times he gazed at Juemin and Juehui admiringly, but they paid no attention to him. Deeply moved by what Qin had said — as well as for another reason — he sighed:

"If only Big Brother had been able to marry Miss Mei, it would have been a perfect match."

Qin glanced at him warmly, then turned her eyes away. Jianyun treasured the brief look like a blessing. He delicately savoured her reply:

"That's how we all felt."

"I don't know who stirred up the trouble between our mother and Mrs. Qian, but they certainly ruined Mei's and Big Brother's happiness once and for all!" Juehui said angrily.

"You don't know? Well, I do. Ma told me the whole story. Even Big Brother himself doesn't know it," Qin said in a mournful voice. "Your father had already sent a matchmaker and Mrs. Qian had consented. But then she took their horoscopes to a fortune-teller who said that they were ill-mated and couldn't marry; that if they did, Mei would die young. So Mrs. Qian refused the match. But there was also another reason. She and your stepmother had a tiff over a mahjong game. Mrs. Qian felt very much abused and used breaking the match as a form of retaliation. Your stepmother had been quite fond of Mei — so was your whole family, for that matter — and she was put out when it was called off. Later, when Big Brother's engagement to a girl of the Li family was announced, Mrs. Qian was displeased too. The relations between the two mothers grew worse. Finally they stopped seeing each other altogether."

"So that's the way it was! We didn't know," said Juemin, surprised. "We didn't know that their marriage had been proposed. In fact we blamed our father and stepmother for not knowing what was in Big Brother's heart and not caring about his happiness. It wasn't their fault after all."

"That's right. We all wanted Big Brother to marry Cousin Mei. When we heard of the engagement with the Li family, we felt that a cruel wrong had been done to Mei. We thought Big Brother should have resisted. Instead, he gave in, like a fool," cried Juehui hotly. "After that, Cousin Mei stopped coming to our house. Then, not long afterwards, she left Chengdu. When Big Brother married Sister-in-law, we were sorry for Cousin Mei and secretly blamed him. It's funny when you come to think of it. We seemed to be more upset about the thing than Big Brother. . . . At the time we thought he and Mei were fated for each other." Juehui smiled in spite of himself.

"I'm afraid we can't say they were really in love. It's just that they were about the same age and well suited to each other temperamentally," mused Juemin. "That's why Big Brother wasn't too hurt after they parted."

"You are the limit!" said Juehui. " 'About the same age and well suited to each other temperamentally!' What else do you want?"

Everyone sighed, including Jianyun.

"What's wrong with *you*, Jianyun?" asked Juemin, startled.

There was no reply from Jianyun. It was as if he had not heard.

"He's always like that," said Juehui with a laugh.

Jianyun suddenly became aware of the three pairs of eyes fixed upon him, and he dropped his head. But he immediately raised it again and looked timidly at Qin with mournful gaze. When Qin made no attempt to avoid his scrutiny, he lowered his eyes at once. Shaking his head, he said softly:

"None of you understand Big Brother, you simply don't understand him. Big Brother hasn't forgotten Cousin Mei. I've seen it for a long time. He's always thinking about her."

"Then why haven't we seen any sign of it? He hardly ever even mentions her name. According to you, the more one loves in his heart, the colder an appearance he should present to the world!" Juemin thought he was making a crushing retort.

"Yes. Only it's not a question of should or shouldn't. In cases like that, sometimes the person doesn't know what he feels," Jianyun explained.

"I don't believe it!" said Juehui firmly.

"Nor I," said Qin earnestly. "I don't think there could be a situation like that. Love is shining and righteous; there's nothing hidden about it. If a man's heart is really ardent, how can he give the appearance of being cold and disinterested?"

Jianyun blanched as if stricken by a severe blow. His lips trembled and his eyes, the light gone out of them, gazed vacantly at the wall. He lowered his head and remained silent.

Looking through a new book on the desk, Qin hadn't observed his changed expression. The brothers, whose eyes were all on Qin, were not aware of it either. But at last Qin noticed him.

"Mr. Chen, what's wrong?" she cried, rising to her feet in astonishment.

Jianyun's body twitched, and he turned and looked at Qin with a doubtful expression. Then he smiled and his eyes shone again, but with their usual melancholy light. Soon the smile faded and gloom quickly overcast his features, as if he had never smiled at all.

The gaze of the two brothers had gone with Qin's stare at Jianyun's face. They observed the play of emotions there but couldn't imagine what was the cause of them.

"Nothing, nothing," replied Jianyun in a somewhat pained tone. A smile returned to his face momentarily. "I was only thinking of something. Something I can't figure out."

"Can you tell us what it is — this thing you can't figure out?" Qin asked him pleasantly.

Jianyun looked very ill at ease. His eyes on Qin's pretty face, he couldn't bring out a single word. Blushing, he finally stammered, "I hardly know, myself. My brain is too weak. Sometimes I don't know what I'm thinking." He smiled a dismal smile.

"Why be so modest, Mr. Chen?" smiled Qin. "We're not strangers."

"It's not modesty. I really am useless. Compared with you people, why, I'm miles behind. I don't even deserve to be in your company." Jianyun's face was red, not with embarrassment, but with the earnestness of his speech. He spoke with a special effort for fear that his words might not be believed.

"Don't talk like that. We don't like to hear it. Let's talk about something else," Qin ordered. Her tone was still friendly, for she knew Jianyun was a little queer and no amount of explanation would do any good.

Juemin said nothing. His eyes were watching Qin, at times shifting for a glance at Jianyun. Listening carefully to their conversation, he smiled occasionally with satisfaction.

Juehui paid no attention to what the others were saying, but buried himself in his *New Tide*.

Jianyun's expression kept changing constantly. It was difficult to guess what was going on in his mind. Qin's "We" had hurt him. He repeated it to himself several times, but in a voice so low that even Qin couldn't hear him.

"All right, I won't say any more. I must be going. I have something to do." Jianyun stood up abruptly and walked towards the door.

Qin watched him in surprise, but didn't say anything. It was Juemin who urged:

"Why not stay a while? It's nice, chatting together like this. Big Brother will be back soon."

"Thanks very much, but I have to go," Jianyun said resolutely, after a moment's hesitation. He nodded to them and went out.

"What does he have to do?" queried Qin dubiously.

Juemin's reply was brief. "Heaven only knows!"

"Something definitely is troubling him. Otherwise, why has he become so strange? He used to be a little better before."

"Yes. He's getting queerer all the time. I don't know what's bothering him," Juemin answered. "Probably because he's poor, he's easily upset; that's what makes him so peculiar."

"I want to be nicer to him, but every time I meet him, he shuts up like a clam — as if he's hiding some secret he's afraid people will discover." Qin spoke warmly, almost argumentatively. When the brothers did not reply, she continued: "How can you get close to a person like that? Sometimes, when we meet, he seems to limit our talk deliberately to idle chatter. The moment I try to discuss anything serious with him, he does his best to change the subject, as if he were afraid of something."

"Maybe he's harbouring some secret heart-break. Unfortunately for him, he's living in the wrong age," Juemin said mockingly. "Yet sometimes he reads new books!" he added in wonderment.

"Oh, forget him!" Juehui closed his magazine and banged it down on his knee. "The world is full of people like that. Can you worry about them all?"

The room was silent for a while. A face peered in through the door, looked around, then withdrew, muttering, "Oh, Young Master Gao has gone out."

"I've already decided to take the exam for your school," Qin suddenly announced to Juemin. "I'm working hard on my lessons now. Would you be willing to help me review my English?"

"Of course. What a question!" Juemin cried happily. "But what about the time?"

"That's up to you. In the evening, naturally. We both have

classes during the day. . . . I don't think we have to wait till
school starts next year. We can begin right now."

"Fine. I'll call at your house later and we can talk it over. —
They've come back." Juemin had heard the voices of Juexin
and Mrs. Zhang outside.

And indeed it was Juexin who held aside the door curtain
and let Mrs. Zhang enter first, he himself then coming in, followed by Zhang Sheng, carrying the packages.

"Let's go, Qin. It's getting late." Mrs. Zhang had just sat
down and taken a few sips of tea, when she addressed these
words to her daughter. To Zhang Sheng, who was still in the
room, she said, "Call a couple of sedan-chairs for us and get
everything ready."

With a word of assent, Zhang Sheng departed. A few minutes later Qin and her mother left. Juexin escorted them to
the office door. Then the two younger brothers walked with
them to the entrance of the arcade and saw both ladies safely
seated in their sedan-chairs.

8

After leaving the West Sichuan Mercantile Corporation, Juehui
and Juemin separated. Juemin went to visit Qin; Juehui intended to call on a friend.

Juehui had walked a few blocks when he ran into his classmate Zhang Huiru at an intersection. Breathing heavily, Huiru
was hurrying along with his head down. Juehui grabbed him
by the arm.

"What's up, Huiru? You're in such a rush you don't even
recognize your friends!"

The triangular-faced youth stared at Juehui, perspiration
beading his forehead. He was panting so hard, for the moment
he couldn't speak. At last he gasped, "Awful . . . thing's . . .
happened!"

"What is it?" Juehui asked in alarm.

Huiru's breathing was a bit more even now, but his voice still quavered with anger and excitement. "We had a fight with the dog-faces today . . . in the Wanchun Theatre."

"What? Tell me about it — quick!" Juehui's blood froze in his veins. He shook Huiru's arm with a hand that trembled. "You mean the soldiers attacked the students? Give me the details!"

"I'm going back to school to tell the rest of the boys. Come along. I'll tell you as we go. . . ." Huiru's eyes were blazing with anger.

Automatically, Juehui turned and walked with Huiru. His heart was beating wildly; his body was beginning to burn. He silently bit his lips.

"Today we were putting on our plays in the Wanchun Theatre," Huiru said in an agitated voice, as the two boys walked quickly together. "I was just one of the audience. When the first play started, three soldiers tried to get in without buying tickets. The man at the door told them this wasn't one of the usual Wanchun Theatre performances; that they couldn't go in unless they paid. There was no reasoning with them, and when they still insisted, our people drove them away. Not long afterwards, they came back with a dozen more dog-faces, all demanding free admission. Our people were afraid they'd disturb the audience with the racket they were making, so they let them in, just to keep them quiet. After they took their seats, they began cheering and yelling and behaving even worse than they usually do in theatres.

"Finally our people couldn't stand it any longer and asked them to be quiet. But they still kept on. We warned them they'd either have to behave or get out. That made them mad; they began to fight. Some of them climbed on the stage and wrecked the props. The riot lasted until a company of soldiers came from the garrison command. But the theatre was already a shambles. Several of the students had been hurt. The rioters all got away; they didn't catch a single one. A whole company of armed troops can't nab a couple of weaponless dog-faces! What fool would believe that? Obviously, the whole thing was planned in advance. . . ."

"Of course. They planned it all together!" Juehui press-ed his hands against his chest. It felt ready to burst, the anger was seething within him so! "There've been plenty of rumours lately that the authorities were cooking up something against the students. We've been too much of a headache to them the last few years — demanding checks on stores to see whether they were selling Japanese goods, holding parades and demonstrations, our movement growing bigger and stronger all the time. . . . They just had to put us in our place. That's why they sicked the dog-faces on us. And this is only the first step. Wait and see. There'll be more to follow!"

"We immediately held a meeting of everyone who was there, in Shaocheng Park. We've decided to call on all students of the schools still in session to go in mass with a petition to the governor. The demands have already been agreed upon. Are you with us?" Huiru quickened his pace.

"Naturally!" replied Juehui. They had arrived at the school, and they strode into the grounds in a highly excited state.

Many students had already gathered on the athletic field, conversing noisily in groups. The whole school seemed to be up in arms. Evidently they had already heard about the fight with the dog-faces. Huiru observed Huang Cunren, who played the role of the father in *When a Girl Marries*, the first of the two plays to be performed that day. *When a Girl Marries* was already over when the rioting started, and Cunren must have gone back to school directly with the news.

Juehui and Huiru joined one of the groups and listened to what the students were saying. Huiru told them everything he knew of the situation, and was still heatedly speaking when the time came for the students to set forth.

Shaocheng Park was the rallying place. When the students from Juehui's school arrived they found boys from other schools already there. But because it was a Sunday, it has not been possible to notify everybody; what's more, several schools were in the middle of their winter vacations. Many less than the entire student body were present, and these were only from the more important schools. The turn-out was much smaller than for previous demonstrations. In all, there was a total of only about two hundred students.

Dusk had fallen. Lamps were being lit in the gathering gloom. The students began their march to the office of the governor.

Juehui looked around him tensely as he walked. Knots of people lined the streets, gazing at the students curiously. A few made guarded remarks; some timidly hurried away.

"They must be out for another blasted check on enemy goods. Which store is going to catch it this time?" Juehui caught the sound of an out-of-town accent. He turned to look at the speaker and found himself confronted with a pair of small shifty eyes in a small pasty face. Scowling, Juehui bit his lips. He couldn't be sure he had heard correctly, so he continued to march.

It was night by the time they reached the governor's headquarters. The pressing darkness increased the tension in every student's heart, assailing them with a nameless fear. They had the peculiar feeling that this was not merely the darkness of night, but the darkness of society and the political situation. Against all these, alone among an indifferent populace, they pitted their youthful hearts.

On the field in front of the governor's compound a platoon of soldiers stood awaiting them with levelled bayonets gleaming, chest high. The soldiers watched in grim silence as the students excitedly demanded to be let in. Neither side was willing to fall back. The students held a conference and decided to send a deputation of eight, but these too were stopped by the soldiers. Finally a junior officer emerged and addressed them curtly:

"Please leave, gentlemen. The governor has gone home."

The deputies replied courteously but firmly that if the gov-

ernor was not in, his secretary would do just as well. But this
was not of the slightest avail. The junior officer shook his head
in a cold, pompous manner, as if to say — The power is in my
hands now; I can handle you students myself!

When the deputies reported the results of this conference to
their mates, the students were furious.

"Nothing doing," they shouted. "The governor must come
out!"

"We're going in! We're going in!"

"If the governor's not here, let his secretary come out!"

"Charge! Let's go in first and talk afterwards!"

Heads were bobbing all over the field. A few students began
to push forward but were held back by their mates.

"Quiet down a bit, fellows. Order. We must keep order!"
one of the deputies shouted.

"Order!" "Order!" Others took up the cry.

"Never mind about order," someone yelled. "The first thing
is to get inside!"

"It can't be done. They've got guns!"

"Order! Order! Listen to our deputies!" was the cry of the
majority.

Gradually the hubbub subsided. In the dark night, a fine
drizzle began to fall.

"Fellows, they won't let us in, and the governor refuses to
send anyone out to see us. What shall we do? Shall we go
back? Or shall we wait here?" So that everyone might hear
him, a deputy shouted at the top of his lungs, his voice going
hoarse with the effort.

"We won't go back!" roared the students.

"We insist on seeing someone in authority. Our demands
must be met. We're not falling for any tricks!" several of the
students cried.

The junior officer approached the deputies. "It's raining,"
he said in a more conciliatory tone. "I urge you to go home.
I promise to deliver your requests to the governor. There's no

use your waiting out here all night." The deputies relayed his words to the students.

"No, we're not going!" was the noisy response. The whole field seethed with agitation. Finally, quiet was slowly restored.

"All right then. We're all staying right here," a deputy shouted through cupped hands. "We deputies will make another try at reasoning with them. We're not leaving till they meet our demands!"

A few students clapped their hands, and in an instant the whole assembly burst into applause. The deputies set out. This time, eight of them were permitted to enter the governor's compound.

Juehui clapped with all his might as rain drenched his hatless head. Though at times he shaded his eyes with his hand or held his wrist over his forehead, his eyes continued to be blurred by the rain. He looked at the bayonets of the soldiers, at the two big lanterns hanging in the entrance-way, at the sea of heads all around him. Uncontrollable anger welled up within him. He wanted to shout; he was suffocating. The soldiers' attack in the theatre had been too sudden. Although there had been rumours that the authorities were planning some action against the students, no one had guessed it would take the form that it did.

How despicable! "Why are they treating us like this?" he asked himself. "Is love of country a crime? Are pure, sincere young people really harmful to the nation?" He didn't believe it.

A watchman's gong sounded twice in the distance. Ten p.m.!

Why haven't our deputies come back yet? Why is there still no news? the irritated students wondered. They began to stir uneasily. The rain was coming down hard now, soaking them from head to foot. Juehui could feel the cold seeping into his bones. He shivered. Then he thought — Is a little discomfort like this going to bother me? . . . Placing his hands in his sleeves, he raised his chest.

All around him, students stood with hunched shoulders, their hair plastered on their foreheads by the rain. But they were not dismayed. One was saying to a classmate:

"If we don't get any results, we won't go back. We can be just as brave as the Beijing students. When they go out to make speeches, they bring packed suitcases with them — ready to go to jail. You mean to say we can't stand here one night to get our demands?"

Juehui heard these words clearly. He was moved almost to tears. He wanted to take a good look at the speaker, but the mist in his eyes prevented him from seeing clearly. Juehui felt a strong admiration for the boy, although he had said nothing out of the ordinary, nothing different from what Juehui himself might have said. Juehui forgot everything — his well-lit home, his warm bed. He would have been willing to do anything for the boy who had just spoken, even if it meant going through fire and water!

By the third watch — midnight — the deputies still had not returned, and there was no news. It was growing much colder. Cold and hungry, and, most of all, weary of the indecision, boys were beginning to ask, "How much longer do we have to wait?"

The bayonets of the soldiers lined up before the entrance gleamed dully, as if in warning.

"Let's go back. We can decide on our next step tomorrow. Hanging around here won't do any good," a few of the weaker boys suggested.

But none of the others responded. It looked as if the majority were willing to wait out the night.

After a long, uncomfortable period, someone said, "The deputies are coming out." A deep hush fell on the entire field.

"Fellows, the Department Chief is going to say a few words to us," announced one of the deputies.

"Gentlemen, the governor left for home hours ago. I'm sorry we had to keep you waiting all this time," said a crisp unfamiliar voice. "I have already conferred with your deputies, on his behalf, and I have received your demands. Tomorrow I

shall present them to the governor. He, of course, will attend
to them; you gentlemen may rest assured of that. He will also
send a representative to call on the students who were hurt.
And now it is getting late. Please go home. We don't want
any of you catching cold. You know the governor has the
greatest concern for all you gentlemen, so please go home. We
wouldn't want anything unfortunate to happen to you."

The voice stopped and, at once, the students began talking
among themselves.

"What is he saying? What does he mean by 'unfortunate'?"
a classmate asked Juehui.

"He says the governor will attend to our demands; that we
should go home. He doesn't take any responsibility himself.
Pretty slick!" Juehui retorted indignantly.

"We might as well go home. Standing here won't get us anywhere. . . . And that last thing he said — it's worth thinking
over."

Another deputy came forward and addressed the students.
"Did you hear what the Department Chief said, fellows? He
has received our demands and the governor will attend to them.
Why not wait and see? Now that we've got results, we can
go home."

"Results? What results?" a number of students demanded
hotly. But most of the boys cried, "Let's go home, then." It
was not because they believed the words of the Department
Chief, but rather because they realized that to stand all night
in the open would be a useless sacrifice. The temperature was
still falling and the rainfall was growing heavier. Everyone was
cold and hungry. They had had enough.

"All right, we'll go home. We can talk some more about
this tomorrow," was the feeling of most. Only a few wanted
to stick it out, but there were not enough of them to make their
view prevail.

The two hundred students began to leave the field.

Large raindrops pelted them without mercy, striking their

heads and bodies fiercely, as if intent on leaving an indelible impression on their memories.

9

Because even the promise that a representative of the governor would call on the students who were hurt was not kept, two days later, the students in all schools called off classes. But actually this was only a gesture since most of the schools were already closed for winter vacation.

The second day of the strike, on the insistence of the Foreign Languages School and the Higher Normal School, the Students' Federation formally issued a strike proclamation, which contained a few disrespectful remarks about the governor. Several days of terror followed. There were frequent clashes between soldiers and students; the citizenry were highly apprehensive that the soldiers might once again turn into undisciplined mobs. Students did not dare appear on the streets alone, but walked only in organized groups of five or six. A student was badly beaten by three soldiers at dusk near the city's South Gate, while a policeman looked on from the sidelines, afraid to intervene.

Disorder reigned everywhere, but the authorities turned a blind eye. The governor seemed to have forgotten the students completely, perhaps because he was busy making preparations for his mother's birthday celebration. Soldiers grew increasingly arrogant, particularly demobilized wounded soldiers. Thrown out on their own, subject to no discipline whatsoever, the "wounded veterans" roved the streets at will. No one dared to interfere.

But the students were not so easily bullied. They launched a heated "Self-Defence Drive to Preserve Respect for Students," they turned out leaflets, they made speeches. The Students' Federation went into action with telegrams to leading social organizations all over the country requesting support; it sent representatives to other cities to explain the students' position; most important of all, it enlisted the co-operation of other students' federations. The drive grew to impressive proportions. But there was still no sign of any action by the governor.

Juehui was much more active in all this than Juemin, who was occupied helping Qin review her English and was not very interested in anything else.

One afternoon, on returning home from a meeting of the Students' Federation, Juehui was summoned into his grandfather's room.

Well over sixty, the old man lay in a reclining chair. His body looked very long to Juehui. Sparse white stubble sprouted on the jaws of his long, dark face, and there was a fringe of grey hair around his shiny bald head. Lying with eyes shut, the Venerable Master Gao dozed, snoring slightly.

Juehui stood timidly before his grandfather, afraid to call the old man, yet not daring to leave. At first Juehui was very uneasy; the whole atmosphere of this room oppressed him. He stood in silence, hoping that his grandfather would awaken soon so that he could quickly leave. But gradually his fear diminished, and he gazed with interest at the old man's dark face and bald head.

As long as Juehui could remember, there had always been a picture of a stern grandfather in his mind. A severe, forbidding man whom all feared and respected. Juehui seldom exchanged more than a few words with his *Ye-ye*. Except for the two times during the day, once in the morning and once in the evening, when he formally called briefly to pay his respects, Juehui had little opportunity to come into contact with him. Juehui avoided him as much as possible, for he always felt awkward and overawed in his presence. The old man seemed to him a person devoid of any affection.

At the moment, his grandfather, lying weakly in the reclining chair, looked very worn-out. *Ye-ye* probably wasn't always such an irritable old stick, thought Juehui. He recalled that many of his grandfather's poems had been dedicated to singsong girls, quite a few girls at that. Picturing how the old man probably looked in his youth, Juehui smiled. He must have been a dashing sort then; it was only later he acquired his pious air. . . . Of course that was thirty years ago. As he grew old, he turned into a crusty Confucian moralist. . . .

Yet even now, his grandfather still played around with the young female impersonators in the opera. The old man once invited one of them to the house and had his picture taken with him. The actor had worn his costume for the occasion. Juehui recalled seeing him putting on his powder and woman's wig in their guest room.

Of course nobody looked askance at that sort of thing in Chengdu. Not long ago, a few old-timers who had been officials under the deposed Qing Dynasty — pillars of the Confucian Morals Society, too — made a big splash in the local press, publishing a list they had composed of the "best" female impersonators in the opera. Patronizing these actors was considered a sign of "refinement." Juehui's grandfather, as a well-known gentleman who had several collections of poems published, a connoisseur of ancient books and paintings, could not go against the fashion.

Yet how can you reconcile this "refinement" with the defence of "Confucian Morals"? Young Juehui couldn't figure it out.

His grandfather kept a concubine — Mistress Chen, a heavily made-up woman who always reeked of perfume and simpered when she talked. She was not in the least attractive, but the old man, who bought her after his wife died, seemed to like her. They had been living together for nearly ten years. She had given birth to a son, but he fell ill and died at the age of five. . . .

Mentally comparing his grandfather's elegant tastes in books and paintings with his fondness for this coarse woman, Juehui had to laugh.

People are certainly inconsistent, he mused. The more he

puzzled over it, the less he understood the old man. His grand-father was an unfathomable mystery to him.

Suddenly the old man opened his eyes. He stared at Juehui in surprise, as if he didn't recognize him, and waved at him to leave the room. How strange! Had his grandfather summoned him and let him stand so long only to send him away without a word? About to ask, Juehui thought better of it when he saw his grandfather's irritated expression. But as he walked towards the door, his grandfather called him:

"Come back here. I have something to say to you."

Juehui turned and walked back.

"Where have you been? We've been looking all over for you." The old man's low voice was dry and harsh. He was sitting up now.

The question took Juehui by surprise. He knew he couldn't say he had been at a Students' Federation meeting, but for the moment his quickness of wit failed him and he was unable to think of an answer. His grandfather's stern eyes were scrutiniz-ing him, and Juehui felt his face reddening. "I went to see a classmate," he finally managed, after some hesitation.

The old man laughed coldly. His eyes swept Juehui's face. "Don't lie," he snapped. "I know all about you. People have told me. The students and the soldiers have been brawling the last few days, and you've been in it. . . . School is over, but you're out every day at some students' federation or other. . . . Mistress Chen just told me she heard from one of my sedan-chair carriers that he saw you handing out leaflets on the street. . . .

"You students have been much too reckless right along — checking stores for Japanese goods, seizing merchants and parading them through the streets — completely lawless! The soldiers would be quite right to beat you. Why do you provoke them with such nonsense? . . . I hear the authorities are plan-ning to take strong measures against the students. If you keep rioting around like this you're liable to riot your foolish young life away!"

After each few sentences, the old man paused or coughed. But whenever Juehui tried to answer, he went on with his lecture. Now he concluded his remarks with a veritable fit of coughing. Mistress Chen hastened in from the next room to drum her fists lightly on his back.

Ye-ye's coughing slowly subsided. But the old man's anger was again aroused when he saw Juehui, still standing before him.

"You students don't study, you just make trouble. The schools are in a terrible state. They produce nothing but rioters. I didn't want you boys to go to school in the first place. The schools make you all go bad. Look at your uncle Keding. He never went to school, he only studied at home with a tutor. But he reads the classics very well, and he writes better than any of you."

"It's not that we want to make trouble. We've been concentrating on our studies right along. We only started this drive in self-defence. The soldiers attacked us for no reason at all. Naturally, we couldn't let them get away with it," Juehui replied evenly, repressing his anger.

"How dare you argue! When I talk, you listen! . . . From now on, I forbid you to go out brawling! . . . Mistress Chen, call his Big Brother in." The old man's voice was trembling, and he began to cough again. Gasping, he drew long, shuddering breaths.

"Third Young Master, look at the state you've got your *Ye-ye* in! Please stop arguing with him and let him get a little rest," rasped Mistress Chen, her face darkening. Her frown made her long face look even longer.

Though stung by the unfairness of her implication, in the presence of his coughing grandfather Juehui could only hold back his retort and hang his head in silence, biting his lips.

"Call his brother, Mistress Chen," the old man said in a calmer voice. He had stopped coughing.

Mistress Chen assented and went out, leaving Juehui standing alone before his grandfather. The old man did not speak. His misty old eyes stared vacantly around the room. Then he half closed them again.

Juehui gazed at his grandfather stubbornly. He examined the old man's long, thin body. A peculiar thought came to him. It seemed to him that the person lying in the cane reclining chair was not his grandfather but the representative of an entire generation. He knew that the old man and he — the representative of the grandson's generation — could never see eye to eye. He wondered what could be harboured in that long thin body that made every conversation between them seem more like an exchange between two enemies than a chat between grandfather and grandson. Gloomy and depressed, Juehui shook himself defiantly.

Finally Mistress Chen returned, a crafty smile on her heavily powdered face. Juehui saw her high cheekbones, her thin lips, her darkly pencilled eyebrows. She reeked of perfume. Then Juexin came in, and the two brothers exchanged unhappy glances. Juexin realized at once that Juehui was in some sort of fix, but he approached their grandfather calmly.

At the sound of the footsteps, the old man opened his eyes. "Where is Third Elder Master?" he asked Mistress Chen.

"He's gone to his law office," she replied.

"More interested in handling other people's litigation than in the affairs of his own family," the old man fretted. He turned to Juexin. "I'm entrusting Third Young Master to you. Look after him carefully. He's not to be allowed out of the compound. I'm holding you responsible." Although *Ye-ye*'s voice was still stern, it was much milder than a few minutes before.

Juexin made respectful noises of assent, and shot a glance at Juehui indicating that he shouldn't try to argue. The younger boy's face was expressionless.

"All right, take him along. He's given me enough of a headache," the old man said listlessly, after a pause. He closed his eyes.

Juexin again murmured his compliance. At a signal to Juehui, the two brothers walked quietly out of the room.

After crossing the great hall, they entered the courtyard. Juehui drew a deep breath and said ironically, "Now at last I feel I'm my own master again." Juexin gave him a reproachful look, but he was unaware of it. Suddenly, Juehui asked seriously, "Well, Big Brother, what about it?"

"What else can we do? We'll have to carry out Ye-ye's orders. You just won't go out for a few days." Juexin helplessly spread his hands.

"But our students' drive is at its height. How can I stay home quietly at a time like this?" cried Juehui, aghast. He was beginning to realize that this thing was serious.

"That's what the old gentleman wants. What can we do?" said Juexin, unruffled. Lately he had been refusing to be upset by anything, big or small.

"There's your 'policy of non-resistance' again. Why don't you become a nice, docile Christian? When someone slaps your left cheek you can offer him your right," Juehui said hotly. He was letting out on Juexin all the emotion his grandfathers' abuse had pent up in him.

"You *are* excitable," Juexin replied with a calm smile. "Why get angry with me? What's the good?"

"I insist on going out! I'm going to leave here right now! Let's see what he can do about it!" Juehui stamped furiously.

"All that will happen is that I'll be scolded and lectured a few more times," said Juexin in a melancholy tone. Like his brother, he seemed more to be talking to himself than for others to hear.

Juehui gazed at him in silence.

"Let's speak frankly," urged Juexin, but his voice was even. "I hope you'll stay home a few days and not make Ye-ye angry. . . . You're still young and impetuous. When Ye-ye talks to you, you ought to listen. Just let him talk. After he's finished and calmed down a little, say 'Yes' a couple of times and walk out. Then you can forget the whole thing. It's much easier that way. Arguing with him will get you nowhere."

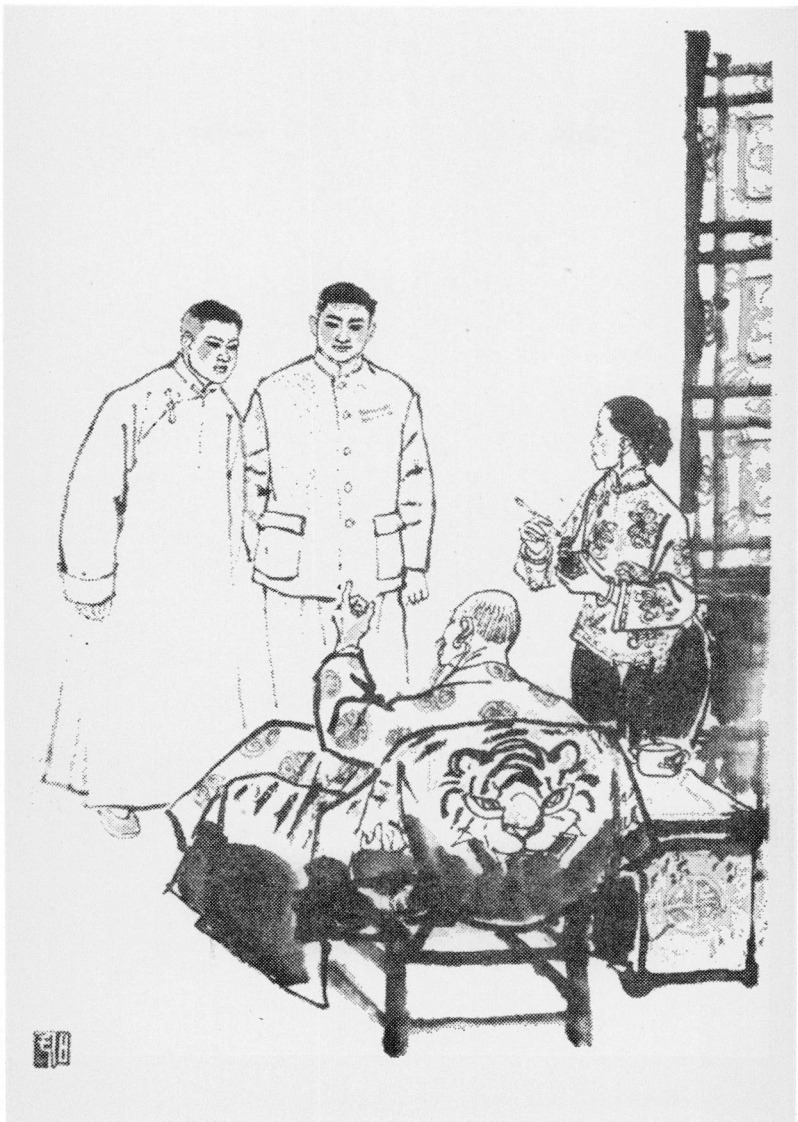

"All right, take him along. He's given me enough of a headache."

Juehui did not reply. He raised his head and looked at the blue sky. Though he didn't at all agree with his brother, he didn't want to argue. And there was something in what Juexin said. What was the point of wasting energy on something from which no good could come? But how could his young mind be for ever weighing fine questions of possible personal profit and loss? Big Brother plainly didn't understand him.

It made Juehui's heart ache to see the clouds drift by. He was torn by conflicting desires. But finally he made up his mind.

"I won't go out for a few days," he said to his brother. "Not because I want to obey Ye-ye, but to save you trouble."

"Thanks very much," said Juexin with a smile of relief. "Of course, if you wanted to go out, I couldn't stop you. I'm at the office all day, usually. I just happened to have come home early today, and ran into this business of yours. In all fairness to Ye-ye, he wants you to stay home for your own good."

"I know that," Juehui replied mechanically. He stood in the courtyard and watched Juexin walk away, then gazed idly at the potted flowers along the path. A few blossoms still remained on the plum trees; their fragrance drifted to his nostrils. Breaking off a small branch, he snapped it into sections, then plucked off the blossoms and ground them to a soggy pulp between his palms. His hands, stained yellow with the juice, were steeped in perfume.

This act of vandalism somehow satisfied him. Some day, when his hands were bigger, if he could crush the old order between them in the same way, how wonderful that would be. . . .

Then his mood changed, and he grew sad. He couldn't take part in the student movement.

"Contradictions, contradictions," he muttered. He knew contradictions existed not only between him and his grandfather, between him and his brother. There were also contradictions within himself.

10

You can lock up a person physically, but you cannot imprison his heart. Although Juehui did not leave home for the next few days, his thoughts were always with his schoolmates and their struggle. This was something his grandfather could not have foreseen.

Juehui tried to envisage what stage the student movement had reached; he avidly searched the local paper for news. Unfortunately, there was very little. He was able to get hold of a mimeographed weekly, put out by the Students' Federation, which contained quite an amount of good news and a number of stirring articles. Gradually the tension was subsiding, gradually the governor was relenting. Finally, the governor sent his Department Chief to call on the students who had been injured in the riots, and issued two conciliatory proclamations. Moreover he had his secretary write a letter in his name apologizing to the Students' Federation and guaranteeing the safety of the students in the future.

Next, the local press carried an order by the city's garrison commander forbidding soldiers to strike students. It was said that two soldiers who confessed to having taken part in the theatre brawl were severely punished. Juexin saw the proclamation posted on the streets, and he told Juehui about it.

With the news improving from day to day, Juehui, a prisoner in his own home, grew increasingly restless. He paced alone in his room, too fretful at times even to read. Or he lay flat on his bed, staring up at the canopy above.

" 'Home. Home, sweet home!' " he would fume.

Hearing him, Juemin would smile and say nothing.

"What's so funny!" Juehui raged, on one of these occasions. "You go out every day, free as a bird! But just watch out. Some fine day you're going to end up like me yourself!"

"My smiling has nothing to do with you. Can't I even smile?" retorted Juemin with a grin.

"No, you can't. I won't let you smile! I won't let anyone smile!"

Juemin closed the book he had been reading and quietly left the room. He didn't want to argue.

"Home, a fine home! A narrow cage, that's what it is!" Juehui shouted, pacing the floor. "I'm going out. I must go out. Let's see what they're going to do about it!" And he rushed from the room.

Going down the steps into the courtyard, he spied Mistress Chen and Aunt Shen (the wife of his uncle Keding) sitting on the veranda outside his grandfather's room. Juehui hesitated, then made a detour around his brother Juexin's quarters and entered the large garden.

Passing through a moon-gate, he came to a man-made hill. The paved path he was following here forked into two branches. He chose the one to the left, which went up the slope. Narrow and twisting, it led through a tunnel. When Juehui emerged again on the other side, the path started downward. A delicate fragrance assailed his nostrils, and he struck off in the direction from which it seemed to be coming. Moving down slowly through the bushes, he discovered another small path to the left. Just as he was turning to it, the view before him suddenly opened up, and he saw a great sea of pink blossoms. Below was a plum tree grove with branches in full flower. Entering the grove, he strolled along the petal-strewn ground, pushing aside the low-hanging branches.

In the distance, he caught a glimpse of something blue shimmering through the haze of plum blossoms. As he drew nearer, he saw it was a person dressed in blue coming in his direction over the zigzag stone bridge. A girl, wearing a long braid down her back. Juehui recognized the bondmaid, Mingfeng.

Before he could call to her, she entered the pavilion on the isle in the middle of the lake. He waited for her to emerge on the near side. But after several minutes there was still no sign of her. Juehui was puzzled. Finally, she appeared, but she was not alone. With her was another girl, wearing a short purple jacket. The tall girl's back was towards him as she chatted with Mingfeng, and he could only see her long plait, not her face. But as they came closer over the zigzag bridge leading from the near side of the isle, he got a look at her. It was Qianer, bondmaid in the household of his uncle Ke'an.

As the girls neared the shore, he hid among the plum trees.

"You go back first. Don't wait for me. I still have to gather some blossoms for Madam Zhou," said Mingfeng's crisp voice.

"All right. That Madam Wang of mine is a great talker. If I'm out too long she'll grumble at me for hours." Going through the grove of plums, Qianer departed along the path by which Juehui had just come.

As soon as Qianer disappeared around a bend, Juehui stepped out and walked towards Mingfeng. She was breaking off a low-hanging branch.

"What are you doing, Mingfeng?" he called with a smile.

Concentrating on her task, Mingfeng hadn't seen him approach. She turned around, startled, on hearing his voice. She gave a relieved laugh when she recognized him. "I couldn't imagine who it was! So it's you, Third Young Master!" She went on breaking the branch.

"Who told you to gather blossoms at this hour of the day? Don't you know that early morning is the best time?"

"Madam Zhou said Mrs. Zhang wants some. Second Young Master is going to take them over." Mingfeng stretched for a branch that was heavily laden with blossoms, but she couldn't reach it, even standing on tiptoe.

"I'll get it for you. You're still too short. In another year or so you might make it," said Juehui, grinning.

"All right, you get it for me, please. But don't let Madam know." Mingfeng stepped aside to make room for Juehui.

"Why are you so afraid of Madam Zhou? She's not so bad. Has she scolded you again lately?" Juehui reached up and twisted the branch back and forth, twice. It snapped off. He handed it to Mingfeng.

"No, she doesn't scold me very often. But I'm always scared

I'll do something wrong," she replied in a low voice, accepting the branch.

"That's called — Once a slave, always a slave! . . ." Juehui laughed, but he wasn't intending to deride Mingfeng.

The girl buried her face in the blossoms she was holding.

"Look, there's a good one," Juehui said cheerfully.

She raised her head and smiled. "Where?"

"Don't you see it? Over there." He pointed at a branch of a nearby tree, and her gaze followed his finger.

"Ah, yes. It has lovely blossoms. But it's too high."

"High? I can take care of that." Juehui measured the tree with his eye. "I'll climb up and break the branch off." He began unfastening his padded robe.

"No, don't," said Mingfeng. "If you fall you'll hurt yourself."

"It's all right." Juehui hung his robe over a branch of another tree. Underneath, he was wearing a close-fitting green padded jacket. As he started up the tree, he said to Mingfeng, "You stand here and hold the tree firm."

Setting his feet on two sturdy branches, he stretched his hand towards the blossom-laden branch he was after. It was out of reach, and his exertions shook the whole tree, bringing down a shower of petals.

"Be careful, Third Young Master, be careful!" cried Mingfeng.

"Don't worry," he responded. Cautiously manoeuvring himself into another position, he was able to grasp the elusive branch. With a few twists, he snapped it off. Looking down, he saw the girl's upturned face.

"Here, Mingfeng, catch!" He tossed her the branch. When it was safely in Mingfeng's hand, he slowly climbed down the tree.

"Enough," she said happily. "I've got three now; that's plenty."

"Right. Any more and Second Young Master won't be able

to carry them all," laughed Juehui, taking up his robe. "Have you seen him around?"

"He's reciting by the fish pond. I heard his voice," Mingfeng replied, arranging the flowers in her hand. Observing that Juehui had only draped his robe over his shoulders, she urged, "Put it on. You'll catch cold that way."

As Juehui was putting his arms through the sleeves, the girl began walking off along the path. He called after her:

"Mingfeng!"

Stopping, she turned around and asked with a smile, "What is it?" But when he didn't answer, and only stood smiling at her, she again turned and walked away.

Juehui hastily followed, calling her name. Again she halted and turned. "Yes?"

"Come over here," he pleaded.

She walked up to him.

"You seem to be afraid of me lately. You don't even like to talk to me. What's wrong?" he asked, half in jest, toying with an overhanging branch.

"Who's afraid of you?" Mingfeng replied with a gurgle of laughter. "I'm busy from morning till night. I just haven't the time for talk." She turned to go.

Juehui held out a restraining hand. "It's true. You *are* afraid of me. If you're so busy, how do you have time to play with Qianer? I saw you two just now in the isle pavilion."

"What right have I to chat with you? You're a Young Master; I'm only a bondmaid," Mingfeng retorted distantly.

"But before we used to play together all the time. Why should it be any different now?" was Juehui's warm rejoinder.

The girl's brilliant eyes swept his face. Then she dropped her head and replied in a low voice, "It's not the same now. We're both grown up."

"What difference does that make? Our hearts haven't become bad!"

"People will talk if we're always together. There are plenty of gossipers around. It doesn't matter about me, but you should

"It's true. You are afraid of me."

be careful. You have to uphold your dignity as one of the masters. It doesn't matter about me. I was fated to be just a cheap little bondmaid!" Mingfeng still spoke quietly, but there was a touch of bitterness in her voice.

"Don't leave. We'll find a place to sit down and have a long talk. I'll take the blossoms." Without waiting for an answer, he took the branches from her hands. Surveying them critically, he broke off two or three twigs and threw them away.

He set off along a small path between the plum grove and the edge of the lake, and she silently followed him. From time to time, he turned his head to ask her a question. She answered briefly, or responded with only a smile.

Leaving the grove, they crossed a rectangular flower terrace, then went through a small gate. About ten paces beyond was a tunnel. The tunnel was dark, but it was quite straight and not very long. Inside, you could hear the gurgling of spring water. On the other side of the tunnel, the path slanted upward. They mounted about two dozen stone steps, followed a few more twists and turns, and at last reached the top.

In the centre of the small gravelled summit was a little stone table with a round stone stool on each of its four sides. A cypress, growing beside the flat face of a large boulder, spread its branches in a sheltering canopy.

All was still except for the chuckling of a hidden brook, flowing somewhere beneath the rocks.

"How peaceful," said Juehui. He placed the blossoms on the table; after wiping the dust off one of the stone stools, he sat down. Mingfeng seated herself opposite him. They couldn't see each other clearly because of the blossoms heaped between them on the little table.

With a laugh, Juehui shifted the branches to the stool on his right. Pointing to the stool on his left, he said to Mingfeng, "Sit over here. Why are you afraid to be close to me?"

Silently, Mingfeng moved to the place he had indicated.

They faced each other, letting their eyes speak, letting their eyes say the many things words would not express.

"I must go. I can't stay too long in the garden. Madam will scold me if she finds out." Mingfeng stood up.

Taking her arm, Juehui pulled her down again to the seat. "It doesn't matter. She won't say anything. Don't go yet. We've just come. We haven't talked at all. I won't let you go!"

She shrank a bit from his touch, but made no further protest.

"Why don't you say anything? No one can hear us. Don't you like me any more?" Juehui teased. He pretended to be very downcast.

The girl remained silent. It was as if she hadn't heard him.

"You're probably tired of working for our family. I'll tell Madam that you're grown up now, to send you away," Juehui said idly, with affected unconcern. Actually he was watching her reaction closely.

Mingfeng turned pale, and the light went out of her eyes. But her trembling lips did not speak. Her eyes glistened like glass, and her lashes fluttered. "You mean it?" she asked. Tears rolled down her cheeks.

Juehui knew his teasing had gone too far. He hadn't meant to hurt her. He was only testing her; and he wanted to pay her back for that cold remark. It had not occurred to him that his words could cause her so much pain. He was both satisfied and regretful over the results of his experiment.

"I'm only joking," he laughed. "You don't think I'd really send you away?" But his laughter was forced, for he had been very moved by her emotion.

"Who knows whether you would or not? You masters and mistresses are all as changeable as the winds. When you're displeased there's no telling what you'll do," sobbed Mingfeng. "I've always known that, sooner or later, I'd go the road of Xi'er, but why must it be so soon?"

"What do you mean?" Juehui asked gently.

"What you said. . . ." Mingfeng still wept.

"I was only teasing you. I'll never let that happen to you," he said earnestly. Taking her hand and placing it on his knee, he caressed it soothingly.

"But suppose that's what Madam Zhou wants," demanded Mingfeng, raising her tear-stained face.

He gazed into her eyes for a moment without replying. Then he said firmly, "I can take care of that, I can make her listen to me. I'll tell her I want to marry —" Mingfeng's hand over his mouth cut him short. He was quite sincere in what he was saying, although he hadn't really given the matter much thought.

"No, no, you mustn't do that!" the girl cried. "Madam would never agree. That would finish everything. You mustn't speak to her. I just wasn't fated. . . ."

"Don't be so frightened." He removed her hand from his mouth as he said this. "Your face is all streaked with tears. Let me. . . ." He carefully wiped her face with his handkerchief. This time she did not draw back. Wiping the tear-stains, he said with a smile, "Women cry so easily." He laughed sadly.

Mingfeng smiled, but it was a melancholy smile, and she said slowly, "I won't cry any more after this. Working for your family I've shed too many tears already. Here together with you, I certainly shouldn't cry. . . ."

"Everything will be all right. We're both still young. When the time comes, I'll speak to Madam. I definitely will work something out, I mean it," he said comfortingly, still caressing her hand.

"I know your heart," she replied, touched. Somewhat reassured, she went on, half in a reverie, "I've been dreaming about you a lot lately. Once I dreamed I was running through the mountains, chased by a pack of wild animals. Just as they almost caught me, someone rushed down the slope and drove them away. And who do you think it was? You. I've always thought of you as my saviour!"

"I didn't know. I didn't realize you had so much faith in me." Juehui's voice shook. He was deeply moved. "I haven't taken nearly good enough care of you. I don't know how to face you. Are you angry with me?"

"How could I be?" She shook her head and smiled. "All

my life I've loved only three people. One was my mother. The second was the Elder Young Miss — she taught me to read and to understand many things; she was always helping me. Now both of them are dead. Only one more remains. . . ."

"Mingfeng, when I think of you I'm ashamed of myself. I live in comfort, while you have such a hard time. Even my little sister scolds you!"

"I'm used to it, after seven years. It's much better now, anyhow. I don't mind so much. . . . I only have to see you, to think of you, and I can stand anything. I often speak your name to myself, though I'd never dare say it aloud in anyone else's presence."

"You suffer too much, Mingfeng! At your age, you ought to be in school. A bright girl like you. I bet you'd be even better than Qin. . . . How wonderful it would be if you had been born in a rich family, or even in a family like Qin's!" Juehui said regretfully.

"I never hoped to be a rich young miss; I'm not that lucky. All I want is that you don't send me away, that I stay here and be your bondmaid all my life. . . . You don't know how happy I am just seeing you. As long as you're near me, my heart's at ease. . . . You don't know how I respect you. But sometimes you're like the moon in the sky. I know I can't reach you."

"Don't talk like that. I'm just an ordinary person, the same as everyone else." His low voice trembled and tears rolled from his eyes.

"Be quiet," she warned suddenly, grasping his arm. "Listen. Someone's down there."

They both listened. The sound, when it reached them, was very faint. Mingled with the babble of the hidden spring, it was difficult to distinguish clearly. They finally recognized it as the voice of Juemin singing.

"Second Young Master is going back to the house." Juehui rose and walked to the edge of the hilltop. He could see a small figure in grey flitting through the pink haze of the plum blossoms. Turning to Mingfeng he said, "It's Second Young Master, all right."

Mingfeng hastily rose to her feet. "I must go back. I've been out here too long.... It's probably nearly dinner time."

Juehui handed her the plum blossoms. "If Madam Zhou asks why you're so late, make up an excuse — anything will do.... Say I asked you to do something for me."

"All right. I'll go back first, so we won't be seen together." Mingfeng smiled at him, and started down the slope.

He walked with her a few steps, then stood and watched her slowly descend the stone stairway and disappear around the face of a bluff.

Alone, he paced the hilltop, all his thoughts devoted to Mingfeng. "She's so pure, so good . . ." he murmured. Walking over to the little table, he sat down opposite the place she had just vacated, and, resting his elbows on the stone surface, supported his head in his hands and gazed off into the distance. "You're pure, truly pure . . ." he whispered.

After a while, he rose abruptly, as if awakening from a dream. He looked all around him, then hurried down the path.

*   *   *

The moonlight was lovely that night. Juehui couldn't sleep. At one in the morning, he was still strolling about the courtyard.

"Why aren't you in bed, Third Brother? It's cold out here." Juemin had come out and was standing on the steps.

"With a beautiful moon like this, sleep is a waste of time," Juehui replied carelessly.

Juemin walked down the steps into the courtyard. He shivered. "It's cold," he repeated, and raised his head to look at the moon.

There wasn't a cloud in the night sky. A full moon sailed through a limitless firmament, alone, chaste, its beams lulling all into slumber, coating the ground and the roof tiles with silver. The night was still.

"Lovely," Juemin sighed. "A perfect example of 'moonlight like frost.'" And he joined Juehui in his stroll. But the younger boy remained silent.

"Qin is really intelligent . . . and brave. A fine girl," Juemin couldn't refrain from commenting, a pleased smile on his face.

Juehui still said nothing, for his mind was occupied by another girl. He walked slowly behind his brother.

"Do you like her? Are you in love with her?" Juemin suddenly grabbed him by the arm.

"Of course," Juehui replied automatically. But he immediately amended, "Who are you talking about? Sister Qin? I don't really know. But I think *you* love her."

"That's right." Juemin was still gripping his arm. "I love her, and I think she could love me too. I haven't said anything to her yet. I don't know what to do. . . . What about you? You said you also love her."

From the sound of his voice and the way his fingers trembled on Juehui's arm, the younger boy could tell that his brother was highly agitated, even without seeing his face. Lightly he patted Juemin's hand and said with a smile, "Go to it. I'm not competing with you. I wish you success. I love Qin only like an elder sister."

Juemin did not reply. He stared at the moon for a long time. At last, when he had calmed down somewhat, he said to Juehui, "You're really a good brother. I was wrong about you; it got me all upset. I don't know what makes me so jealous lately. Even when I see Jianyun and Qin talking together, I feel annoyed. Do you think I'm silly? Are you laughing at me?"

"No, I'm not laughing at you," Juehui answered sincerely. "I sympathize with you. Don't worry. I don't think Jianyun will compete with you, either." Then in another tone of voice, "Listen, what's that?"

A sound like quiet, subdued weeping spread softly, pervading every corner of the moonlit night. It was not a human voice, nor was it the cry of a bird or insect. The sound was

much too light, too clear, for that.   At times it seemed to rise
in pitch, a persuasive plaint issued directly from the soul.   Then
it slowly faded again until it became almost inaudible, like
the merest hint of a breeze.   But one was still aware of a
vibration in the atmosphere, charging the very air with sadness.

"What is it?" Juehui repeated.

"Big Brother playing a bamboo flute.   The past few nights,
he's been playing only when it's very late.   I hear him every
night."

"What's troubling him?   He wasn't like this before.   That
bamboo flute has such a mournful sound!"

"I don't know exactly.   I think it's probably because he's
heard that Cousin Mei has came back to Chengdu. That must
be it.   He keeps playing those same mournful tunes, and
always so late at night. . . .   He probably is still in love with
her. . . .   I haven't been sleeping well the past few nights.   I
keep hearing his flute.   It seems to carry a warning, a
threat. . . .   I'm in practically the same situation with Qin now
as Big Brother was with Cousin Mei.   When I hear that flute
I can't help fearing I'll go the same road as he.   I don't dare
to even think about it.   I'm afraid I couldn't live if it ever came
to that. I'm not like him." Juemin's voice shook with emotion.
He was almost in tears.

"Don't worry. You'll never go Big Brother's road," Juehui
consoled him. "Times have changed."

He looked up again at the full moon, bathing the night with
its limitless radiance.   An irresistible strength seemed to well
up within him as he thought of Mingfeng.

"You're so pure," he murmured. "You alone are as unsullied
as the moon!"

I I

The storm over the clash between the soldiers and the students
gradually subsided.   Out-of-town students returned home for

the New Year holidays. Among those who lived in Chengdu, a number began reviewing for exams. The student strike dragged on, overlapping into the winter vacation. The school authorities wound up their work for the term and prepared to celebrate the New Year. On the surface, at least, the students had won.

During this period, Juemin continued calling at his aunt's house every night to teach Qin English. Juehui continued hanging around the house reading the newspaper. The paper was full of items in which Juehui had no interest. Its coverage of the student strike dwindled steadily until there was no news at all. By that time, Juehui had stopped reading even the newspaper.

"You call this living! A prisoner in a narrow cage!" he would fume. Often he grew so exasperated he didn't want to see any member of his family. To add to his troubles, Mingfeng seemed to be avoiding him. He seldom had an opportunity to speak to her alone.

As usual, he went every morning and every evening to pay his formal respects to his grandfather. He could not avoid seeing the old man's exhausted dark face and Mistress Chen's crafty powdered one. In addition, he also frequently encountered a number of expressionless, enigmatic visages. Juehui felt ready to burst. "Just wait," he would mutter. "The day is coming. . . ."

Exactly what would happen when the day finally came, he wasn't quite sure. All he knew was that everything would be overthrown, everything he hated would be destroyed. Again he looked through his *New Youth* and *New Tide* magazines. He read an article entitled "Impressions of an Old-Style Family," and its biting attack pleased him immensely; it was almost as if he had already gained his revenge.

But his joy was only momentary, for when he tossed the magazine aside and came out of his room, he was confronted with all the things he so disliked. Lonely and bored, he returned to his room.

It was mostly in this manner that he whiled away his days.

Although Juemin and Juehui shared the same room, the older boy was always busy with his own affairs. Even when he was home, he spent most of his time reading in the garden. He was also quite occupied helping Qin with her lessons. Juehui didn't like to disturb him.

"It's so lonesome here," Juehui would sigh, alone in his room. He had not looked at any of the new periodicals for several days, having lost interest; reading them made him feel even more lonely. Idly he turned through the pages of his diary. He hadn't made any entries in a long time. Taking up his pen he began to write:

> This morning I went to pay my respects to Ye-ye. He was in the study, telling Uncle Ke'an to write on a pair of scrolls a birthday greeting that Uncle Keding had composed and send it to old man Feng Leshan who is going to celebrate his sixtieth birthday. After Uncle Ke'an left, with a slight smile on his dark, tired face, Ye-ye handed me a book and said, "You should read this carefully."
> "Yes," I said. On my way out, I saw Mistress Chen in the next room combing her hair. I left as quickly as I could. I always feel much better once I get out of Ye-ye's room. I don't know why, but somehow it reminds me of a magistrate's inquisition chamber.
> I had only to look at the title of that book he gave me and my head ached: "On Filial Piety and the Shunning of Lewdness." I threw the thing on the table and went out for a walk in the garden.
> I saw Sister-in-law in the plum grove, picking blossoms with her little son Hai'er, who is not quite four. It made me feel good just to see her healthy affectionate face, and that lively pair of big kindly eyes.
> "You're out early this morning, Sister-in-law," I said to her. "If you want blossoms, why not let Mingfeng get them for you?"
> She broke off another branch and smiled at me. "Your Big Brother likes plum blossoms. Haven't you noticed his room? He's got vases full of them.... I'd rather pick them for him myself than ask Mingfeng to do it. I'm afraid she wouldn't choose the right ones."
> Sister-in-law told Hai'er to greet me and wish me good morning. Hai'er is very intelligent. He's obedient too. We all like him. But then another thought came to me and I said:
> "Big Brother has always loved plum blossoms."
> Blushing faintly, she answered, "I sketched a plum blossom design to embroider the side runner of our bed canopy. You must come and see it." She smiled proudly, and two dimples appeared in her cheeks. Her voice is very warm whenever she mentions Big Brother.

I know she loves him a lot, but I'm beginning to worry about them. If she knew why he's so fond of plum blossoms, what they signify to him, she'd be terribly hurt.

"Third Brother, you don't look very happy. I know these past few days have been hard on you. They've got you locked up at home and won't let you out. But *Ye-ye* must be over his anger by now. You'll be free in another day or two. Don't take it so hard. Brooding too much will make you ill."

Here she was trying to comfort me, while all the time I was thinking — It's because of you I'm brooding. You don't know Big Brother whom you love so dearly is in love with another woman! A woman whose name means "plum blossom"!... But seeing her calm, sympathetic face, I didn't have the courage to tell her.

"I must go back and boil an egg for your Big Brother," she said, taking Hai'er by the hand. She smiled at me. "Come over after a while and we'll play chess. I know you're bored, home all day."

I nodded and watched her walk away. I felt I was falling in love with her. But this would not harm Big Brother, for I loved her like an elder sister. Of course I'd be too embarrassed to tell this to anyone, even Juemin — Juemin whom I trusted so.

Juemin is very partial to Qin; he's told me so. But, from what he says, apparently he still hasn't revealed his feelings to her. He's been turning rather queer lately. He never gives a thought to home. He leaves early in the morning for Qin's place and doesn't even come home for supper. I'm afraid sooner or later the gossipers around here are going to notice, and then....

Whenever he speaks to me now, it's always about Qin. He gives you the impression that Qin belongs to him alone. Well, it's none of my business. He was not very interested in our student strike either. Qin seems to be his whole world. He's much too happy. I'm afraid he's riding for a fall, but I certainly hope it doesn't happen.

I strolled in the plum grove for a long time and Juemin came and chatted with me a while. After he left, I remained there until Mingfeng called me to lunch.

She seems to be avoiding me lately, I don't know why. Today, for instance, when she saw me coming, she turned and walked the other way. I ran after her and asked, "Why are you avoiding me?"

She stopped and looked at me timidly, but the light in her eyes was warm. Then she dropped her head and said in a low voice, "I'm afraid ... I'm afraid Madam and the others will find out."

Very moved, I raised her face and, smiling, shook my head. "Don't be afraid. It's nothing to be ashamed of. Love is very pure." I let her go. Now, at last I understand.

After lunch I went back to my room and started reading the English translation of *Resurrection* that Juemin had just bought. Suddenly I grew frightened, and couldn't go on. I was afraid that book might become a portrait of me, even though its hero's circumstances are very different from mine.... Lately, I've been daydreaming a lot, wondering how families like ours are going to end....

I'm so lonely! Our home is like a desert, a narrow cage. I want activity, I want life. In our family, I can't even find anyone I can talk to.

That book *Ye-ye* gave me — "On Filial Piety and the Shunning of Lewdness" — was still on the table. I picked it up and skimmed through a few pages. The whole thing is nothing but lessons on how to behave like a slave. It's full of phrases like "The minister who is unwilling to die at his sovereign's command is not loyal; the son who is unwilling to die at his father's command is not filial," and "Of all crimes, lewdness is the worst; of all virtues, filial piety is the best." The more I read, the angrier I became, until I got so mad I ripped the book to pieces. With one less copy of that book in the world, a few less people will be harmed by it.

I felt depressed and weighted down with all manner of unpleasant things. Everything in the room is so dull and tasteless; outside my window too, it's always so gloomy. I wished I could sprout wings and fly away, but the silent house engulfed me like a tomb. I threw myself on the bed and began to groan.

"Third Brother, are you coming over for a game of chess?" the voice of Sister-in-law called from the next flat.

"All right, I'll be right over," I answered. I wasn't the least interested in chess, but I knew she was trying to cheer me up, and I couldn't be ungracious. After a few minutes, I went over. I became so interested in the game I forgot everything. Sister-in-law plays a better game than Big Brother, but she's not as good as me. I beat her three games in a row. She didn't mind a bit — just as pleasant and smiling as ever.

The nursemaid brought Hai'er in, and Sister-in-law played with him, while continuing to chat with me. As I wandered about the room, my eye was caught by the embroidered bed canopy, with its plum blossom design.

"That's a nice design, Sister-in-law," I said. I really liked it, though I don't really know much about art. I thought it was the best sketch she had ever done.

"I don't draw very well, but I took a lot of pains with that one. Your Big Brother pleaded with me several times to do a plum blossom design." A pleased smile appeared on Sister-in-law's face. "I'm very fond of plum blossoms too."

"You mean because Big Brother likes them?" I teased her.

A faint blush coloured her cheeks and she smiled. "I won't tell you now. When you're married, you'll understand for yourself."

"What will I understand?" I pretended to be puzzled.

"Don't press me like that. In the future, you can ask your wife!"

There were sprigs of plum blossom in the small vase on the table and in the big vase on the desk. The golden yellow of the flowers

hurt my eyes. I pictured the sad and beautiful face of Cousin Mei —
"mei" for "plum blossom"! I wanted to say to Sister-in-law, "Take
care that these plum blossoms don't steal a part of Big Brother's
love away," but I didn't have the courage.

"It's been a long time since I've done any sketching. The past two
or three years I've been so busy with Hai'er, I've forgotten everything I ever studied," Sister-in-law was groping for words; her eyes
shone with memories of dreams past.

I wondered whether she remembered the days before her marriage, days as beautiful as a rainbow. It seems to me she hasn't
changed much in appearance, but her manner is much more open
now, and her girlish shyness is gone.

I asked her, "Do you ever think of the time when you still lived
with your parents?"

She nodded. "Sometimes.... It all seems like a dream now.
Things were very different then. Aside from my elder brother, I
had a sister who was three years older than me. She and I used
to practise drawing and writing poetry together. Father was the
head of Guangyuan County then, and we lived in the Official Residence. My sister and I had a room on the upper floor, looking
out over a large garden with many mulberry trees. Magpies used
to perch in the branches and wake us early in the morning with
their chatter.

"At night, the moonlight would shine in through our window
and it was very still. My mother always went to bed quite early,
but my sister and I loved the moonlight, so we often stayed up
quite late. We used to open the window and gaze at the moon,
while we chatted or made up poems. Sometimes, in the deep of the
night, we would hear the sound of a distant horn. That meant the
courier was coming. You know, in those days, all important official
documents were always sent by special messenger who changed
horses at relay stations. He would blow his horn while he was
still a long way off, so that the people at the relay station would
get a fresh horse ready for him. The sound of the horn was very
mournful. It would wake us in the middle of the night, and we
wouldn't be able to fall asleep again....

"My mother raised silkworms, and we girls helped her. We
would take a lantern late at night and go down the stairs and out
to the breeding shed to see whether the silkworms had eaten all
their mulberry leaves and needed more. I was still very young then,
but nearly grown up. Those were wonderful days.

"Then the 1911 Revolution came, and father resigned his post
as an official for the Manchus and took us all back to Chengdu.
We were young ladies by then. Father said our painting was not
bad, and arranged for us to do paintings on fans for a fan shop.
We used the money we earned to buy more paints and some poetry
collections.

"Later, my sister got married. We had been very close to each
other and hated to part. The night before she left, we cried together

all night. Less than a year later, she had a miscarriage and died.... We heard that her mother-in-law treated her badly, and it made her furious. She always had a nasty temper. At home, mother used to pamper and spoil her. She just couldn't learn to accept her in-laws' abuse. It burned her up inside; the aggravation is what finally killed her.

"Looking back on those things now, they all seem to have happened in a dream," Sister-in-law concluded in a sad voice. Her eyes were moist.

I was afraid she was going to cry, but my stupid brain couldn't think of anything to comfort her. "Have you had any news from your mother or brother lately?" I asked.

Sister-in-law's face was unhappy. "Brother writes that they're both well, but they won't be able to come back to Chengdu for another year or two."

We talked a while longer, and then I said I had to review my lesson and returned to my own room. I was still thinking of the things she had told me, but at last I calmed down and began to review *Treasure Island*. After reading more than twenty pages, I was worn out. I lay down on my bed and slept.

When I awoke it was already dark, and I felt cold. The faint glow of the sixteen-watt electric bulb in my room did nothing to warm my heart. Again I was oppressed with the dullness of my family life. Pacing the floor, I thought of the many exciting things going on outside. I can't stand this kind of life any more. There's nothing but oppression for me here in this house. I must fight to the finish.

At dinner I heard my stepmother and Big Brother discussing the battle tactics of Aunt Wang and Aunt Shen. Though they were speaking quite seriously, I couldn't help laughing. Later I talked with Big Brother in his room about filial piety. He's too weak and he's full of reservations. I'm very dissatisfied with him because he's slipping backward day by day. Just as our argument was getting warm, Aunt Shen's maid Waner called him to play mahjong with the ladies, and he agreed without the least hesitation.

"You mean you're going?" I asked in some annoyance.

"What else can I do?" he replied simply, and walked out with Waner. Those are his battle tactics.

I have two brothers. One plays mahjong to get on the good side of certain people; the other stays all day at my aunt's house teaching Qin English and doesn't even come home for supper. I must never become like them.

What a life! This is how I spent today. If I keep on like this, I'll have wasted my youth away.

I won't put up with it. I must resist, go against my grand-father's orders. I've got to get out of here.

The above was one day's entry in Juehui's diary. The next morning, he did indeed leave the compound.

12

The traditional New Year Holiday was fast approaching, the first big event of the year, and everyone, except those who owed heavy debts — which traditionally had to be paid off before the end of the year — was enthusiastically looking forward to it. It slowly drew nearer, with each day bringing a new harbinger of its coming. The whole city bubbled with life. More people than usual were on the streets. Many lanterns and toys appeared. Everywhere the sound of festive horns could be heard.

Although the Gao compound was located on a relatively quiet street, this gentry family, while outwardly calm and reserved, was also beginning to stir. Preparations for New Year ceremonies were being set in motion; a great many things had to be got ready. The servants, of course, were as busy as their masters; they were impatiently awaiting holiday festivities, and the traditional gifts of cash that came their way each New Year.

Every evening, the cook bustled about the kitchen making glutinous rice dumplings. During the day, all the females of the family — young and old — gathered in the room of the Venerable Master and folded gold and silver paper into the shape of ingots — these were to be burned at memorial services, and thus "sent" to ancestors for their use in the next world; the women also cut intricate pictures and designs out of red and green paper — these were to be pasted on the paper windows or on the oil-lamp cups.

The Venerable Master Gao was seldom at home during the day. If not at the theatre, he was visiting friends and playing mahjong. He and his cronies had organized what they called "The Nine Old Men's Club" and each took turns at playing host to the others, displaying his prized books and paintings, his antiques.

Juexin and his uncle Keming were busy supervising the family's large body of servants, preparing for the New Year. Large red lanterns were hung in the main hall; on each of the side walls were placed panels of embroidered red silk. Portraits of departed ancestors were invited out of the chests in which they had been resting, and carefully hung on the hall's middle wall, there to enjoy the respects that would be paid them during the New Year Festival.

It was the Gao family tradition to have a large banquet two nights before the New Year. The afternoon of the banquet, Juemin and Juehui went to call on Big Brother at his office, bringing with them a few new magazines they had picked up at the bookstore. They had also bought a translation of Turgenev's novel *On the Eve*.

As they neared Juexin's door, they could hear the clicking of his abacus counters. Pushing aside the door curtain, they entered.

Juexin looked up, and was surprised to see Juehui. "You're out?" he asked.

"For several days already. Didn't you know?" Juehui grinned. He was entirely at ease.

"What if *Ye-ye* finds out?" asked Juexin, worried. Again he bent over his abacus.

"I can't be bothered about such details. I don't care if he does!" Juehui said coolly.

Juexin looked at him silently, then, frowning, continued with his calculations.

"It's all right. *Ye-ye* is sure to have forgotten by now," Juemin said soothingly. He stretched out on the cane reclining chair beside the window.

Juehui sat down near the wall, and began to read aloud from *On the Eve*:

> *Love is a great word, a great feeling . . . but what kind of love are you talking about?*
>
> *What kind of love? Whatever kind of love you like, so long as it's love. For my part I confess that there just aren't different sorts of love. If you fall in love — then love with all your soul.*

His two brothers were looking at him in surprise, but Juehui
was unaware of it. He continued to recite:

It's the thirst for love, for happiness, nothing else.
We're young, we are not monsters, not fools. We'll con-
quer happiness for ourselves.

A surge of warmth swept through Juehui's body; his hands
trembled with emotion. Unable to go on, he closed the book
and took several large swallows from his teacup.

At this moment, Jianyun slowly entered.

"What were you saying just now with so much passion, Juehui?" he asked in his dry rasping voice.

"I was only reading," Juehui replied with a bitter laugh.
Again he opened the book, and read aloud:

Nature awakens the need for love, but it is not capable of
satisfying it.

The room was very quiet. Even the sound of the abacus was
stilled.

In Nature there is Life and Death. . . .
In Love there is Life and Death.

"What does that mean?" Jianyun asked in a low voice. No
one replied. His face showed doubt, then fear, but the expressions were fleeting.

A nameless terror began to flutter in the small room, but
gradually it vanished, and a common misery gripped each of
the four young men.

"In this kind of society, what other kind of life can you
have!" Juehui burst out angrily. "This kind of existence is
simply a waste of youth, a waste of life!"

He had been increasingly tortured by this feeling, of late.
Ever since childhood, he had been consumed by a craving to be
entirely different from the men of his elder generation. As a
boy, he had travelled a great deal with his county prefect
father, and had seen many odd things. He often dreamed of
running away to distant exotic lands, of pursuing unusual ca-

reers. There had been something dreamlike about the life in his father's yamen. Later, when they returned to Chengdu, he was brought into closer contact with reality, and he began to have a new recognition of the world.

In the Gao family, servants and sedan-chair carriers alone came to several dozen. These "underlings," though coming from many different places, were bound together by a common fate. People who originally were strangers to one another, for a pittance of a wage now served the same masters, living together like some large tribe — peacefully, even affectionately — because they were the same kind of people; they had only to anger their master today, and tomorrow they would not know where their next meal was coming from.

Sympathizing with them, Juehui spent much of his childhood among them, and he earned the servants' love and respect. He would lie on the bed of one of the sedan-chair carriers, watching, in the light of an opium lamp, a lean porter smoking his opium pipe, listening to him tell his favourite stories. Juehui loved to sit around a brazier in the servants' quarters and hear tales of bold and masterly swordsmen, dreaming of the day when he would be grown up, when, holding a sword like his heroes, he would rob the rich and give to the poor, a gallant wanderer with no family ties.

Later, when he entered middle school, his world again began to change. From his books, from the words of his teachers, he gradually became inspired with an ardent love of country and strong reformist sentiments. He became a devoted reader of the agitational articles by Liang Qichao, who demanded constitutional reforms. He read books like *The Soul of China*, and supported the proposal advocated by Liang Qichao in his *Citizen's Guide to Elementary Politics* that national military conscription replace the prevailing practice among the various warlords of hiring mercenaries. Juehui even considered leaving school to become a soldier.

But when the May Fourth Movement erupted in 1919, he seemed to be brought into a new world. He lost his admiration for Liang Qichao and embraced newer and much more progressive theories. It was then he earned the title his Big Brother ironically bestowed upon him — "The Humanitarian." The main reason for the nickname, so far as Big Brother was concerned, was that Juehui refused to let himself be carried in a sedan-chair. The boy had been influenced by a number of articles in the magazine *New Tide* on the purpose and meaning of life as a member of society, and was starting to think about these things for the first time. In the beginning, Juehui had only the haziest conceptions. But gradually, as he gained more experience — particularly through his recent "imprisonment" — and after much internal struggle and the study of many books, his vision widened and he began to understand the significance of life and how a real man should behave.

And so Juehui was pained by this waste of his youth. But the more he hated the life he was leading, the more intangible barriers he found hemming him in, preventing him from breaking away from it.

"What a cursed life!" he fumed. His eye accidentally caught Juexin's confused gaze, and he quickly looked away. He observed Jianyun, melancholy and resigned, then turned to look at Juemin. Second Brother appeared engrossed in his magazine. The room was still, deathly still. Juehui felt as if something were gnawing at his heart. He could bear it no longer.

"Why don't you speak?" he shouted. "You all deserve to be cursed too . . . every one of you!"

The others gazed at him in astonishment.

"Why?" Juemin asked mildly, closing his book. "We're all trying to get along in an old-fashioned family, the same as you."

"That's exactly the reason!" Juehui retorted hotly. "You're all so docile. You don't put up the slightest resistance. How much abuse can you take? You talk a lot about opposing the patriarchal family system, but actually you support it. Your ideas are new but your conduct is still the old kind. You're all spineless! You're full of contradictions!"

Juehui forgot for the moment that he was full of contradictions himself.

"Third Brother, calm down a little. What's the good of raising such a row? You're not going to solve anything all in one sweep," Juemin asserted. "What can you accomplish alone? You ought to know that the patriarchal family system exists because it has its economic and social foundation." Juemin had just read this last sentence in his magazine, and it rolled off his tongue very naturally. "You're not necessarily any worse off than the rest of us," he added.

Again Juehui happened to catch Juexin's gaze. Juexin was looking at him in a melancholy and somewhat reproachful manner. Juehui's wrath slowly subsided and he went back to reading his book. After an interval of quiet, he again read aloud in a low voice:

Let them be! My father was right when he said: "We're not Sybarites, my boy, we're not aristocrats, the spoilt children of destiny, we're not even martyrs — no, we're just workers, workers, workers. Put on your leather apron, worker, and get to your bench in your dark workshop! Leave the sunshine to other people. There's pride and happiness even in our obscure existence."

That could be a description of me, thought Jianyun. But where is my pride, my happiness? All an illusion!

"Happiness? Where can it be found? Is there actually such a thing?" sighed Juexin.

Juehui looked at him, then leafed back a few pages to a place he had dog-eared. He read aloud, as though in answer to his brother's question:

We're young, we are not monsters, not fools. We'll conquer happiness for ourselves!

"Third Brother, please don't read any more," Juexin begged.

"Why not?" Juehui persisted.

"You don't know how badly I feel. I'm not young — I

never had a youth. I never had any happiness, and I never will." Another person might have said these words angrily, but Juexin's tone was only sad.

"Just because you never had any happiness, are you afraid to hear someone else even talk about fighting for it?" Juehui demanded rudely. He was very dissatisfied with his Big Brother's weak-kneed attitude towards life.

"Ah, you don't understand, your situation is different from mine," said Juexin, pushing aside his abacus and looking at Juehui with a sigh. "You're quite right. I'm afraid to hear others talk of happiness. That's because I no longer have any hope of attaining it. My life is finished. I don't fight back because I don't want to. I'm willing to be a victim. Once, like the rest of you, I had my beautiful dreams, but they all were shattered. Not one of my hopes was fulfilled. I have no one but myself to blame. I was quite willing to assume the burdens *Die*[1] left me. . . .

"I remember the day before he died. He was very ill. That day our little sister passed away; she was only five, and the news hurt him badly. He wept and holding my hand, said, 'When your mother died she entrusted all you six children to me. But I've let her down. Today I lost one of you.' The tears ran from his eyes, and he said, 'I haven't much chance of recovering. In case anything happens, I'm turning your stepmother and brothers and sisters over to you. Take good care of them for me. I know your character well. You won't disappoint me.'

"I couldn't help bursting into loud sobs. *Ye-ye*, who was passing by, thought *Die* had died, and he came rushing in. He scolded me for upsetting a sick man, then he gave *Die* a few words of comfort. Later, he called me to his room and questioned me in detail on what had happened. When I told him, he wept too. He seemed to want to say something but, whatever it was, he couldn't get the words out. Finally, he waved me away, telling me to take good care of the patient.

---

[1] Father.

"That night *Die* summoned me to his bedside to write his will. Stepmother held the candle and Elder Sister the ink box. I wrote as he dictated and, as I wrote, I wept. The next day he died, and his burdens fell on my shoulders. I still cry whenever I think of how he died. I had to sacrifice myself for him. What else could I do? I'm quite willing to be the victim. Even so, I've let him down, for I lost Elder Sister. . . ."

Tears ran down Juexin's face as he told this story, and he was more and more wracked with sobs. Finally, unable to go on, he lay his head on the desk and wept unrestrainedly.

Juehui was almost weeping too. He held back his tears with an effort. He saw that Jianyun was mopping his eyes with a handkerchief and Juemin had hidden his face behind his magazine.

In the arcade outside the window, footsteps kept approaching, then passing on and fading away.

Juexin took a handkerchief from his pocket and wiped his tears.

"Don't feel badly, Big Brother," came the voice of Juemin from behind his magazine. "We understand you."

Juehui could no longer restrain his tears, but an instant later he stopped himself. What's past is dead and buried, he thought. Why dig it all up again now? Yet he couldn't help grieving for his departed father.

"Those lines you just read are very apt, Third Brother," said Juexin with a mournful smile. He had recovered his calm somewhat. "I'm not a wastrel or the spoilt child of destiny. I'm only a worker. I put on my leather apron and work in my own dark workshop. . . . I'm a worker without pride or happiness. I —" Juexin suddenly paused, a startled look on his face. He had heard a familiar cough outside the window.

"*Ye-ye's* coming," he said to Juehui in a low voice. "What are you going to do?"

Juehui felt a brief flurry of panic, but he suppressed it immediately. "Why get excited?" he said coolly. "He won't eat me."

The door curtain was pushed aside and the old man entered, followed by a servant who waited in the doorway. The four young men rose in greeting, and Juemin offered the cane chair in which he had been sitting.

"So you're all here," said the Venerable Master Gao, a pleasant smile on his dark countenance. He looked more affectionate when he was cheerful. "You can all go home early. We're having our New Year's banquet tonight." He sat down in the cane chair beside the window, but at once rose to his feet again.

"Juexin, I want to do some shopping. Come along with me," he directed. Walking sedately in his cotton-padded black cloth shoes, he stepped across the threshold as Juexin held aside the door curtain. Juexin and the servant followed him.

The moment they were gone, Juemin blew out his breath in relief and grinned at Juehui. "He's forgotten all about you."

"If I were as docile as Big Brother, I'd probably be locked up at home for ever. It's a good thing I had a little courage," said Juehui. "As a matter of fact I was silly not to have come out earlier. *Ye-ye* gets mad, and then it's over and forgotten. How would he remember that I was still suffering, pent up at home? Let's go. There's no need to wait for Big Brother — we're walking and he'll be taking a sedan-chair. Besides if we start back early, we can avoid bumping into *Ye-ye* again."

"Right," Juemin agreed. "What about you?" he asked Jianyun.

"I've got to go back too. I'll walk along with you."

On the way home, Juehui was very happy. He had closed the tomb of the past and sealed the door tight. He said to himself:

"I'm young. I'm not a monster, not a fool. I'll conquer happiness for myself."

Once again he was grateful that he was not like his Big Brother.

13

Dusk had already fallen in the Gao family compound. In the main hall, in addition to the hundred-watt electric bulb which had just been installed, suspended from the central beam was an "eternal flame" lamp that burned vegetable oil, a large kerosene lamp, and four lamps with picture glass panels. Their combined light brilliantly illuminated the pictures on the wall and the portraits of the Qing Dynasty ancestors resting on the altar. Even the cracks in the coloured-tile floor were made visible.

Eating utensils had been neatly laid on two large round tables placed in the centre of the hall. The chopsticks were of ivory; the bowls, spoons and plates were silver. Beneath each plate was a red slip of paper on which a place name had been written. Four servants waited on each table; two to pour the wine, two to serve the food. Cooked dishes were brought from the kitchen to a large service table outside the hall, from there passed by an older woman servant to the male servants, who carried the food to the round tables. The bondmaids from all the households were also there to help.

After eight varieties of cold-cuts and two plates of melon seeds and almonds had been set upon the tables, the diners were invited to enter. Led by the Venerable Master Gao, everyone, old and young, gathered in the hall; then, at the old man's signal, found their places and took their seats.

The members of the elder generation all sat at the main table, each according to rank. First was the Venerable Master Gao, then Mistress Chen, Madam Zhou, Third Elder Master Keming and his wife Madam Zhang, Fourth Elder Master Ke'an and his wife Madam Wang, Fifth Elder Master Keding and his wife Madam Shen, plus the old man's daughter Mrs. Zhang, mother of Qin. At the second table were Juexin, his wife Ruijue, Qin, Juemin and Juehui, plus the boys' male cousins — Jueying and Jueren of the Third Household; and Juequn, Jueshi and Juexian

of the Fourth Household.   Also present were all the girls of
the "Shu" generation — the boys' young sister Shuhua, their
fifteen-year-old cousin Shuying of the Third Household, seven-
year-old cousin Shufen of the Fourth Household and twelve-
year-old cousin Shuzhen of the Fifth Household. Because the
old man wanted all four generations represented at the banquet,
Juexin's wife Ruijue held their son little Haichen on her lap for
a while and let him eat with the grown-ups.

Winecup in hand, the old man gazed around at the smiling
celebrants crowding the tables — his children, his grandchildren, his great-grandson.   His wish to see "four generations
under one roof" had been fulfilled.   A satisfied smile on his
face, he drank deeply of his wine.   He looked at the younger
generation at the next table, laughing, drinking, calling for more
wine in their fresh clear voices, the two male servants rushing
around, refilling the cups from small wine kettles.

"Not too much wine, don't get drunk," he called with a smile.
"Eat more food."

He heard Juexin's sound of assent, and unconsciously the
old man raised his cup again and took another carefree sip.
All the winecups at the table of the Venerable Master Gao rose
in unison with his; when he placed his cup back on the table,
the other diners followed suit.   It was quiet and restrained at
the old man's table.   The Madams and Elder Masters sat stiffly
correct.   They took up their chopsticks when the old man raised
his; they returned theirs to the table as soon as he put his
down.   They spoke to one another rarely, and then only a word
or two. Finally the old man took notice. Slightly tipsy, he urged:

"Don't be so formal.   Relax, all of you.   Talk, laugh.   See
how gay they are at the next table.   We're much too quiet.
There's no need to stand on ceremony.   We're all one family."
Lifting his cup, he drained it, then said, "I'm very happy tonight."

The old man's unusual high spirits brought a breath of life
to his table.   Wine began to flow and the food was attacked in
earnest.

It did the old man's heart good to see the excited flushed faces, to hear the noisy laughter accompanying the winedrinking games. He took another sip from his refilled cup. He thought back on the past — his early struggles to get an education, his success as a scholar, his service as an official for many years. Starting empty-handed he had accumulated vast farmlands, built houses, raised this large family. All had gone well. If the family continued to prosper at this rate, who could tell how affluent the Gaos would be in another generation or two.... Smiling, he took another big swallow of wine, then put down the cup and announced:

"I've had enough. It takes only two cups to get me drunk. But the rest of you go on." And he ordered the servants: "Refill the cups of the gentlemen and ladies here."

The second table was indeed, as the old man had said, much more gay. The chopsticks of the diners seldom rested. A new dish had only to appear, and in a few minutes the platter was clean. The little boys Juequn and Jueshi, who were still unable to manipulate chopsticks successfully, knelt on their chairs and helped themselves from the platters with their spoons. The young men and women ate and drank and laughed with complete abandonment right up to the very end of the banquet. Most of them were a little drunk by the time it was over.

Qin and her mother left first. Originally, Juemin, Juehui, their sister Shuhua and their cousin Shuying had pleaded with Madam Zhou to let Qin stay as their guest over the holidays. But Mrs. Zhang said they had things to do at home, and took Qin off with her. Ruijue went back to her room to look after Haichen. Juexin, Juemin and Shuhua all had drunk too much; they went to their rooms to sleep it off.

By then, the zest had gone out of the party, and the other youngsters had no choice but to return to their own households. Quiet descended on the big compound. Only a few servants remained in the large hall, clearing off the tables and sweeping the floor.

Juehui, also, was feeling the wine he had drunk. His face

burned, his heart felt very hot. On the street, firecrackers were bursting like the staccato hoofbeats of stampeding horses. Juehui couldn't sit still. He went out into the cold air of the hall's ante-room. A few sedan-chairs stood waiting, while three or four carriers sat on the high threshold of the gatehouse, talking in low tones. A string of firecrackers rattled in the compound next door.

After standing for several minutes, Juehui started towards the street. Just as he reached the main gate of the compound, the sound of fireworks ceased, except for an occasional scattered burst. The smell of powder filled the air; corpses of exploded firecrackers littered the street. Two large red paper lanterns hung in the gateway, casting only hazy red shadows on the ground in spite of the large candles burning inside.

The streets were quiet. Scattered remains of fireworks lay ignored and disappointed, emitting their last warm, sulphurous breath. From somewhere came the sound of soft weeping.

Why should anyone be crying at a time when everyone else is happy? wondered Juehui. He was growing sober again. Peering around in the darkness, he observed a dark shadow near the large stone vat on the right side of the compound gate. Curious, he approached.

A tattered beggar child was leaning his head on the edge of the vat, weeping, his tousled hair dangling into the water within. The child looked up at the sound of Juehui's footsteps. Although they could not see each other clearly in the darkness, they stood staring, face to face, neither speaking a word. Juehui could hear the child's laboured sobs.

It was like a dash of cold water to Juehui. He could distinctly sense the silver coins clinking in his own pocket. A rare emotion possessed him, and he drew out two silver half-dollars and placed them in the beggar child's moist hand.

"Take these," he said distractedly. "Find yourself some place warm. It's cold out here, very cold. Look how you're shivering. You'll feel better after you've bought a bit of hot food."

Juehui turned quickly and strode back into the compound, as if running from something shameful. Passing through the main gate into the courtyard he could visualize his Big Brother's mocking smile and hear him scoff — "Humanitarian!" As Juehui neared the main hall after going through the inner compound gate, a voice seemed to shout at him in the silence:

"Do you think deeds like that are going to change the world? Do you think you've saved that beggar child from cold and hunger for the rest of his life? You — you hypocritical 'humanitarian'; what a fool you are!"

Terrified, he fled to his own room. Sinking down weakly on to his bed, he kept repeating to himself, "I'm drunk, drunk."

14

Next day was the last day of the old lunar year. Juehui woke quite late that morning. Sunlight already filled his window and the room was very bright. Juemin, standing by his bedside, said with a teasing smile:

"Just see how you slept last night."

Throwing back the covers, Juehui found that he had not undressed. He grinned at his brother and sat up. The sunlight was painful. He rubbed his eyes. Mama Huang, the boys' maid, came in, carrying a basin of hot water for Juehui to wash his face.

"You were so drunk last night you didn't even take your clothes off," she scolded. "It's very easy to catch a chill in weather like this. When I covered you, you were snoring away, dead to the world. And you slept right through till this morning!" Her wrinkled face was wreathed in smiles. She often berated the boys, but with such motherly affection that they always took it in good grace.

Juemin smiled, and Juehui couldn't suppress a grin.

"You do love to chatter, Mama Huang," Juehui teased her.

"Everyone was so happy last night. What was wrong with drinking a little? I saw you glaring at me every time I raised my cup. It took all the fun out of it. You ought to loosen up a bit during holidays. You're much stricter with us than Madam Zhou!"

"It's because she's not strict enough with you that I have to be so strict," retorted the old lady as she made the bed. "I'm over fifty this year. Been working in this family for more than ten years, looking after you two. I watched you grow up. You've been good to me too. Never a harsh word. I've been thinking of going home for a long time, but I can't bear to leave you. I've seen all sorts of things in this compound. It's not as good now as in the old days. I keep thinking — Leave. When you're used to living in clear water, it's not worth staying after it gets muddy.... But I can't part with you two. Who would take care of you after I've gone? Both you Young Masters are very good — just like your mother. She'd be happy if she could see how well you've grown. I know she's still protecting you, up there in heaven. In another few years, after you've finished school, you'll both become big officials. That will be a great honour for me too!"

Juehui grinned. "If we really become big officials, we'll probably have forgotten all about you by then. How could we think of you at a time like that?"

"I know you'd never forget me. Not that I'd want anything from you. I'll be old and useless by then. All I want is to hear that you've done well in your studies and come up in the world, and I'll be satisfied," the old lady said, gazing at the boy's affectionately.

"Of course we won't forget you, Mama Huang," Juemin assured her, patting her on the shoulder.

The old lady smiled at him and took up the wash basin which Juehui had finished using. At the doorway she paused to warn them:

"No more drinking tonight."

"A little bit won't hurt," was Juehui's laughing rejoinder. But the old lady was already out of earshot.

"What a nice woman," said Juemin. "Servants as good as she are hard to find."

"So you've made the great discovery that servants have feelings and consciences, the same as their masters," Juehui twitted him.

Juemin sensed the mild sarcasm, but he made no reply. He started walking towards the door.

"Going to Qin's house again?" Juehui called after him.

Juemin, at the threshold, turned and gave his brother a reproachful look. But his reply was moderate.

"No. I'm going for a walk in the garden. Would you like to come?"

Juehui nodded and joined him. Passing the door of Juexin's flat, they heard Qianer, bondmaid of the Fourth Household, apparently looking for their elder brother, calling, "First Young Master!" They walked on into the garden.

"Let's stick to the right. *Ye-ye* is in the plum grove, supervising the servants cutting branches," said Juemin when they passed through the moon-gate.

The boys followed a winding covered walk, enclosed on one side by a whitewashed wall inlaid with plaques of decorative marble. A bit further on, a number of windows were cut in the wall — behind these was the drawing-room. Running along the outer side of the covered walk was a stone balustrade, beyond which a large man-made hill and a long stretch of garden could be seen. There was also a low terrace where a few bare peony bushes braved the cold. The end of each branch was wrapped in a layer of cotton padding.

"That's the way to be," said Juehui, nodding approvingly at the peonies. "Standing out in the icy breeze, never shivering a bit. We ought to be like them, not like the little grass that falls withered at the first frost!"

"There you go, making speeches again," laughed Juemin. "Even though peonies weather the winter, grow leaves and put forth blossoms, in the end they still can't avoid *Ye-ye's* shears."

"What of it? The next year they put out new blossoms all over again!"

Emerging from the covered walk, the boys went down a flight of stone steps into a garden filled with misshapen boulders. Some looked like bent old men, some like crouching lions, some like long-necked cranes. At the other end of the garden, the boys mounted some stone steps to a bamboo fence and went through a gate so narrow that only one person could pass at a time. They were confronted with what at first glance seemed an impassably dense thicket of growing bamboos. Then they entered upon a small twisting path which took them through. Nearing the end of the thicket, they first heard, then saw, a little brook flowing out from beneath the man-made hill. Its waters were very clear — you could see plainly the pebbles and fallen leaves lying on the bottom.

A wooden bridge took the boys to the opposite side, where they entered another garden. Here, in the centre, was a pavilion with a thatched roof before which grew a few cassia trees and camellia bushes. Beyond the pavilion was another whitewashed wall, with a small gate leading through its left corner. As the boys crossed the gateway, the sound of waves struck their ears, and a cold breeze made them shiver, but they pressed on.

They had entered a maze of fences, through which they twisted and turned for a long time before finally finding their way out again. Before them stood a grove of tall cypresses. They could hear the wind moaning through the grove; the sky was darkening. Halfway through, to the right where the trees were not so dense, they could see the gleaming windows of a dull red pavilion. At last they reached a clearing on the other side of the grove. Ahead were the shining waters of a crescent-shaped lake, embracing the opposite bank in its curve. A zigzag bridge led to a small isle with a pavilion in the lake's middle.

The boys halted at the edge of the lake and stood gazing at the ripples. They picked up stones and tried to fling them across, but each time, although they were at a relatively narrow section of the lake, their throws fell short, and the stones dropped into the water.

"Let's go over to the other side and find a place to sit down," Juemin suggested.

The boys traversed a small hump-backed bridge to the opposite shore.

Then, crossing a narrow strip of lawn, they mounted stone stairs to a large garden of magnolia trees. A path paved with stones of different sizes ran through the centre, flanked on each side by a row of four glazed earthen stools. Going up a few more steps, the boys came to the recently repaired pavilion they had seen through the cypresses. Except for its tile roof, its whole exterior had been painted vermilion. It was very attractive. A horizontal plaque over its door bore the building's name — "Fragrance at Eventide." The inscription had been written by their uncle Ke'an.

Juemin sat down on one of the glazed earthen stools and gazed appreciatively at the plaque.

Juehui stood on the steps of the building. "Let's climb the back of the hill," he suggested to his brother with a smile.

The older boy refused to get up. "Suppose we rest a while first," he countered.

"All right. I'm going in to take a look around." Juehui pushed open the door of the building and entered.

He gave only a cursory glance at the room's furnishings and the paintings on the wall. Walking towards the rear, he went up the stairs to the upper storey. There he found Big Brother lying on a brick bed. His eyes half shut, Juexin looked worn out.

"What are you doing here, all alone?" Juehui asked, surprised.

Juexin opened his eyes and gazed at him wearily. "I've come for a rest," he replied with a forced laugh. "The last

few days have been too much for me. I can't have any peace
at home. People are always coming to me for one thing or
another. We're going to be up all night again tonight. If I
don't get some rest, I won't be able to last."

"Qianer was looking for you a while back. I don't know
what she wanted."

"You didn't tell her I was here?" Juexin asked in alarm.

"No. I didn't see her. I just heard her calling you in your
room."

"Good," said Juexin, relieved. "I know Uncle Ke'an wants
me for something. I'm glad I was able to get away."

Evidently Big Brother's tactics had changed. Juehui wondered
whether his new methods of placating everyone would be any
more successful.

"You had quite a lot to drink at dinner last night. You
never used to like drinking, and your health's none too good.
Why drink so heavily?" Juehui was not one to beat about the
bush.

"You're always laughing at my battle tactics. Well, this is
one of them," Juexin sat up and replied with a wry smile.
"When things get too much for me I drink some wine, and
the world becomes pleasantly hazy. It makes life much easier."
Juexin paused. "I admit I'm a weakling; I haven't the courage
to face life. The best I can do is make myself befuddled; it's
only in that state that I can get along."

What can you do with a man who admits he's a weakling?
thought Juehui bitterly. He began by pitying his Big Brother
and ended by sympathizing with him. Afraid that anything
more he might say would only add to his brother's unhappiness,
Juehui turned to leave.

"Wait a minute, Third Brother. There's something I want
to ask you," said Juexin.

Juehui walked back and faced his brother. Juexin looked
at him, his eyes gleaming.

"Have you seen Cousin Mei?"

"You know she's in Chengdu?" replied Juehui, surprised. "I haven't seen her, but Qin has."

Juexin nodded. "I've seen her too — a few days ago, at the entrance of the Xinfaxiang Department Store in the arcade."

Silently, Juehui also nodded, trying to read his brother's face.

"She was coming out with her mother. Her mother stopped to talk to someone inside and Mei stood in the doorway looking at some clothing material. I nearly called out. Mei turned around and looked at me. She nodded in half a greeting, then faced towards the interior of the store. Following her gaze, I saw that her mother was there inside. I didn't dare to come any closer, I just stood looking at her from a distance. Her limpid eyes were fixed on me for a long time, her lips trembling. I thought she was going to say something. But she turned and walked back into the store without so much as another glance."

A peal of children's laughter flew in from outside the building, then subsided. Juexin continued:

"Meeting her like that brought everything back again. I had already forgotten. Ruijue is wonderful to me, and I love her. But now Mei's return is stirring up old memories. Living in these surroundings, how can I help thinking of her? I wish I knew how she felt about me. Perhaps she hates me for having led her on. I know that she married, and that she's a widow now, that she's gone back to live with her mother. . . ." Juexin's voice was choked with emotion. Pain and regret contorted his face. He sighed.

"I'm sure she doesn't hate you after all this time and after everything that's happened. Why do you keep torturing yourself with the past? The past should be buried and done with. It's the present we should be thinking of, and the future. Cousin Mei has probably forgotten all about you by now." As Juehui spoke the last sentence, he knew in his heart he was lying.

"You don't understand." Juexin shook his head. "How could she have forgotten what happened between us? Women remember everything. If life had been better for her, if she had a husband who loved her, perhaps she could have forgotten, and I wouldn't worry about her. But Fate had to rule otherwise! Now she's a young widow, a companion for life to her crochety old mother, living like a recluse in a nunnery. How can I help worrying about her?

"But when I think of her, I feel I'm not being fair to Ruijue. Ruijue loves me. Why must I turn around and love someone else? If I go on like this, I'll hurt both of them. I'll never forgive myself. . . . Life is too cruel; that's why I have to dull my brain, that's why I've taken to drink. But it wears off quickly, so I hide myself away from Ruijue after I drink, and quietly weep, for my past sins haunt me even worse then. I curse myself for being such a coward!"

Juehui felt like saying, "You brought it on yourself. Why didn't you fight back? When they wanted to choose a bride for you against your will, why didn't you speak up? You only got what you deserved!" But when he saw his brother's tragic countenance, he only said softly, "It may work out all right. If Cousin Mei falls in love and marries again, everything will be solved."

Juexin shook his head and smiled bitterly. "That only happens in those new books of yours. You ought to open your eyes and take a look at reality. How could a thing like that happen in a family like hers? Not only would her mother oppose it — she herself would never even consider such a thing."

There seemed to be nothing more Juehui could say. He didn't want to argue with Juexin; the distance between their ways of thinking was wider than ever. He didn't really understand Juexin. If a thing was right, why couldn't it be done? It was a useless sacrifice to throw away one's happiness because of conditions, which were capable of being changed. It did no one any good and only served to extend the life of an old-fashioned family a few hours longer. Why couldn't Cousin Mei remarry? Since Big Brother loved her, why did he marry

Ruijue? After marrying Ruijue why was he still thinking of Cousin Mei?

Juehui understood, and yet he didn't. Everything about his patriarchal family was a tangled knot to him; his ardent, direct young mind had no way to unravel it. As he stood gazing at his brother's agonized expression, he was struck by a frightening thought: It was a tragic truth that for people like Juexin there was not a shred of hope; they were beyond saving. Bringing new ideas to them, opening their eyes to the true aspects of the world only intensified their misery. It was like resurrecting a corpse and letting it view its own putrefying flesh.

This bitter truth tormented his young mind. Everything seemed clear to him now; he had a premonition of a still unhappier future. He could see an unfathomable chasm yawning before people like his Big Brother. They were stepping into it without any hesitation, as if they didn't know it was there. It was just as well that they didn't, for they were beyond redemption.

Though he could see them walking towards the chasm, he was powerless to save them. What a tragedy! Juehui's spirits sagged. He felt trapped in a narrow lane, unable to find his way out. The laughter of the children playing outside seemed to be mocking him.

Enough, he said to himself. How many problems can I cram into my one small brain after all? Let everything take its natural course. As long as I behave like a man, that's plenty. That seemed the best solution, and he refused to think any further.

He put his head out of the window and looked around. There were his two boy cousins Jueying and Juequn, his sister Shuhua, his girl cousins Shuying, Shuzhen and Shufen. His brother Juemin was there too. The children were taking turns kicking up a small feathered pad with the inner side of the foot. The point of the game was to see who could kick it up the most times without letting it fall to the ground.

Juehui hailed them with a cheerful shout. His sister Shuhua, who was busy kicking the pad and counting at the same time, turned her head instinctively at his call. As a result, in spite of her desperate effort to retrieve it in mid-air with her foot, it thudded to the ground. And she had just reached a score of one hundred and forty-five, too!

Juemin and the children had also been counting, growing rather anxious as her score mounted. Now, when she missed, they set up a great cheer. Shuhua was furious. She stamped her foot and said it was all Juehui's fault.

"Why is it my fault?" teased Juehui. "I wasn't talking to you!" Turning to come downstairs, he discovered that Juexin was no longer there. Slowly he descended to the ground floor.

He could hear Big Brother's voice. By the time he got outside, Juexin was already kicking the feathered pad. His awkward gestures were quite funny to behold, and the children hooted with laughter. Although Juexin kept a straight face, he was obviously enjoying himself immensely.

Juehui watched, marvelling at how easy it was for people to forget. Within a short time, a person could have a complete change of mood. Could it be that this ability to forget is what enables us to bear up under adversity? Juehui was beginning to have some understanding of this Big Brother of his. Juexin could open the tomb of the past, then close it again and promptly forget all about it.

15

When darkness fell that day, firecrackers began to pop, first sporadically, then bursting all over the neighbourhood. The quiet street resounded with explosions, the boom of big crackers shaking the earth. There was so much sharp, agitated sound it was impossible to tell which direction it was coming from. The noise was like ten thousand stampeding horses, a roaring tidal wave.

After the evening meal, all the Gaos gathered in the family hall. Everyone wore new clothes. The men stood on the left side of the hall, the women on the right. Lights in the hall were burning bright as day, but the two big doors were wide open. Before the ancestral shrine stood a rectangular altar table, covered with a red velvet cloth. In a large basin in front of the altar, several dozen chunks of charcoal, piled up like a mountain, glowed hotly with a bright red flame. Two or three balsam branches sizzled noisily in the fire, emitting an acrid smoke that stung the eyes and nostrils. More branches were scattered on the large, deep-yellow carpet spread upon the floor. A large cushion for kneeling had also been placed before the flaming basin; this cushion was covered with a red velvet cloth.

A pair of tall candlesticks and a big incense burner stood near the outer edge of the altar table. Along the inner edge and at both ends of the table were a great many winecups; only a few members of the family knew exactly how many. Because the Venerable Master Gao was too old to conduct the tiring ceremony, his son Keming had been put in charge.

Wearing long gowns and wide-sleeved jackets, Keming and his brother Ke'an slowly filled the cups with fine white liquor, and lit the incense sticks and inserted them in the burner. Then Keming went to the inner room and invited the Venerable Master Gao to come out and start the ceremony.

A hush fell on the assembly when the old man appeared. Keming issued the order to start the fireworks. A servant hurried out to the inner compound gates — also opened wide — and shouted, "Set them off!" A thunderous burst of fireworks shattered the air.

The women then left the hall by a side door and the men lined up with their backs to the altar table. Facing the main door, the Venerable Master Gao knelt and kowtowed his respects to the gods of Heaven and Earth. He was followed by his three sons who knelt in a line and also kowtowed. Juexin had been out carrying a lighted incense stick to the kitchen, symbolizing the Kitchen God's return after his annual New

Year's report to Heaven on the way the family had been con-
ducting itself. Now Juexin entered the family hall just in time
to join his two brothers and his three male cousins lining up to
kowtow to the gods of Heaven and Earth. This done, all the
men turned and stood facing the altar table. The women, who
had been peeking from the side door, hastily filed back into the
hall.

In accordance with custom, the Venerable Master Gao was
the first to kowtow to the ancestral shrine, after which he retired from the hall. The others followed in this order: Madam
Zhou, the boys' uncles and aunts, then Mistress Chen. They all
kowtowed slowly, consuming a full half hour. Next came the
male children of Juexin's generation — nine in all. The ceremony took place only once a year and the youngsters were quite
awkward at it. They were supposed to kneel, kowtow three
times, rise, then repeat the whole process twice more. But the
nine couldn't co-ordinate their movements. The little boys
Juequn and Jueshi were too slow. Before they finished their
first three kowtows, the others had already risen. Juequn and
Jueshi scrambled to their feet, but the others had already knelt
for the second set. Some of the watchers chuckled, and Madam
Wang, mother of the two youngsters, kept urging them to hurry.
Amid general laughter, the nine young heads quickly bobbed
to a finish. They were capable of much greater speed than their
elders.

Ruijue led four girls to the velvet kneeling cushion — Shuying, Shuhua, Shuzhen and Shufen. Their movements, though
naturally a little slower, were considerably more orderly than
the boys'. Even Shufen, though only seven, was quite graceful.
Ruijue then brought forward her little son Haichen, to pay his
respects.

The servants removed the velvet cover from the kneeling
cushion, and Keming went to the next room to invite the
Venerable Master Gao to emerge again. After the old man
came out, all the men and women of Keming's generation knelt
around him in a circle and kowtowed. They were followed by

the grandsons and granddaughters. The old man received their respects with a smiling face, then he retired to his own room.

A festive air filled the hall after the old man left. The men and women of the older generation formed a semi-circle on the velvet carpet and kowtowed to one another. Grandchildren kowtowed to their parents, then bent the knee to their aunts and uncles. Finally, at Madam Zhou's suggestion, everyone gathered in a large circle, joking and talking only of "auspicious" things. The children and young people then ran off to play, but Juexin and his wife remained with the older generation to receive the respects of the servants.

Juemin and Juehui ran from the hall through the side door and hurried towards their room to avoid the servants' obeisances. But they were caught as they were passing Madam Zhou's flat. First, old Mama Huang made them a very respectful curtsey and wished them well from her heart. Moved, the boys clasped both hands before their faces, and swung them down as they bowed. Three other women servants followed.

Last came Mingfeng. There was a faint sprinkling of powder on her face and the dark braid of her hair shone lustrously. Over her cotton-padded jacket, she wore a new short coat of fine cloth with a rolled edge-trimming. After curtseying to Juemin, she turned to Juehui with a smile. "Third Young Master," she hailed him, and bent her body in a brief bow. Happily, Juehui returned her greeting.

During that instant as they openly smiled at each other, he forgot the past, and the world seemed a beautiful place. It was quite reasonable that he should feel this way, for everywhere in the compound were the sounds of joy and merriment. As to the broad world beyond the compound walls, young Juehui didn't give it a thought. He even forgot the little beggar child he had seen the night before.

A servant came down the steps outside the family hall and shouted, "Set off the fireworks!" A voice further away relayed his command. From the outer courtyard between the front gate and the inner gate, a dazzling display of pyrotechnics shot into the sky. One burst followed another, eight or nine times in succession. These fireworks had been presented by Qin's mother, Mrs. Zhang. The Venerable Master Gao sat on a chair placed for him in the doorway of the family hall. Surrounded by his daughters-in-law, he watched and made critical comment on the show.

Juehui and his young boy cousins went to the main hall in the front courtyard where they could get a better view. The youngsters had already bought some fireworks of their own — "Drops of Gold," "Scurrying Mice" and "Miraculous Book and Arrows" — and were waiting to set them off.

When the display ended, the elders in the family hall departed. Juexin and his three uncles called for sedan-chairs and left to pay their Year's End respects to socially prominent friends. Juehui stood outside the main hall watching his young cousins set off their fireworks.

In the old man's room a game table was placed, and the Venerable Master Gao, Madam Zhou, Madam Zhang and Madam Wang played mahjong. The heavily made-up Mistress Chen, who had just removed her pink outer skirt, sat beside the old man, helping him with the game. Women servants and bondmaids stood around to fill the water-pipes and serve tea.

Ruijue, Shuying, Shuhua and Madam Shen played mahjong in Juexin's room. As hostess, Ruijue offered to relinquish her place to Juemin. But he refused and was only willing to stand behind her and watch her play one game. Then he left.

Instead of returning to his room, Juemin joined Juehui and his young cousins outside the main hall. Juehui was setting off a "Miraculous Book and Arrows" for the boys. A fiery ball shot up over the roof-tops, where it disappeared in mid-air — a dud. Juemin walked up to Juehui and said quietly in his ear:

"Let's go and see Qin."

Juehui nodded and the two brothers walked off, ignoring the pleas of their young cousins that they stay and finish the fireworks.

From the eaves of the front gateway, the large lanterns still shone with a hazy red glow that shimmered in the cold air. The old gatekeeper, seated on an ancient straight-backed wooden armchair chatting with a sedan-chair carrier who sat on a bench opposite, rose respectfully to his feet as the brothers walked by.

Crossing the high iron-bound threshold, they noticed a thin dark face beside the stone lion to the right of the gate. Not recognizing the countenance of their former servant, Gao Sheng, in the dim light of the lantern, they strode on into the street.

Gao Sheng had served in the Gao family for over ten years. Then he became addicted to opium smoking and stole some pictures belonging to the Venerable Master Gao and sold them. When the theft was discovered, he spent a term in jail. On his release, he drifted about from place to place, begging. But at every important holiday he returned to the home of his former master to plead for the small cash gift customarily given to servants at such times. Too ashamed of his tattered clothes to enter the compound, he would wait outside the main gate until a servant who had worked together with him would come out, and beseech the man to relay his request. Because his requests were always very modest, and made at a time when his former master was in good spirits, he usually attained his purpose. As time went on these hand-outs became an established custom.

Today, he had received his small gratuity, as usual. But this time he did not leave immediately. Instead, he remained concealed behind one of the stone lions, rubbing his hand over an icy flank that did not shrink from his caress, picturing the festivities he knew must be going on inside the compound.

When the two brothers emerged, he had recognized them. He remembered Juehui particularly well, for the Third Young Master used to lie on his bed and listen to him tell stories in the light of the opium lamp. He wanted to come forward, to talk with them, fondly. But then, conscious of the shabby state of his clothes, and recalling his disgrace, he drew back, squatting behind the lion to avoid being seen.

Only after the brothers were well down the street did he rise and stare after them, keeping his misty eyes upon them until they were out of sight. He stood in the centre of the street, oblivious of the merciless wind biting through the thin garments covering his bony frame. A loneliness such as he had never felt before gnawed at his heart, and he walked listlessly away, one hand holding the money his master had given, the other clutching his chest.

At this very moment, Juemin and Juehui were striding along, light-hearted and gay, stepping over the remains of fireworks. They walked through quiet streets and noisy, past shops in front of which burned pairs of huge candles, until they finally reached the home of Qin and Mrs. Zhang. Their minds were filled with many cheerful things, and they gave never a thought to the man named Gao Sheng.

The Zhang home had a cold appearance. A lonely kerosene lamp hung from a beam in the gateway, revealing its bareness.

Although not very large, the compound was shared by three families. The heads of two of these families were widows, and there were only two or three adult men in the entire compound, so that life here was quiet. Even on New Year's Eve the place was only a bit more lively than usual.

And the Zhang family was the most quiet of all, for it consisted of only mother and daughter. Qin also had a grandmother who lived in a nunnery, but she seldom came home. The family was served by a man and a woman who had been with the Zhangs for over ten years.

As the boys entered the east courtyard in which the Zhangs lived, the man servant came forward to greet them. Outside Mrs. Zhang's window, the boys called "Aunt!" and they heard her respond. They then went in and knelt before her, saying, "Our respects to Aunt on the End of the Year." Although she protested that such courtesy was "unnecessary," it was too late to stop them. Qin also came in, and the boys clasped their hands and bowed to her ceremoniously. Mrs. Zhang invited them to sit in the family parlour, while the woman servant, Sister Li, went to make some tea.

The boys learned from Mrs. Zhang that their brother Juexin and their uncle Keming had already paid her a formal call, but had left early. They chatted a while with Mrs. Zhang and asked her to spend the New Year Holiday in the Gao compound, the home of her childhood. She said she first had to take Qin to visit her grandmother at the nunnery, but that they would come to the Gaos on the second. She herself would stay only a day or so, because she preferred quiet, but she would let Qin remain a few days more. This made the boys very happy, Qin asked them to come to her room for a while. They followed as she led the way.

To their surprise, they found another girl there. Slim, wearing a rust-coloured satin vest over a pale blue silken gown, the girl sat on the edge of the bed reading beside an oil lamp. She raised her head at the sound of their footsteps, then put down the book and stood up.

The boys stared at her, speechless.

"Don't you recognize her?" asked Qin, surprised.

The girl smiled at them, a sad, helpless smile that deepened the furrow on her forehead, a furrow that somehow heightened her beauty and intensified her melancholy air.

"Yes, of course," replied Juehui wryly. This girl had left a permanent impression on the boys. Time had passed quickly, yet here she was before them, as beautiful and as sad as ever, still slim, with the same thick head of fine hair, the same limpid eyes. Only the furrow in her brow was deeper now, her long braid of hair had been done up in a married woman's bun, and her face was slightly powdered. They had never expected to see her here.

"Are you all well? . . . It's been a long time!" Though her words were ordinary, Mei had to make a great effort to speak them.

"We're all fine, Cousin Mei. And you?" Juemin replied warmly. He forced a laugh.

"Still the same. Except that the last few years I've become even more sensitive. I'm very easily hurt. I don't know why." Mei knit her brows. She was still the same disturbing personality. "I always have been on the melancholy side," she added.

"Environment makes a difference," said Juehui. "But you don't look any different."

"Why don't you sit down? What are you all standing for?" Qin interrupted. "Just because you haven't seen each other for a couple of years, that's no reason to become so formal."

Everyone sat down, Qin seating herself beside Mei on the bed.

"I thought of you often after we parted. The last few years have been like a bad dream. Well, now it's over, and I'm left with nothing but an empty heart," said Mei. Then she immediately corrected herself: "No, I'm dreaming yet. Who knows when I'll really awake? I have no regrets for myself. I'm only sorry I delayed the happiness of someone else."

"You shouldn't be so pessimistic, Cousin Mei. You're still young. Who can predict what the future will bring? Happiness will come to you too. There's no need for such gloomy talk!" said Qin, patting Mei's shoulder. "We're entering a new age. It may be bringing you happiness." Smilingly Qin added a few words in Mei's ear.

Mei coloured slightly, and her brows relaxed. A touch of brightness flitted across her face. Looking at Qin, she pushed a lock of hair back into place. But then her features were again overcast, and she said to Qin with a melancholy smile:

"I think there's a lot in what Third Brother says — environment does make a difference. Our circumstances are very different. I can't be like you. I can't keep up with the changing times. All my life I've been a plaything of Fate. I was never allowed to make up my own mind about anything. What hope have I for happiness?" Squeezing Qin's hand, Mei cocked her head to one side and gazed at her friend approvingly. "I certainly envy you. You have courage and strength. You never let yourself be pushed around."

Qin was pleased with Mei's admiration, but her feeling of satisfaction drifted by like a passing breeze. She was left only with the sad smile that some girls use when confronted with an insoluble problem. Though praised for her "courage and strength," Qin had no choice but to resort to that kind of a smile now.

"Circumstances are certainly important, but why can't we change them?" Juehui interjected heatedly. "Circumstances are man-made to begin with, and man must struggle against them constantly. It's only by conquering our environment that we can win happiness for ourselves." There was much more he wanted to say, but didn't.

In Juemin, Mei aroused varying emotions — sadness, pleasure, alarm, pity, fear. Not only for Mei, but for himself as well. Yet seeing the firm expression on Qin's face, he recovered his calm. He was even able to find words of comfort for Mei.

"You've had a great deal of trouble the past few years, so you're often downhearted. But in the next few years, things are sure to change, and you'll change too. Actually, Qin's situation isn't much better than yours, except that you've been married — let's say you've had one more bad dream than she. The world is the same, the difference is that you look at the dark side and she looks at the bright. That's why you're so easily hurt, while nothing deters Qin."

"Cousin Mei, why not read more of the new books? Qin has some here." said Juehui. He thought the new books could solve all problems.

Mei smiled sadly. She did not answer at once, but looked at them with her limpid eyes. They couldn't guess what was in her mind. Suddenly she withdrew her gaze and stared at the lamp flame and sighed. . . . She started to speak, then hesitated and silently bit her lip. Finally she said, "You all mean well, but it's no use. What's the good of reading new books?" She paused, then went on again, "Everything is beyond redemption. No matter how the times change my situation will never change."

Juemin had nothing more to say. He knew she was right — everything was beyond redemption; she had married and Big Brother now had Sister-in-law. No change in the times could bring them together again. Moreover, their mothers had become enemies.

Even Juehui was beginning to realize that the solution to many problems could not be found in books.

Everyone sat trying to think of an appropriate remark. It was Mei who finally broke the silence.

"I was just looking at some of Qin's *New Youth* magazines. Of course, there are some things in them I don't understand, but there's a lot I do. They have some good articles. I know, because I've suffered. But reading them only makes me feel bad. They talk about another world, a world that has nothing to do with me. Although I admire it, I know I can never reach it. I feel like a beggar standing outside the garden wall of some wealthy home and hearing the laughter inside, or smelling the fragrance of meat cooking as I pass the door of a restaurant. It's sheer agony!"

The furrow in Mei's brow deepened. She drew a handkerchief from her bosom and coughed into it a few times, then smiled mournfully. "I've been coughing a lot lately. At night I can't sleep. My heart pains me."

"Forget about the past, Cousin Mei," Qin begged. She was close to tears. "Why torture yourself? You should take care of your health more. Our hearts ache too to see you this way."

Mei gave Qin a smile and nodded gratefully, but her voice was still sad. "You know my disposition. I can never forget the past. It seems engraved upon my heart. You don't know how I spend my days. My home is much the same as yours, except that in addition to my mother I also have a younger brother. He's busy preparing for his entrance exams; mother is either playing mahjong or visiting friends. I'm alone in the house. I sit reading poetry, without a single person I can tell my troubles to. . . .

"I see fading flowers and I weep. The waning moon hurts my heart. Everything recalls unhappy memories. It's a year now since I left my husband's family and returned to my mother. There's a tree outside my window that I planted when I went away to be married. It was budding then, but by the time I returned, its branches were bare. I often think — that tree symbolizes me. . . . There was a storm a few nights ago, and I lay on my bed, unable to sleep. The rain beat incessantly on the roof tiles and windows. In the dim lamplight, I thought of the lines of a poem:

> *The wind and rain recalls to my heart*
> *The past, so like a misty dream. . . .*

You can imagine how I felt! Tomorrow, tomorrow — you all have a tomorrow, but what kind of tomorrow have I? I have only yesterday. The events of yesterday are painful things, but they are all I have to console myself with."

Suddenly the tone of Mei's voice changed, and she asked the boys, "How is Big Brother? Is he well?"

The boys had been quite moved, listening to her talk, and this abrupt change of mood took them by surprise. Finally, Juehui, the more quick-witted of the two, managed a brief reply.

"Not bad. He said he saw you the other day."

Only Mei understood the meaning of this. Qin and Juemin stared at Juehui in astonishment.

"It's true, we have already met. I recognized him the moment I saw him. He looks a bit older. Perhaps he's angry with me for avoiding him. I wanted very much to talk to him, but I was afraid of stirring up old memories. He would be hurt and so would I. Besides, my mother was there. He came here a little while ago. I heard his voice, but I was afraid to look at him through a crack in the door. Only when he was leaving did I steal a glance at him as he walked away."

"I'm sure he's not angry," said Juehui.

"Don't talk about those things any more," urged Qin. "I was afraid you'd feel lonely over the New Year. That's why I invited you here. I didn't know it would only make you think of the past even more. It's all my fault for bringing the boys in to see you."

Gradually, Mei's melancholy lightened. Although her brows were still slightly knit, her face brightened and she smiled, "It doesn't matter. Getting all this off my mind has done me good. At home I have no one to talk to. Besides, I enjoy talking about the old days."

Then she asked the boys many solicitous questions about their Big Brother and their Sister-in-law.

16

It was past eleven when Juemin and Juehui left the Zhangs, but there was still considerable activity in the streets. Walking along the cobble-stoned thoroughfare and observing the brightly burning lamps in the stores and wine shops that lined the way, they shook off the depression their meeting with Mei had engendered.

Anxious to get home, they walked rapidly and in silence. Their own street, when they reached it, was quiet and littered with the remains of fireworks. But as they neared the stone lions flanking the gateway of the Gao compound, they could already feel the gaiety and activity seething inside.

All of the doors of the gatehouse were open. Servants and sedan-chair carriers were crowded around a dimly lit table, noisily playing a dice game. The doors of the family parlour were open too, and the boys could see their aunts and uncles, or most of them, surrounding a well-lit table, engrossed in a dice game of their own. Uncle Keding and Aunt Wang were the most boisterous of the lot.

Hearing the clatter of mahjong pieces in Juexin's room, Juehui stopped by and watched the game for a little while, then left. The clicking of dice, the clink of coins, laughter and chatter, swept after him in gusts of sound. He stood on the steps, like a spectator at a play, and watched the revellers move about, laugh, shout.

Suddenly he felt lonely and far removed from all this festivity. A chill enveloped him and he was weighed down by a nameless despair. No one sympathized with him or cared about him. He seemed completely isolated.

Juehui found these peculiar surroundings increasingly difficult to comprehend. On previous New Year's Eves he had been able to join in the festivities, merrily, whole-heartedly, forgetting everything as he laughed and played with the other young people. But today he stood alone in the darkness listening to the laughter of others. He seemed to be living in another world.

Has this place changed, or have I? he asked himself. Though he had no definite answer to the question, he knew that he and this big family were travelling in two opposite directions. He recalled Mama Huang's remark about "clear and muddy water."

To calm the confusion in his mind, he came down the steps to walk along paths that were unobstructed.

Passing through a corridor, he turned into an inner courtyard. The sound of laughter was gradually left behind him. He stopped, and discovered that he was outside the room of his sister Shuhua. On the other side of the courtyard the flat of his uncle Ke'an stood brightly illuminated. A wistaria vine clambered over a trellis arbour in the garden separating the two dwellings. Juehui sat down on a straight-backed chair outside his sister's window and gazed dully at the kitchen in the corner diagonally opposite. Through the open door of the kitchen, he could see women servants bustling about.

He heard a low familiar voice in Shuhua's room say, "I hear they're going to pick one of us two. . . ." The speaker was

Waner, bondmaid in the Third Household of Juehui's uncle Keming, a long-faced girl about a year older than Mingfeng, who spoke rather quickly.

The remark came suddenly, and it drew Juehui's attention. Sensing that there was something unusual behind it, he listened with bated breath.

"Needless to say, you'll be the lucky one," said the voice of Mingfeng, with a giggle.

"I'm serious. How can you have the heart to laugh at me?" Waner retorted hotly.

"I congratulate you on your good fortune — does that make me heartless?" laughed Mingfeng.

"Who wants to be a concubine!" Waner's anger mounted, and there was misery in her voice.

"A concubine's life is not so bad. Look at the Venerable Master's Mistress Chen."

"Got an answer to everything, haven't you? Just wait, we'll see who they pick. Your turn is coming sooner or later," Waner replied in agitation. She laughed spitefully.

Juehui's heart pounded. Repressing an urge to cry out, he listened intently, waiting to hear what Mingfeng would say.

Apparently realizing that this was no joking matter, Mingfeng remained silent for a long time. The only sound was the steady ticking of the clock on the wall. Juehui was growing impatient, but he couldn't tear himself away.

"If they choose me, what shall I do?" Mingfeng asked despairingly.

"All you can do is go, cursing your fate," was Waner's bitter response.

"No, no, I can't go, I couldn't. I'd rather die than be that old man's concubine!" Mingfeng cried desperately, as if already faced with the prospect. Her voice shook tragically.

"Maybe it's not true. Maybe someone has only made it up of scare us. If it ever really came to that, we could still think of a way out. We could ask Madam Zhou to help us," said Waner, somewhat mollified by Mingfeng's words. She seemed to be trying to console herself as much as to soothe the younger girl.

Juehui sat motionless in the straight-backed chair, oblivious to time and place, deaf to the maids laughing and chatting in the kitchen. Servants carrying platters of food occasionally passed by Uncle Ke'an's window. They never gave Juehui a glance. The laughter in the kitchen grated on his ears; it sounded raucous, mocking.

"I have an idea that you're in love with someone. Am I right?" Waner asked Mingfeng softly. She spoke more slowly than usual.

Mingfeng didn't answer, and Waner gently pressed, "You are in love, aren't you? You've been acting rather strange lately. Why don't you tell me the truth? I won't tell anyone. I'm like your elder sister. You shouldn't hold anything back from me."

Mingfeng whispered a few words in Waner's ear. Though Juehui listened with all his might, he was unable to hear what she said.

"Who is it? Tell me," Waner demanded with a laugh.

Electrified, Juehui strained his ears.

"I won't tell you." Mingfeng's voice shook a little.

"Is it Gao Zhong?" Waner persisted. Gao Zhong was the young servant who worked for Uncle Keding. Juehui released his breath and a weight seemed to drop from his heart.

"Him? Ha! Why should anyone love him! You're the one who's after his heart but you won't admit it," laughed Mingfeng.

"I was asking you in earnest. How can you say such things?" Waner retorted. "Are you sure Gao Zhong isn't in love with you?"

"Oh, good sister, no more nonsense!" Mingfeng pleaded. "Let's talk sensibly."

Then in a lowered tone she continued, "You can't guess, and I won't tell you. I'm the only one who knows his name."

She felt safe and secure when she thought of him, and happiness crept into her voice.

The girls' voices dropped lower and lower, until Juehui could catch only snatches of it, interspersed with muffled laughter. He gathered that Waner was talking about her own romance. One of the older women servants shouted for her from one of the front buildings, but Waner paid no attention and went on with her story. Only when the calls drew very close and it seemed that the older servant was about to enter the room where the girls were hiding did Waner reply.

"We're at their beck and call all day long. Even on New Year's Eve we can't get any rest," she grumbled as she walked out.

Mingfeng was left alone in the room. She sat silent, motionless.

Juehui knelt on his chair and, poking a small hole in the paper window, peered inside. Mingfeng was sitting on a cane chair, her elbows on the desk, supporting her face in her hands, the little finger of her right hand tucked in the corner of her mouth. She was staring at the pewter oil lamp whose stem was festooned with cedar twigs and clusters of peanuts.

Suddenly she sighed. "What is the future going to bring?" She leaned forward and buried her head on the desk.

Juehui tapped lightly on the small pane of glass in the centre of the window. There was no response. He rapped more loudly, and called in a low voice, "Mingfeng, Mingfeng."

The girl raised her head, and looked around. Seeing nothing, she sighed again. "I must have been dreaming. I thought I heard someone calling me." Listlessly, she pushed herself up from the desk and rose to her feet. The lamplight cast the shadow of her early-ripening young form against the bed canopy.

Juehui rapped harder and called her name several times. When she at last determined where the sound was coming from, Mingfeng hurried over and knelt on the chair beside the window. Leaning against the chair back, she asked, "Who is it?"

"It's me," Juehui replied quickly. His voice was low. "Lift the curtain. I want to ask you something."

"It's you, Third Young Master?" cried Mingfeng, surprised. She raised the paper curtain, painted with grass and flowers, and saw the tense face of Juehui pressed against the pane of glass. "What's wrong?" she asked in alarm.

"I heard what you and Waner were saying just now —"

Blushing, Mingfeng cut him short. "You heard us? We were only joking."

"Don't try to fool me," Juehui replied excitedly. "Suppose there really comes a day when they want to marry you off. What will you do then?"

For several minutes Mingfeng did not speak. Suddenly tears began to roll from her eyes. She did not wipe them away but, taking a grip on herself, said with utmost determination, "I won't go. I'll never go to another man. I give you my vow!"

Juehui hastily pressed his hand against the glass, as if to seal her mouth. "I believe you," he assured her. "You don't have to swear."

Like one awakening from a dream, Mingfeng remembered where they were. Urgently she rapped on the glass, pleading, "Go away, Third Young Master. Someone is liable to see you."

"I won't go until you tell me what's happening."

"All right, I'll tell you. But then you must go, please, dear Young Master. . . ."

Juehui nodded.

"They say your grandfather's old friend Feng is looking for a concubine. Mrs. Feng came here to help him find one among us bondmaids. Waner heard from her mistress that the Venerable Master had agreed, and she told me. As to how we feel, well, you just heard us. . . . Now please go. It would be bad if anyone saw you here." Mingfeng firmly pulled the curtain back into place and refused to open it again, no matter how Juehui rapped and called.

Defeated, he got down from the chair and stood dully on the

steps.   His mind was alive with many things.   Though his eyes
were facing the kitchen, he saw nothing.

Inside, Mingfeng remained kneeling on the chair. Thinking
Juehui had gone, she cautiously raised the curtain and peeked
out.   When she saw him still standing there, she was touched.
Unconsciously, she pressed her face against the glass and gazed
abstractedly at his back.

17

When Juehui returned to his room, the sound of dice rolling in
a bowl had already stopped, but many people remained chatting
around the game table.   Although the mahjong tiles were still
clicking in Juexin's room, they were not nearly so noisy.   The
sky was beginning to lighten.   The year was ending.   The old
was disappearing with the darkness, and the new and bright
was emerging.

At the hour for prayers to the gods, Juehui went to the family
hall.   Because young Juequn had let slip an unlucky remark
there, the Venerable Master Gao wrote the phrase "A child's
words cannot prevent good fortune and prosperity" on a piece
of red paper and pasted it on the door post. Juehui couldn't
help smiling.

Firecrackers began bursting outside the main hall.   Three
long strings in succession were set off; they were still popping
when the last of the worshippers had entered the hall.   It was
then already daylight.

Juexin and his three uncles got into sedan-chairs and went
off to pay their New Year calls.   The women of the family,
stepping over the remnants of exploded firecrackers, walked
smilingly through the main gate and out on to the street.   This
was the women's annual comedy of "going abroad." It was only
during this brief interval each year that they were permitted to
travel freely in public, other than in closed sedan-chairs.   The

women feasted their curious eyes on the sleepy little street. Then, fearful of meeting any strange men, they hurried back into the compound. The firecrackers were finished, the laughter was stilled. For a short time, the street again lapsed into silence.

With the important events of the day over, most of the Gao family, having been up all night, went to bed early. Except for people like Juexin and his uncle Keming, who had many social functions to perform, nearly everyone slept through until the evening prayer service. A few, like Juemin and Juehui, didn't even get up for dinner.

The days of the New Year Holiday thus passed smoothly. Each day's programme was arranged in advance, much the same as in previous years. Gambling went on apace; the sound of dice and mahjong almost never stopped. Even Jianyun, who considered gambling pointless, also took part, unhesitatingly acting against his own desires for the sake of pleasing others. In these intervals he was able to shake off a bit of his melancholy and enjoy a pittance of fun.

On the second day of the New Year, Qin and her mother arrived. Mrs. Zhang remained three days, then returned home, permitting Qin to stay on until the sixteenth.

Having Qin with them greatly added to the young people's enjoyment. All day they played games in the garden or told stories. They would each contribute and send one of the servants to buy spicy and salty delicacies which they would take to the foot of the hill behind the "Fragrance at Eventide" building, and heat up picnic lunches on a small stove. The girls Ruijue, Shuying and Qin were good cooks, and they took turns at preparing the meals, with the rest of the young folks helping out. When the food was ready it would either be brought into "Fragrance at Eventide," or to some other clean, quiet spot, and placed upon a table. Then everyone would set to eating with a will, to the accompaniment of noisy win-drinking games.

One day they had a visitor — Xü Qianru, a classmate of Qin. Qianru lived in a compound diagonally opposite the

Gaos. She was a plump girl of eighteen or so, outspoken, with
a free and easy manner, very much the modern schoolgirl. Like
Qin, she was dying to get into the boys' school. She was anxious to meet Juehui and Juemin and ask when their school
was going to lift its ban against girls.

Qianru's father was active in the Tong Meng Hui Society
(a forerunner of the Kuomintang). In his youth, he had attended a university in Japan. Later, he managed a revolu-
tionary newspaper advocating the overthrow of the Manchus.
He now held a post in the Bureau of Foreign Affairs of the
Sichuan Provincial Government. He was much more advanced
in his thinking than the average man of his day.

Qianru's mother, who had also studied abroad, had died two
years before, but her father had not remarried. An only daughter, Qianru was still looked after by an old nursemaid who
had cared for her ever since she was born.

Brought up in this enlightened environment, it was inevitable
that Qianru should be quite different in personality from
Qin. But the two girls were very good friends.

Jianyun also spent a few days with them. He seemed somewhat happier, and although Juemin could not entirely conceal
his dislike, the other boys were very good to him.

On the evening of the eighth, after the young people had
prepared for two whole days, they invited their elders to the
garden to watch some fireworks. Unable to resist the youngsters' ardent entreaties, the grown-ups, with the exception of
Ye-ye, who couldn't take too much of the evening cold, arrived on time.

All the electric lights in the garden were blazing. In addition, small lanterns of red and green and yellow burned on the
branches of the bamboo and cypress trees. The illuminated
railings of the arched stone bridge joined their reflections in
the water to make perfect circles. Big panelled red lanterns
with dangling tassels hung from the eaves of "Fragrance at
Eventide," casting soft pink shadows that evoked a dreamlike
atmosphere.

The audience took their seats inside the building beside the widely opened windows. Except for a few faint coloured shadows here and there, outside all was dark.

"Where are the fireworks? You've fooled us," said Madam Zhou with a laugh.

"You'll see them in a minute," replied Qin, smiling. She looked around and observed that the boys had already disappeared.

In the inky stillness beyond the windows, suddenly, from a somewhat lighter patch of darkness, came a piercing sound, and a ball of red flame rose high into the black sky, burst into a shower of golden rain, then melted back into the night. Immediately a snow-white thing like a goose egg shot heavenward. There was a shattering explosion, and silver sparks flew in all directions. Then a blue light streaked up into the sky, where it changed colour and came down in droplets of red, quickly turning into a shower of green. The last was so brilliant that even after it vanished, the audience still saw green shadows before their eyes.

"How lovely," said Madam Zhou. "Where did you buy them?"

Qin only laughed, but did not reply. In the light of the dazzling fireworks that followed, a small boat was revealed near the opposite shore of the lake.

"So that's where they've been setting them off. No wonder they seemed to rise from a different place each time," Madam Wang remarked to her husband Ke'an. He nodded and smiled.

For a time the lake was absolutely still. The watchers craned their necks, but their eyes couldn't pierce the darkness.

"Is it over?" Keding asked regretfully. As he started to rise, the lake burst into light.

A myriad of fireworks streaked and flowered all over the sky. After a while, darkness again descended. The air trembled and the clear notes of a bamboo flute sailed up from the lake, to the muted accompaniment of a bow on a two-stringed *hu qin*, lulling its listeners with a melody that charmed like an ancient fairy tale, making them forget their petty cares, evoking old dreams, dreams that were never fulfilled.

"Who is that, playing so well?" asked Madam Zhou, when the tune was nearly over.

Listening entranced, Qin was a bit shaken by the sudden question. "Cousin Shuying," she whispered quickly. "And that's Big Brother on the *hu qin*." She returned her attention to the concluding performance.

The flute stopped, and in the distance there was applause and laughter. Striking the quiet surface of the lake, they were at once swallowed up, and did not float to the surface again. Only a few sounds that had escaped the water reached the audience on the wings of a breeze; and these were already very faint, dying with the lingering echoes of the melody's last few notes.

Then the mellow tones of the flute again soared forth in a lively and cheerful air, and a strong male voice joined in song, penetrating the dark night, driving away the echoes of the earlier melody. The listeners in the building were awakened from their misty reveries; they recognized the voice of Juemin.

The singing did not last very long. Soon, together with the sound of the flute, it faded away in the darkness. Then Juemin's voice rose again, this time in a popular operatic aria. As he launched into the second line, he was joined by a chorus of mixed voices. But even as these blended together, it was still possible to distinguish the individual singers; the crisp soprano of Shuying was not drowned out by the vibrant baritone of Juemin. The forceful music struck the audience like a blow in the face. It poured into their ears; overflowing, it flew all around them; it seemed to rock the very building they were sitting in.

Then, just as the audience's tension was at its height, the singing abruptly stopped. But this was immediately followed by a great roar of laughter — the audience wasn't given a moment's rest. The laughing voices collided with one another in mid-air. Some splintered into thready slivers, shattered beyond repair; a new laugh would rise, pursue one that was still intact, and smash it to bits. To those in the building it seemed as though the laughter was battering, leaping, chasing through the darkness.

Little red and green lanterns began to appear, floating on the lake, one after another. Before long, the patch of water which the audience was watching was covered with lanterns. They moved slowly, reflecting strange colours on the surface of the water, changing, bobbing, all without a sound. Suddenly, there was a flurry of activity, and the lanterns separated to leave a lane in the middle. Again there was laughter — this time more subdued. A small boat loaded with laughter slowly drew near, and stopped beside the bridge. The laughing voices were now much clearer to the people in the building; they could see Juexin and his brothers coming ashore. The boat then passed under the hump-backed bridge and approached the near bank. To the surprise of the audience, there was another boat behind it. This one remained at the bridge, and several girls got out — Shuying, Shuhua and Shuzhen, all carrying lanterns.

As the young people came into the building, the atmosphere grew lively.

"Well, how did you like it?" cried Juexin with a laugh.

"Excellent," commended Uncle Keding. "Tomorrow night I'm inviting you all to see a dragon dance. I'm preparing the 'fire tubes' myself."

Jueying excitedly clapped his hands, and the other young people joined in with exclamations of approval.

The performance that night had indeed brightened the lives of the older folks like a rainbow. But in a little while everything returned to its original form, and the garden again stood quietly in the chill darkness.

18

On the ninth day of the New Year, the young boys Jueying, Juequn and Jueshi were extremely busy. From early morning, they laboured all through the day, helping the sedan-chair carriers make fireworks and discussing the coming dragon dance.

That morning Uncle Keding's carriers had cut down two thick bamboos and sawed them into segments. With the aid of the other carriers, these were packed with gunpowder, fuses and bits of copper coins — the last because they would stick to the skin of their human targets and burn without dropping off. Everyone worked with a will, and the dozen-odd tubes were soon ready. The tubes were then placed on exhibition in the gatehouse for all to admire. Proudly lined up on a long bench, they stonily awaited their victims.

Time seemed to drag interminably, but dusk came at last. After the prayer services were over, Uncle Keding took charge of the servants in making final arrangements. In the inner compound, a number of tables were set up and chairs placed on top of them to serve as a temporary grandstand. Keding personally sealed the packets of coins to be awarded to the performers. He made several trips to the main gate to see if they were coming, while dispatching a servant to stand on the street corner to keep a lookout for them.

A quarter of an hour later, the whole compound stirred with excitement. By then the entire family, with the exception of the Venerable Master Gao, had taken their seats on the grandstand. The dragon dance troupe, beating drums and cymbals, entered the outer compound. The main gate was promptly closed behind them, to keep outsiders from slipping in under cover of the general tumult.

To the pounding beat of the drums and cymbals, the dragon began to dance. From head to tail, the dragon consisted of nine sections, made of paper pasted over bamboo frames and painted to resemble scales. Each section contained a lit candle, and was manipulated by a dancer who held it aloft by a bamboo handle. Ahead of the dragon pranced a youth twirling a staff with a big ball of coloured paper streamers at one end. The dragon bounded after the ball, rolling on the ground, or wagging its tail or shaking its head as if in great satisfaction, leaping and cavorting like a real dragon, while the beat of cymbals and drums seemed to add to its awesomeness.

A sharp report like the crack of a rifle bullet split the air. Firecrackers began to pop, and the dragon danced more wildly, as if angered. As firecrackers fell and exploded on its body, it dodged and twisted from left to right and made several startled leaps. The drums and cymbals roared more loudly, like the cries of a wounded dragon.

Perched on a ladder against the compound wall, Gao Zhong, a young male servant, extended a long bamboo pole with a string of bursting firecrackers dangling from one end, over the dragon's body. A few sedan carriers who had been standing by, waiting with a powder-filled "fire tube," now ignited it and took turns spraying the flying sparks against the bare torsos of the dragon dancers. The maddened dragon rolled desperately on the ground trembling from head to tail, trying to ward off the shower of hot sparks. People shouted, while the drums and cymbals crashed incessantly. The sedan-chair carriers laughed. The gentry on the grandstand laughed too, though in a much more refined way, of course.

Now the chair carriers attacked the dragon with four or five "fire tubes" from both sides. It was impossible for the dragon to escape. No matter how it writhed and rolled, the sparks streamed against the bare flesh of the dancers, some of the flame adhering to their bodies, making them halt their dancing and cry out loudly. Finally the dancers stood stock-still and, holding the poles by which they had manipulated their segments of the dragon end up like walking staffs, they struck bold poses and let the carriers spray them. Their only defence was to shake their bodies violently to throw off the sparks. The audience laughed approvingly, and the carriers moved in closer with their fire-spitting tubes, determined to make the dragon dancers beg for mercy.

Though strong, powerful men, the dancers made no attempt to defend themselves. In spite of the pain, they uttered fierce defiant cries.

"If you've got any more 'fire tubes,' bring them on!" they yelled.

But the dancers were only flesh and blood. When the flaming tubes came closer and closer, they broke and fled, the awesome dragon disintegrating into nine parts, as each man ran off with the segment he had been manipulating. The dragon's scales had been burned away completely, from head to tail, and all that remained of the segments were the bamboo frames.

Some of the dancers, carrying the empty frames on their shoulders, ran for the main gate. But it was already closed, and they had no choice but to steel themselves and return. At their master's signal, the chair porters again attacked with fresh "fire tubes." The compound was flat, offering no concealment, and several of the dancers ran towards the inner compound gate. But the gateway was jammed tight with spectators, presenting a solid screen of nothing but heads. As the dancers drew near, Uncle Keding suddenly stepped forward with a flaming tube and sprayed, catching the youth who twirled the stick with the ball of coloured paper streamers. Uttering a sharp cry of pain, the boy turned and fled, only to be headed off and driven back by a servant armed with another "fire tube." The boy shook his body violently to ward off the burning sparks; his forehead was beaded with sweat.

Uncle Keding, pursuing the dancer who had manipulated the dragon's tail, suddenly observed the trembling youth. "Are you cold?" he asked with a grin. "Here, this will warm you up a bit!" And he directed the full force of his fire against the boy at close range.

By instinct the youth raised his staff defensively, exposing the ball of paper streamers. The paper burst into flame; in a moment it was demolished by the blaze. Servants and chair carriers with spewing tubes of sparks were closing in now on the youth and the tail dancer, determined to make them beg for mercy. But just then the tubes burned out, and it was discovered that there were no more reserves; so the merrymakers were forced to desist.

The main gate was then opened. Carrying their clothes, the dancers again formed into ranks, took up the skeletal remains of the dragon and, to the bedraggled beat of drums and cymbals, wearily marched out of the compound. The youth who twirled the coloured ball had been hurt. He was muttering under his breath as he limped away.

Uncle Keding had finished handing out the packets of money gratuities to the dancers. "Too bad we didn't have enough 'fire tubes,' " he said regretfully. "Were you satisfied? I'll invite you all to watch another show tomorrow night."

"I've had enough. I don't want to see any more," said Juehui coldly.

Keding looked at him uncomprehendingly. Other people, more polite, added, "I's not necessary."

The three young boys, Jueying, Juequn and Jueshi, who had had the best time of all, were already lost in the crowd. The rest of the gentry, well pleased, strolled back to the inner compound, while the servants quickly dismantled the temporary grandstand.

Juemin and Juehui lagged behind with Qin. Juehui asked her, "Did you find it interesting?"

"I didn't see anything interesting about it."

"Well, what was your reaction?"

"Nothing in particular."

"It was dull," Juemin interposed. "I used to like these shows a lot as a kid; not any more."

"You mean neither of you was the least bit moved?" Juehui demanded sternly.

Juemin didn't know what his young brother was driving at. "It's just a low-class carnival act. How could it move anyone?" he protested.

"You didn't feel even a touch of sympathy?" Juehui asked heatedly.

"What has sympathy got to do with it?" inquired Qin. "Uncle Keding and his friends enjoyed themselves, and the dragon

dancers got their money.   Everybody was satisfied.   What's
wrong with that?"

"Spoken like a true daughter of the rich!" Juehui laughed
coldly.   "Why can't an intelligent girl like you understand?
Do you really think enjoyment should be based on others'
pain?   Do you think just paying money entitles you to sear a
man's flesh?   You talk as if you look at things with your eyes
only half open!"

Qin did not reply.   It was her habit when confronted with
a question she could not answer to remain quiet and think,
instead of plunging into an argument.   She did not know that
this was a problem to which her young girl's mind could never
find a solution.

19

The weather was exceptionally fine the night of the fifteenth.
A lovely full moon like a white jade platter hung suspended
in the dark blue sky amid a sprinkling of bright stars and a few
wisps of white clouds.   Riding slowly through the heavens, the
moon spread its rays on the world below.

That evening, the usual prayer service was concluded early.
The little boys went out to the street to watch other dragon
lanterns being burned up.   The young people were gathered in
Juexin's room, discussing how to spend the last night of Qin's
visit.   The New Year Holiday would end on the fifteenth day
of the first lunar month, and though Qin lived nearby they
seldom had an opportunity to visit together for several full
days at a time.   They all agreed with Juexin's suggestion that
they go rowing on the lake.

Originally, Ruijue was also going, but the baby began to cry
just as they were leaving, and she stayed behind to look after
him.   The party consisted of Juexin and his two brothers, their
sister Shuhua and her two girl cousins, and Qin, with Mingfeng
bringing a small hamper of food.

Slipping into the garden one after another, like a school of fish, they travelled along the covered walk. Shuzhen, the most timid of the girls, stuck close to Mingfeng. It was very quiet, and the scattered electric bulbs glowed dim and lonesome. A swath of moonlight in the long garden was mottled over with dark shadows.

The young people moved on slowly, chatting as they walked. As they reached the flower terrace, they suddenly heard a strange noise, and a dark shape leaped from the artificial hill to the tile roof of the covered walk, terrifying Shuzhen so that she shrank behind Mingfeng.

"What was that?" cried Shuhua in a startled voice.

Everyone stood still. In the surrounding darkness nothing moved. Juehui stamped his foot, but there was no response. He stepped across the railing, walked over to the flower terrace, picked up a few pebbles and tossed them on to the tile roof of the covered walk. A cat miaowed, then was heard scampering away.

"Only a cat," laughed Juehui. Vaulting the railing back into the promenade, he noticed Shuzhen cringing behind Mingfeng. "Aren't you ashamed?" he twitted her. "Scared of nothing at all."

"My ma says there are ghosts in the garden," the girl replied in a quavering voice. She was clutching Mingfeng's hand tight.

"Ghosts? Who ever saw a ghost? Your mother was only teasing you, and you fell for it. What a simpleton!" Juehui laughed.

"Why did you come with us if you're afraid of ghosts?" asked Juexin.

Shuzhen dropped Mingfeng's hand. "It's fun to be with you," she replied timidly. "I just had to come."

"Well said, dear. That's the way to talk," Qin commended with a smile. "Come on, I'll protect you. Don't worry. With me at your side, no ghost will dare come near you." Qin took her by the hand, and the two girls walked on together.

"Old Master Jiang, the famous ghost exorcizer, is here. All

spirits disperse!" cried Shuhua sarcastically, and everybody laughed.

They entered the bamboo grove. Although there were no electric lights here, the moonlight illuminated a small winding path. The grove was not very dense, and the sky was bright overhead. The bamboos rustled slightly in the breeze. From somewhere came the sound of running water; near the end of the grove the young people discovered a little brook.

To show his contempt for ghosts, Juehui deliberately lagged behind, walking with Mingfeng. Suddenly he dashed into a bamboo thicket. At the noise, everyone turned around, and Juemin asked:

"Third Brother, what are you up to?"

Juehui made no reply, but uprooted a young bamboo and, breaking off the thin end, shaped it into a staff. He rapped it experimentally against the ground, and said with satisfaction, "This will make a good walking stick." Then he rejoined Mingfeng.

The others laughed. "Is that all?" grinned Juemin. "I thought you had gone crazy and rushed off to dig for buried treasure!"

In high spirits, the group entered a grove of pines. Little of the moonlight filtered through the dense pine needles, and in the deepest part of the grove the path seemed to vanish completely. But they all knew the way well. With Juehui in the lead, feeling out the twists and turns with his bamboo staff, they were able to proceed. The soughing of the pines somehow gave them a feeling of terror, a fear of the unfathomable darkness. Tensely, they moved slowly forward, Qin holding Shuzhen closely to her.

Gradually, the path ahead lightened, and then they saw the lake, silver and glistening in the moonlight. The reflection of the full moon, floating on the surface of the water, was pulled at times into an oval shape by the spreading ripples. Occasionally, a leaping fish splashed. Not far to the right was the hump-backed bridge. In the distance on the left, the twisting stone bridge leading to the pavilion in the centre of the lake was vaguely discernible.

Halting at the water's edge, the young people relaxed in the cool tranquillity. A stone, flung into the water, broke the moon's reflection, rippling it out into a large circle. Although the mirrored moon quickly resumed its original shape, the ripples continued to widen until they vanished.

Juemin turned around to see Juehui standing behind them, grinning.

"So it's you again," Juemin snorted.

"What are you all hanging around here for? The boat's over there." Juehui pointed to a small craft moored to a willow on the opposite side of the bridge.

"No need for you to tell us. We saw it long ago," said Shuhua. She pulled her long braid forward over her shoulder. Toying with it, she looked up at the moon and began to sing an old tune.

Just as she had sung the first line, "When is the moon at its brightest," Juemin's vibrant voice joined in, then Qin and Shuying sang too. Juexin began to accompany them on his flute. At this point, Shuying borrowed Juemin's piccolo, saying:

"That flute's too reedy. This is sharper." Then the long clear notes of the piccolo pressed down on the thin, weakly piping flute. But some of the flute's mournful tears seeped through, and could still be heard.

Juehui slowly strolled along the lake's edge towards the bridge, after beckoning Mingfeng to come with him. They exchanged a few brief words as they walked a distance, then Mingfeng turned around and rejoined the others. It wasn't until Juehui had almost reached the bridge that he realized he was alone. He turned and went back to the group.

The beautiful surroundings suddenly irritated him. He felt he was somehow different from his brothers and his girl relatives. It seemed to him that under its peaceful exterior, his family harboured a smouldering volcano.

The song concluded, Shuying raised the piccolo to her lips to begin another. Juehui stopped her.

"Let's wait till we get in the boat. What's the rush?"

With Juehui in the lead and Mingfeng bringing up the rear, the young folk walked along the lake to the bridge and went across.

Juexin untied the boat and held it while everyone got in. Then, pushing off, he jumped into the stern and, taking up the tiller oar, started the boat moving.

Slowly passing under the hump-backed bridge, the boat entered the broad bosom of the lake. In the prow, Mingfeng opened the small hamper she had brought, and took out some bits of salted vegetable, melon seeds and peanuts. She also produced a bottle of rose wine and some little winecups. She passed all these to Shuying and Shuhua, who laid them on the small round table in the middle of the boat. Juemin pulled the cork from the bottle and poured the wine. In the bright rays of the moonlight, the young people set to eating and drinking.

Moonlight draped the now distant hump-backed bridge like shimmering gossamer, and the electric lights at the bridge's either end could be seen only dimly. Imperceptibly, the boat had slowly turned. The young people had been gazing up at the moon, and when they next looked around they discovered quite a different section of the lake. On one side was a sharp towering cliff; on the other, a building stood overlooking the water. The pavilion on the isle in the centre of the lake was now entirely visible, etched against the moonlight.

Juehui's heart was bursting with things he wanted to say. To relieve the pressure, he let out an exuberant shout that rang and echoed against the cliffside.

"You certainly have a big voice," laughed Juexin, and he launched into a Beijing opera aria.

Rounding the cliff, the boat passed the fishing pier. The building overlooking the water was now screened by a dense growth of low trees.

The surface of the water suddenly darkened, and the sky

took on a greyish cast as clouds hid the moon. Except for the rhythmic splash of the rudder oar, all was still.

"A little slower," Juexin directed.

As the waters of the lake turned and narrowed, the trees and house gradually disappeared. On both sides were man-made hills, a small hut leaning out from the hilltop on the right. The water flowed more rapidly here, and the boat soon drifted through the narrow passage. With Juexin cautiously operating the oar which he had taken over, the boat described a wide circle to the rear of one of the artificial hills. Here the span of water was short. On one side was a low wall; on the other, the man-made hill, looking extremely high and blocking out some of the moonlight.

Mist, creeping over the lake, cast a veil over everything. It was beginning to get chilly. The young folk finished the wine in their cups and sat closer together. A gong, clashing faintly in the distance, seemed to be in another world. Juexin and Mingfeng plied the oar vigorously.

"Has the question of your schooling really been settled?" Qin asked Shuzhen. "I hear your teacher is coming tomorrow."

The past few days, with Qin's encouragement, Shuhua and Shuzhen had been bombarding their mothers with pleas that they be allowed to study. The women finally consented to let them join the class conducted by the private tutor of their young boy cousins.

"It's settled," Shuzhen replied promptly. "I'm all ready."

"I didn't think you'd succeed so easily," remarked Qin.

"There's nothing strange about that," Juehui interposed. "It's not costing her parents a penny — the tutor gets the same fee no matter how many pupils he teaches in one family. With other people's daughters learning how to read and write, you can't be very proud of yourself when your own daughter's practically illiterate. As long as Shuzhen's mother agreed, her father doesn't care; he never bothered about such things anyhow. Ye-ye's always worried that he'll lose face by some female member of our family doing something conspicuous in public, but he doesn't mind them studying at home, particularly since they only read the 'works of the sages'. . . ." Just mentioning the "works of the sages" caused Juehui's flesh to creep; he couldn't suppress an uncomfortable laugh.

Juehui's recital made the whole thing as clear as day to the others. They had no need for further explanation.

White-capped waves tossed and a mist covered the lake as the boat neared the hump-backed bridge, seen dimly through the fog. The electric bulbs on the shore gleamed red and yellow in the mist. The young people had made a complete circuit of the lake.

From the slowly moving boat, they found the picture of the moon shining through the fog intriguing. As they silently gazed around them, their craft sailed past the "Fragrance at Eventide" pavilion. Juexin asked whether they wanted to go back.

"It's getting late," said Juehui, "and there are sweet dumplings waiting for us at home."

Since no dissenting opinion was expressed, Juexin steered for the bank. When the boat was again moored to the willow tree and everyone was ashore, the group walked across the bridge.

"I never enjoyed an evening more in my life," Juemin commented, and several of the others voiced their agreement.

But Juexin was thinking — If only Mei had been here with us. . . .

And Qin was saying to herself — I must bring Mei to join one of our outings some time. . . .

As the group emerged from the garden, the two young boys, Jueying and Juequn, puffing hard, came running to meet them. To Juexin, Jueying cried excitedly:

"Have you seen the newspaper 'extra,' Big Brother? They've started to fight!"

Juexin was mystified. "Which extra? Who's started to fight?"

"Here, see for yourself," said the boy, proud to be the bearer of such important tidings. He thrust a "Special Edition" of the *National Daily* into Juexin's hand.

"The governor has ordered a punitive campaign against General Zhang," Juexin read with a growing feeling of tension. "Hostilities have already commenced."

20

"Is there any news?" Ruijue asked Juexin as he entered the house. There was a worried look on her face.

"The situation has worsened," he replied, shaking his head despondently. "The provincial troops suffered another bad defeat. They say the attacking General Zhang has already reached the city's north gate." Juexin walked over to the window and sat down on a wicker chair.

"I hope there won't be any street fighting," Ruijue said in alarm.

"Who knows? That depends on whether the governor is willing to step down." Juexin was worried, but to soothe Ruijue he added, "But I think they'll be able to solve this thing peacefully." Actually he hadn't the faintest idea how it would end.

Ruijue walked into the adjoining room and listlessly seated herself on the edge of the bed where little Haichen was sleeping. There was a faint smile on his face. She lightly caressed his rosy cheeks with her fingers. He seemed especially precious to her at this moment. It was as if someone wanted to snatch him away from her. She couldn't bear to let him go and sat guarding him, her eyes staring blankly at the window. The compound was very still, and the rhythmic ticking of the clock struck her heart like little blows.

Rapid footsteps hurried into the next room. Obviously someone was bringing an urgent message. Frightened, Ruijue rose to her feet, and hastened to see who had come. She found Juemin standing beside the desk talking to Juexin.

"What is it?" she asked from the doorway, very upset.

"I just saw them carrying wounded soldiers into the city, two and three at a time. I don't know how many there are," said Juemin excitedly. "It's simply terrible. They're on stretchers, all bloody, some with shattered hands, some with broken legs, dripping blood and groaning. I saw one fellow with a gash an inch long in his temple. His face was as white as paper. It's really terrible. . . ." Juemin paused, then went on, "The battlefield can't be far from the city. If they lose another battle, we're sure to have fighting in the streets."

"Will we be all right here?" Ruijue asked quickly, frightening pictures flashing into her mind.

"Maybe. Let's hope the routed soldiers don't set fire to everything like they did the last time!" replied Juemin.

"We've only had two or three years of peace, and now this had to happen. They just won't leave you alone! What kind of life do you call this?" Juexin suddenly burst out, rising to his feet. He strode from the room, leaving Juemin and Ruijue alone and frightened.

Then Juehui and Shuhua came in.

"The circus has begun again." Juehui's bright voice broke the silence.

"Aren't you afraid, Third Brother?" Juemin asked fretfully. "You seem quite happy."

"What's there to be afraid of?" replied Juehui breezily. "It's been much too quiet around here. A little military acrobatics will liven things up a bit. I'm afraid our school will have to suspend classes tomorrow, though."

Ruijue was surprised. "How can you be so brave!"

"When you've seen this same show often enough, even the timidest person becomes brave. They've been fighting for years, but I'm still me. Why should I be afraid?"

But Juehui's words couldn't drive away their fears. When Mingfeng, who raised the door curtain just then, called them to dinner, none of them had any appetite.

"I'm not hungry," Ruijue replied apathetically.

"Me either," said Shuhua.

"You girls are really useless creatures, scared of your own shadows. Hear a little news and you can't even eat," laughed Juehui, as he left for the dining room.

After dinner, the three brothers decided to go out and see if they could pick up any news. But they found the big doors of the compound gate closed and bolted with a great wooden bar. It was very dark in the gateway. The old gatekeeper told them the streets were already closed to traffic.

As they turned and walked back into the interior of the compound, they discussed the relative strength of the two contending military forces.

"We're sure to hear gunfire tonight," said their uncle Keding, meeting them at the entrance to the inner courtyard.

The compound was much quieter than usual that night. Everyone seemed afraid to speak in a normal tone; people even walked more softly. The least sound was enough to set hearts pounding. The kitchen fires had been banked early; no one felt much like eating. The women wrapped their valuables and hid them in the basement or concealed them on their persons. In every room parents and children, staring at one another with tired, frightened eyes, sat in vigil through the long, long night.

A serious-visaged Keming went from room to room, announcing the instructions of the Venerable Master Gao. Everyone was to act with caution. It would be best for all to wear their clothes to bed so as to be able to flee at a moment's notice.

These orders heightened the tension even more, as if some tremendous calamity was just about to happen. Juehui began to lose a bit of his self-assurance.

"Flee? Where to?" he asked himself. A picture suddenly appeared in his mind: A rifle bullet ricocheting off the cobbled street hits a servant standing beside a stone vat. The servant clutches his wound, utters a piercing cry, falls writhing to the ground and dies in a pool of blood. This was something Juehui had seen with his own eyes. Although several years had elapsed since, the scene was still etched in his memory. He too was full of life; but, like all the people around him, he was only flesh and blood. Juehui felt uncomfortable and a little frightened recalling that terrible day. The glaring light of the electric bulb irritated him. He wished it would vanish and leave him buried in the darkness.

At about ten o'clock, a clear sharp report rang out, the air vibrating briefly with its trailing echo.

"They've commenced firing." Juemin raised his head from the desk. He spoke in a hushed voice. His eyes were dull in an ashen face.

Three or four more shots sounded, this time much closer.

"From the look of things, the situation isn't too serious yet. That was just soldiers on the city wall firing to scare off the enemy." Juehui forced himself to speak calmly. But before he had finished, more shots were fired, loudly and rapidly. Then another brief silence, followed by very heavy firing, like a squall of rain. Bullets sang over the rooftops, a few striking and smashing the tiles. Haichen, awakening in the next room, began to cry. Outside, a tragic voice wailed someone's name.

"Awful, it's awful," sighed Ruijue in the adjoining room. Haichen stopped crying. The old man, in his room in the central building, coughed loudly.

"Boom!" A tremendous sound like a clap of thunder shattered the air, followed by a hiss like pouring gravel. The whole house shook with the explosion.

"They're firing shrapnel shells!" Ruijue's low voice trembled.

"Boom! Sssh! Sssh!" Three times in succession, and with the last a huge crash somewhere behind the Gao compound, like a wall collapsing. The house shuddered long and violently.

"We're finished. They're using such heavy artillery — we're all goners!" Juexin, in the next room, could be heard stamping his foot in anguish. "That last crash sounded like a wall coming down. I'd better go to the back and see if Uncle Keming and the others are all right."

"Don't go. It's even more dangerous outside. I won't let you go!" cried Ruijue tearfully.

Juexin sighed. "The three of us together like this — one shell can finish us all off."

"Shells have no eyes. You can be killed outside just as easily as in here. If we have to die, I'd rather we die together," sobbed Ruijue. Haichen began to cry again, loudly, and the artillery shells again commenced to boom.

"This is torture! Let's die and get it over with!" Juexin's voice was tragic, hopeless, frightened.

Juehui couldn't bear to listen to it any longer. He covered his ears with his hands, pressing hard to blot out every bit of sound.

A piercing mournful wail cut through the air, as if intent on tormenting the weak of heart. Suddenly, the electric lights went out, and the whole compound was plunged into darkness.

"Light the oil lamps!" The cry seemed to rise from every building simultaneously. There was much confusion and scrambling about in the rooms.

But Juehui lay on his bed; Juemin sat beside the table. Neither of them moved.

There was a momentary lull in the pounding of the artillery, but rifle fire was still quite heavy. Suddenly, many people were heard shouting in the distance. Were they uttering cries of joy, or of warning, or of sorrow? To the brothers the noise evoked a terrible picture: Soldiers running down the streets, driving gleaming bayonets into the backs of fleeing citizens, who dropped dead to the ground as the bloody blades were ripped out again; in a fury of sparks from burning buildings, the mad soldiers, howling like animals that had tasted blood, savagely searching for more victims. . . .

In the compound there was only darkness and terror. Everyone waited in silence for the decision between death and survival. On the fields and hills outside the city, thousands were locked in mortal combat, fighting, struggling, dying. This thought would not let the brothers rest for a moment. In the darkness of their room, red and white shadows danced constantly before their eyes.

"What a terrible age we live in!" Juexin sighed bitterly in the next room, his cry evoking a sympathetic echo in his brothers' hearts.

"Isn't there anything we can do?" moaned Ruijue. "We must think of something!"

"Don't talk like that. You only make me feel worse," Juexin pleaded. "Try to sleep a little. You look exhausted."

"How can I close my eyes at a time like this? A shell might land on us at any moment."

"Calm yourself, Ruijue. If we're fated to die, there's nothing we can do about it. You must try and get some sleep." Juexin forced himself to speak in a soothing voice.

Next door, Juemin struck a match and lit the oil lamp. Its small wick flickered weakly, illuminating only a small part of the room. When his lacklustre eyes fell on Juehui's white face, Juemin cried in surprise:

"What's wrong? You look awful!"

Juehui lay motionless on his bed. "You don't look so good yourself," he replied softly.

The two brothers gazed at each other in silence. Bullets continued flying over the roof, while thundering artillery shook the house to its foundations. Haichen again began to cry.

"There's no use just waiting around like this. Let's get some sleep, I say," said Juehui with determination, rising to his feet and starting to unbutton his clothing.

"That's a good idea, but we'd better keep our clothes on," advised Juemin.

But the younger boy had already removed his outer garments and slipped between the covers. He pulled the comforter over his head; sure enough, before long the sound of the firing began to fade from his ears.

*   *   *

The next day dawned bright and clear, and the new rays of the sun, radiating up from the horizon, revealed that the Gao compound was quite unharmed — except for a few broken roof tiles and a piece that had been knocked off the roof of the left wing. There was only desultory firing now, and the general atmosphere was fairly peaceful.

Juemin and Juehui went to see their stepmother, Madam Zhou, and found Uncle Keming's wife and daughter Shuying there with her, looking weary and rather bedraggled. The room was very messy, with four square tables pushed together in the centre over a thick carpet. The two women and the girl had slept beneath the tables the previous night, tightly barricading themselves on all sides with quilt comforters, hoping that this would protect them from bullets. Madam Zhou said Shuying and her mother had moved over after a shell had landed in the garden behind their house, knocking down a section of the courtyard wall.

"It must have been about three o'clock in the morning. A shell seemed to have struck the roof of your wing and broke many tiles. Ruijue came running over here, crying, carrying Haichen," Madam Zhou said to the boys. "I was afraid your room had been hit, and I called and called to you, but nobody answered. Bullets were flying thick and fast. No one dared to go out and look. Finally, Mingfeng went over and found your door locked but your room undamaged. It was only then we knew you were all right and stopped worrying. Don't go to sleep like that again tonight whatever you do. You must be ready to run at any minute."

Madam Zhou ordinarily spoke quite quickly, and this speech she uttered without stopping for breath. The words came sliding out of her mouth like pearls rolling down a smooth surface.

"I usually wake at the least noise. With all that racket going on outside, I don't understand why I slept so soundly," laughed Juemin.

At this point Juexin and Keming came in. Their calm appearance soothed Madam Zhou.

"Is everything all right now?" she asked them.

"It's probably all over," replied Keming in his usual measured tones. "The streets are passable again. There isn't a soldier in sight. Things are quiet outside. They say the attacking troops took the arsenal last night and the provincial authorities asked the British Consulate to act as intermediary. They asked him to say that they were willing to make concessions and that the governor would resign. I don't think there will be any more fighting. Last night we all had a needless scare."

Turning to his wife, Keming urged her to go home and get some rest. "You were up all night," he said. "You look worn out. . . ." And to Madam Zhou he courteously added, "You ought to rest too. We put you to a lot of trouble last night."

After a few more words, Keming and his wife and daughter departed. The two brothers remained to chat with their stepmother.

The day passed uneventfully. Everyone assumed that the trouble was over. But towards evening the situation suddenly changed again.

Except for the Venerable Master Gao, the whole family was sitting in the courtyard, discussing the happenings of the previous night. A servant rushed in, out of breath, and announced tensely:

"Madam Zhang has come."

A moment later, Madam Zhang, Qin and another young woman entered through a side gate. They were dressed in the ordinary clothing that women wore around the house, rather than in the more formal dress for making calls. Although their expressions were different, they all appeared rather frightened.

Everyone rose and greeted them in turn. But just as Mrs. Zhang was about to explain the reason for their sudden arrival, there was a noise like a clap of thunder. A fiery streak flew across the sky, followed by a tremendous explosion, then several more. Men, women and children hastily left the courtyard for the shelter of the family hall.

After four or five rounds, the artillery fire stopped, and rifle bullets began to sing. These came from the northeast corner of the city, thick as a squall of rain. The chatter of machine-guns joined the fray, and it was soon impossible to distinguish this sound from the rapid popping of rifles. Suddenly, the noise grew in intensity, like the wild rush of a large army, and the cannon mounted on the city walls commenced firing. The racket was no less deafening than the night before, with over a dozen big guns, quite nearby, roaring simultaneously. The ground shook and the windows rattled as if the compound had been struck by an earthquake.

Inside the family hall, frightened speechless, people turned pale and looked at one another distractedly. They knew that their lives were hanging by a thread, and they waited silently — without a sigh, without a groan, without a struggle. The fear of extinction overrode all other emotions. They simply did not react to Juexin meeting Mei again, to her coming to this compound again with Mrs. Zhang after several tumultuous years. Their only thought was of the fiery harbingers of death streaking through the sky above them.

Slowly, the daylight faded. There was a lull in the artillery barrage, although the heavy rifle fire continued. People began to worry: "How are we going to get through this night?" Just then an enormous explosion made the walls tremble. A noise followed like the sputter of firecrackers and the smashing of tiles.

"Finished, we're finished!" cried Madam Zhou in a quavering voice, instinctively rising to her feet. Walking to the door that led to her room, she almost collided with Mingfeng who came running in.

"What is it? What's happened?" several voices demanded at once.

Mingfeng's face was bloodless. She was gasping so hard she couldn't speak.

The door curtain was pushed aside and the Venerable Master Gao entered, followed by Mistress Chen. Everyone rose.

"What's wrong?" the old man asked.

"I was in Shuying's room . . . a big shell landed . . . and

knocked a hole in the eaves. . . . It broke all the windows too. . . . The courtyard was full of smoke. . . . I ran. . . ." Mingfeng stammered, very frightened.

"Crowding together like this won't do at all. One shell in here could finish off the whole family. We'll have to think of something better," the old man warned. He started coughing.

"I say it's best for us to separate, leave the compound. Each household can go and live with relatives in other parts of the city. *Die* can move in with the Tang family. It's quite safe there," suggested Keming.

"There's no way to get through to the East Gate section. But the sections near the South Gate and West Gate might be a bit better," said Mrs. Zhang. She and the girls had fled by way of the East Gate after her house had been taken over by the military. Mei, who was visiting the Zhangs, was intending to go home, but when the road was cut, she had come with them to the Gao's, instead.

Before Mrs. Zhang had finished speaking, another shell howled over the roof. It exploded somewhat further off than the previous one — probably in the next compound.

Everyone rushed towards the entrance; but they were stopped by servants at the main hall, who explained that the big gate was already bolted — the streets were full of soldiers and all traffic had been halted.

There was no choice but to return. For the want of a better shelter, at Juexin's suggestion, everyone went into the large garden.

It was like entering another world. They could still hear the firing, but their surroundings helped them forget their terror. Green grass, flowers of red and white — everywhere expressions of gentle life. Veiled in the twilight mists, the garden had an air of mystery. Although people were overwrought, they could not help noticing these beauties of nature.

Passing through the grove of pines, they came to the edge of the lake. The sunset clouds, the colour of the rambling rose, were reflected in the pale blue water, which was already draped with twilight mists. Without pausing, they followed along the edge of the grove where it skirted the lake and proceeded towards the "Lakeside Retreat" pavilion.

Thickets of slim bamboos screened the dark grey tiles of the building's roof. A few magnolias, in the clearing before the front door, were in full blossom, and their white flowers gave out a heady fragrance.

Keming, opening the door, invited the Venerable Master Gao to enter first; the others filed in behind him. A servant lighted a hanging kerosene lamp. The old man was exhausted. He lay down on a bed, while everyone else found chairs and benches. Besides this middle room, the "Lakeside Retreat" also had two side-rooms which the servants now quickly set in order, preparing one for the men and one for the ladies.

By this time the big guns were silent. The rifle fire dwindled, then stopped altogether. In these peaceful quiet surroundings the recent terror seemed merely a bad dream. From the windows overlooking the lake, people gazed at the clear water. The fresh breeze drifting in seemed to blow away much of their anxiety. A new moon cast pale silver beams on the surface of the lake, adding to its coolness. Opposite, the "Fragrance at Eventide" pavilion rose chastely in the moonlight; before it spread a swath of white flowers. The man-made hills, the cliffs, the plum trees, the willows — each with its own distinctive colour and shape — touched by the moon's silvery rays, became clothed in an air of the deepest secrecy.

"I came here once about five years ago." Mei, who had been worrying about her mother and brother at home, now relaxed a bit in these pleasant surroundings and sat staring at the "Fragrance at Eventide" pavilion on the opposite shore as if in search of something there. After a while her gaze had shifted to the line of willows along the bank and, with a sigh, she had addressed this remark to Qin.

Standing beside Mei, Qin was silently watching the moon sail slowly through clouds resembling billowy white waves.

She turned and looked at Mei, who pointed at the willows and said:

"Those trailing willow strands are knotted around my heart. . . . And now spring has come again."

Changing the subject, Qin tugged at Mei's sleeve and said cheerfully, "We all went boating here on the first full moon of the New Year. Everyone said what a pity it was you couldn't be with us. Who would have thought that you could come so soon. . . ."

But Mei's response was still sad. With tears in her eyes she took Qin's hand. "I'm very grateful for your good intentions. But what's the good of my coming here? Don't you know how I feel? Nothing has changed here. Every tree, every blade of grass, brings back painful memories. Even though my heart has turned to cold ashes, I can't forget the past completely."

Qin gave Mei a startled glance, then looked around quickly to see whether anyone had overheard her. "You shouldn't talk that way here," Qin whispered. "They might hear you. Even if it is hard to forget, you shouldn't torment yourself like this."

Just then, Qin heard footsteps behind her. She turned quickly to see Ruijue approaching, leading little Haichen.

"What were you two whispering about that was so secret?" Ruijue asked with a laugh.

Mei blushed and made no reply. Qin said jestingly, "You've come just at the right moment. We were finding fault with you!"

Even Mei laughed at this. "Don't you believe her," she said to Ruijue.

"Of course I can't compare with Qin," smiled Ruijue. "She's read many books, she goes to a new-type school, she's good-looking, courageous —"

"And what else?" Qin demanded, with mock sternness.

"And, and . . . oh, and lots more!" Ruijue burst out laughing.

Then, in a more serious tone, she said to Mei, "I've been wanting to meet you for a long time — I've heard so much about
you — but I never had the good fortune. What lucky wind
brings you here today? I can't tell you how glad I am. But
haven't I seen you somewhere before?"

"Her photograph perhaps?" Qin suggested.

"No. I'm sure I've seen her somewhere. I just can't remember where. . . ."

Mei moved her lips in a tight little smile. "I haven't been
fortunate enough to have known Sister-in-law before," she said
courteously. But she immediately added in a friendly voice,
"You're a bit plumper than your picture, though." Taking the
little boy by the hand, she asked, "And this must be Haichen?"

"Yes," smiled Ruijue. To Haichen she said, "Say hello to
aunty."

The little boy, his eyes fixed on Mei, promptly responded.

Mei smiled at the child fondly and bent to embrace him.
Patting his cheek, she remarked, "He looks just like Big Brother,
especially his bright eyes. How old is he? Four?"

"Not yet."

Mei pressed her cheek against Haichen's, kissing him and
calling him "darling" several times before finally returning
him to Ruijue. "You're really fortunate to have such a
wonderful son," she said quietly, in a somewhat different tone
of voice.

Sensing the change, Qin quickly began to talk of something
else. As the three young women chatted, Ruijue suddenly realized that she was attracted to Mei, in spite of the fact that
this was the first time they had met.

That night everyone went to bed early. Keming and Juexin
returned to their own quarters so as to be able to keep an eye
on the compound. Juemin and Juehui felt very restricted oc-
cupying the same room as their grandfather; they too went back
to their own room where they could have more freedom. Having already been through a few shellings, they were much
braver now.

21

No one slept well that night. As the sky was turning light, the Venerable Master Gao began to cough. He coughed loudly and incessantly, waking the others, who decided they might as well get up early too.

Qin and Shuying, after washing their faces and combing their hair, took Mei on a tour of the grounds, pointing out the changes that had been made during the years she had been away. The girls also talked of some of the events in their own lives in that period.

The garden had not been damaged much by the bombardment. Only two pine trees had been knocked down by a shrapnel shell.

Outside, the streets were still not open to traffic, but the restrictions were a bit more relaxed than the day before. Although soldiers remained on duty at every intersection and sentries stood at regular intervals along the streets, individual pedestrians, if not stopped by the sentries, could travel within limited areas.

The Gao family cook could find little in the vegetable market. Because all the city gates had been closed for two days, peasants had been unable to bring in their produce from the surrounding countryside. Although the cook exercised all his ingenuity, the meals that day were necessarily rather skimpy.

Lunch was served in the "Lakeside Retreat." Two large round tables were set up in the middle room, with the elder generation sitting at one and the younger folks at the other. Although no one had eaten well for two or three days, the few dishes which now appeared on the table looked so uninspired that most people lost their appetite. After a couple of listless mouthfuls, they put their bowls down again and left the table.

Only Juemin and Juehui did justice to the food. Juexin stole glances at Mei, seated diagonally opposite, and their eyes met several times. Mei quickly lowered her head or looked away, blushing, her heart beating fast. She didn't know whether the surge of emotion she felt was joy or sorrow. Fortunately, everyone was so engrossed watching the voracious way the two younger brothers were cleaning out their bowls that no one noticed her reactions.

"Your appetites aren't bad at all," Shuhua twitted her brothers after her grandfather had left the room. She addressed her remark to Juemin. "The food is gone, but you're still holding on to your rice bowls."

"Naturally we're not the same as you girls," Juehui retorted, swallowing a large mouthful of rice and putting his bowl down. "You have to have chicken or duck or fish or meat at every meal. Do you know what our lunch at school consists of? Green vegetables, cabbage, beancurd, bean paste.... Now you have to suffer too. I hope we're cut off another few days just to see whether you can take it."

He was preparing to go on, but Juemin joggled his elbow, signalling him to be quiet. Juehui, also noting the displeased expressions on the faces of some of his elders, lapsed into silence. He pushed back his chair and got up.

"I was talking to Second Brother," snapped Shuhua. "Who asked you to butt in?" Turning her head, she refused to pay any more attention to him.

The meal over, the three brothers went out to the street to see whether there was any news. They also intended to have a look at the house of Mrs. Zhang, if they could get there.

Few pedestrians were abroad. People were gathered in groups of four or five at the front gates of their compounds, craning their necks to look up and down the street and engaging in earnest discussion. Every ten yards or so, a soldier in full battle dress stood beside the wall or paced slowly back and forth, holding his rifle. But none of the sentries challenged the brothers, and they strode on freely.

Beside a barrier at a fork in the road, they came upon half

a dozen men reading an announcement posted on the wall. It was the governor's resignation. As the governor modestly expressed it, his "virtues were insufficient to serve the people and (he) lacked the talent to alleviate their distress." As a result, a battle took place which "brought suffering to my officers and men and hardship to the people." He had therefore decided to retire, so as to avoid "prolonging the fighting and bringing devastation to the land."

"Now that the enemy soldiers are camped outside the city walls, he makes pretty speeches," Juehui laughed. "Why didn't he resign long ago?"

Juexin hastily looked around. Fortunately no one was standing nearby, and the remark had not been overheard. He tugged at Juehui's sleeve and warned in a low voice, "Be a little more careful in what you say. Don't you want to live?"

Juehui made no reply. With his two brothers he passed through an opening in the barrier. In front of an old temple, a dozen soldiers, their faces expressionless, stood near their stacked rifles. Next door, the little general store had a few copies of that day's newspaper on sale. The boys picked up a copy and glanced through it. The paper's attitude had already begun to change. Although it still had kind words for the retiring governor, it no longer referred to the enemy army as rebels. Enemy leaders whom it formerly had designated as "insurrectionists" and "bandits" it now described politely as General this or Commander that. The same Merchants' Association, the same Society for the Preservation of Ancient Morals, which had previously published denunciations of the "vile bandits," in today's paper announced their welcome to the officers and generals about to enter the city.

"It looks like the trouble is over," said Juexin. By then the boys had already walked two blocks and were entering the intersection of a third.

The barrier ahead of them was shut tight, guarded by two armed soldiers. The boys had no choice but to turn back. They tried to make a detour through a back lane, but they again found themselves confronted by a sentry where the lane rejoined the main street.

"Where do you think you're going?" the thin-faced soldier demanded savagely.

"We want to visit a relative who lives a few blocks beyond here," Juexin replied courteously.

"You can't get through." The sentry clamped his mouth tight. He looked with satisfaction at the rifle in his hands and the bright blade affixed to the end of it. "If you come one step nearer," he seemed to indicate, "I won't waste any more words. I'll let this bayonet do the talking."

Silently turning away, the three brothers retraced their footsteps through the small lane and sought another entrance to the main street. But all their efforts were in vain. Sentries blocked every intersection.

They decided to go home. Worried that the road back might be cut off, they walked quickly. There were few people on the streets. Shops and homes were silent, their doors shut. It was much quieter than when the boys had set out, and this increased their apprehension. Each time they passed a sentry their hearts pounded, fearful that he would stop them. Luckily, this did not happen, and they finally arrived home.

Most of the family were in the garden. The brothers hurried to join them. They found their grandfather and their aunts playing mahjong at two tables in the "Lakeside Retreat." Juehui marvelled at their interest in the game at a time like this. Noticing that Juemin had disappeared, he slipped out too. Juexin remained standing beside his grandfather's chair where he reported what little news they had been able to obtain.

This news naturally pleased the older folks considerably. Mrs. Zhang was still rather uneasy that Juexin was unable to tell her the condition of the house she had been forced to abandon, but then she drew a good hand and promptly forget about her worries.

When the older people became engrossed in their game, Juexin took the opportunity to depart. He stood a while beneath a magnolia tree, feeling rather silly, as if longing for something he knew he couldn't attain, though it was right in front of his eyes. - Life seemed empty, futile. Leaning against the tree trunk, he gazed at the greenery stretching before him.

Birds sang in the trees. A pair of grey thrushes fluttered on a branch above, bringing a shower of snow-white magnolia petals down on Juexin's head. He watched the thrushes fly off to the right. He would have given anything to change into a bird and soar with them aloft into the vast firmament. An intoxicating fragrance assailed his nostrils; when he bent his head to look around, magnolia petals dropped from his head and shoulders. One still adhered to his chest. He gently picked it off with two fingers and, releasing it, watched it sail languidly to the ground.

A woman's figure came rounding the artificial hill. She walked slowly, head lowered, a willow branch in her hand. Suddenly, she looked up and saw Juexin standing beneath the tree. She halted, her mouth trembling a little, as if about to speak. But no sound came from her lips, and she silently turned and walked away. Over a jacket of pale green silk she wore a black satin vest. It could be no one but Mei.

Juexin felt chilled all over, as if drenched with a bucket of cold water. Why was she avoiding him? He had to know. He set off in pursuit, walking softly.

As he rounded the artificial hill, he saw flowers and shrubs, but there was no sign of Mei. Strange. Then, off to the right, through a cleft of the adjoining man-made hill, he observed her black satin jacket. Making a circuit of that hill too, he came to a small oval-shaped lawn fringed with a few peach trees. She stood beneath one of the trees, her head down, looking at something in the palm of her hand.

"Mei!" The cry escaped him as he walked quickly towards her.

She looked up. This time she did not turn away, but gazed at him blankly, as if she didn't recognize him.

Coming up to her, he demanded in an agitated voice, "Mei, why are you avoiding me?"

She lowered her head and gently stroked the dying butterfly cupped in her hand. It was still feebly moving its wings. Mei made no reply.

"Haven't you forgiven me yet, Mei?" he asked painfully.

She looked up and gazed at him steadily, then replied coldly, "You haven't injured me in any way, Big Brother."

Only those few words.

"That means you won't forgive me." His tone was almost tragic.

She smiled. But it was a sad, not a happy, smile. Her eyes, softening, caressed his face. She placed her right hand on her breast and said quietly, "Don't you know what's in my heart? Could I ever have hated you?"

"Then why do you avoid me? We've been parted so long, but now, at last, when we're able to meet again, you're hardly even willing to talk to me. How do you think I feel? How can I help thinking you still hate me?" Juexin demanded tearfully. He drew out a handkerchief and mopped his eyes.

Mei did not weep. She only bit her lips, and the furrow in her brow deepened. "I never hated you," she said slowly, "but it's better that we don't see much of each other. There's no use stirring up the past."

Juexin, sobbing, was unable to speak. Mei bent and gently placed the butterfly on the grass. "What a shame," she said in a voice filled with love and pity. "Who could have put you in such a state?" Although this might be taken in two different ways, Mei had not intended any hidden meaning. She walked away in the direction of the "Lakeside Retreat."

When Juexin looked up, through the tears that filled his eyes he could see the bun on the back of Mei's head and the pale blue woollen cord that held the hair in place. She was about to disappear behind the hill. A cry burst from his lips.

"Mei!"

She paused and waited for him to catch up.

"What is it?" she asked, assuming a cool air.

"Are you really so cruel? You have pity to give a butterfly. Don't I deserve any pity at all?" He was sad and disappointed.

Mei remained silent. Head down, she leaned against the face of the man-made hill.

"You may be leaving tomorrow. We may never have a chance to see each other again, living or dead. We seem to be in two different worlds. Can you really walk off from me like this without a word of farewell?" sobbed Juexin.

She still did not reply, but her breathing was rapid.

"Mei, I've wronged you, hurt you . . . though I couldn't help myself. After I got married, I forgot about you. . . . I didn't think of how you must be suffering." His voice was still low but broken with agitation. Though he held a handkerchief, he did not wipe his eyes, and tears coursed down his cheeks.

"Later, I heard what you've been through these last few years, all because of me. After that, how could I live in peace? I've been suffering too, Mei. Can't you even say that you forgive me?"

This time when Mei looked up tears stained her face and her eyes glistened. She was weeping softly after all. "My heart is tangled like flax. . . . What do you want me to say?" she kept repeating. She pressed her hand to her breast and began to cough.

Her distress wrenched Juexin's heart. Forgetting himself, he drew near to her and dabbed her tears with his handkerchief.

For a moment she permitted this. Then she pushed him back. "Don't," she said miserably. "You mustn't arouse any suspicion." She started to walk away.

He grasped her hand. "Who can suspect anything? I'm a married man already, the father of a child. I shouldn't make you suffer so. You must take care of your health." He wouldn't release her. "You can't go back looking like that. So many tears," he said tenderly. Juexin forgot his own unhappiness completely in his pity for Mei's tragic fate.

Gradually her weeping subsided. She took the handkerchief

"What a shame. Who could have put you in such a state?"

from him and wiped her tears, then returned it to him. "I've thought of you every minute these past few years," she said sorrowfully. "You don't know what a comfort it was getting a glimpse of you at Qin's house the day before New Year. I was very anxious to see you after we came back to Chengdu, but I was afraid. That day at the Xinfaxiang Store I avoided you. Later I was sorry. But I couldn't help it. I have my mother. You have Sister-in-law. I was afraid recalling the past would only hurt you. I don't care about myself. My life is already over, but I don't want to cause you any pain. . . .

"At home, my mother doesn't know how I feel. She only sees things from her own viewpoint. She loves me, but she doesn't think of me as a person. To her I'm just a soulless thing. She can't possibly understand my tragedy." Mei sighed. "I'd rather die early than go on like this."

Juexin massaged his chest. His heart pained him terribly. They stood looking at each other. Juexin smiled mournfully and pointed at the grass.

"Do you remember as children how we used to roll on this lawn? When an insect bit my hand, you sucked the bad blood out. We used to chase butterflies here and dye our fingernails with the juice of red balsam flowers. The place is still the same, isn't it? . . . Once when there was an eclipse of the moon, we took a bench and sat in the garden. We offered to accept the pain so that the moon wouldn't have to suffer while it was being eaten. . . . Remember? . . . And those days when you studied together with us at our house. How happy we were then. Who would have believed that we'd end up as we have today?"

He spoke as if in a reverie, as if straining to recapture the joy of the past.

"I live almost entirely on my memories now," Mei said, softly. "Memories sometimes can make you forget everything. I'd love to return to those carefree days. Unfortunately, time cannot flow backwards. . . ."

Footsteps were heard approaching, then the voice of Shuhua

spoke. "We've been looking for you all over, Cousin Mei. So this is where you've been hiding!"

Mei quickly stepped back a bit from Juexin and turned around.

Qin, Shuying and Shuhua were coming her way. As the three girls drew near, Shuhua noticed Mei's face and cried in mock alarm, "Has Big Brother been picking on you? Why are your eyes all swollen with crying?" Then she peered at Juexin who hastily drew back. But she had already seen.

"Oho, you've been crying too? Meeting again after so many years you both ought to be happy. Instead you hide here and weep at each other. Very peculiar."

Mei blushed, while Juexin looked away muttering something about "my eyes hurt."

Shuying laughed. "That's strange. They never hurt you before. Why should the pain start just when Cousin Mei arrives? Funny you should both be suffering together!"

Qin was tugging at her sleeve, indicating that she should be quiet for Ruijue was approaching, leading the baby. But Shuying couldn't stop in time, and Ruijue overheard her.

Ruijue didn't know what to make of it. Smiling, she brought little Haichen to Juexin and asked that he carry him. To Mei she said, "Don't feel badly, Cousin Mei. Let's go for a walk. I'm afraid you take things too seriously." Affectionately, she took Mei by the arm and led her away to the other side of the hill.

Shuying and Shuhua wanted to follow, but Qin stopped them. "They probably have something private to discuss," she admonished. "I think they'll become good friends. Sister-in-law is very fond of Cousin Mei." Although addressing the girls, Qin intended her remark for the ears of Juexin.

22

Two days later, the streets were opened to traffic again. The invading army, under General Zhang, was encamped outside the city walls. It was rumoured that the governor was departing from the city that day, leaving the newly appointed garrison commander temporarily in charge of public security. Although the fighting had ceased, the city was badly disorganized, and people were very uneasy.

Small groups of soldiers of the defeated army roved the streets. They were a sorry sight — their hats gone, their leg wrappings undone, their uniforms unbuttoned. Some had torn off their unit designation. They carried their rifles in their hands, on their shoulders, across their backs — any old way. But they hadn't lost their usual insolence. Their scowling, belligerent manner was a constant reminder of the evil they had done before under similar circumstances; it intensified the atmosphere of fear hanging over the city.

Eearly in the morning Zhang Sheng, man-servant of Qin's mother Mrs. Zhang, came to the Gao compound. He reported that the soldiers who had been quartered in the Zhang compound had departed, except for two or three who, it was said, would be leaving soon. None of the soldiers had been billeted in any of the women's rooms, so nothing of value had been damaged. Zhang Sheng added that Mei's family had sent someone to inquire about her; and he had told the man that she was staying at the Gao's.

Mrs. Zhang and Qin were very relieved to learn that everything was all right, and they said no more about returning home.

In the afternoon Mei's mother Mrs. Qian sent a servant with a note to Madam Zhou, thanking her for her kindness in looking after Mei. Mrs. Qian said she was extremely grateful and that in a few days, when things were more peaceful, she would come to offer her thanks in person. The servant also brought a message to Mei from her mother saying that all was well at home, she needn't worry. There was no necessity for her to come home immediately; she could stay at the Gaos a few more days if she wished.

At first Mei was going to return with the servant but, unable to resist the importunities of Madam Zhou and Ruijue, she finally agreed to remain.

In spite of the tense atmosphere on the streets, it was quiet and serene in the Gaos' garden. A few walls seemed to mark the separation between two different worlds. Time passed quickly in this peaceful environment. Soon, before anyone was aware of it, evening came.

A half-moon hung in the sky, and the air was filled with the fragrance of dusk. Gradually, as the blue of the sky deepened, the rays of the moon grew richer. It was a warm, beautiful night.

Suddenly, the tranquillity was shattered. The parents of Fourth Household's Madam Wang sent someone to bring her home immediately. The man said there were many rumours. It was feared there might be looting that night. The Gaos were the richest family in the North Gate neighbourhood; their compound was bound to be one of the first invaded. . . . Madam Wang and her five children quickly departed in three sedanchairs.

Next, the family of Madam Shen of Fifth Household sent for her and her daughter Shuzhen, for the same reason.

This alarmed Madam Zhang of Third Household. Without waiting to be called, she departed for her mother's house with her three children, Shuying, Jueying and Jueren.

Only Madam Zhou and Ruijue remained of the Gao family womenfolk. Their parents did not live in Chengdu and they had no place to go. There were a few distant relatives with whom they might have sought refuge, but they didn't know them very well. Besides, by the time Madam Zhou and Ruijue heard of the danger, the streets were already deserted. Except for the soldiers, no one dared to venture out.

The Venerable Master Gao had gone to call on a cousin that morning. His concubine, Mistress Chen, was visiting with her old mother. Ke'an and Keding had quickly disappeared, though their brother Keming remained, writing letters in his study. The only intact household was Juexin's. In time of crisis, this rich old family, which depended on ancient morality to sustain itself, revealed its inner emptiness. No one cared about anyone else. Each was concerned solely with his own personal safety.

Mrs. Zhang had always been partial to Juexin's household. Even if she had been able to go home — which she was not — she would not have been willing to abandon them.

"I'm not so young any more," she said to Juexin, "and I've seen many things in my time. But I've never seen good people suffer evil retribution. Your father was a good man all his life. No calamities could ever happen to his children. I know that Heaven is just. Why should I be afraid to remain with you?"

But the others were unable to share her confidence, and as time passed she herself grew worried. Although the night was still young, the streets outside were completely silent. A dog began to bark. Usually, they seldom heard him, but this night his barking sounded particularly loud.

Time dragged on with unbearable slowness. Every minute seemed a year. At the slightest sound, they imagined pillaging soldiers had broken in. Immediately they pictured all that this entailed: bayonets, knives, blood, fire, naked female bodies, money scattered on the ground, strong-boxes ripped open, corpses lying in pools of blood. . . . With hopeless desperation they struggled against this irresistible, shapeless force. But terror was closing in on them and they were weakening steadily.

They wished they could close their eyes to everything, end all sensation. As it was, even the feeble glow of the lamp hurt their eyes. It reminded them of the dilemma they were in. They prayed that time would pass quickly, that the sun would rise a little earlier. Yet they knew that the quicker time passed, the sooner the things they dreaded might occur. They were like prisoners awaiting execution. Although they were men and women with different personalities and ideas, in their fear of death they were the same. It was worse for the women, who faced an anguish more terrible than death.

"Cousin Mei, if the soldiers really break in, what shall we do?" asked Qin. They were all gathered in Madam Zhou's

room. When Qin uttered the words "what shall we do," her
heart trembled. She didn't dare let herself think any further.

"I have only this one life to lose," retorted Mei coolly, but
there was a note of sadness in her voice. She quickly covered
her face with her hands. Her mind was growing hazy. Before
her eyes there seemed to be a vast stretch of water, rolling on
and on, without end.

"What shall I do?" Ruijue asked herself in a low voice. She
knew what Mei meant. She felt it was the only way out for
her too. But she didn't want to kill herself. She didn't want to
leave those she loved. As she looked at little Haichen, playing
at her feet, a dozen knives seemed to plunge into her heart.

Qin silently rose to her feet and began slowly to pace the
room, fighting against her rising fear. "You could never do
it," a voice inside her said. Although she could think of no
other alternative, she felt there must be one. All her new ideas,
her new books and periodicals, Ibsen's social dramas, the
writings of the Japanese author Akiko Yosano — had vanished
from her mind. She could see only outrage and humiliation,
leering at her, mocking her. The shame would be something
she could not live with. She had her pride.

Qin looked at Mei, seated on the reclining chair, her hands
over her face. She looked at Ruijue, holding Haichen's hand
and weeping. She looked at her mother. Mrs. Zhang was
standing with her back to the lamp, sighing. Qin looked at
Shuhua, at Juemin, at the others. It was hopeless; none of
them could save her. Yet they all were infinitely precious to
her; she couldn't bear to leave them. Weary, despondent, for
the first time Qin began to think she was no different from
women like Mei and Ruijue. She was just as weak, after all.

She sat down and lay her head on the tea table and wept
softly.

"Qin, what is it?" cried Mrs. Zhang. "Do you want Ma to
feel any worse than she does already?" Tears sprang to Mrs.
Zhang's eyes.

The girl didn't answer, but continued to sob with her head

on the table. She wept for herself, for the shattered dream she had fought so hard and long to attain. Now, just as she was beginning to see a glimmer of hope that she might become a strong and self-reliant woman, a "human being," like Nora in Ibsen's *A Doll's House*, she had collapsed, weak and frightened, at the first real danger she had to face. What was the use of all her fine ringing phrases? She used to think she was brave, and others had praised her for her courage, yet here she was, waiting like a lamb to be slaughtered, without even the strength to resist.

Her mother couldn't understand what was going on in her mind, nor could the others, even Juemin — who believed he knew her best. They assumed she was weeping because she was afraid. They too were tormented by fear, and they could find no words of comfort for her, though her sobbing cut them to the quick. Juemin wanted to take her in his arms, but he didn't have the courage.

Unable to sit still, Juehui got up and went out. He was shocked to see a pale red glow in the sky to the east, a glow that was slowly spreading, accompanied by occasional sparks shooting heavenward.

"Fire!" The shout escaped him, and his blood seemed to congeal in his veins. He stared stupidly at the sky, unable to move a step.

"Where?" several voices in the room cried in alarm. "Where's the fire?" Juexin was the first to come rushing out, followed by Shuhua. Soon they all were standing outside on the steps.

The sky was blood-red. Each of them suddenly had the feeling that his life was fading, as if something were eating it away.

A cloud hid the moon, and the brightness of the flames was accentuated in the ensuing darkness. The crimson glow now covered half the sky, reddening the flagstones and the tiles on the roofs. Sparks flew wildly. Viewing this holocaust, they gave up hope of living.

"Those must be pawn shops on fire," said Mrs. Zhang. She sighed. "After they've looted them clean why can't they at least leave people a place to live?"

"What's going to become of us?" cried Ruijue, stamping her foot frantically.

"Why don't we change into old clothes and make a run for it?" suggested Juemin.

"Where would you run to? And who would look after the compound? If no one in charge stays here and the soldiers come, they'll burn the place to the ground," countered Juexin. He didn't know what to do either.

Suddenly, sharp rifle reports broke the silence. Dogs began to bark wildly. There was shouting too, but it seemed to come from a distance.

"We're finished. This time we'll never get away," cried Juexin. Then he said loudly, "Must we all wait around to die? We've got to think of some way to get out of here."

"But where can we go?" Madam Zhou queried tearfully. "If we run into any deserters on the streets, we're sure to die. We're better off remaining at home."

"If we're staying here, we still have to find places to hide. If we can save even one of us, it will be better than none. Our household must leave someone to continue the family line," said Juexin in a voice filled with sorrow and anger. After a pause, in a different tone, he addressed Juemin and Juehui.

"Second Brother, Third Brother, take the womenfolk into the garden. Hurry. There are places to hide there. If all else fails, there's always the lake. Your Sister-in-law knows how to preserve her honour." He looked longingly at Ruijue, then gave a glance to Mei. Juexin trembled violently and tears rained from his eyes. Although he seemed to have made up his mind, he was struggling desperately to control himself.

"What about you?" the others demanded.

Juexin was silent for half a minute. Finally, regaining some semblance of calm, he said, "Never mind about me. Just go. I can take care of myself."

"Nothing doing. If you don't go, we won't go either," retorted Juehui decisively.

Rifles again cracked, but the intensity of the firing had not increased.

"Third Brother, why are you only concerned about me? The women are important!" Juexin stamped his foot with anxiety. "If no one in charge stays here and the soldiers come, they'll be sure to search the garden."

Ruijue, who had been sitting holding Haichen without a word, now put the child down and walked over and firmly took a stand beside Juexin. "You'd better hurry and take the other women into the garden," she said to the younger brothers. "Please take the baby for me, too. I'll stay here with Big Brother. I know how to look after him."

"You — you'll stay here with me? What's the meaning of this?" Startled, Juexin lightly pushed her away. In a worried voice he added, "What would be the good? Go quickly, before it's too late!"

Ruijue grasped his arm. "I won't leave you," she sobbed. "If you're going to die, I want to die with you."

Little Haichen came over and tugged at Ruijue's jacket, beseeching, "Mama, let me stay too."

Juexin was nearly beside himself. He clasped his hands and swung them repeatedly in obeisance. "For the sake of our child, please leave me," he begged. "What purpose is served in our dying together? Besides, I may not die. If they come, I know how to deal with them. But if they should see you here, who knows what they'd do. You must preserve your purity. . . ." Juexin couldn't go on.

Ruijue stared at him dully, blankly, as if she didn't recognize him. She stood before him and let his anxious gaze caress her face a moment longer, then said in a mournful and tender voice, "Very well, I'll do as you wish. I'll go."

At her instructions, Haichen said, "Goodbye, Papa." Then mother and child turned and walked away.

*　　　　*　　　　*

That night, everyone except Juexin slept in the "Lakeside Retreat." Through the open windows they could see the chill moonlight shining on the water. The red glow in the sky was gradually fading. Everything was the same as before, only the barking of the dogs was unusually frightening. All was the same, but to the dull eyes of the watchers the waters of the lake, rippling slightly in the moonlight, appeared more mystic, colder. They wanted to plumb its depths. Some even wondered: What would it be like to sleep far down beneath its surface?

They looked at one another, but could think of nothing to say. Finally, Madam Zhou, observing how tired Juehui looked, told him to go to sleep.

Juehui got into bed. Just as he was dozing off, Madam Zhou came and opened the mosquito netting. Leaning her round face down, she whispered into his ear:

"The firing has started again. It seems to be very near. You must be careful. Whatever you do, don't sleep too soundly. If anything happens, I'll call you."

Her breath warmed his cheek, and there was a concerned, affectionate look on her face. She tucked him in, closed the netting, and softly walked away.

Although the news she had brought was not good, Juehui was very comforted. He felt he had a mother again.

* * *

After three or four days of tension, order was restored on the streets, and everyone felt much better. Those who had left for places of safety in other parts of the city began to return. The compound was once again alive and bustling.

Mrs. Zhang's man-servant, Zhang Sheng, came to take her and Qin home. Mei also wanted to go back, but Madam Zhou prevailed on her to remain a few days longer. In the afternoon, Mei's mother, Mrs. Qian, arrived in a sedan-chair to pay her respects to Madam Zhou.

Elderly women are naturally inclined to be forgetful. Besides, Madam Zhou and Mrs. Qian were distant relatives. In the few

years since they had last seen each other they had completely
forgotten their differences. Madam Zhou received Mrs. Qian
with the fullest cordiality, and the two women had a long chat.
Later, they sat down for a game of mahjong, in which Mei and
Ruijue joined.

When Juexin returned, Ruijue relinquished her place at the
table to him. He found himself sitting opposite Mei. They
spoke very little. Occasionally they exchanged a mournful
glance. Juexin's heart wasn't in his game, and he made several
bad plays. Ruijue came and stood behind him, to try and help.
He turned his head and smiled at her. He and Ruijue were
both entirely natural and quite affectionate in their manner to
each other.

Mei, observing, felt a pain in her heart. If she had only told
her mother how she felt about Juexin before he became engaged
to Ruijue, perhaps she, not Ruijue, would be standing behind
him now. Ah, how wonderful it might have been. But today
it was too late.

She saw the close bonds between Juexin and Ruijue, and
thought of her own unhappy life and the lonely years ahead.
The mahjong tiles blurred before her eyes. Her heart ached
unbearably.

She stood up and asked Ruijue to take her place, saying there
was something she had to attend to. Ruijue gave her a friendly
look, then sat down on her vacated chair. As Mei walked slowly from the room, Ruijue gazed after her thoughtfully.

Mei went to Shuhua's room, which she was sharing with the
younger girl. Fortunately, no one was there, and she lay down
on the bed and reviewed her past, carefully, in detail. The
more she thought, the worse she felt, until finally she burst
into tears. Muffling her sobs for fear of being overheard, she
cried a long time. She felt better then, although she still
couldn't see even a thread of hope. Her past, her present, were
crushing her like a weight. She felt weak, unable to stir. At
last, she drifted off into slumber.

"Cousin Mei," a warm voice called her. She opened her eyes. Ruijue was standing beside her bed.

"Aren't you playing mahjong, Sister-in-law?" Mei asked with a weary smile. She tried to sit up, but Ruijue gently held her down and sat beside her on the edge of the bed while gazing at her affectionately.

"I let Aunt Shen take over for me." Then, surprised, Ruijue said, "But you've been crying! What's the matter?"

"No, I haven't," said Mei, trying to smile.

"Don't pretend. Your eyes are all swollen. Tell me what's troubling you," Ruijue insisted, squeezing her hand.

"I had a bad dream, that's all," replied Mei airily, but the hand which Ruijue held was trembling.

"Don't try to fool me. There must be something wrong. Why won't you tell me the truth? Don't you believe I really care about you? I want to help you." Ruijue's voice was full of sympathy.

Mei made no reply. Fixing her mournful gaze on Ruijue's friendly visage, she frowned slightly and shook her head. Her eyes glistened suddenly and she blurted, "You can't give me any help." She lay her head on the pillow and wept softly.

There was a lump in Ruijue's throat. She patted Mei's quivering shoulder. "I understand, Cousin Mei," she said sorrowfully. "I know what's in your heart." Ruijue wanted to cry too. "I know he loves you, and you love him. You would have made a fine couple. . . . He shouldn't have married me in the first place. . . . Now I know why he loves plum blossoms so — because that's what your name means. I love him too, I love him more than life. . . . But, Mei, why didn't you marry him? . . . You and I — he too — we've done wrong, we've fallen into a tragic muddle. I've been thinking. I ought to step out of the way and let you two have your happiness. . . ."

Mei had already stopped her tears. She looked around when she heard Ruijue weeping. With one hand pressed against her chest, she listened intently to what Ruijue was saying, then immediately turned her head, not daring to look at Ruijue's tear-stained face. But at those last few sentences, she quickly sat up and covered Ruijue's mouth with her hand.

Ruijue buried her head on Mei's shoulder and sobbed.

"Sister-in-law, you're wrong. I don't love him," said Mei, then promptly contradicted herself. "No, I do love him. I don't have to fool you. . . . Our mothers wouldn't let us marry. Fate must have ordained it that way. We just weren't meant for each other. . . . We separated, and that's the end of it. Suppose you gave him up, what would be the use? He and I will never be together again in this life. . . . You're still young, but I, emotionally, am already old and feeble. Haven't you seen the wrinkles on my forehead? They show what I've been through. . . . I'm tired of this world. I'm fading, while you are only beginning to blossom and bear fruit. I truly envy you, Sister-in-law. . . . I no longer live; I just exist. My life is only a burden to others."

Mei smiled bitterly.

"You know the saying, 'There is no greater tragedy than the death of the heart.' Well, my heart is already dead. I shouldn't have come to your compound again. I only upset people. . . ."

Her voice had changed. Ruijue could feel her trembling.

"How can I possibly feel at ease here?" she cried despondently. But then she went on quietly with a mournful smile, "If there ever was a case of 'woman's wretched fate,' I'm a perfect example. No one understands me at home. My mother is interested only in her own affairs. My brother is still very young. Who can I pour out my bitterness to? . . . Sometimes, when the misery is more than I can bear, I hide alone in my room and cry, covering my head with the bedding so that no one will hear. . . .

"You shouldn't laugh that I weep too easily. It's only the past few years that I've become this way. It began when my mother quarrelled with his stepmother and broke us up. Later, after we left Chengdu, I cried many times. It was all fated, but sometimes I think things might have been different if his own mother hadn't died. She was related to my mother, and they were good friends. . . . But who wants to hear my complaints? No one understands me. The best thing for me is to swallow my tears. . . ."

Mei paused, pressing her handkerchief to her mouth to smother a few coughs. "Later, I married, much against my will. I had no choice in the matter. I lived for a year with my husband's family. It was simply awful. Even today I still don't know how I managed to exist. If I had to spend another year or two in that house, I'm afraid I wouldn't be here today. . . . Weeping was an actual pleasure for me then. I wasn't permitted to do a thing. Everything was forbidden, but weeping — that was all right. . . . I don't cry nearly so much now. Maybe my tears are running dry. Du Fu said, '*Though you weep till my bones show through your eyes, there is no mercy in heaven or on earth.*' But what other consolation have I except to weep?

"You mustn't feel badly because of me, Sister-in-law. I'm not worth your pity. I didn't intend to ever see him again. Something seems to have drawn us together. Yet, at the same time, something is driving us apart. Even though I know there's no hope for me in this life, the last few days I've been acting as if there might be. Please don't hold it against me. Anyhow, I've decided to leave. You can treat the whole thing as a bad dream. Just forget about me. . . ."

Tears of blood were running into her heart, but Mei did not weep. She only smiled sadly.

Every word of this tragic tale weighed heavily on Ruijue's tender feminine heart. She listened intently, unwilling to miss a single syllable, gazing quietly at Mei's mournfully smiling face. The tear-stains on Ruijue's lightly powdered cheeks in no way detracted from her beauty.

When Mei finished speaking, Ruijue shook her head, for all the world like a mischievous little girl. Her dimples deepened and she smiled, a sad, moved smile. She forgot her own misfortune completely. Placing both hands on Mei's shoulders, she said in a clear affectionate voice:

"... You are only beginning to blossom and bear fruit. I truly envy you, Sister-in-law...."

"Cousin Mei, I didn't know you were suffering so. I shouldn't have led you to talk about it. I was too selfish. Your situation is much worse than mine. Promise me that you'll come here often. I like you very much, Cousin Mei — it's the truth. You say no one understands you. I hope you'll let me be the one. I had a sister once, but she died. If you won't refuse me, I hope we can be sisters. I can comfort you. I'll never be jealous. As long as you're happy, I'll be pleased from the bottom of my heart. You must come to visit with us often. Promise that you'll come. That's the only way to prove you don't dislike me, that you've forgiven me."

Gazing at Ruijue with loving tenderness, Mei removed Ruijue's hands from her shoulders and pressed them tightly, then leaned wearily against her. For a moment she was too moved to speak. Finally she said:

"I don't know how to thank you, Sister-in-law." She kept stroking Ruijue's plump ripe hands. She coughed several times.

Ruijue looked at her in concern. "Do you cough very much?"

"Sometimes. Mostly at night. I've been a little better lately, but my chest always pains me." Mei's voice was melancholy.

"Are you taking any medicine? That kind of ailment it's better to cure in the early stages."

"I was taking some medicine. It helped a little, not much. Now there are some pills; I swallow a few every day. My mother says it's nothing to worry about — I'll be all right with a tonic and a good rest at home."

Overwhelmed with pity, Ruijue looked avidly at Mei's face, while tightly squeezing her hand. Both young women were gripped by an emotion that would have been difficult for them to describe. They put their heads together and talked softly for some time.

Finally, Ruijue rose to her feet. "We'd better be going back." She went to the mirror, combed her hair and powdered her face, then helped Mei do the same. Hand in hand, the two young women walked from the room.

23

Tension quickly subsided in the city. The battle soon became only a memory. Peace was again restored. At least on the surface people once more lived in peace. The fighting seemed only a bad dream.

Some real changes began to be put into effect. General Zhang was chosen military commander of the combined conquering forces, after which he became civil administrator. With the administrative power in his hands, he indicated that he was willing to institute reforms.

In this new atmosphere, the students came to life and put out three new periodicals. Juemin, Juehui and some of their classmates published a weekly magazine which they called *Dawn*, containing news of the new cultural movement, introducing new ideas and attacking all that was unreasonable in the old.

Juehui was very enthusiastic. He wrote many articles for the magazine. Of course most of his material came from the new periodicals published in places like Shanghai and Beijing. He had not yet made either a really thorough study of the new theories or a careful analysis of society. All he had was a little experience in life, some knowledge derived from books, and the ardour of youth.

As to Juemin, he was busy with his classes at school all day; in the evening he went to tutor Qin. That left him little time for anything else. Except for writing a short article once in a while, he wasn't of much help to the magazine.

The magazine was very well received by the young people. Its first issue of a thousand copies sold out in less than a week. The second issue did the same. By the time the third issue was published, the magazine already had nearly three hundred subscribers. The backbone of the magazine's staff were three of Juehui's best friends, and their fine work earned his deepest admiration.

With the advent of the magazine Juehui's life became more interesting and active. For the first time he found an outlet for his pent-up energies. His ideas were put into print and a thousand copies were distributed at a time. People everywhere knew what he was thinking; some of them even wrote in expressing agreement. In his ardent eyes the fanciful, lofty joy he experienced was something precious to the extreme. But although he was more than willing to devote his free hours to the magazine, he was afraid his grandfather would find out, or that his participation would get his Big Brother into trouble.

But in the end he was discovered. One day his uncle Keming came across an issue of the magazine in Juehui's room containing one of his articles. Keming made no comment; he only smiled coldly and walked out. Though Keming did not report the matter to *Ye-ye*, from that time on Juehui increased his caution. His activities, his work, his desires were things he revealed to no one in his family. He didn't even confide in Juexin. He knew his Big Brother was weak, and not necessarily in sympathy with what he was doing.

As his interest mounted in his new life, Juehui's youthful fervour knew no bounds. In a short time a group for the study and propagation of the new culture had been built up around the magazine. They met every Sunday in the park, twenty of them, sitting around a few tables under a big mat canopy, drinking tea and heatedly debating every conceivable social question. Or they would gather in small groups in the homes of various students and discuss plans to help others — for they had become imbued with the spirit of humanitarianism and socialism. They had already taken on their shoulders the burden of reforming society and liberating mankind.

The galley proofs, the rhythmic motion of the printing press, the beautiful printed pages, the many letters from people he had never met — these were all wonderfully new and stimulating to Juehui. They were things he had never dreamed of, yet today they were all reality, tangible, forceful, meeting his young thirst for action.

Juehui gradually became more deeply immersed in his new environment; at the same time the distance between him and the members of his family widened. He felt they were incapable of understanding him. His grandfather's visage was eternally stern; the powdered face of Mistress Chen never lost its crafty expression. His stepmother remained courteous and cool. Big Brother continued to practise his "compliant bow" philosophy. Sister-in-law, pregnant again, was beginning to lose her blooming vitality. Behind Juehui's back his aunts and uncles complained that he was too proud; he showed them none of the respect due from a nephew. They protested to his stepmother, demanding that she scold him. Yet whenever he met them, they greeted him with hypocritical smiles.

The only one in the family Juehui was close to was his brother Juemin. But Juemin had his own aspirations, his own work. Even in his thinking, he was different from Juehui.

There was one other person. Every time Juehui thought of her, his heart melted with tenderness. He knew at least one person in the compound loved him. The girl's selfless devotion was a source of constant happiness to him. Whenever he looked into her eyes — more expressive than any pair of lips, burning with the clean flame of love — hope surged in his breast. All the world was in those eyes; in them he could find his life's purpose. At times he was so overcome by emotion, he wanted to cast everything aside for their sake; he felt they were worth any sacrifice.

But when he walked out into the world, entered his new environment, met with his new friends — his vision widened. He could see the great world before him; in it was room for his smouldering fire; it was there he should concentrate his energies. Life was not so simple; he knew that well. Comparing the wide world with a girl's eyes was really too silly. How could he give everything up for them?

Recently he had read a forceful article in *Struggle*, a bimonthly published in Beijing. The writer had said that the youth of China must not be idlers living only for enjoyment; they ought to lead a Spartan existence. Chinese society was dark, and their responsibility was a heavy one. It was up to them to face the social problems and solve them. Naturally this would require all their energies. In conclusion, the writer warned his young readers: "You must guard against falling in love. Don't become emotionally involved."

Although the theoretical basis of the article was weak, at the time it influenced many of the young people who read it, especially those who were anxious to devote themselves to the service of society.

It made a strong impression on Juehui too. He read it with a trembling heart. It moved him so, he was ready to vow that he would be exactly the kind of youth the author demanded. His mind was filled with the vision of an ideal society. He forgot completely the pure love of the young girl.

But his forgetfulness was only temporary. True, he did forget her when he was busy outside. But as soon as he returned home, when he again entered that compound silent as the desert, he was bound to think of her. And thinking of her he was sure to feel troubled. Two thoughts struggled for supremacy in his mind — or perhaps we could say the struggle was between "society" and Mingfeng. But since the girl was alone, and pitted against her were the whole system of feudal morality and the Gao family clan, in Juehui's mental battle, Mingfeng was doomed to defeat.

Of course Mingfeng herself knew none of this. She still loved him, secretly but unreservedly. She was happy for his sake. She waited, praying that one day he would rescue her from the miry pit of her existence.

Her life was somewhat easier than before. Her masters were much kinder to her. She was sustained by her love. It brought her beautiful daydreams in which she could take refuge. Yet she remained very humble. Even in her dreams she did not conceive of living with Juehui as equals; she wanted only to be a faithful slave, but the slave of him alone. It seemed to her that this would be the greatest possible happiness.

Unfortunately, reality is often the exact opposite of what people desire; it smashes their hopes, mercilessly, swiftly.

24

One night, after the electric lights in the compound had been turned off, Mingfeng was called to the apartment of Madam Zhou. The fat face of the older woman was expressionless in the feeble glow of an oil lamp. Although she could not guess what Madam Zhou was going to say, all day Mingfeng had a premonition that something bad was about to happen to her. She stood before Madam Zhou with trembling heart and gazed at her unsteadily. They both were silent. The fat face seemed to swell gradually into a large, round object that wavered before Mingfeng's eyes, increasing her feeling of fear.

"Mingfeng, you've been with us for several years. I think you've worked long enough." Madam Zhou began very deliberately, though still speaking more quickly than most people. After these first few words, her speed increased, until the syllables were popping from her lips like little pellets.

"I'm sure you also are quite willing to leave," she continued. "Today, Venerable Master Gao instructed me to send you to the Feng family. You are going to be the concubine of the Venerable Master Feng. The first of next month is an auspicious day; they will call for you then. Today is the twenty-seventh. That still leaves four days. From tomorrow on, you needn't do any work. Take things easy for the next few days, until you go to the Feng family. . . .

"After you get there, be sure to take good care of the old man and the old lady. They say he's rather strange; his wife's temper is none too good either. Don't be stubborn; it's best to go along with their whims. They also have sons and daughters-in-law and grandchildren living together with them. You must respect them too.

"You've been a bondmaid in our family for several years, but you haven't gained anything from it. To tell you the truth I don't think we've treated you very well. Now that we've arranged this marriage for you I feel much better. The Feng family is very rich. As long as you remember to act according to your station, you'll never want for food or clothing. You'll be much better off than Fifth Household's Xi'er. . . .

"I'll think of you after you leave. You've looked after me all these years and I've never done anything to reward you. Tomorrow I'll have the tailor make you two new sets of good clothing and I'll give you a little jewelry." The sound of Ming-feng's weeping interrupted her.

Although every word cut the girl's heart like a knife, she could only let them stab. She had no weapon with which to defend herself. Her hopes were completely shattered. They even wanted to take away the love she depended upon to live, to present her verdant spring to a crabbed old man. Life as a concubine in a family like the Fengs could bring only one reward: tears, blows, abuse, the same as before. The only difference would be that now, in addition, she would have to give her body to be despoiled by a peculiar old man whom she had never met.

To become a concubine — what a disgrace. Among the bondmaids "concubine!" was one of the worst imprecations they would think of. Ever since she was very small Ming-feng felt that it was a terrible thing to be a concubine. Yet after eight years of hard work and faithful service that was her only reward.

The road ahead looked very black. Even the thread of light which her pure love had brought her, even that was snapped. A fine young face floated before her. Then many ugly visages leered at her, horribly. Frightened, she covered her eyes with her hands, struggling against this terrifying vision.

Suddenly she seemed to hear a voice say, "Everything is decided by Fate. There is nothing you can do about it." An overwhelming disappointment took possession of her, and she wept broken-heartedly.

Words were flying from Madam Zhou so fast it was difficult for her to stop at once. But when she heard the girl's tragic weeping, she paused in surprise. She couldn't understand why Mingfeng was so upset, but she was moved by her tears.

"What's wrong, Mingfeng?" she asked. "Why are you crying?"

"Madam, I don't want to go!" sobbed Mingfeng. "I'd rather be a bondmaid here all my life, looking after you, and the young masters and the young mistresses. Madam, don't send me away, I beg you. There's still a lot I can do here. I've only been here eight years. I'm still so young, Madam. Please don't make me marry yet."

Madam Zhou's maternal instincts were seldom aroused, but Mingfeng's impassioned pleas struck a responsive chord. The older woman was swept by a feeling of motherly love and pity for the girl.

"I was afraid you wouldn't be willing," she said with a sad smile. "It's true, the Venerable Master Feng is old enough to be your grandfather. But that's what our Venerable Master has decided. I must obey him. After you get there, if you serve the old man well, things won't be so bad. Anyhow you'll be much better off than married to some poor working man, never knowing where your next meal is coming from."

"Madam, "I'm willing to starve — anything but become a concubine." As Mingfeng blurted these words, the strength drained from her body, and she fell to her knees. Embracing Madam Zhou's legs, she begged, "Please don't send me away. Let me stay here as a bondmaid. I'll serve you all my life. ... Madam, have pity, I'm still so young. Pity me. You can scold me, beat me, anything — only don't send me to the Feng family. I'm afraid. I couldn't bear that kind of life. Madam, be merciful, pity me. Madam, I've always been obedient, but this — I can't do it!"

Endless words were welling up from her heart into her throat, but something seemed to be stopping her mouth, and she could only swallow them down again and weep softly. The more she cried the more stricken she felt. The tragedy was too overwhelming. If only she could cry her heart out, she might have some relief.

Looking at the girl weeping at her feet, Madam Zhou was reminded of her own past. Sadly, maternally, she stroked Mingfeng's hair.

"I know you're too young," she said sympathetically. "To tell you the truth, I'm against your going to the Feng family. But our Venerable Master has already promised. He's the kind who never goes back on his word. I'm only his daughter-in-law. I don't dare oppose him. It's too late. On the first, you must go. Don't cry. Crying won't do any good. Just gather your courage and go. Maybe your life will be comfortable there. Don't be afraid. People with good hearts always get their just rewards. Get up now. It's time for you to be in bed."

Mingfeng hugged Madam Zhou's legs tighter, as if they were the only things that could save her. With her last strength she cried despondently, "Don't you have even a little pity for me, Madam? Save me. I'd rather die than go to the Feng family!"

Raising her tear-stained face, she looked into Madam Zhou's eyes and stretched forth her hands pleadingly. "Save me, Madam!" Her voice was tragic.

Madam Zhou shook her head. "There's nothing I can do," she replied sadly. "I don't want you to go, myself, but it's no use. Even I can't go against the decision of the Venerable Master. Get up now, and go to bed like a good girl." She pulled Mingfeng to her feet.

Mingfeng offered no resistance. All hope was gone. She stood dazedly before Madam Zhou, feeling that she was in a dream. After a moment, she looked around. Everything was dim and dark. She was still sobbing soundlessly. Finally, she brought herself under control. In a dull, melancholy tone she said, "I'll do what you say, Madam."

Madam Zhou rose wearily. "Good. As long as you're obedient I won't have to worry about you."

Mingfeng knew it was no use to remain any longer. She had never been so miserable in her life. "I'm going to bed, Madam," she said listlessly. She slowly walked from the room, her hand pressed to her breast. She was afraid her heart would burst.

Madam Zhou sighed as she watched the girl's retreating back, sorry that she was unable to help her. But, half an hour later, this comfortable, well-fed lady had forgotten all about Mingfeng.

The courtyard was dark and deserted. Feeble lamplight gleamed in Juehui's window. Originally Mingfeng had intended to return to the servants' room but now, seeing the light, she walked softly towards Juehui's quarters. The light was seeping through the tiny openings in the curtain, casting a pretty pattern on the ground. That curtain, the glass windows, that room, now seemed particularly adorable to Mingfeng. She stood on the stone porch outside the window and gazed unwinking at the white gauze curtain, holding her breath and being as quiet as possible so as not to disturb the boy inside.

Gradually, she imagined she could see colours on the white curtain; they became even more beautiful. Beautiful people emerged from the maze of colour — boys and girls, very handsomely dressed, with proud and haughty bearing. They cast disdainful glances at her as they passed, then hurried on. Suddenly, the one she thought of day and night appeared in their midst. He gazed at her affectionately and halted, as if he wanted to speak to her. But crowds of people came hurrying and pushing from behind him, and he disappeared among them. Her eyes sought him intently, but the white gauze curtain, hanging motionless, concealed the interior of the room from view.

Mingfeng drew closer, hoping to get a look inside, but the window was higher than her head, and after two unsuccessful

"Save me, Madam!"

attempts, she stepped back, disappointed. As she did so, her hand accidentally bumped against the window-sill, making a slight noise. From within the room came a cough. That meant he wasn's asleep. She stared at the curtain. Would he push it aside and look out?

But inside it became quiet again, except for the low sound of a pen scratching on paper. Mingfeng rapped softly against the window-sill. She heard what sounded like a chair being shifted, then the scratching of the pen again, a bit faster. Mingfeng was afraid if she rapped any harder, she might be overheard. Juemin slept in the same room. Clutching a final hope, she again tapped, three times, and called softly, "Third Young Master." Stepping back, she waited quietly. She was sure he would come out this time. But again there was nothing but the rapid scratching of the pen and the low surprised remark, "Two a.m. already? . . . And I've a class at eight in the morning. . . ." And the sound of the writing resumed once more.

Mingfeng stood dully. Tapping again would be no use. He wouldn't hear it. She didn't blame him, in fact she loved him all the more. His words were still in her ears, and to her they were sweeter than music. He seemed to be standing beside her — so warm, so very much alive.

He needed a girl to love him and take care of him, and there was no one in the world who loved him more than she. She would do anything for him. But she also knew there was a wall between them. People wanted to send her to the Feng family, soon, too, in four days. Then she would belong to the Fengs; she'd have no opportunity to see him again. No matter how she might be insulted and abused, he'd have no way of knowing. He wouldn't be able to save her. They'd be separated, for ever separated. It would be worse than if they had been parted by death.

Mingfeng felt that a life of that kind was not worth living. When she had said to Madam Zhou, "I'd rather die than go to the Feng family," she had meant it. She was really considering death. The Eldest Young Miss had often told her that suicide was the only way out for girls who were the victims of Fate.   Mingfeng believed this fully.

A long sigh from the room broke in on her wild thoughts. Mournfully, she looked around.   All was still and very dark. Suddenly she remembered a similar scene of several months ago.   Only that time he had been outside her window, and the conjecture he had overheard then had today become a reality. She recalled all the details — his attitude towards her, how she had said to him, "I'll never go to another man.   I give my vow."

Something seemed to be wringing her heart, and she was blinded by tears. The lamplight from the window shone down on her head pitilessly.   Eagerly she gazed at the beams, a hope slowly forming in her breast.   She would cast all caution to winds, rush into his room, kneel at his feet, tell him her whole bitter story, beg him to save her.   She would be his slave for ever, love him, take care of him.

But just then, everything went black.   The lamp had been turned out.   She stared, but she could see nothing.   Rooted to the spot, she stood alone in the night, the merciless night that hemmed her in from all sides.

After a few moments, she finally was able to move.   Slowly she groped her way through the disembodied darkness towards her own room.   After a long time, she reached the women servants' quarters.   She pushed open the half-closed door and went in.

A wick was sputtering feebly in a dish of oil.   The rest of the room was all darkness and shadows.   Beds on both sides of the room were laden with corpse-like figures.   Harsh snores from the bed of the fat Sister Zhang struck out in every direction in a very frightening manner.   They halted the startled Mingfeng in the doorway, and for a moment she peered anxiously around.   Then with dragging feet she walked over to the table and trimmed the wick.   The room became much brighter.

About to take off her clothes, Mingfeng was suddenly crushed by a terrible depression.   She threw herself on her bed and began to cry, pressing her head against the bedding and soaking it with her tears. The more she thought, the worse she felt. Old Mama Huang, awakened by the sound of her weeping, asked in a muzzy voice, "What are you crying about?"

Mingfeng did not answer. She only wept. After offering a soothing word or two, Mama Huang turned over and was soon fast asleep again. Mingfeng was left alone with her heartbroken tears. She continued to cry until sleep claimed her.

By the next morning Mingfeng had changed into a different person. She stopped smiling, she moved in a leaden manner, she avoided people. She suspected they knew about her; she imagined they were smiling disdainfully, and she hurried to get away. If she saw a few servants talking together, she was sure they were discussing her. She seemed to hear the word "concubine" everywhere, even among the masters and mistresses.

"Such a pretty girl," she thought she heard the Fifth Master say. "It's a shame to make her a concubine of that old man."

In the kitchen she heard the fat Sister Zhang angrily comment, "A young girl like that becoming the 'little wife' of an old man who's half dead! I wouldn't do it for all the money in the world!"

It got so that Mingfeng was afraid to go anywhere for fear of hearing contemptuous remarks. Except when she had to join the other servants for her two meals a day, she hid in her room or in the garden, alone and lonely. Once in a while, Xi'er or Qianer came to see her. But they were both very busy, and they could only steal out briefly for a comforting word or two.

Mingfeng wanted very much to speak to Juehui, and she was constantly seeking an opportunity. But lately he and Juemin were busier than usual. They left for school very early each morning and came home late in the afternoon. Sometimes they had dinner out. But even when they ate at home, they would go out again immediately after the evening meal and not return until nine or ten at night. Then they would shut themselves in their room and read, or write articles. On the one or two occasions she happened to meet Juehui, he gave a tender glance or a smile, but did not speak to her. Of course these were signs of his love, and she knew he was busy with serious affairs; even though he had no time for her, she did not blame him.

But the days were passing quickly. She simply had to speak to him, to pour out her troubles, to seek his help. He didn't seem to have any inkling of what was happening to her, and he gave her no chance to tell him.

Now it was the last day of the month. Not many people in the compound knew about Mingfeng. Juehui was completely in the dark. He was all wrapped up in the weekly magazine. Even the hours he spent at home were devoted to study and writing; he had no contact with anyone who might have told him about Mingfeng.

To Juehui the thirtieth was the same as any other day. But for Mingfeng it was the day of reckoning: Either she would leave him for ever or serve him for ever. The latter possibility was very slim, and Mingfeng knew it. Naturally she was hopeful that he would be able to save her and that she could remain his devoted servant always. But between them was a wall which could not be demolished — their difference in status.

Mingfeng knew this very well. That day in the garden when she had said to him, "No, no. I just wasn't fated," she already knew. He had replied that he would marry her. But his grandfather, Madam Zhou and all the elders were arrayed against them. What could he do? Even Madam Zhou didn't dare go against a decision of the Venerable Master Gao. What chance would a grandson stand?

Mingfeng's fate was irrevocably decided. But she couldn't give up the last shred of hope. She was fooling herself, really, for she knew there wasn't the slightest hope, and never could be.

She waited to see Juehui that day with trembling heart. He came home after nine in the evening. She walked to his window. Hearing the voice of his brother, she hesitated, afraid to go in but unwilling to leave. If she gave up this last opportunity, whether she lived or died, she would never be able to see him again.

At long last Mingfeng heard footsteps. Someone was coming out. She quickly hid in a corner. A dark figure emerged from the room. It was Juemin. She waited until he was some distance away, then hurried into the room.

Juehui was bent over his desk, writing. He did not look up as he heard her enter, but continued with his work. Mingfeng timidly approached.

"Third Young Master," she called gently.

"Mingfeng, it's you?" Juehui raised his head in surprise. He smiled at her. "What is it?"

"I have to speak to you." Her melancholy eyes avidly scanned his smiling face. Before she could go on, he interrupted:

"Is it because I haven't talked with you these last few days? You think I've been ignoring you?" He laughed tenderly. "No, you mustn't think that. You see how busy I am. I have to study and write, and I've other things to do too." Juehui pointed at a pile of manuscripts and magazines. "I'm as busy as an ant. It will be better in a day or two. I'll have finished this work by then. I promise you. Only two more days."

"Two more days?" Mingfeng cried, disappointed. As if she hadn't understood, she asked again, "Two more days?"

"That's right," said Juehui with a smile. "In two more days I'll be finished. Then we can talk. There's so much I want to tell you." He again bent over his writing.

"Third Young Master, don't you have any time now, even a little?" Mingfeng held back her tears with an effort.

"Can't you see I'm busy?" said Juehui roughly, as if reproving her for persisting. But when he observed her stricken expression and the tears in her eyes, he immediately softened.

Taking her hand he stood up and asked soothingly, "Has someone been picking on you? Don't feel badly."

He really wanted to put aside his work and take her into
the garden and comfort her. But when he remembered that he
had to submit his article by the next morning, when he recalled
the struggle the magazine was waging, he changed his mind.

"Be patient," he pleaded. "In another two days we'll have
a long talk. I definitely will help you. I love you as much
as ever. But please go now and let me finish my work. You'd
better hurry. Second Young Master will be back in a minute."

. Juehui looked around to make sure that they were alone,
then took her face in his hands and lightly kissed her lips.
Smiling, he indicated with a gesture that she should leave
quickly. He resumed his position at the desk, pen in hand, but
his heart was pounding. It was the first time he had ever kissed
her.

Mingfeng stood dazed and silent. She didn't know what she
was thinking or how she felt. Her fingers moved up to touch
her lips — lips that had just experienced their first kiss. "Two
more days," she repeated.

Outside, someone was heard approaching, whistling. "Go,
quickly," Juehui urged. "Second Young Master is coming."

Mingfeng seemed to awake from a dream and her expression
changed. Her lips trembled, but she did not speak. She gazed
at him longingly with the utmost tenderness, and her eyes suddenly shone with tears. "Third Young Master," she cried in
an anguished voice.

Juehui looked up quickly, only to see her disappearing
through the doorway.

He sighed. "Women are strange creatures." He again bent
over his writing.

Juemin came into the room. The first words out of his
mouth were, "Wasn't that Mingfeng who just left here?"

"Yes." Juehui continued writing. He did not look at his
brother.

"That girl isn't the least bit like an ordinary bondmaid. She's intelligent, pure, pretty — she can even read a little. It's a shame that *Ye-ye* is giving her to that old reprobate for a concubine. It's a real shame!" sighed Juemin.

"What did you say?" Juehui put down his pen. He was shocked.

"Don't you know? Mingfeng is getting married."

"She's getting married? Who said so? She's too young!" "*Ye-ye* is giving her to that shameless old scoundrel Feng to be his concubine."

"I don't believe it! Why, he's one of the main pillars of the Confucian Morals Society. He's nearly sixty. He still wants a concubine?"

"Don't you remember last year when he and a couple of his old cronies published a list of 'Best Female Impersonators' and were bitterly attacked by *Students' Tide*? His kind are capable of anything. He gets away with it, too — he's got money, hasn't he? The wedding day is tomorrow. I certainly am sorry for Mingfeng. She's only seventeen."

"Tomorrow? Why wasn't I told before? Why didn't anyone tell me?" Juehui jumped to his feet and hurried out, clutching his hair. He was trembling all over.

"Tomorrow!" "Marry!" "Concubine!" "Old Feng!" The words lashed against Juehui's brain till he thought it would shatter. He rushed out; he thought he heard a mournful wail. Suddenly he discovered a dark world lying at his feet. All was quiet, as if every living thing had died. Where was he to go in this misty space between heaven and earth? He wandered about, tearing his hair, beating his breast, but nothing could bring him peace.

Suddenly a torturing realization dawned upon him. She had come to him just now in the utmost anguish, to beg for his help. Because she believed in his love and because she loved him, she had come to ask him to keep his promise and protect her, to rescue her from the clutches of old man Feng. And what had he done? Absolutely nothing. He had given her neither help nor sympathy nor pity — nothing at all. He sent her away without even listening to her pleas. Now she was gone, gone for ever. Tomorrow night, in the arms of that old man, she would weep for her despoiled springtime. And at the same time she would curse the one who had tricked her into giving her pure young love and then sent her into the jaws of the tiger.

It was a terrifying thought. Juehui couldn't bear it. He had to find her, he had to atone for his crime.

He walked to the women servants' quarters and lightly tapped on the door. Inside it was pitch dark. He called "Mingfeng," twice, in a low voice. There was no answer. She must be asleep, he thought. Because of the other women, he couldn't very well go in.

Juehui returned to his room. But he couldn't sit still. Again he came out and went to the servants' quarters. Pushing the door open a trifle, he could hear only snoring inside. He walked into the garden and stood for a long time in the dark beneath the plum trees. "Mingfeng!" he shouted. Only the echo replied. Several times he bumped his head against the low-hanging plum branches, scratching his forehead and drawing blood. But he felt no pain. Finally, disappointed, he slowly walked back to his own room. As he entered his room, everything began to spin.

Actually, the girl he sought was not with the women servants, but in the garden.

When Mingfeng left Juehui's room she knew that this time all hope was gone. She was sure he loved her as much as ever; her lips were still warm with his kiss, her hands still felt his clasp. These proved that he loved her; but they were also symbols of the fact that she was going to lose him and be cast into the arms of a lecherous old man. She would never see him again. In the long years ahead there would be only endless pain and misery. Why should she cling to a life like that? Why should she remain in a world without love?

Mingfeng made up her mind.

She went directly to the garden, groping her way through the darkness with a great effort until she reached her objective —

the edge of the lake. The waters darkly glistened; at times feeding fish broke the placid surface. Mingfeng stood dully, remembering many things of the past. She recalled everything she and Juehui had ever said and done together. She could see every familiar tree and shrub — so dear, so lovely — knowing that she was going to leave them all.

The world was very still. Everyone was asleep. But they were all alive, and they would continue living. She alone was going to die.

In the seventeen years of her existence she had known nothing but blows, curses, tears, toil in the service of others. That plus a love for which she now must perish. Life had brought much less happiness to her than to others; but now, despite her youth, she would leave the world first.

Tomorrow, others had their tomorrow. For her there was only a dark empty void. Tomorrow birds would sing in the trees, the rising sun would gild their branches, countless pearls would bubble on the surface of the water. But she would see none of it, for her eyes would be closed for ever.

The world was such an adorable place. She had loved everyone with all the purity of a young girl's heart, wishing them all well. She had served people without pause; she had brought harm to no one. Like other girls she had a pretty face, an intelligent mind, a body of flesh and blood. Why did people want to trample her, hurt her, deny her a friendly glance, a sysmpathetic heart, even a pitying sigh?

She had never owned nice clothes, nor eaten good food, nor slept in a warm bed. She had accepted all this without complaint. For she had won the love of a fine young man, she had found a hero whom she could worship, and she was satisfied. She had found a refuge.

But today, when the crisis came, reality had proved it was all an illusion. His love couldn't save her; it only added to her painful memories.

He was not for her. His love had brought her many beautiful dreams, but now it was casting her into a dark abyss. She loved life, she loved everything, but life's door was closing in her face, leaving her only the road to degradation.

Thinking of what this meant, she looked at her body in horror. Although she could not see clearly in the darkness, she knew it was chaste and pure. She could almost feel someone casting her into the mire. Painfully, pityingly, she caressed her body with soothing hands.

Mingfeng came to a decision. She would hesitate no longer. She stared at the calm water. The crystal depths of the lake would give her refuge. She would die unsullied.

About to jump, a thought came to her, and she paused. She should't die like this. She ought to see him once more, pour out her heart to him. Perhaps he could save her. His kiss still tingled on her lips, his face still shimmered before her eyes. She loved him so; she couldn't bear to lose him. The only beauty in her life had been his love. Wasn't she entitled even to that? When everyone else went on living, why did a young girl like her have to die?

She pictured an idyllic scene in which she chatted and laughed and played with rich girls her own age in a beautiful garden. In this wide world she knew there were many such girls and many such gardens. Yet she had to end her young life — and there was no one to shed a sympathetic tear, or offer a word or two of comfort. Her death would bring no loss to the world, or to the Gao family. People would quickly forget her, as if she had never existed.

Has my life really been so meaningless? she thought, stricken. Her heart filled with an unspeakable grief, and tears spilled from her eyes. Strength draining from her body, she weakly sat upon the ground. She seemed to hear someone call her name. It was his voice. She halted her tears and listened. But all was quiet; all voices were stilled. She listened, hoping to hear the call again. She listened for a long, long time. But there was no sound in the night.

Then she knew. He was not coming. There was a wall eternally between them. He belonged to a different sphere.

He had his future, his career. He must become a great man. She could not hold him back, keep him always at her side. She must release him. His existence was much more important than hers. She could not let him sacrifice himself for her sake. She must go, she must leave him for ever. And she would do so willingly, since he was more precious to her than life itself.

A pain stabbed through her heart, and she rubbed her chest. But the pain persisted. She remained seated on the ground, her eyes longingly roving over the familiar surroundings in the dark. She was still thinking of him. A mournful smile flitted across her face and her eyes dimmed with tears.

Finally, she could not bear to think any longer. Rising tottering to her feet, she cried in a voice laden with tenderness and sorrow, "Juehui, Juehui!" — and she plunged into the lake.

The placid waters stirred violently, and a loud noise broke the stillness. Two or three tragic cries, although they were very low, echoed lingeringly in the night. After a few minutes of wild thrashing, the surface of the lake again became calm. Only the mournful cries still permeated the air, as if the entire garden were weeping softly.

25

Juehui slept badly that night and got up late the next morning. He and Juemin hurried to school, but classes were in session for over ten minutes by the time they arrrived.

Mr. Zhu, their tall, thin English teacher, was reading aloud from *Resurrection*. Juehui and the other students listened carefully, preparing to answer questions that would be asked on the passage being read.

But Juehui's mind kept going back to Mingfeng, and thinking of her made him tremble inwardly. Not that he had determined to hold on to her. No. After pondering the matter all night, he was ready to let her go. It was a painful decision, but he felt that he could carry it through. There were two things in the back of his mind with which he was already consoling himself for Mingfeng's loss. One was that he wanted to devote himself entirely to serving society. The other was that a person of his position could never really marry a bondmaid — his petty-bourgeois pride would not permit it.

The day at school passed quickly. On the way home, Juehui was again torn by conflicting thoughts. Though he said nothing, his brother could tell from his face that something was troubling him, and did not try to draw him into conversation.

Just as they were going through the inner gate of their compound, they saw the sedan-chair the Feng family had sent for Mingfeng departing, accompanied by two servants. Tragic weeping came through the sedan-chair curtains. Although it was barely audible, it went straight to Juehui's heart. She was leaving, and she would never return.

Servants who had seen the sedan-chair off were still gathered in the garden. Juehui was sure they were discussing Mingfeng. He didn't dare to look at them. Hurriedly, he walked on. A mournful voice greeted him as he entered the inner compound:

"You're home early today." The speaker was Jianyun. His long thin face was cast in its usual melancholy lines. He had been standing on the steps talking with Juexin, but came towards the two younger brothers when he saw them approaching. Juexin silently turned and went back to his own apartment.

"We've been having only one class in the afternoon lately, because we're getting ready for exams," replied Juemin.

Jianyun, followed them into their apartment and sat down on a cane chair. He sighed deeply.

"Why are you always so gloomy, Jianyun?" Juemin asked him. As for Juehui, he tossed his books on the desk and lay down on his bed without a word to anyone.

"Life is too cruel!" Jianyun sadly shook his head.

Juemin was about to twit him for having such easily wounded sensibilities. But then he remembered Jianyun's remark about his bad health and how he had lost his parents at an early age, and he changed his mind. Instead, he urged kindly:

"Don't take everything so hard, Jianyun. Why must you always dwell on things that make you unhappy?"

"Too cruel, too cruel!" Jianyun didn't seem to have heard Juemin. "I just happened to drop in, and there she was, struggling, weeping, as they forced her into the sedan-chair. I cried too. After all, she's a human being. Why should she be treated like some lifeless object and sent to that old —"

"Who do you mean? Are you talking about Mingfeng?" Juemin asked sympathetically.

"Mingfeng?" Jianyun looked at Juemin in surprise. "I'm talking about Waner," he said heatedly. "The sedan-chair just left. Didn't you see it?"

Juehui sat up quickly on the bed. "Then Mingfeng didn't go?" he asked delightedly.

"Mingfeng. . . ." Jianyun's voice trailed off. He turned his hazy eyes on Juehui and said quietly, "Mingfeng . . . drowned herself in the lake."

"What? Mingfeng killed herself?" Juehui leaped to his feet in horror. Clutching his hair, he paced the room distractedly.

"So they say. Her body has already been carried out of the compound. I didn't see it. Well, she's probably better off than Waner. . . ."

"Ah, so that's it. Mingfeng killed herself, and Ye-ye sent Waner in her place. Bondmaids aren't persons in Ye-ye's eyes, just things he can hand out as gifts," Juemin cried, half in anger, half in pity. "I didn't realize that Mingfeng was a girl of such strong character. To do a thing like that!"

"The result is that Waner is out of luck," said Jianyun. "It would have made anyone weep to see the way she struggled. I think she might have chosen the same path as Mingfeng, but the thing happened too suddenly. She had no idea they were going to send her. And they watched her every minute. . . ."

"I never thought Ye-ye could do such a thing! One is dead,

so he sends another. These girls are people's daughters. How can they be treated so brutally?" Juemin demanded hotly.

"Tell me, how did Mingfeng kill herself?" Juehui suddenly walked up to Jianyun, grabbed his arm and shook it savagely.

Startled, Jianyun looked at him, unable to comprehend his passion. In his usual emotional tone, he replied: "I don't know. I'm afraid nobody knows. One of the servants discovered her body. He called a few others and they fished her out, then they carried her away, and that was the end. . . . This life, this world . . . it's too cruel."

Juehui stared at Jianyun's gaunt visage, ravaged by long years of grief. His own face was expressionless. Roughly, he dropped Jianyun's arm, turned without a word and ran out.

"What's wrong with him?" Jianyun was confused.

"I'm beginning to understand," Juemin nodded.

"Maybe you do, but I don't!" Jianyun again lowered his head and lapsed into his own thoughts. He was eternally timid, eternally humble.

"Can't you see that love is at the bottom of it?" Juemin shouted. There was no answer. The room was still. Occasional footsteps outside seemed to be stamping on his heart.

After some minutes, Jianyun again slowly raised his head. His misty eyes travelled about the room, and he said to himself in a shaking voice, "I . . . understand."

Juemin rose and paced the floor with large strides. Suddenly he sat down on the chair beside the desk and fixed his gaze on Jianyun's face. The eyes of the two young men met, exchanging some unhappy thoughts. Jianyun was the first to lower his head.

"It was all for love," Juemin said bitterly. "Third Brother and Mingfeng. . . . I suspected they were interested in each other. . . . Who knew it would come to this? I never dreamed that Mingfeng could be so strong-willed! . . . What a pity. She was a fine girl. If only she had been born in some rich family. . . ." Juemin couldn't go on. His internal struggle was reflected on his face.

It was some time before he could say in a shaken voice, "Love, all for love. . . . Big Brother is much thinner lately. The last few days, his spirits have been very low. . . . And isn't it love that's making him that way? . . . I used to think that love brought happiness. Why does it cause so much misery? . . ."

There were tears in Juemin's trembling voice. Thinking of his own love affair, he was ready to weep. He could see dark shadows lying ahead. The fate of Big Brother was a terrible example of what might happen to him too.

26

With lowered head, Juehui walked along the lake front. At times he stopped and stared at the calm surface of the water, or, heaving a long sigh, turned to walk with large strides in the other direction. He was quite unaware of the approach of Juemin.

"Third Brother," Juemin called as he emerged from the plum grove.

Juehui halted and gazed at him silently.

Coming near, Juemin said in a moved voice, "You look terrible. Is something troubling you?"

Juehui did not answer and began to walk away. Juemin hurried after him and grabbed his sleeve.

"I know all about it," Juemin said in a trembling voice. "But since things have come to this, what can you do? The best thing is to forget."

"Forget? I'll never forget," Juehui retorted angrily, his eyes flashing. "Many things in this world are hard to forget. I've been standing here looking at the water for a long time. This is her grave; it's here that I've been searching for a last trace of her. But the water shows me nothing at all. How hateful! After swallowing her body how can the lake look so peaceful?"

He threw off his brother's restraining hand, and raised a clenched right fist as if to strike the water. "She can't be gone without a trace. Every shrub and blade of grass can tell me how she ended her life. I don't dare to think what was in her heart when she died, but I must. I'll remember it for ever, for I am her murderer. But not I alone. There's also our family, the society we live in!"

Taking Juehui's hand and pressing it, Juemin said sincerely, "I understand you, Third Brother, and I sympathize with you. These days I've been thinking only of my own happiness, my own future, my own love. That was wrong. I remember when we were small and took lessons with a tutor in our library. We did everything together then. Whoever finished his lesson first always waited for the other. Everyone praised us for being such devoted brothers. It was the same when we entered middle school and, later, the Foreign Languages School. At home, we helped each other prepare our lessons. We shared our joys, we shared our sorrows. But the past half year, I've been so involved in my own affairs, I've grown away from you. Why didn't you tell me about Mingfeng earlier? Together, we might have worked something out. Two heads are better than one. Isn't that what we always used to say?"

There were tears in the corners of Juehui's eyes. He laughed bitterly. "I remember too, Second Brother. But it's too late. A person is always short of courage, acting alone. I never thought she'd take that road. I truly loved her. But under the circumstances, how could I marry her? Maybe I was too self-ish. Maybe I was dazzled by other things. Anyhow, I killed her. She ended her life in the waters of the lake, and another girl, weeping, went to the Feng family to bury her youth, to satisfy the passions of a lustful old dog. With that always in my mind, do you think I'll ever be able to live in peace?"

A look of hatred and regret appeared on Juemin's face, and tears rolled down from behind his gold-rimmed spectacles. "Too late," he muttered painfully. He gripped Juehui's hand hard.

"Second Brother, do you remember the night of the fifteenth

"Forget? I'll never forget."

of the first lunar month?" Juehui asked in an agitated tone.
When Juemin silently nodded, he continued, "How happy we
were that night! It seems only yesterday. But where is she
now? . . . Her voice, her face — where can I seek them? She
was sure I could have her, but I let her down. I didn't have
the courage. . . . I used to blame you and Big Brother for
being spineless. Now I know I'm not any different. We're all
sons of the same parents, raised in the same family. None of
us have any courage. . . . I hate everyone. I hate myself!"

Juehui was too agitated to go on. He was panting, his body
was hot as fire. There was a lot more he wanted to say, but
the words stuck in his throat. His heart seemed to tremble.
He punched himself in the chest, and when Juemin grabbed
his wrist to restrain him, he struggled like a madman to extricate
himself. He didn't know what he was doing; he struggled
blindly. Only with the greatest effort was Juemin able to hold
him and finally push him to the plum grove beside the path.
There he stood, leaning limply against a tree, gasping for breath.

"Why carry on like this?" Juemin, his face flushed with
exertion, stood on the path gazing at him pityingly.

"This family! I can't live here any longer!" Juehui said,
more to himself than to his brother. Head down, he was wringing his hands.

Juemin's expression changed. He wanted to speak, but
couldn't. He looked from Juehui to the grove of plum trees.
A magpie was calling from a branch. Gradually, Juemin's eyes
brightened, and a smile returned to his face. But there were
tears in that smile, tears which rolled from his eyes.

"Why don't you trust me like you used to?" he asked. "You
used to talk everything over with me. We shared the bitter
with the sweet. Why can't we still be that way today?"

"Because we've both changed. You have your love. I've lost
everything. What is there left for us to share?" Juehui was
not trying to hurt Juemin, he was only releasing some of his
pent-up emotion. He felt he was separated from his brother
by a damp and dripping corpse.

Juemin opened his mouth as if to make a loud reply, then stopped himself. After a long silence, he said in a voice that was almost a plea, "Haven't you forgiven me yet? Can't you see how sorry I am? Let's help one another again, just like before, and stride down life's road together. I promise I'll never leave you."

"What would be the use? I don't want to walk down life's road any more." Juehui seemed to have cast off his armour. His anger was gone. Only despair remained.

"Can this be you speaking? Would you really throw everything aside because of a girl? That's not like you at all!"

"No, I don't mean that," Juehui started to argue. Avoiding Juemin's eyes he said slowly, "It's not only because of her." With sudden anger, he added, "I'm just sick of this kind of life."

"You have no right to say that. We're still young. We don't really know what life is all about yet."

"I suppose we still haven't seen enough! Just wait. The worst is yet to come! I predict it!" Juehui's face was red with anger.

"You're always so excitable! The thing is over with. What can you do about it? Can't you think of the future? It's strange that you should have already forgotten those lines you liked so much."

"Which lines?"

"We're young, we are not monsters, not fools. We'll conquer happiness for ourselves."

Juehui made no reply. The rapidly changing expressions on his face reflected the struggle raging within him. Frowning, he said heavily to himself, "I am young." Then he repeated angrily, "I am young!" After a moment, he asked tentatively, "I am young?" And he added with conviction, "I am young! No question about it, I am young!"

He grasped Juemin's hand and gazed into his brother's eyes. That affectionate grasp, that firm gaze, told Juemin what was in Juehui's heart. Reassured, he returned the pressure of his young brother's handclasp. They understood each other again.

After an early dinner that evening, the two brothers went out for a walk. As they strolled along the street, they talked animatedly of many things. It was over six months since their last good talk together.

Dark clouds gathered in the evening sky. It was quite cool. Only a few people were abroad on the lonely streets, but at some compound gates servants and sedan-chair carriers stood around in groups, chatting idly.

Two or three blocks further on, the brothers came to a corner compound enclosed by a brick wall. Beside the gate a large yellow placard with green lettering read: "Law Office of Gao Keming."

"How did we ever wander in this direction?" asked Juemin.

They turned off into a small twisting lane. It was paved with cobble-stones that were hard on the feet. Tall locust trees in the compounds hung their branches over the earthen walls lining the lane. Here and there were elms. Unfortunately, blossom time was already over. Only a few withered pomegranates remained on the green leafy branches of pomegranate trees.

This section of the town was very quiet. Most of the small black lacquered compound gates were shut. Rarely did anyone emerge.

"Let's go back. It's too dull around here. Besides, it looks like it's going to rain," said Juehui, observing the black clouds piling up in the sky.

"It's raining already," said Juemin, as a drop of water struck his forehead. The boys quickened their steps.

"We'd better hurry. It's going to pour in a minute," urged Juehui, breaking into a trot.

The brothers ran for home, but the rain caught them. By the time they reached their compound, they were soaked.

"Mingfeng, bring some hot water," Juehui shouted, outside the window of the women servants' quarters.

"You're calling Mingfeng? But she's —" Juemin stopped himself.

Juehui turned and looked at him, his face suddenly falling. After a moment, he called in a despondent voice, "Mama Huang!" When she answered he said, "We want to wash our faces." Dully he entered his room and changed his wet clothes, his high spirits completely gone.

Mama Huang soon came with a basin of hot water. When she saw what the boys looked like, she began to scold. She was close to tears.

"If your mother were still alive, she'd never let you run wild like this. For her sake, you two ought to take better care of your health. If it weren't for you boys, I would have left this place long ago. Now that Mingfeng is gone, I'm the only one left to look after you. I don't know who could take care of you if I should die too. The waters here have become muddy. I really don't want to live in this compound any longer."

The old lady said all this in a heartsick voice. Her words so upset the boys that they did not dare to answer for fear of weeping.

Having had her say, and after seeing to it that the brothers put on dry clothes, Mama Huang sighed and left the room.

Juehui went out into the garden. The rain had stopped, and the air was fresh and cool. He paused on the steps to look around at the lights burning in the other apartments, then walked towards the main hall. He could hear young voices intoning lessons from the ancient feudal philosophers:

Children should not live in the best section of the house, nor sit at the centre of the table, nor walk in the middle of the road.

. . . That was Jueying's voice.

Of all the major crimes, the worst is violation of filial piety.

. . . That was Juequn's voice.

If you laugh, do so quietly. Do not raise your voice in

anger. When seated, do not show your knees. When walk-
ing, do not sway your body. . . .
That was Shuzhen's girlish voice.

Juehui couldn't stomach it. He turned and started to walk
back, the voices following him. After two paces he halted,
miserable. Gazing around, he doubted his own eyes. All he
could see was false and empty shadows. All he could hear was
false and empty voices. He didn't know where he was.

"That's what they call education!" a harsh voice abruptly
broke upon his ears.

Startled, Juehui turned to see his brother standing beside
him. Juehui clutched him with the joy of a man in the track-
less desert suddenly meeting an old friend. Juemin was a bit
mystified by the fervent reception.

Thus, in silence, the brothers returned to their room, two
lonely hearts alone in the great wide world.

27

The death of Mingfeng and the marriage of Waner were quickly
forgotten in the spacious confines of the Gao family compound.
Neither of these events had any effect on the daily life of the
family. Two bondmaids were gone, that was all, and the
masters quickly bought new ones to replace them. Qixia took
the place of Mingfeng; Cuihuan filled Waner's job. Numerical-
ly, there was no change. (Qixia was from the country. Cuihuan was the same age as her young mistress,
Shuying. She had been sold after the death of her
father — her last remaining close relative.) Before long, people
stopped even mentioning Mingfeng's name. But in the hearts
of Xi'er, Qianer, Mama Huang and a few others, the girl was
a constant unhappy memory.

Juehui never spoke of her either. He appeared to have
forgotten her. But she left a wound that would never heal. He
had little time to mourn her, however, because of something
new which developed.

After the sixth issue of *Dawn* was published, a rumour started that the officials were going to close the progressive weekly down. It was said that the Confucian Morals Society was behind the move. This story naturally aroused Juehui and his friends but, being inexperienced, they didn't take it very seriously. What's more, they didn't believe that General Zhang, the new governor, would permit his subordinates to do such a thing.

The seventh issue appeared as usual. There were some new subscribers. The magazine had rented an upstairs shop in the market arcade, and members of its staff met there every night. During the day (with the exception of Sunday) they kept the place shut, so that even Juexin, whose office was in the same arcade, didn't know that Juehui was a frequent visitor.

The more important enterprises occupied the ground floor shops; most of the upper stories were empty. The magazine office had no neighbours; all of the surrounding rooms were vacant.

Every evening, two or three young students would take down the shutters, turn on the light and set the office in order. Soon there would be half a dozen of them, mostly boys, though girls like Xu Qianru also dropped in once or twice. They would sit around and talk. Anything they could not mention at home, here they discussed without reservation. They were smiling, relaxed. The office was their club.

Juehui came often, sometimes accompanied by Juemin. Tuesday evenings, Juehui was sure to come, because the magazine went to press Wednesday mornings. On Tuesday, he, Zhang Huiru and Huang Cunren edited the final copy.

The day the copy of the eighth issue had to be prepared for press was the day after Mingfeng's death. That evening, Juehui went to the office as usual. He found Xu Qianru reading a newspaper item aloud to the others. It was a Police Department proclamation prohibiting girls from bobbing their hair. Short hair was considered much too "modern" and "rebellious."

Qianru flung the paper down angrily and threw herself into

a wicker armchair. "Of all the piffle!" she cried.

"Why don't we print it as it is, in the 'About Face!' column of our next issue?" suggested Cunren, with a grin.

"Fine!" said Qianru.

The others agreed. Huiru thought there ought to be a critical article to go with it. Everyone asked Huiru to write it himself, but he passed the job over to Juehui. For Juehui, it was a chance to give vent to the bitterness filling his heart over Mingfeng's death. He took up his pen and began writing without a word.

He soon finished; the article was rather short. He read it aloud to the others, and they said it would do. Cunren made a few small changes, then announced that the piece would appear on page one of issue number eight. Only one of the older boys sounded a note of caution: "This is going to make a real noise."

"Let it," said Huiru jubilantly. "The louder the better!"

The eighth issue of *Dawn* appeared in print on Sunday morning. In the afternoon, Juehui and Juemin paid their customary visit to Juexin's office. They didn't stay long. Huiru soon slipped away to the magazine's headquarters. Huiru, Cunren and two or three others were already there. Juehui asked them how the issue was selling; they said they had checked at one or two outlets and were told the magazines were being bought almost as quickly as they appeared on the stands.

"You haven't paid your dues," Cunren suddenly said to Juehui.

Juehui felt through his pockets. "I'll have to do it tomorrow," he said apologetically. "I didn't bring any money with me."

"Tomorrow at the latest, then!" smiled Cunren.

"He's great at squeezing money out of people. He's been after me too," Huiru interjected, walking over to them. There was a grin on his impish face. "This morning, before I left home, I put on a new padded gown. My sister thought I was crazy to wear anything so warm in this weather. I insisted I was cold and walked out. . . ."

Everyone laughed, and Huiru laughed with them. He continued:

"I nearly fried in the sun with that gown on. Luckily the pawn shop isn't far from my house. I left the gown there. I was much cooler and lighter when I came out, and I had money to pay my dues with, too!"

"What will your sister say when you get home?" Juehui asked.

"I've got it all figured out. I'll just say I felt too warm and left the gown at a friend's house. If she doesn't believe me, I'll just tell her the truth. Maybe she'll give me the money to get it out of pawn!"

"I certainly admire your nerve —" Juehui laughed. Before he could finish, he was interrupted by the entrance of two policemen.

"Do you have any more copies of the latest issue?" asked the older one. He had a moustache.

Cunren handed him a copy. "Three cents apiece."

"We don't want to buy them. We have orders to take them with us," the younger policeman said. He picked up two bundles of magazines that were stacked on the floor.

"You boys will have to come along with us to the station. Not all of you — two will be enough," said the older policeman. His tone was not unfriendly.

The startled boys looked at one another. Then they all stepped forward, each insisting that he wanted to go.

"That's too many. Two is all we need." The older policeman looked rather distressed. Finally, he selected Huiru and Juehui. The two boys left the room with the policemen, the others trailing behind. When they reached the head of the stairs, the older policeman suddenly changed his mind.

"Forget it," he said to Juehui. "We don't need you two. You can go back."

"What's going on anyway?" Huiru demanded hotly. "By what right are you confiscating our magazines?"

"We've got our orders," retorted the younger policeman, continuing down the stairs with the bundles. The older man, about to follow him, paused to give the boys some friendly advice.

"You're young and don't understand much. Better stick to your studies. Don't put out any magazines and bother with things that don't concern you."

He slowly descended the stairs. The boys returned to their office.

They began a heated discussion, with no two opinions alike. While they were still arguing, another policeman arrived and brought them a letter from the police authorities. It was unusually polite, but very firm:

Because the agitational nature of your periodical disturbs public order and security, we regret that we must ask you to cease circulation immediately....

The life of *Dawn* was thus abruptly brought to an end.

A mournful silence followed. The announcement came as a severe blow to the boys. They had put a lot into the magazine, pooling their feeble resources in an attempt to show the average person a glimmer of light. Working together had also brought them friendship, comfort and strength. Was it all over after only two short months?

"I know now — they're all hypocrites!" cried Huiru. "And the new governor is no different from the rest!"

"The old reactionary forces have powerful roots." Cunren stood up and scratched his close-cropped hair irritably. "There's no use expecting anything from Governor Zhang. Ten like him wouldn't make any difference!"

"That's just what I'm saying." Huiru continued. "All his talk of wanting reforms is a fake. The only 'new' thing he's done is to hire a couple of men who studied abroad as his advisers, and pick up a few girl students for concubines!"

"Yet, last year, before he took office, he invited a lot of people with advanced ideas from Shanghai and Nanjing to come and give talks," mused Cunren.

Huiru laughed scornfully. "Have you forgotten his speech at the meeting to welcome them? His secretary wrote it all out for him, but he memorized it so badly that his meaning came out the exact opposite of his script. He's pulled plenty of boners like that!"

Cunren said nothing. As to Huiru, not only did his outbursts fail to solve the present main problem, they didn't even relieve his anger. He was furious. There was a great deal more he wanted to say to the world.

"Let's change the name and put out another magazine with exactly the same content!" Huiru proposed. "How can they stop us?"

"I'm for it!" Juehui, who had been silent until now, suddenly spoke up.

"But we have to plan our moves carefully," said Cunren, raising his head. He had been deep in thought.

The boys again began a long discussion. This time they arrived at a decision: They would send out a circular notifying their subscribers of the suspension of *Dawn*. At the same time they would prepare the publication of their new magazine. They also would convert the office into a public reading-room to which the boys would contribute all of their progressive books and periodicals. Anyone could come in and read, free of charge. This would help spread the new culture.

With a new programme mapped out, everyone promptly sloughed off his gloom and set to work. What a wonderful thing enthusiasm is! It enabled the boys to conquer their difficulties in a very short time. By the following day, they had already set up the reading-room. Two days after that, the preparatory work of the new magazine, *For the Masses,* was well advanced.

There were no classes on Tuesday; the examination period had begun. Juehui and Juemin, after attending the opening celebration of the new reading-room, returned home for lunch.

Juehui had never felt so happy. Never had conversation and laughter, friendship, ardour and faith, seemed so beautiful. About a dozen young people had been at the party; they were like one family. Only they were bound together not by ties of flesh and blood, but by the same good intentions and ideals.

"How fine it would be if life could always be like this!" Juehui had said excitedly to Juemin at the party. The older brother had nodded emotionally.

The boys talked of many things on the way home. Juehui's heart was still warm and glowing. But the moment he set foot in the family hall, he was plunged into a chill abyss. Here the old society was all around him. There was virtually no one of the new generation here, no one to whom he could talk.

"How lonely! How insufferably lonely!" he sighed. His bitterness increased.

The faces around the table at dinner that night also bore the scars of bitterness. His stepmother was complaining about the strife between Aunt Shen and Aunt Wang. Somewhere in the rear, Aunt Wang was upbraiding her bondmaid, Qianer. Aunt Shen and Mistress Chen were cursing each other in the courtyard.

Juehui finished eating quickly, threw down his chopsticks and ran out, as if pursued by something fearful.

Juemin left the dining-room at the same time. "Where are you going?" he asked, concerned by the wild look on his younger brother's face.

"I want to walk around a little. I feel awful."

"All right. But come back soon," said Juemin soothingly. "You have exams the day after tomorrow. You'd better do some reviewing."

Juehui nodded. He went into the big garden. With the change in surroundings, his heart eased a trifle. He strolled slowly in the moonlight.

Crickets chirped mournfully. A fragrance spread through the night like a soft net, enveloping all in its folds. Everything was blurred, illusory, secretive. It was like walking in a world of dreams.

Gradually, Juehui calmed down. He strolled, enjoying the scenery, following the same path he and the other young folks had taken the night they went boating on the lake.

On the hump-backed bridge, he halted and leaned on the railing, gazing at his dark reflection in the waters below. The lake was a deep blue sky in which a half-moon rode, shimmering. Suddenly a lovely face appeared in the water, a face that he adored. Juehui turned and fled.

Crossing a lawn at the edge of the lake, he came upon a rowboat moored to a willow tree. This too recalled memories. He hastily recrossed the hump-backed bridge and returned to the opposite shore.

He followed the path that skirted the grove of cedars near the bank until he came to "Lakeside Retreat." About to go in and rest a while, he suddenly observed a glow of flame from behind the artificial mountain. He almost cried out in surprise. Pausing by the magnolia tree, he watched. There was a steady glow, but it did not grow any larger. Gathering his courage, Juehui walked forward softly to investigate.

Rounding the artificial mountain, he found nothing. The glow was coming from behind another man-made hill, diagonally opposite. Again he advanced. Behind the second hill, he saw a girl kneeling on the ground, burning "ingots" of gold and silver paper.

"What are you doing here?" he demanded loudly.

Startled, the tall girl quickly rose to her feet. When she recognized Juehui, she saluted him respectfully, "Ah, Third Young Master!"

It was Qianer, bondmaid in the Fourth Household.

"So it's you," said Juehui. "You nearly scared the life out of me! Why are you burning sacrifice money here?"

"Please don't tell anyone, Third Young Master. My mistress would be sure to scold me if she knew."

"But why are you doing it?"

Qianer lowered her head. "Today is the seventh day after Mingfeng's death. . . . She died so pitifully. I thought I'd send her a little money, so she won't go cold and hungry in the next world. . . ." Qianer was almost crying.

"Go ahead," said Juehui. "I won't tell anyone." He pressed a hand against his chest. There was a pain in his heart. He watched Qianer burn the "money" expressionlessly. She couldn't guess what was going on inside him.

"Why are you burning two piles?" he asked.

"This one is for Waner."

"Waner? But she's not dead!"

"She asked me to. As she was getting into the bridal sedan-chair, she said to me, 'Sooner or later, I'm going to die too. Even if I live, my life will be worse than death. Consider me dead. When you burn money for Mingfeng, burn some for me too.' And that's what I'm doing."

Hearing Qianer's tragic voice and recalling those two unhappy events, could he simply laugh at her superstitious ceremony? Of course not. Juehui struggled to control his emotions. Finally, he wrenched out:

"Burn it! You're doing the right thing!" He staggered away, not daring to turn his head for a last look.

"Why is there so much misery in the world?" he muttered. Rubbing his aching heart, he came out of the garden.

As he passed Juexin's flat and saw the lights burning in the windows, and heard the warm human voices, he felt as if he had returned from another world. He remembered what his French teacher had said the other day: "In France, youngsters your age don't know the meaning of tragedy."

But he was a youth of China, and already tragedy was weighing him down.

28

It was summer holiday time. Juemin had much more opportunity to meet Qin. Juehui had much more time to spend with his young friends, all talking and working together. With renewed strength, the boys put out the new magazine, won new readers. All was going well.

That summer a big event was celebrated in the Gao family compound — the sixty-sixth birthday of the Venerable Master Gao.

Preparations began early. It was to be a gala occasion. At the suggestion of Keming, who handled the accounts, and with the approval of the old man, a large sum of money was allotted from the family funds. As Keming put it: "We collect such a huge amount of rent every year, we have more money than we know what to do with. What difference if we spend a little extra!"

Naturally, no wealthy family would let slip such a good opportunity to show off its affluence.

The festive day was fast approaching; gifts flowed in like a tide. A special office had to be set up to accept them and issue invitations. Many people were kept busy day and night. Juexin took a fortnight's leave from his office to help out. The gardens were hung with lanterns and bunting; extra electric lights were added. In the main hall, a stage was built, and the best actors in the city were hired to perform three days of opera. The dramas to be presented were chosen by Keding, who was an expert in such matters.

Everyone was busy except Juemin and Juehui, who spent most of their time away from the compound. They were home only the three days of the formal celebration, when they had no choice.

Those three days were a new experience for them. Although they ordinarily disliked their family compound, at least they were familiar with it. Now, during the celebration, it changed beyond recognition. It became a theatre, a market-place — crowded with people, noisy, full of unnatural grinning faces. Even their own room was given over to some guests whom they knew only slightly. Here a band of zither-playing blind musicians chanted birthday greetings; there another group sang

lewd verses to the accompaniment of two-string fiddles. Still
a third group performed behind a curtain; the leering tones of
the male and female voices were highly erotic; young people
were not permitted to listen.

The operas began in the afternoon of the first day. Except
for a few special birthday plays, the rest were all pieces which
required skilful and subtle interpretation and were not originally included on the programme. These had been specially requested by several of the honourable guests. Whenever a
portion was performed that brought blushes to the women and
the young folks in the audience and smirks to the grown men,
a servant with a stentorian voice would come out on the stage
and read from a festively red slip of paper: "The Honourable
Mr. So-and-so presents to such-and-such an actor the sum of
so-much!" And the lucky actor (invariably a female impersonator) would at once profusely thank his donor, while the
beneficent gentleman beamed with pompous satisfaction.

But even this did not satisfy the honourable guests. When
an opera was over, the actors who had been rewarded had to
drink with them at their tables, still wearing their make-up and
costumes. The honourable gentlemen fondled the performers
and filled them with wine; they behaved with such crass vul-
garity that the younger guests were shocked and the servants
whispered among themselves.

Venerable Master Gao, the shining light of all these festivities, sat up front. He gazed around briefly at what was going
on, and smiled, then turned his eyes back to the stage, for the
old man's favourite female impersonator had just made his
entrance.

Keming and the other two sons of the Venerable Master
Gao circulated among the guests, looking after their wants with
fawning solicitude, while Juexin trailed in their wake.

To Juemin and Juehui it was all absolutely sickening. In this
family, in these surroundings, they felt like strangers. The
noisy, riotous, drunken sots seemed to them some strange
species. A few faces looked vaguely familiar, yet closer ex-

amination made the boys wonder whether they had ever really seen them before.   They felt completely out of place, but they were not allowed to leave because they were supposed to be acting as hosts.   Like the supernumeraries in an opera, they were placed at a table with lesser guests, where they were expected to smile and drink and eat, more like machines than human beings.

Juehui stuck it out the first day; that night he had bad dreams.   The second day was just too much.   He stayed away all afternoon between lunch and dinner.   The young friends whom he visited first laughed at him, then consoled him.   He finally worked up enough courage to go back and receive fresh insults (the word was Juehui's).   But the third day, he was unable to escape.

Mei had come with her mother, Mrs. Qian, but had gone home early because she was ill.   She was growing thinner by the day, and although her frailty was not yet extreme, sensitive people were touched by it, for they knew it was a sign that this lovely star would soon fall.

There were few enough sensitive people in the Gao family, but Juexin certainly was one of them.   He was perhaps the most concerned about Mei.   Yet there were so many invisible barriers between them — at least he thought there were — that they could only gaze at each other and converse wordlessly at a distance.   They avoided all opportunities to speak together in private, thinking they could thus diminish the pain.   The result was just the opposite.   Juexin lost weight steadily and Mei's illness became worse; she began to cough blood.

Madam Zhou was very fond of Mei, but because she didn't know what was in Mei's heart, she had no way of comforting her.   Actually, there was no one who could comfort Mei — not even Ruijue, who recently had grown very close to her and knew her best.

Qin had also come to the party, and also gone home pleading illness — though hers was feigned. The next day she secretly sent a note to Juemin, asking him to call.

Juemin stole away at the first opportunity, and he and Qin had a long talk. On the way home, he was very happy. Juexin met him at the entrance to the main hall and, to Juemin's surprise, asked:

"You've been to Qin's, haven't you?"

Juemin could only nod, mutely.

"I saw her servant slipping you a note; her illness wasn't real. I know all about you two." Juexin spoke in a low voice, a wry smile on his face.

Juemin said nothing. He too was smiling, only his was a smile of satisfaction.

Juexin saw Keming approaching. He exchanged a few words with the elder man. When his uncle had walked on, he again turned to Juemin.

"You're happy," he said softly. "You can do the things you want. I'd like to visit a sick person too, but I don't even have that much freedom. She's very ill. I know she needs me. . . ." His face twisted into an odd expression that could have been either a smile or a grimace of pain.

Moved, Juemin didn't know what to say. "Why don't you forget Mei?" at last he blurted awkwardly. "You're only torturing yourself. And what about Ruijue? You love her too, don't you?"

Juexin's face drained of colour. He stood looking at his brother in stricken silence. Suddenly he became angry. "So you too want me to give her up? You're the same as the others! You can still talk that way at a time like this! . . ." Juexin tore himself away and walked off quickly.

Juemin realized that he had not given Juexin the answer he was seeking. But what other answer could he have given? Juexin said one thing, but did another. Juemin couldn't understand the discrepancy between his Big Brother's words and his deeds. For that matter the whole family was a puzzle to him.

His eyes wandered to the stage, where a short clown and a tall, stately beauty were engaging in a subtle exchange of dialogue. The guests burst into guffaws at some filthy innuendo — the honourable, the not-so-honourable, and the completely dishonourable, guests. Juemin laughed scornfully.

He forgot about Juexin. Slowly, he paced back and forth, his mind filled with his own affairs. For the first time, his prospects looked bright.

Of course it all had to do with Qin. He was very optimistic; she gave him courage and confidence. Not only did she trust him — she had already made it plain that she would not disappoint him. Everything was going smoothly.

At first, when they finished studying English together every day, they had chatted about things in general. Gradually their talk had become more personal, until they understood one another completely, until they had grown so close together that they felt unable to part. Cautiously they spoke of love — the love affairs of their relatives and friends, of Mei and Juexin. Only much later did their conversation get around to their own emotions. Juemin remembered how Qin had blushed and toyed with the pages of a book, trying to appear calm, when she told him how much she needed him. She said she had determined to take the new road, but that there were many obstacles in her path; she needed someone like him, someone who could understand and help her.

He and Qin already knew what was in each other's heart. All that was lacking was an open declaration. When she sent for him today, he felt his chance had come, and he told her what he had never dared say before, announcing heroically that he was willing to sacrifice everything for her sake.

Then she had replied. Actually, one of them had only to speak ten per cent and the other understood the remaining ninety. They had faith in one another, faith in their future. Their latest meeting had parted a curtain; they had made their relationship plain. And this wonderful thing, thought Juemin, had happened only today, practically just a minute ago!

His dreams for the future were very rosy and, of course, quite exaggerated. Blinded, he could see none of the difficulties ahead. Standing on the stone platform outside the main hall, he glanced again at the flirtatious actors on the stage inside. Now the short clown and the stately beauty had been replaced by a handsome hero and a pert young maid. Again the audience roared with laughter at some vulgar sally. Juemin smiled contemptuously. People like this couldn't stop him.

He gazed off into the distance, picturing an ideal life. A slap on the shoulder from a familiar hand brought him back to reality. Juemin turned to find his younger brother, Juehui, standing grinning behind him.

"So you've run out on them too," said Juemin.

"Naturally," replied Juehui with a satisfied laugh. "And you . . . have another chance to sneak out!" He had guessed what Juemin was contemplating from the expression on his face.

Juemin reddened slightly. He nodded. "It's all settled between me and Qin. We've taken the first step. The problem now is the next one." His somewhat weak eyes peered happily at Juehui from behind his gold-rimmed spectacles.

A fleeting smile crossed Juehui's face. Even though he had told Juemin he thought of Qin only as a sister, even though he had loved another girl who had died for his sake, even though he had hoped that one day Juemin might make Qin his sister-in-law, yet when he heard that she now belonged to another, he couldn't help feeling a stab of jealousy — for he had secretly been in love with her. But at once he berated himself for harbouring such an emotion, particularly where his brother was concerned.

"Be careful. Don't take too much for granted." Though there was reason in Juehui's words, they were still motivated a bit by jealousy.

"Everything's fine." Juemin was not in the least discouraged. "You're usually very bold. What makes you so cautious all of a sudden?"

Plainly Juemin had no inkling of what he was thinking. Juehui immediately felt ashamed. He laughed. "You're absolutely right. I wish you luck."

From the stage came a deafening uproar of cymbals and drums, as bare-torsoed warriors somersaulted about in a battle scene. This was followed by a fight between three generals with painted faces. Juehui could see his grandfather, seated up front, chatting with a grey-bearded old man beside him. The sight of the guest's mottled, wrinkled face and his sausage-like nose infuriated Juehui. Clenching his fists, he grated through his teeth:

"So he had the nerve to come!"

"Who?" asked Juemin, surprised.

Juehui pointed. "That murderer — old man Feng!"

"Not so loud! People will hear you!" said Juemin agitatedly.

"So what? I want them to hear! Don't you admire boldness?" Juehui laughed coldly.

While Juemin tried desperately to think of a way to quiet him, an interruption distracted Juehui's attention. The boys' younger sister Shuhua and their young girl cousin, Shuzhen, arrived breathlessly with a bit of news.

"Old man Feng's new concubine is here," said Shuzhen, tugging at Juemin's sleeve. "Let's go see her!"

"But I don't know her. How can I speak to her?" replied Juemin, surprised.

"Do you mean Waner?" queried Juehui. Suddenly he understood. "Where is she?" he demanded, as if asking about someone who had just come back from the grave.

"In my room. No one else is there. Do you want to go?" asked Shuhua with a conspiratorial smile.

"Yes," said Juehui. He went off with the girls. Juemin remained behind.

They found Waner alone — alone except for Ruijue, Shuying and half a dozen bondmaids. Waner was beautifully dressed, but her face was pitifully haggard. She was telling them something, and Ruijue and Shuying were crying. As soon as Waner saw Juehui enter, she stood up and greeted him, trying to smile.

"Third Young Master has come."

Juehui nodded and smiled. "Why are you standing? You're not our servant any more; you're a concubine of the Feng family." Though he jested, Juehui felt miserable. Waner was suffering the fate Mingfeng had died to escape.

Waner silently hung her head. Ruijue, seated on the edge of the bed, reproved him gently, "Look what they've done to her, Third Brother. How can you have the heart to laugh?"

"I'm sorry. I didn't mean anything." He remembered what Qianer had told him in the garden when he found her burning sacrifice money, and he felt very sorry for Waner. He wanted to do something to make amends.

"You're a fine one to scold!" he said to Ruijue. "Instead of you all sitting around crying the first time she comes back, why don't you take her out to see some of the operas?"

"Who can out-talk that sharp tongue of yours?" said Ruijue, pretending to be angry. Shuhua and Shuzhen laughed.

"If you can't out-talk him, let me try!" Shuying interrupted. Noticing that Waner was still standing, she urged, "Please sit down. You needn't be so polite to him." By then Juehui had already seated himself on a stool, so Waner silently resumed her seat. Shuying addressed herself to Juehui.

"Those operas aren't fit to be seen. Some of our guests ought to be ashamed of themselves — choosing nothing but dirty plays. Waner has very little chance to visit here. She wanted to talk to Qianer and some of her other friends privately, so we arranged for them to meet in this room. Now, just as they're getting started, you barge in. Who asked you to come along and play the young master anyhow?"

"I gather that you'd like me to get out," grinned Juehui, but he made no move to go.

"You needn't feel so cocky, Third Brother. They've already picked a bride for Second Brother. Your turn is next," Shuhua inserted.

"What? Who's picked him a bride?" Juehui demanded sceptically.

"The Venerable Master Feng. I hear it's his grandniece. They say she's got a fierce temper, and she's not so young either," said Shuying.

"Why, that old bastard!" Juehui stood up. "I'm going to tell Second Brother!" He cast a final glance at Waner, as if bidding her goodbye for ever, and hurried from the room.

As he passed the main hall, Juehui saw something that depressed him exceedingly. There was Juemin standing before his grandfather and old man Feng. The Venerable Master Feng was smilingly questioning him and Juemin was answering respectfully.

"How can you be polite to that old murderer?" Juehui fumed to himself. "Don't you realize he's your enemy, that he's going to drag you and Qin apart!"

Juemin finally heard the news not only from Juehui but also from his Big Brother. Juexin, while informing Juemin of their grandfather's orders, also asked him how he felt about the matter. This inquiry was not the old man's idea — he issued commands and, naturally, they had to be obeyed. Juexin thought so too, although he did not approve of his grandfather's methods.

While shaken by the blow, Juemin was not afraid. His reply was simple. "I will decide whom I am to marry. Right now, I'm too young. I still have to finish my studies. I don't want to get married." There was a good deal more he wanted to say, but he kept it to himself.

"I can't very well tell *Ye-ye* that you want to make your own decisions. It's better to stress the youth aspect. But I'm afraid that won't convince him either. In our family nineteen isn't considered too young for marriage," Juexin said doubtfully. It was difficult to tell what he really advocated.

"According to you, it's hopeless, then!" said Juemin angrily.

"I didn't mean that," Juexin said quickly, but he had nothing to add.

Juemin stared at him fixedly, as if trying to read his mind. "Don't you remember what you said to me this afternoon?" the younger brother demanded. "Do you want me to re-enact your tragedy?"

"But *Ye-ye*. . . ." Juexin agreed with Juemin completely, yet he felt their grandfather's orders had to be obeyed.

"Don't talk to me about *Ye-ye*. I'm going to travel my own road," Juemin snapped. He turned and went into his room.

Juemin and Juehui discussed the problem far into the night. Finally they agreed upon a plan of action: Resist. If that fails, run away. In any event, never give in.

Juehui encouraged him, first because he sympathized with Juemin, and second because he wanted him to set a precedent, to blaze a new trail for other young men in the same position.

Fired with enthusiasm, Juemin immediately wrote a note to Qin, intending to send it to her the following day, concealed between the pages of a book. The note read:

Qin:
　　No matter what you may have heard, please do not believe a word of it. People are trying to make a match for me, but I have given my heart to you and I will never go back on my pledge. Please have faith in me. You will see how courageously I can give battle, how I will fight for and win you!
Juemin

Juemin read the note over twice. This is an important memento in the annals of our love, he thought. He showed the note to Juehui. "How's that?" he asked proudly.

"Splendid," replied Juehui sarcastically. "Straight out of the middle ages!" And to himself he mocked: We'll soon see how courageously you "give battle"!

Now that the Venerable Master Gao's birthday celebration was over, old man Feng sent a matchmaker to formally propose the marriage of his grandniece to Juemin. The Venerable Master of course was entirely in favour. Madam Zhou was only his daughter-in-law and Juemin's stepmother, not his mother; she did not think it proper to express an opinion.

Juexin felt the marriage would be a serious mistake, ruining
the life of another young couple. But he hadn't the courage
to oppose his grandfather. He could only pray that some miracle might occur.

The matchmaking was done secretly, without Juemin's
knowledge. Such matters were always conducted in secret; the
persons involved were mere puppets. Those, who had been
puppets in their youth, today were making puppets out of others.
That was how it had been in the past, and that was how it
always would be — or so people like the Venerable Master Gao
thought. But they were mistaken in Juemin's case. He wasn't
the type to submit to being a puppet.

In contrast to the older generation, Juemin took active measures concerning his marriage. Without the least shyness, he
made inquiries about the proposed match. Juehui became his
scout. Together with Qin the two brothers formed a com-
mittee of three. They discussed tactics — how to block the
match with old man Feng's grandniece, how to publicize the
relationship between Juemin and Qin.

As the opening stage of the battle, Juemin made his attitude
plain to his Big Brother. Juexin replied that it was not up to
him. Juemin requested his stepmother to cancel the match.
Madam Zhou said the decision rested with his grandfather.
But Juemin couldn't approach the old man directly and he could
find no one with influence to help him. In this family, the
Venerable Master Gao passed final judgement.

A few days later, Qin's mother requested him to stop calling. Mrs. Zhang was the old man's daughter. Although she
sympathized with Juemin, as a member of the Gao family she
could not and would not help him. There was already a
rumour going around among the Gaos that Juemin was being
supported in his actions by his aunt Mrs. Zhang because she
wanted her daughter to marry him. Qin was so furious when
she heard this, she cried.

After the preliminary skirmish ended in total failure, Juemin began the second phase of his tactics. He spread the story that unless the family respected his wishes, he would take drastic measures. Since this threat was never permitted to reach the old man's ears, it did not produce any results either.

Then Juemin learned that his horoscope and that of his proposed bride were about to be exchanged, after which a date would be set for the engagement. He heard this news only two weeks after the Venerable Master Gao's birthday celebration.

It was then that Juexin had given the old man some indication of Juemin's feelings, but to no avail.

"How dare he disagree?" the patriarch had retorted angrily. "What I say is final!"

Juemin paced the garden for hours that day. His determination wavered a bit. If once he decided to run away from home, there would be no turning back. Earning his own living would be a big problem. He was very comfortable at home; he was well provided with food and clothing. But on the outside, how would he live? He had not made any preparations for such a move. Yet now the problem was upon him; he had to make up his mind.

Seeking out Juexin, he came directly to the point. "Is there any hope of changing *Ye-ye's* mind?"

"I'm afraid not," said Juexin mournfully.

"Have you really tried to think of every possible way?" asked Juemin, disappointed.

"I really have!"

"What do you think I ought to do?"

"I know what's on your mind but, honestly, there's nothing I can do to help you. The best thing is to do what *Ye-ye* wants. In this day and age, we're fit only to be sacrificed," said Juexin sadly. He was almost weeping.

Juemin laughed coldly. "Still the same old policy of non-resistance! A fine philosophy!" He turned on his heel and left.

29

The following morning when Juexin went to pay his respects to his grandfather, the old man announced triumphantly that the marriage with the Feng family girl was all arranged. The Venerable Master said it could take place after two months and selected an auspicious day in his almanac. He told Juexin to go ahead with exchanging the horoscopes. Mumbling an assent, Juexin left, just as Juehui was entering, a cryptic smile on his face.

No sooner had Juexin reached his quarters than a servant came after him with a summons from the Venerable Master Gao to return at once. Hurrying to his grandfather's study, he found the old man, seated on a sofa, berating Juehui, while Mistress Chen, dressed in a light green, wide-sleeved blouse in crepe silk, her face heavily powdered and her hair smoothly done, sat perched on the arm of the patriarch's chair, and massaged his back with drumming fists. Juehui stood before the old man not saying a word.

"The rebel! That such a thing could actually happen! You find Juemin and bring him back!" shouted the Venerable Master Gao when he saw Juexin enter. Big Brother was mystified.

The old man burst into a paroxysm of coughing and Mistress Chen increased the tempo of her drumming. "Calm yourself, Venerable Master," she pleaded. "At your age you shouldn't get yourself all worked up. They're not worth it!"

"How dare he disobey me? How dare he oppose me?" gasped the old man, red in the face. "Doesn't like the match I made for him, eh? Well, he'll have to! You bring him back here. I'm going to punish him."

Juexin murmured an assent. He was beginning to understand.

"Going to school has ruined him. I wanted you boys to take private tutoring at home, but you wouldn't listen to me. Now look what's happened! Even Juemin had gone bad. He actually dares to rebel. From now on, no son of the Gao family

is permitted to attend an outside school!   Do you hear that?"
The patriarch began to cough again.

Juexin stood flustered, his grandfather's words crashing about
his head like thunder.

Juehui, lined up beside his Big Brother, was quite unperturb-
ed.   Roar away, he thought, smiling inwardly.   You'll soon be
exposed as a paper tiger!

The old man's coughing finally ceased.   Worn out, he lay
back and closed his eyes.   For a long time he did not speak.
He looked as if he were asleep.   The brothers continued standing before him respectfully, waiting.   Only when Mistress Chen
signalled for them to go did they tiptoe out of the room.

"Second Brother left a note for you," Juehui said to Juexin
when they got outside.   "It's in my room.   Come and read
it."

"What in the world did you say to *Ye-ye*?   Why didn't you
tell me first, instead of running to him?   How could you be
so stupid!"

"I wanted him to know!   I wanted him to realize that we're
human beings, not lambs that anyone can lead to the slaughter!"

Juexin knew the barb was directed against him.   It struck
home, but he could only bear the pain in silence.   No matter
how sincerely he explained, Juehui would never believe him.

In Juehui's room, the boy handed him the letter.   It was
hard for Juexin to find the courage to read it, but at last he
did:

Big Brother,
    I'm doing what no one in our family has ever dared to do be-
fore — I'm running out on an arranged marriage.   No one cares
about my fate, so I've decided to travel my own road alone.   I'm
determined to struggle against the old forces to the end.   Unless
you cancel the match, I'll never come back.   I'll die first.   It's still
not too late to save the situation.   Remember our brotherly love
and do your best to help me.
                                                            Juemin
                                        Written at 3 in the morning.

Juexin turned pale.   The note dropped from his trembling

fingers to the floor. "What shall I do?" he stammered. "Doesn't he understand my position?"

"It has nothing to do with your position," said Juehui stiffly. "The question is what are you going to do about it?"

Juexin rose quickly, as if he had received a shock. "I'm going to bring him back," he said simply.

"You'll never find him," said Juehui with a cold laugh.

"Never find him?" echoed Juexin, confused.

"No one knows where he's moved to."

"But surely you know his address. You must know. Tell me, where is he? Please tell me," Juexin begged.

"I do know. But I certainly won't tell you," said Juehui firmly.

"Don't you trust me?" Juexin angrily demanded.

"It doesn't matter whether I trust you or not. Your 'policy of non-resistance,' your 'compliant bow' philosophy would be sure to bring Second Brother to grief. In a word — you're too weak!" said Juehui hotly. He paced the floor with large strides.

"I must see him. Tell me his address."

"No, absolutely no!"

"You'll have to reveal it. They'll make you. *Ye-ye* will make you."

"I won't tell them! Even in this family, I don't think they'd resort to torture," said Juehui coolly. He was aware only that he was achieving some measure of vengeance against his family. He gave no thought to what his Big Brother might be suffering.

Despondently, Juexin walked out. Before long he came back and had another talk with Juehui, trying to evolve a plan. But he failed. He could offer no compromise that would satisfy both Juemin and his grandfather.

Later that day, a small family council was held in Madam Zhou's room. Present were Madam Zhou, Juexin, his wife Ruijue, his sister Shuhua, and Juehui. Juehui stood on one side; the others arrayed themselves opposite him. They urged him to reveal Juemin's whereabouts; they wanted him to per-

suade Juemin to come home. They made many attractive promises — including an assurance that if Juemin returned a way
would be found, in time, to call off the match.

But Juehui was adamant.

Since no information could be obtained from Juehui, and
since Juemin's demands could not be accepted, Madam Zhou
and Juexin could only worriedly seek out Keming and ask him
to delay the exchange of the horoscopes a few days, without
letting the old man know.   At the same time they sent people
out to try and discover where Juemin was hiding.

The search proved fruitless.   Juemin was well concealed.

Keming called Juehui to his study and gave him a lecture —
to no avail.   He offered friendly guidance — to no avail.   He
tried argument and exhortation — to no avail.   Juehui insisted he knew nothing.

Madam Zhou and Juexin worked on Juehui next. They pleaded with him to bring Juemin back.   They said all Juemin's
conditions could be met — provided he returned home first.
Juehui was firm. Unless he got guarantees in advance, he didn't
trust anyone.

Madam Zhou scolded Juehui, then she wept.   Although she
usually left the boys to their own devices, she was genuinely
interested in their welfare.   The situation was serious.   She
didn't want anything bad to happen to them, but she was even
more concerned with her reputation if this scandal should leak
out.   She disapproved of Juehui's disrespectful attitude towards
his elders, and was very dissatisfied with Juemin's flying in
the face of the decision of the head of the family. But no matter
how she tried, she couldn't think of any solution.

Confronted with a difficult problem, Juexin's only recourse
was to weep.   He knew that Juemin was right.   Yet not only
couldn't he help him — he had to help their grandfather oppress
him.   And now Juehui considered him an enemy. Unless he
brought back Juemin, he would be unable to placate the old
man.   But if he did make him return, he would be wounding
Second Brother grievously.

No, that was something he could not do! He loved Juemin. His father had entrusted his two younger brothers to him on his death-bed. How could he go back on his pledge to love and cherish them? Juexin broke into sobs. He wept so bitterly that tears also came to Ruijue's eyes.

The Venerable Master Gao knew nothing of this. All that interested him was that his orders had to be obeyed, his face preserved. What others suffered as a consequence meant nothing to him. He demanded that Juemin be produced. He swore at Juexin. He swore at Keming. At times he even swore at Madam Zhou.

But all of his ranting evoked no sign of compliance from Juemin. His pressure was useless; Juemin wasn't there to be subjected to it. By now the scandal was known to everyone in the compound. Great effort was made to keep it from spreading outside.

The days passed. The Venerable Master Gao was in a perpetually bad temper. A pall of gloom hung over Juexin's household, while the other households sneered privately at his misfortune.

One day, Juehui returned home after a secret meeting with Juemin. Leaving his desperately struggling brother was like leaving the world of light. The Gao compound depressed him dreadfully. The place was a desert; or perhaps it would be more accurate to call it a bastion of reaction, the main base of his enemy. Juehui immediately sought out Juexin.

"Are you willing to help Second Brother or not?" he demanded irritably. "A whole week has already gone by."

"What can I do?" Juexin spread his hands despondently. Now you're the one who's anxious, he said to himself.

"Are you just going to let the thing drag on like this?"

"Drag on, nothing! Ye-ye says if Juemin doesn't return in another half month, he can stay away for ever. He'll put an announcement in the papers disowning him," said Juexin unhappily.

"Do you think Ye-ye would have the heart to do a thing

like that?"   Juehui asked bitterly.   He was still angry.

"Why wouldn't he?   He's absolutely furious.   He won't allow his orders to be disobeyed.   Second Brother's resistance can't win."

"So you say that too.   No wonder you won't help him!"

"But how can I?" Juexin considered himself the unluckiest man in the world.   He had no strength whatsoever.

"When our father was dying, didn't he tell you to look after us?   He'd be very disappointed in you today!"   There were angry tears in Juehui's eyes.

Juexin made no reply.   He began to sob.

"If I were in your position, I'd never be so weak and useless, I tell you that!   I'd cut the match with the Feng family with one slash of the knife, that's what I'd do!"

"But what about Ye-ye?"   Big Brother asked, finally raising his head.

"Ye-ye's era is over.   Are you going to let Second Brother become a sacrifice to Ye-ye's prejudice?"

Juexin again lapsed into silence.

"You are a weakling!"   Juehui stalked out angrily.

Alone in the room, Juexin was weighted down with misery. His "compliant bow" philosophy and his "policy of non-resistance" had failed him; he had not been able to make peace in the family.   In an effort to satisfy everyone, he had given up his own happiness, but it had not brought him peace.   He had willingly accepted the burden entrusted to him by his dying father; he had made every sacrifice for his younger brothers and sisters.   The result was that he had driven one brother away, while the other cursed him for a weakling.   What could he say to comfort himself?

After brooding thus for some time, he took up his pen and wrote an earnest letter to Juemin, vivisecting his own sincerity, and setting forth all his difficulties and tragic circumstances. He spoke of his love and friendship for his brothers, concluding with a plea that Juemin return, for the honour of their departed father, for the sake of peace in the Gao family.

Then he went to Juehui and asked him to deliver the letter to Juemin.

Juehui read the letter and wept. Shaking his head unhappily, he placed the missive back in the envelope.

Juemin's reply, of course, was brought by Juehui. This is what it said:

> After waiting so long, I frankly was very disappointed to get a letter like this from you! All you can say is — Come back, come back! As I write this, I am sitting in a little room, like an escaped prisoner, not daring to go out for fear of being caught and brought back to my jail. The jail I mean is our home, and the jailers are the members of our family — they have banded together to destroy me without mercy.
>
> Yes, you all want me to come home. That would solve your problems. There would be peace in the family and another victim would be sacrificed. Of course you would all be very happy, but I would be sunk in a sea of bitterness.... Well, you can just forget it. I won't come home unless my demands are met. Home is nothing to me but a lot of unpleasant memories.
>
> Perhaps you wonder what makes me so bold? I wonder myself sometimes. It's my love that sustains me. I'm fighting for the happiness of two people — hers and mine.
>
> I often think of our garden, how we played there as children together. You are my Big Brother. You must help me, for the sake of our father. For Qin too. And don't forget Cousin Mei. There's been enough heartbreak over her. Please don't let Qin become another Mei.

Tears coursed down Juexin's cheeks, but he was not aware of them. He was plunged into a dark abyss, without a ray of light, without a shred of hope. "You don't understand me," he kept mumbling. "No one understands me."

Juehui stood watching him, torn between anger and pity. He not only had already read Juemin's letter — he had helped him write it. He had hoped the letter would move Big Brother, stir him into action, yet this was the result. He wanted to berate Juexin, but then he thought — What would be the use? Big Brother had become a man with no will of his own.

"This family is absolutely hopeless. The sooner I get out of here the better," Juehui said to himself. From that moment on, he was no longer pessimistic over the chances of Juemin's success. This new idea intrigued him. It was a sprout that had just emerged into his consciousness, but it might grow very, very quickly.

Quite a number of people were suffering because of Juemin's escapade, Juemin himself among them. He was hiding in the home of his schoolmate, Cunren, and although he was comfortable enough and Cunren was very good to him, he hated being cooped up in a small room. Unable to do the things he wanted to do, unable to see the people he wanted to see, tormented by fear and longing, Juemin found life very difficult.

All day long he waited for news, but the only news Juehui had been able to bring him so far was bad. Gradually, his hope dwindled. But it was not yet completely extinguished, and he still had the courage to go on. Juehui constantly encouraged him with a promise of final victory. Qin's love, her image, gave him strength. He was sticking it out; he had no intention of surrendering.

Qin was always in his mind; he dreamed of her day and night. The more depressed he felt, the more he thought of her. And the more he thought of her, the more he longed to see her. But although she lived quite near to Cunren's house, he couldn't visit her because her mother was home.

He wanted to send her a note via Juehui. But when he took up his pen he found he had too much to say — he didn't know where to start. At the same time he was afraid if he didn't write her in detail, she would become worried. He decided to wait for an opportunity to talk to her face to face.

It came sooner than he expected. Juehui arrived one day with the news that Mrs. Zhang had gone out; he took Juemin to see Qin.

Leaving Juemin waiting outside the door, Juehui went in first. "I've brought you something good, Cousin Qin," he announced cheerfully.

Qin had been lying down, reading, half-asleep, but she sat up quickly. Smoothing her hair, she asked listlessly, "What is it?" She looked pale, too tired even to smile.

"How thin you are!" Juehui exclaimed in spite of himself.

"You haven't seen me in several days." Qin smiled wryly. "What about Second Brother? Why haven't I received even a single letter from him?"

"Several days? Why, I was here only the day before yesterday!"

"You don't know how time is dragging for me. Tell me quickly. What's happening with him?" Qin stared at him with large, worried eyes.

"He's given in!" Juehui succumbed to an irresistible impulse to tease her.

"No! I don't believe it!"

Just at that moment, a young man stepped into her room, and Qin's eyes lit up.

"You!" she cried. Whether it was doubt, or surprise, or joy, or reproach that she felt, she didn't know herself. She rushed towards him, then checked herself abruptly and stood gazing at him, her eyes aglow.

"Yes, Qin, it's me." There was both joy and sorrow in his voice. "I meant to come much sooner, but I was afraid of running into your mother."

"I knew you'd come, I knew you'd come," she said, weeping tears of happiness. She looked reproachfully at Juehui. "How could you try to fool me like that, Third Brother? I knew he'd never give in. I have faith in him." She gazed at Juemin lovingly, with no trace of shyness.

Juehui was favourably impressed. He hadn't realized that Qin had grown so mature. Smiling, he looked at Juemin, who plainly was feeling very heroic at the girl's exaggerated praise. Juehui acknowledged to himself that he was wrong. He had expected their meeting would be attended with tears and weeping and all the other trappings of tragedy. Such scenes were common in families like theirs.

But contrary to his expectations, they seemed to fear nothing, sustaining each other with an all-powerful mutual faith. He was delighted with them. They were a gleam of light in a dark

world; they gave him hope. They didn't need his encouragement any more. Juemin would never bend the knee.

How easy it was for an ardent youth like Juehui to believe
in people!

"All right, you can quit talking like a couple of stage actors
and get down to business. If you've got anything to say, say
it quickly. We haven't much time." Juehui grinned. "Would
you like me to step out a minute?"

They both laughed but didn't answer. Ignoring Juehui,
they sat down on the edge of the bed, holding hands and talking
affectionately. He idly picked one of Qin's books from the
shelf. It was a collection of Ibsen's plays, dog-eared and under-
scored in places. Apparently, she had recently been reading
An Enemy of the People. She must have found encouragement
in it. Juehui couldn't help smiling.

He stole a glance at Qin. She and Juemin were engrossed in
a lively conversation. Her face was radiantly beautiful. Juehui
felt rather envious of his brother. He turned back to *An Enemy
of the People*.

After reading the first act he looked up. They were still
talking. He read the second act. They still hadn't finished.
He read the play through to the end. Qin and Juemin were
chattering away, with no sign of a let-up.

"Well, how about it? What a gabby pair you two are!"
Juehui was growing impatient.

Qin looked up at him with a smile, and continued talking.

"Let's go, Second Brother," Juehui urged, half an hour later.
"You've said enough."

"Just a little longer," Qin pleaded. "It's early yet. What's
your hurry?" She was holding Juemin's hand tightly, as if
afraid he would leave.

"I must go back," said Juehui, with mock stubbornness.

"Go ahead, then," Qin pouted. "My humble home isn't good
enough for an aristocrat like you!" But when she saw him actually begin walking out, she and Juemin, in chorus, hastily called
him to wait.

"Must you go, Third Brother? Can't you help me out a little?" Juemin asked earnestly.

Juehui laughed. "I was only fooling. But you two are much too cold to me. Qin, you haven't spoken to me, or even asked me to sit down. Now that Second Brother's here, you've forgotten me completely."

The other two also laughed.

"I've only got one mouth. I can only speak to one person at a time," Qin defended herself. "Be good now, Third Brother. Let me talk to him today. Tomorrow, you and I can talk to your heart's content." She coaxed him, as if he were a child.

"Don't try to fool me. I haven't Second Brother's luck!"

Juemin opened his mouth to say something, but Qin cut in. "How's your luck going with Xu Qianru?" she asked slyly. "Qianru's got it all over me. Do you like her? She's a really modern girl."

"Maybe I like her, and maybe I don't. But what's that got to do with you?" Juehui retorted mischievously. He loved this kind of banter.

"They are well matched. I was thinking the same thing, myself," Juemin interposed.

Juehui laughed and waved his hand in refusal. "No thanks. I don't want to become like you two — secret rendezvous and dramatic scenes!" In his heart he was thinking: What I want is you, Qin! ... But this first thought was immediately driven away by a second: I've already sent one girl to her death. I've had enough of love. Outwardly he smiled, but it was a bitter smile.

Juemin's conversation with Qin at last came to an end. Now they had to part. Juemin hated to leave. Thinking of his lonely life in that little room, he hadn't the courage to go back. But Juehui's impelling look told him that he must; there was no other way.

"I have to go," he said sadly, a note of struggle in his voice. But he didn't move. He cast about in his mind for some words to comfort Qin; all he could manage in that instant was: "Don't think about me too much," although that wasn't his meaning at all. As a matter of fact, he hoped she would think about him a great deal.

Qin stood before him, her big, luminous eyes fixed on his face, listening carefully, as if expecting him to say something out of the ordinary. He didn't. She waited, but he spoke only briefly. Disappointed, she clutched his sleeve, urging:

"Don't go yet. Stay a little longer. I still have a lot to tell you."

Juemin gulped down these wonderful words like the tastiest of morsels. He stared at her animated face. "All right, I won't go yet," he said with a smile — a smile so tortured that Juehui, watching from the side, really thought he was going to cry.

To Qin, Juemin's tender gaze seemed to be gently caressing her eyes, her face. "Speak," they seemed to say. "Speak. I'm listening to every word, every syllable." But she couldn't think of anything to say, and she was frantic for fear that he might leave at any moment. Still holding on to his sleeve, she blurted out the first thing that came into her mind:

"Cousin Mei has become pitifully thin lately. She coughs blood every day, though not very much. She's hiding it from her mother, and she doesn't want me to tell anyone, because she doesn't want to be given medicine. She says every day she lives is another day of misery — she'd be better off dead. Her mother is always busy entertaining and playing mahjong; she doesn't pay much attention to Mei. Yesterday I finally found the chance to tell her how sick Mei is; only now has she begun to worry. Perhaps Mei is right. But I can't stand by and watch her die. Don't say anything to Big Brother. Mei begged me not to let him know."

Suddenly Qin noticed the tears glistening behind Juemin's glasses. They were beginning to trickle down his cheeks. His lips trembled, but he could not speak. She understood. He was frightened that their love, too, might end in tragedy.

"I can't say any more!" she cried. She fell back a few paces, buried her face in her hands and wept.

"I really must go now, Qin," said Juemin unhappily. He hadn't imagined that their joyous meeting would terminate with both of them in tears. And they called themselves the new youth, the brave! . . .

"Don't go! Stay!" Qin took down her hands from her tear-stained face and stretched them towards Juemin.

Only Juehui's restraining grasp kept Juemin from rushing to her. Juemin looked at his younger brother. Juehui's eyes were dry, and they burned with a strong, steady light. Juehui jerked his head in the direction of the door.

"Don't cry, Qin, I'll come again," Juemin said in a stricken voice. "I'm living not very far from here. I'll come as soon as there's a chance. . . . Take care of your health. I'll be sending you good news soon."

Steeling himself, he turned and walked out with Juehui. Qin followed as far as the door of the main hall. There she halted and stood with her back against the frame of the doorway. Wiping her eyes, she watched them go.

The brothers reached the street with the sound of Qin's weeping still in their ears. They walked on quickly in silence, and soon arrived at Cunren's house. Juehui abruptly stopped in the middle of the street.

"You and Qin are bound to succeed," he said in a bright, strong voice. "We don't need any more sacrificial victims. We've had enough." Juehui paused, then went on firmly, almost cruelly. "If any more sacrifices have to be made, let *them* be the victims this time!"

30

Juexin's conscience had been bothering him a lot of late. He knew that unless he helped Juemin, he'd regret it all his life.

After talking it over with his wife and stepmother, he went to the Venerable Master Gao and circuitously suggested that the marriage be postponed until Juemin was self-supporting. Naturally, he made no reference to the affair between Juemin and Qin. Juexin spoke quite movingly — he had been preparing for several nights; he had even written his speech out. He was sure he could sway the old man.

But Juexin was wrong. The patriarch was furious. He knew only that his authority had been attacked and stern measures were needed to restore it. A parent's order, the word of a marriage sponsor, the bride chosen by the head of a family — none of these could be questioned by a member of the younger generation. That was an unshakable principle; going against it demanded severe punishment. As to young people's happiness and aspirations, he never gave them a thought. Juexin's plea only increased his rage. He swore the engagement would not be broken. Unless Juemin returned by the end of the month, he would place an announcement in the newspapers publicly disowning him and compel Juehui to marry the girl in Juemin's place.

Juexin didn't dare to argue. Humbly leaving his grandfather's room, he hurried to Juehui and told him what the old man had said. He thought that this might frighten Juehui into urging his Second Brother to return. But Juehui had learned wisdom; what's more he was prepared for something like this. He made no comment, he only laughed coldly. . . . They're certainly not going to make me the victim! he thought.

"You'd better persuade Second Brother to come back," Juexin urged, when Juehui remained silent. "Otherwise you'll be the marriage victim."

"If that's what *Ye-ye* really wants, let him go ahead. He'll be sorry. I'm not afraid. I've got some ideas of my own," retorted Juehui proudly.

Big Brother could hardly believe his ears. He had thought he knew Juehui thoroughly.

"I don't understand why you're so weak, so useless!" Juehui mocked him.

Juexin blushed, then turned pale. He trembled, speechless with anger. At that moment a servant rushed in and breathlessly announced:

"A messenger has just come from Mrs. Qian. Miss Mei is dead!"

"Mei is dead? When did she die?" cried Ruijue, emerging hastily from the inner room.

"About seven this morning," the servant replied.

The clock on the wall struck nine. A heavy silence filled the room. No one could speak.

"Get a sedan-chair ready for me immediately," Juexin directed, his face falling.

"I want to go too," said Ruijue, weeping. She sat down in a wicker chair.

"What are you waiting for?" Juexin said to the servant. After the man had left, he turned to Ruijue and said soothingly, "Don't go. Jue, you're with child. It's bad for you. You'll get too upset."

"I want to see her. . . . That day after I visited her in Qin's house . . . as I was getting into my sedan-chair, she took my hand. She said I must come to see her often. She kept repeating that the next time I must bring Haichen. Her eyes were filled with tears. Who knew that she'd never see us again. I want to go. . . . It's the last time. . . . She was so good to me . . . it's the least I can do."

"Rui, don't carry on so. You must think of your health. You're all I have left. If anything should happen to you, it would be the end of me," said Juexin dismally.

Juehui stood beside the desk, staring at the white gauze curtains. The news hadn't come to him as a surprise. He remembered Qin telling him about Mei, "She says every day she lives is another day of misery — she'd be better off dead." Still, the death of this fragile, lovely young woman was hard to bear.

Bitterness and fury seethed in Juehui's breast. Controlling himself, he said coldly:

"Another sacrificial victim!"

He knew Juexin would understand his meaning. He turned to see Big Brother gazing at him with suffering eyes. "The trouble is far from over," Juehui added. "The worst is yet to come." This too was for Juexin's benefit.

Juexin could hear weeping as he got out of his sedan-chair at the door of the Qian family. He hurried directly to Mei's room.

Mei's mother, Mrs. Qian, was there, and Mei's younger brother, as well as Qin and a bondmaid. They were grouped around the body, crying. All looked up when Juexin came in.

"What am I going to do, First Young Master?" wailed Mrs. Qian. Her hair was dishevelled and tears stained her face.

"We'll have to start arranging for the funeral immediately," said Juexin in a tragic voice. "Has the coffin been bought?"

"I sent Old Wang out to buy one. He hasn't come back yet." (Old Wang was their servant.) Mrs. Qian began to weep again. "Mei's been dead for over two hours, but not a thing has been done. We've no grown men in the family, and Old Wang has been busy notifying people. What am I going to do? Look at the state this house is in!"

"Don't worry, Aunt Qian. Just leave everything to me."

"You're a good man, First Young Master. Mei will be grateful to you in the next world."

The word "grateful" was like a needle through Juexin's heart. He didn't know what to say. He wished he could cry. Why should she be grateful to me? he thought. It was I who brought her to this! He walked to her bedside. She was lying with her eyes closed, her hair spread upon the pillow. Her thin face was white, her lips slightly parted, as if she had been about to speak when she died. She was draped with a coverlet from the waist down.

"I've come to see you, Mei," he said in a low voice. Suddenly he was blinded by tears. Is this how we part for ever?

he wondered. You've gone without a word. You've never forgiven me! Why didn't I come earlier? I could have seen your
lips move, heard your voice. I would have known what was in
your heart. Silently he beseeched her: Mei, I've come. If
you've anything to tell me, say it quickly. I can hear you!

Juexin wiped his eyes. Mei lay like an icy stone. She
wouldn't really be able to hear him even if he shouted himself
hoarse; she would remain motionless. All hope was gone.
They were separated now by eternity, and they would never
be able to bridge the gap. Heartbroken, torn by remorse, he
wept hopeless tears.

His crying started Mrs. Qian sobbing again. Qin came over
to him impatiently.

"This is no time for weeping. You ought to help make the
final arrangements. She's dead. Crying won't bring her back
again. Aunt Qian is nearly beside herself as it is. Your crying
only makes her feel worse. If Mei has any consciousness after
death, you're hurting her too."

I've hurt her so many times already, he thought bitterly, what
difference will one more time make! Restraining his tears with
an effort, he sighed deeply.

"You shouldn't blame First Young Master," said Mrs. Qian.
"He and Mei were very dear to each other. There were people
who proposed that they marry. It's all my fault for not agree-
ing. If I had, we wouldn't have come to this, today!" Mrs.
Qian wept as she spoke. She was incapable of doing anything.
Her mind was in a whirl.

"Hurry and make the arrangements, Cousin," Qin urged Juexin. "Don't leave her exposed so long." She knew Mrs. Qian's
remark had upset Big Brother, and she used this prod to distract
him.

"All right," sighed Juexin. He discussed the details with
Mrs. Qian. Then Mei was dressed in burial clothes and placed
in the coffin. Juexin wanted to lift her out in his arms and
run with her to some distant, deserted place. But he didn't
have the courage.

Finally, steeling himself, he gave the order to close the coffin. Mrs. Qian grasped the edge of the casket and began to wail:

"Mei, I was blind, I didn't know what was in your heart. I broke up your match with Juexin. I made you suffer till you died. I'm sorry, Mei. Can you hear me? Why don't you answer? Do you hate me? Take your revenge on me in your next life. Hurt me as I've hurt you. Only don't leave me. We must be mother and daughter again. Do you agree, my poor darling? Mei, Mei, let me go with you. . . ."

She tried to climb into the coffin, deaf to all exhortations to be calm. They had to pull her away.

The lid was placed on the coffin and sealed tight. Mei was gone from the room. Only the coffin remained, and even that was to be removed the same day.

One by one, the few visitors departed. Madam Zhou had come with Shuhua. Qin's mother, Mrs. Zhang, had also come, and two or three other women. They had sat for a while and departed. Except for Mei's mother and young brother and their servant, Old Wang, the only ones to accompany the body to the funeral hall outside the city were Juexin, Juehui, Shuhua and Qin. Juehui had arrived quite late, but he was in time to take part in the funeral procession.

The funeral hall was in the wing of a large dilapidated temple whose courtyard was overgrown with weeds. Each of the wings flanking the main temple building contained a series of small rooms. Most of these housed coffins and funeral equipment, much of it in a decayed and neglected condition. Ordinarily a coffin was left in a funeral hall until the family could arrange to transport it back to the deceased's native place for burial. But here, in one room were four coffins that had been brought in almost twenty years ago; no one remembered to whom they belonged.

Mei's room was a relatively modest one. They soon set it in order. The coffin was carried in; an altar was put beside it; Mei's "spirit tablet" was placed upon the altar. Old Wang squatted on the stone platform outside the door and burned paper "money." Mrs. Qian leaned against the coffin and wept, her young son sobbing beside her. Qin tried to comfort Mrs. Qian, but when she remembered what good friends she had been with Mei and thought of what had become of Mei now, she herself burst into tears.

Juexin stood dazedly before the altar. He could hear the others weeping. He was crying too, though he hardly knew why. It seemed to him that the one in the coffin wasn't Mei, but someone else. She was still alive, looking at him with a mournful expression, telling him of her sad life. Through his tears the red paper inscribed in black ink and pasted on the "spirit tablet" gradually came into clear focus. "Our Deceased Sister . . . Mei. . . ." The words were merciless, unmistakable. She was dead. Behind the altar, Mei's mother wept and beat upon the coffin; her young brother cried, "Sister, sister. . . ." Qin pillowed her head on her right arm and lay against the coffin, weeping quietly — Qin whose love was menaced by the same fate as Mei's.

Juexin's tears flowed freely. This time he knew why. He wiped his eyes with his handkerchief. He couldn't bear to look any more. Striding out of the door, he paused on the stone platform and watched Old Wang burning sacrifice money. Juehui was just coming out of the main temple; he walked firmly. In spite of his youth, he was the only one who could bolster Juexin's strength in such surroundings. That certainly was how it seemed to Juexin at the moment.

"Let's go back," said Juehui, walking up to Juexin. Old Wang had finished burning the "money." Only a pile of embers and black ashes remained. The wind lifted the flaky ashes, and let them sail down, scattering in all directions.

"All right," replied Juexin listlessly. He turned and went back into the funeral hall. With tears in his eyes, he urged the others not to cry. Qin was sobbing; Mrs. Qian had wept her eyes dry. Only the little brother was still calling, "Sister, sister. . . ."

Each made an obeisance before the altar.   As they were leaving, the little boy suddenly burst out:

"We're going, sister, and leaving you all alone!   How lonely you'll be!"

Tears came to everyone's eyes.   Qin pressed the child's hand and, comforting him, led him outside. Mrs. Qian had just calmed down a bit, but her son's cry again plunged her into misery.   Standing before the altar, she gazed at the candles, the incense, the "spirit tablet."

"Your brother is right, Mei," she moaned weakly.   "This place is too cold, too desolate.   Come home tonight; surely you remember your own house.   From now on, I'll leave a lamp burning in your room every night, to help you find your way. I won't change anything . . . Mei . . . my dear. . . ."

It was a great effort for her to speak.   She wanted to say more, but her chest ached and there was a lump in her throat. She trailed out after the others.

Juexin was the last to get into his sedan-chair; he turned his head many times to look back as they departed.   But the last to leave was Juehui — he wouldn't let any man carry him.   He never rode in sedan-chairs; he walked.

Juehui returned to the small room and made a circuit around the coffin.   He too wanted to bid farewell to Mei. But he didn't weep; he felt no sorrow — only a furious anger.   In a voice that shook with pity and rage, he said:

"To the accompaniment of weeping and words and tears, a sweet young life has been put to rest. Ah, Cousin Mei, if only I could pluck you from your coffin and make you open your eyes, I would prove it to you — You didn't die; you've been murdered!"

31

The following afternoon, Juehui went to see Juemin and told him about Mei. Juemin wept.   They talked for less than an hour, then Juehui left. Juemin saw him to the door. Juehui had already crossed the threshold when Juemin suddenly called him back.

"What is it?" asked Juehui, returning to the door.

Juemin only smiled, but did not speak.

"You're lonely, aren't you?" said Juehui sympathetically. "I am too. Nobody at home understands me. Mama Huang and Sister-in-law and the girls are always hanging around, asking me about you. But their way of thinking is so different from yours and mine. I feel quite isolated. But I know I must be patient, and so must you. You're sure to win."

"I'm a little afraid. . . ." Tears glistened in Juemin's eyes.

"Afraid of what? You can't lose." Juehui forced an encouraging smile.

"I'm afraid of the loneliness. I'm very lonely!"

"But don't you remember — you have two people fighting on your side?" Juehui struggled to maintain his cheerful expression.

"It's because you're both so dear to me that I'm always wanting to see you. But she can't come, and now you're leaving. . . ."

Juehui's eyes smarted. He turned his head so that his brother might not see the moisture in his eyes, and clapped Juemin on the shoulder. "Be patient. It won't be much longer. You're bound to win."

"Why don't you fellows talk inside?" Cunren had come out and was standing beside them. "You shouldn't be too careless," he added with a smile.

Juehui greeted him and said, "I'm going." As he walked away he heard Cunren saying to Juemin, "We'd better go in."

"You're bound to win," he had assured Juemin, but now he wondered bitterly — Is victory really possible? How long would it take to finally attain it? . . . But by the time he reached Qin's house, he made up his mind — Never mind all that. We'll fight to the end, come what may!

After paying his respects to his aunt, he went to Qin's room.

"I've just seen Juemin," he said, coming directly to the point. "He's asked me to tell you — He's fine."

Qin had been writing a letter. She quickly put down her pen and said, "Thank him, and thank you, too. I was just writing to him."

"Needless to say, I'll deliver the letter for you," Juehui smiled. He glanced at the letter and noticed that the words "Cousin Mei" appeared in several places. "You're writing about Cousin Mei? I've already told him. Tell me, what's your reaction to her death?"

"As I've said in this letter, under no circumstances am I going to be a second Mei. My mother won't permit it either. She told me that after seeing all the heartbreak at Mei's funeral yesterday, she was very shaken. She's willing to help me, now." Qin spoke firmly. She had none of the despondency of a few days before.

"That's good news. You should let him know right away." Juehui urged her to finish the letter. They chatted for a few minutes, then Juehui went back to Cunren's house.

Of course both Juemin and Cunren were delighted with the news. They and Juehui talked optimistically for almost an hour. Only then did Juehui return home.

In the compound, he found a small crowd gathered outside his grandfather's window, craning their necks and listening. This sort of thing was very common in the Gao family, and Juehui paid no attention. Walking into the main hall, he was about to enter his grandfather's room, when he heard a woman crying inside. He recognized her voice. It was Madam Shen, wife of his Uncle Keding. Following came the sound of his grandfather swearing and coughing.

I knew there'd be a farce like this sooner or later, Juehui said to himself. He remained outside the door.

"Bring him back immediately! You'll see how I'll punish him! . . . I've had enough of his insolence!" The old man's voice trembled with rage. He lapsed into a fit of coughing which was interspersed with the weeping of Aunt Shen.

A man's voice servilely murmured "Yes" several times. Then the door curtain was pushed aside and Uncle Keming, red-faced, emerged. By then Juehui had already left the hall.

Among the audience outside the window was his younger sister Shuhua. When she saw Juehui, she walked over to him and asked, "Do you know about Uncle Keding, Third Brother?"

"I've known for some time," Juehui nodded. In a low voice he asked, "How did they find out?" He pointed with his lips towards his grandfather's room.

"Fifth Uncle has been keeping a concubine on the outside," the girl replied dramatically. "He rented an apartment for her. Nobody in the family knew. He took all of Fifth Aunt's gold and silver jewelry; he said he loaned it to someone who wanted to copy the designs. When Fifth Aunt pressed him to return it, he said he'd lost it. The last few months, he's been out every day; at night he comes home very late. Fifth Aunt has been so busy with her mahjong games that she didn't notice anything. Yesterday morning she found a woman's picture in his pocket. When she questioned him, he refused to say who it was. By coincidence, Fifth Aunt went shopping yesterday afternoon and saw a woman getting out of Uncle Keding's sedan-chair in front of the arcade, with Uncle Keding's servant Gao Zhong right behind her.

"Today, Aunt Shen found an excuse to keep Gao Zhong at home, and she forced him to tell the truth — Uncle Keding has pawned some of her jewelry; some of it he's given to the woman. Now Aunt Shen has complained to *Ye-ye*. . . . Uncle Keding's concubine is a prostitute. Her name is 'Monday'! . . . Oh yes, they say Uncle Keding has begun smoking opium; he's got the habit. His concubine smokes it too. . . ."

Shuhua rattled on as if she would never stop, plainly relishing the scandal. Juehui was neither much interested nor surprised. He knew the family was hollow and that it was bound to collapse. No one could prevent it — his grandfather or anyone else. The old man himself was already deteriorating rapidly. It seemed to Juehui that he alone was on the threshold of brightness. His moral strength far exceeded that of his tottering family.

Today he was uplifted by enthusiasm as never before. The so-called struggle between parent and child for the right to freedom, love and knowledge was going to conclude happily. The era of tragedies like Mei's would soon be over, giving way to a new era, an era of girls like Qin, or perhaps the still more modern Xu Qianru. It would be Juemin's era, and his own. The youth of this era could never be defeated by corrupt, weak, and often criminal, old-fashioned families. Victory was assured, of that Juehui was confident.

He shook himself vigorously, as if to cast off the burden of years of bitterness and pain. Proudly, fiercely, he gazed around him, and he thought: Wait and see, old family. Your end is coming, soon!

Naturally, Shuhua had no inkling of what was going on in Juehui's mind. He didn't answer her, and she could see that he was bored. She hurried back to her listening post outside the window.

Juehui went to his room. Not long after, through his window he observed Keming returning with Keding in tow. Next, from his grandfather's room, came the sound of thunderous swearing, obviously directed at Keding. Finally, it stopped, and the crowd outside the old man's window stirred with excitement, as if over some unexpected development.

"I always said our family loves a farce," Juehui muttered.

The voices of the people outside rose, and men and women ran breathlessly to spread the news.

"*Ye-ye* is hitting Uncle Keding!" Juequn, one of Juehui's little boy cousins, went tearing across the courtyard, then halted abruptly to announce this news to Jueying, another young boy cousin.

"Really? Then why are you running away?" asked Jueying.

"I've got to get Sixth Brother to come and see this. . . . A big man like Uncle Keding getting a beating!" Juequn laughed, and he rushed off.

His interest aroused at last, Juehui walked to his grand-father's apartment. Three people, watching surreptitiously through the door-curtain, blocked the doorway. Not wanting to squeeze past them, Juehui went outside to the window. Many people were gathered there, listening. A few had brought chairs and were kneeling on them, peering through small holes in the paper panes.

But there was no sound of any beating, only the furious tones of the old man.

"A man of your age, with a daughter growing up — you still haven't learned to behave! A fine example you give to your child! Be ashamed of him, Shuzhen. He's not fit to be your father!"

Juehui couldn't help laughing to himself.

The old man coughed and, after a pause, resumed his angry lecture.

"You're absolutely shameless. What has been the good of your schooling? Fooling your wife into lending you her jewelry and then pawning it! I give you three days to bring it back!" The Venerable Master Gao went on cursing Keding, and finally he said, "You animal, I pampered you because you were a clever child. I never thought you'd turn out to be such a dis-grace. How have you returned my kindness? By deceiving me! Scoundrel! Slap your face! Slap your own face!"

There came the sound of a hand smartly striking a cheek. Juehui walked back quickly to the door of his grandfather's room. "Let me see," he said softly to his sister Shuhua who was leaning forward, peeking through the door-curtain. He edged past her and stood in the doorway.

Keding was kneeling upright, slapping his cheeks, left and right. His usually thin sallow face was quite red from the blows. Although his wife and daughter were before him, he showed no sign of shame. He continued hitting himself.

But this humiliation didn't satisfy the Venerable Master. He demanded that Keding tell his whole dirty story — how he got into bad company and began sliding down hill, his relations with the prostitute, the apartment he rented for her, how he pawned his wife's jewelry.

Cursing himself, Keding revealed all, including things his father had never suspected. He had incurred many debts, some of them debts for gambling, obtaining credit on the old man's name. What's more, he was helped in all this by his brother Ke'an; in fact, Ke'an was partly responsible for his getting into debt in the first place.

The patriarch was astonished. Even Juehui had not guessed that matters had gone so far.

Juehui couldn't help being impressed by the contrast between his Fifth Uncle, Keding, and his brother, Juemin. Juemin, nineteen years old, surrounded by enemies, sustained only by his faith and enthusiasm, was fighting on bravely, the family helpless against him. Keding, over thirty, the father of a thirteen-year-old daughter, knelt on the floor, slapping his own face, insulting and reviling himself, implicating others, offering no resistance by word or deed. He did his father's bidding without hesitation, although he didn't really agree with what the Venerable Master said. In the face of the menace of the stubborn old man, what a difference in reaction between these two different generations! Juehui was proud of his own generation. Looking at Keding, he thought contemptuously: Your type can be found only among people of your generation; they'd never be found in ours. He walked away.

Coughing violently, the patriarch ordered Shuzhen to fetch Ke'an. The girl returned in a few moments, saying her uncle was not at home. The old man cursed and pounded the table. "Where is your Fourth Aunt?" he said to Shuzhen. "Bring her to me."

Madam Wang of the Fourth Household had been listening outside the window. When she saw Shuzhen coming for her, although she was afraid, she had no choice but to take a grip on herself and go in.

The old man asked her in a loud voice where her husband Ke'an had gone. Madam Wang said she didn't know. He then asked when Ke'an would return. She replied she didn't know that either.

"Why don't you?" yelled the Venerable Master, slapping the table. "Muddle-head!"

Angry and embarrassed, Madam Wang hung her head. She thought she saw Mistress Chen making an ugly grimace at her, and she felt like telling the long-faced old concubine a thing or two. But in the presence of the Venerable Master, she didn't dare to move. She didn't even dare to weep.

The old man again broke into a violent fit of coughing. Mistress Chen diligently drummed on his back. "Don't make yourself ill over them," she urged. "They're not worth it!"

Gradually, the patriarch calmed down. His anger was replaced by a depression he had never experienced before. Exhausted, he closed his eyes and lay back on the sofa. He didn't want to see any of them.

"Go away, all of you," he sighed with a weak wave of the hand. "I can't bear to look at you."

Everyone had been longing to be dismissed; they went out quickly. Keding got up off the floor and tiptoed out. The Venerable Master was left alone with Mistress Chen. He didn't want to see her either. All he wanted was a little peace and quiet. He sent Mistress Chen away and lay on the sofa, panting slightly.

He opened his eyes. He seemed to see many forms and faces drifting before him. Not one of them looked at him with any affection. There were his sons, indulging themselves in women and wine, sneering at him, cursing him behind his back. There were his grandsons, proudly going their own new road, abandoning him, old and weak and powerless to stop them.

Never had he felt so lonely and despondent. Had all his hopes been nothing but idle dreams? He had built up the family until it was large and prosperous. Ruthless, dictatorial, he had controlled everything, satisfied in the conviction that the family would continue to flourish. Yet the results of his strenuous efforts had brought only loneliness. Though he was taxing his waning strength to the utmost to keep a grip on things, it was obvious he could not.

No question about it — the family was sliding downhill. He already had some premonition of how it would end. It probably would happen very soon. He had no way to prevent it. Viewing the large wealthy family he had spent so many years in the building the Venerable Master Gao could feel only futile, empty.

Weakly he rested on the sofa, ignored, bitter, lonely. For the first time he became aware of his true position in the family. Not only had he lost his pride — even the people he relied upon to maintain the daily life of the family had proved worthless. For the first time he felt disappointed, disillusioned, sunk in despair. It occurred to him, also for the first time, that he must have made mistakes; but he didn't know what they were. Even if he could discover them, it was already too late.

He seemed to hear Keding wrangling with his wife, Mistress Chen cursing someone. Everywhere were quarrelsome, discordant, grating sounds. He covered his ears, but he couldn't shut them out. He had to find some quiet place to hide! Struggling to his feet, he tottered towards his bed. Suddenly, the room began to spin. He swayed; his eyes went black. He knew nothing more until awakened by the terrified screeching of Mistress Chen.

32

The Venerable Master Gao was ill.

He lay groaning upon his bed, attended by several famous physicians, dosed by dark and bitter potions. The first two days, the doctors said his ailment was not serious. The old man dutifully drank his medicines, but he became worse. The third day, he refused to drink any more, and only relented under the combined pleading of Keming and Juexin.

Keming sat with the old man all day, leaving the affairs of his law office in the hands of his secretary and another lawyer. Ke'an was at home part of the time, but he also went to the theatre and to the private apartment he kept outside.

Keding took advantage of his father's illness to visit his "love nest" where he drank, played mahjong and bantered with his female friends. He saw the old man only in the morning and in the evening when, as usual, he paid his formal respects.

No one in the family was particularly inconvenienced by the patriarch's illness. People laughed, cried, quarrelled and fought as before. Even the few who were concerned about him didn't think his condition was serious, in spite of the fact that he grew weaker day by day.

When medication proved ineffective, the family turned to superstitious quackery. Some pepole, when they begin to lose confidence, seek the aid of the supernatural. This may take very complicated forms — forms contrived by weak-minded people and believed in only by other weak-minded people.

Yet the ceremony proposed by Mistress Chen, and approved by the other ladies in the family, also obtained the full support of the grown men, gentlemen allegedly "well versed in the books of the Sages."

It began with a number of Taoist monks beating drums and cymbals in the main hall, and chanting prayers. At night, when all was still, Mistress Chen prayed in the courtyard. Juehui watched her curiously through his window. Formally attired in a pink skirt, she knelt before a pair of candles and an incense burner, in which nine sticks of incense smouldered, and mumbled prayers under her breath. She kept rising, then falling to her knees — time after time, night after night. But the old man did not improve.

"Stupid woman!" Juehui raged to himself. "All you're fit for is to put on an idiotic show!"

The next device was for the Venerable Master's three sons — Keming, Ke'an and Keding — to offer a sacrifice. Mistress Chen's burner was replaced in the middle of the night by an

altar bearing tall candles, thick incense and sacrificial imple-
ments. The ceremony was conducted seriously, but the solemnity of the three sons was so exaggerated it appeared ludicrous.
Although they too knelt and kowtowed, they finished in a
much shorter time than it had taken Mistress Chen. Juehui felt
the same scorn for them as he had for the old concubine. He
knew that only a few hours before Ke'an had been at the
theatre, dallying with his favourite female impersonator, and
Keding had been gambling and drinking in his "love nest." It
was sheer hypocrisy for them to kneel and pray that they be
allowed to die in their father's place.

Just when Juehui thought the family had exhausted its
ingenuity, a new programme was contrived. A witch doctor
was invited to "drive out the devils."

One night, shortly after dark, Keming ordered that all doors
be shut tight. The compound was converted into a weird and
ancient temple. A thin-faced witch doctor with flowing locks
arrived. Dressed in peculiar vestments, uttering shrill cries, he
scattered burning resin, exactly like an actor impersonating a
devil upon the stage. He ran about the courtyard making all
sorts of frightful noises and gestures. Entering the patient's
apartment, he leaped and yelled and flung things to the floor,
even throwing burning resin beneath the bed. The loud groans
of the old man — induced by the clamour and terror — in no
way deterred the witch doctor. His performance gained in
frenzy. He made such wild menacing thrusts that the old man
cried out in alarm. The room was filled with thick black smoke
and the glare and odour of sputtering resin.

It went on for an hour. Then the witch doctor, still yowling,
departed. After a period of complete silence, normal voices
were again heard in the compound.

But there was more to come. The devils had only been driven
from the patient's room. That wasn't enough. The compound
was full of devils; there were devils, many devils, in all the
rooms. It was decided to have a general clean-out the follow-

ing evening. Only in this way, said the witch doctor, could the old man recover.

Not everyone believed this; some, in fact, were opposed to a second drive against the devils. But not one person had the courage to express his opposition openly. Although Juehui was not afraid to speak his mind, no one paid any attention to him.

The second farce commenced on schedule. Every room was subjected to a ridiculous, yet frightening, treatment. People got out of the witch doctor's way. Children bawled, women sighed, men shook their heads.

Juehui sat in his room, listening to the racket and unearthly howls coming from his sister-in-law's apartment on the other side of the wall. He muttered angry curses. A weight seemed to be crushing him down; he wanted to leap up and cast it off. He couldn't become a party to this preposterous show. Juehui made up his mind. He locked his door, sat down, and waited.

Before long, the witch doctor came to Juehui's flat. Finding the door locked, he rapped sharply; servants helped him knock. No answer. They began to push against the door, calling, "Third Young Master!"

"I'm not going to open!" shouted Juehui. "There are no devils in here!" He lay down on his bed and covered his ears with his hands.

Suddenly, someone shook the door violently. Juehui sat bolt upright, his face scarlet with rage. He seemed to see Mingfeng's tousled hair, her tear-stained face.

"Quit that racket!" he yelled. "What are you trying to do, anyway?"

"Juehui, open the door," he heard his uncle Keming call.

"Third Young Master, open the door," came the loud voice of Mistress Chen.

So you've brought up reinforcements, he thought. "I will not!" he retorted crisply, and walked away from the door. His brain felt ready to explode. "I hate them, hate them! . . ." he muttered.

But they wouldn't let him go. Their angry voices pursued him, louder and louder.

"Don't you want your grandfather to get better? Open the door! . . . Where's your sense of duty!" The shrill voice of Mistress Chen, which Juehui always found so irritating, now struck him like a threatening blow, wounding him and adding fuel to his rage.

"You must be reasonable, nephew," said Keming. "We all want *Ye-ye* to get well. You're a sensible boy —"

Another voice cut his words short: "Open the door, Third Brother. I want to talk to you." It was Juexin.

You too, thought Juehui bitterly. It's not enough that you're a coward yourself. . . . His heart was breaking.

All right, if that's what you want, he said to himself. He swung open the door. Confronting him were red, furious visages. People pushed towards him, the witch doctor, naturally, being the first to advance.

"Not so fast." Juehui stood in the doorway, his cheeks flushed, his voice trembling with anger. "What exactly do you think you're doing?" he asked contemptuously. He swept their faces with hate-filled eyes.

The question stopped them, cold. Keming muttered something about "driving out devils" in a tone that indicated plainly he had no faith whatsoever in what he was saying.

"We are eradicating devils for your grandfather," said Mistress Chen, reeking of perfume and holding herself very erect. She indicated to the witch doctor that he should enter.

"You're out of your mind!" Juehui virtually spat the words in her face. "You're not chasing devils, you're hurrying *Ye-ye* to his grave. You're afraid his illness won't kill him soon enough, so you're trying to exasperate him to death, scare him to death!"

"You —" That was all Keming could say. He was livid with fury.

"Third Brother!" Juexin cried warningly.

"As for you, you ought to be ashamed of yourself!" Juehui

fixed his gaze on his Big Brother. "An educated man like you. How can you be so stupid? A man is sick, and you call in a witch doctor! It's all right if you people enjoy this sort of idiocy, but you shouldn't make *Ye-ye*'s life the butt of your games. You say you respect him. Why don't you let him rest? I saw the way the witch doctor terrified him last night. But you're still not satisfied; tonight you're at it again. I say you're not driving out devils — you're trying to kill him! I'm warning you — the first person to set foot in my room gets a punch in the jaw! I'm not afraid of any of you!"

Ordinarily, such intemperate words might have created a situation ending badly for Juehui. But tonight, it was the very intensity of his attack that brought him victory. He stood grimly blocking the door, his eyes gleaming proud and right-eous. They were his elders and he was heaping them with scorn. But, he felt, they had brought it on themselves by their contemptible behaviour!

Keming, ashamed, was the first to drop his head. He knew Juehui was right. He knew that the devil-eradication perform-ance could only do harm. But for the sake of giving friends and relatives the impression he was a "dutiful" son, Keming was reluctantly taking part. Unable to face Juehui, he walked away without a sound.

Juexin felt angry and humiliated. Tears ran down his cheeks. When he saw Keming leave, he turned and followed.

Mistress Chen was a woman with no courage of her own. She relied entirely on other people's power. Keming's depar-ture left her without support, and she was afraid to open her mouth. But she really believed in the efficacy of driving out devils, and was genuinely concerned about the old man's illness. She couldn't understand Juehui's attitude. She hated him. He had insulted her openly, before many people. But in the absence of the Venerable Master, and now that even Keming had gone, she didn't dare to oppose Juehui. Humiliated, she left the scene, cursing in her heart the grandson who didn't respect his grandfather.

The remainder of the crowd broke up too. No one offered the witch doctor any help. Although the sorcerer grumbled, and some of the ladies of the family privately expressed dissatisfaction, this time Juehui won a total victory. He himself had never expected it.

33

Juehui slept exceptionally well that night. He went to visit his sick grandfather the following morning, expecting a scolding, at least.

Half of the bed curtain had been pulled back, revealing the old man from the waist up. He lay with his bald head propped against high-piled pillows, his face bloodless and thinner than ever, his mouth slackly open. Above high cheekbones, his large eyes were sunken; from time to time he closed them wearily. To Juehui, his grandfather looked weak and pitiful; he no longer resembled the awesome and frightening Venerable Master Gao.

Ye-ye was breathing with difficulty. He opened his eyes wide to gaze at Juehui as he entered. An affectionate smile slowly appeared on the old man's face, a smile that was without strength, pathetic.

"Ah, you've come," he said. He had never greeted Juehui so warmly before. Juehui couldn't comprehend this change in him.

"You're a good boy," the old man said, making a great effort. He forced a smile. Juehui leaned closer to him.

"You're very good," *Ye-ye* repeated weakly. "They say you have a peculiar disposition. . . . Study your books well."

"I understand things better now," he continued slowly. "Do you ever see your Second Brother? I hope he's well." Tears shone in the corners of his eyes. It was the first time Juehui had ever seen him look kind.

Juehui said, "Yes."

"I was wrong. I want to see him again. Bring him home, quickly. I won't make any more trouble for him." The old man wiped his eyes with his hand.

Mistress Chen, who had just finished combing her hair, rouging her face and pencilling her brows, observed this scene as she emerged from the next room. She addressed Juehui reproachfully, "Third Young Master, you're old enough to know better. You shouldn't upset your *Ye-ye* when he's so ill."

"Don't blame him," said the old man quickly. "He's a good boy." Mistress Chen turned away, angry and resentful, while the old man urged Juehui, "Bring your Second Brother back. I haven't seen him in a long time. Tell him I'll say no more about the match with the Feng family. I'm afraid I won't live much longer. I want to see him again. I want to see all of you."

On leaving his grandfather, Juehui went directly to Juexin's room. Big Brother and Sister-in-law were talking about something, and they both looked worried. Juexin, recalling the previous night's fiasco, dropped his eyes in embarrassment when he saw Juehui approaching.

"*Ye-ye* wants me to bring Second Brother back. He admits he was wrong," crowed Juehui, the moment he entered the door.

Surprised and pleased, Juexin raised his head. "Really?" He could hardly believe his ears.

"Of course. *Ye-ye* is sorry now," Juehui said, his face glowing with satisfaction. "I told you we would win. You see — we've won after all!"

"Tell me — what exactly did he say?" Smiling, Juexin walked over and took Ruijue's hand. She tried, unsuccessfully, to pull it away, being unaccustomed to public displays of affection. Husband and wife were both very glad to hear this news. It seemed virtually a miracle to them that such a big problem could be solved so easily. They thought this miracle would bring them good fortune.

Juehui told them the details of his conversation with his

grandfather, growing more elated with every word. Before he
could finish, a maid came in and announced:

"The Venerable Master wants to see the First Young Master."
Juexin left immediately.

Juehui remained to chat with Ruijue. The nursemaid brought
Haichen back from outside, and Juehui played with the little
boy for a while.

Then he ran to where Juemin was living. He literally ran.
At home he hadn't felt any need for haste; he had spent quite
some time gaily talking with Sister-in-law. But as soon as he
left the compound it seemed to him he had delayed too long.
He should have brought the good news to Second Brother as
quickly as possible.

Juemin, of course, was overjoyed when Juehui told him their
grandfather's decision. After a few minutes of conversation
with Cunren, in whose home Juemin had been hiding, the two
brothers quickly left.

First, they went to see Qin. She was extremely happy with
their news, just as they had expected. The prospect of a bright
future seemed more likely than ever to these three young
people; they could almost reach their hands out and touch it.
It was coming to them not by any accident of fate, but through
their own strenuous efforts. And so it appeared to them particularly precious.

Relaxed and cheerful, they talked for a long time. After
lunching together with Qin and her mother, the brothers
strolled home. On the way, Juemin prepared little speeches —
what he would say to his grandfather, to his stepmother Madam
Zhou, to his Big Brother. He was very happy. He was returning home like a conquering hero.

Juemin walked through the main gate, entered the inner
courtyard, then went into the main hall, then walked still deeper
into the compound. He was rather surprised that everything
still looked the same.

But suddenly, he became aware of a change. People were

hurrying in and out of his grandfather's apartment. They all appeared very alarmed, and spoke in hushed voices.

"I wonder what's wrong," said Juehui. He took his brother by the arm and hastened him forward. His heart sank with a dark premonition.

"Maybe *Ye-ye.* . . ." Juemin dared say no more; he dared think no more. He was afraid the bright future which had seemed so close at hand had flown away.

The two brothers entered their grandfather's room. It was filled with people. They couldn't see their grandfather. The people blocked their view. They could hear only a low strange sound. No one paid any attention to them. Finally, they managed to push their way forward. Their grandfather was seated in a large armchair before the bed, his head down, gasping for breath. That was the strange sound they had heard.

Overcome with emotion, Juemin wanted to throw himself on his grandfather, but his uncle Keming restrained him. Keming looked at Juemin in a startled manner, and shook his head.

"*Ye-ye* told me to bring him here," Juehui explained. "He said he wants to see him."

Sadly Keming shook his head. "It's too late," he said in a low voice.

"Too late!" The words struck Juehui like a blow. He didn't seem to understand them. But when he heard his grandfather's painful gasping, he knew indeed that it was too late. The old man was going to depart, with the gap between grandfather and grandson unbridged for ever.

Juehui couldn't stand it. He rushed up to his grandfather, took the old man's hand and cried, "*Ye-ye, Ye-ye!* I've brought Second Brother back to you!"

The old man said nothing. He only continued to fight for breath. People tried to pull Juehui away, but the boy threw himself at the old man's knees and shook him, crying tragically, "*Ye-ye!*" Juemin stood watching.

Suddenly the old man sighed and opened his eyes wide. He

looked at Juehui without recognition. "Why are you making such a row?" he asked in a low voice. He waved his hand weakly, indicating that Juehui should go.

Then the haziness slowly vanished from the old man's thin face. His lips moved, but no sound came out. He looked at Juemin, and his lips moved again. "*Ye-ye!*" Juemin called. The old man didn't seem to hear him. Turning his eyes to Juehui, the patriarch grimaced slightly in what evidently was an attempt at a smile. Tears rolled from his eyes. He patted Juehui on the head and whispered, "You've come. . . . You're a good boy. . . . Your Second Brother? . . ."

Juehui pulled Juemin forward and said, "Here he is."

"*Ye-ye*," said Juemin respectfully.

"You've come back. Good! We won't talk about the match with the Feng family any more. . . . You boys must study diligently. . . ." The old man took a deep breath and went on slowly, "Remember — bring honour to the family name. . . . I'm very tired. . . . Don't go. . . . I'm leaving. . . ." His voice grew weaker and weaker, and he slowly dropped his head. At last he closed his mouth completely.

Keming walked up quickly and called to him, but his father did not respond. He grasped the old man's hand. With tears in his eyes he cried, "His hand is cold!"

Everyone crowded closer, all exclaiming loudly. Then the noise gradually stilled; someone dropped to his knees. Others followed suit, and the room was filled with weeping.

News of death spreads more quickly than any other. In a matter of minutes, the whole compound knew that the old man had passed away. Servants hurried to the homes of the Gaos' relatives to deliver the sad tidings. Guests soon began to arrive. Women guests added volume to the weeping, bewailing their own unhappy fate at the same time.

Then the work commenced. A division of labour was made between the men and the women. Three or four female relatives were assigned to sit by the body and weep. The old man was laid out on the bed, from which the canopy was removed.

The work advanced rapidly; many people were busy. The ancestral tablets, the altar and other equipment were moved to a chamber in the rear of the main hall. Then the coffin was carried in. It had been bought several years before and stored away. The price was reported to be quite reasonable — only a little over one thousand ounces of silver.

The Taoist priest who was to "open the road" to the next world arrived. By divination, he decided on the propitious hour and minute for encoffining the body. The old man was bathed and dressed in his burial clothes, then laid comfortably in the coffin. All the objects the Venerable Master Gao had loved best in life were packed in beside him, filling the casket to the brim.

By now it was almost nightfall. A troupe of Buddhist monks were next called in. Each of these shaven-pated men — one hundred and eight of them — carried a stick of lighted incense. They wandered through the compound, going in and out of rooms, up and down stairs. Behind them trailed Juexin and his three uncles, also holding incense sticks. Juexin walked in the lead, because he was the "first son of the first son."

At ten o'clock in the morning of the following day, the sealing of the coffin took place. This hour, too, had been divined by the Taoist priest. The weeping reached its maximum intensity then; some of it was genuine.

The death of the Venerable Master brought everything in the family to a stop. The family hall became a funeral parlour, hung with mourning bunting; the main hall became a temple of prayer. Women wept in the funeral parlour; monks intoned prayers in the temple. The funeral parlour was hung with eulogy scrolls and odes to the departed; in the temple were Buddhist idols and ten scenes from the Palace of the Afterworld.

Everyone was busy with the final rites for the deceased. Or perhaps it would be more accurate to say everyone was busy using the occasion to maintain face and display his own affluence.

Three days later, the Mourning Period officially commenced. Innumerable gifts came pouring in, dozens of ceremonies were conducted, droves of condolence callers arrived. This was what everyone had been looking forward to, and now the activities were at their height.

Even Juemin and Juehui could not help becoming involved. They didn't want to be, but they felt it didn't matter much. They were set to work "returning courtesies." In other words, whenever a visitor kowtowed to the spirit of the departed, they were required to do the same, while a Master of Ceremonies intoned, "Thanks from the Filial Sons and Grandsons." Then all would rise to their feet and grin at each other sheepishly at the silliness of it all.

The boys couldn't help smiling to themselves, too, when they saw their elder brother and their uncles decked out in mourning clothes — a hempen crown with a long "filial" streamer trailing behind, a white mourning gown covered by a wide hempen vest, straw sandals — holding a mourning staff and walking with solemn tread. To the younger brothers it was like an act from a farce.

After lunch the following day they were able to escape. Juehui left first, and went directly to the reading-room the students had set up. He worked there all day and did not come home until evening. Juemin had not yet returned.

Juehui found the main hall empty. The monks had already departed. The pair of tall candles in front of the coffin of the deceased had burned far down; their wicks were sputtering in pools of tallow. Even the sticks of incense had burned out.

Why is it so quiet? he wondered. Where has everyone gone? . . . He adjusted the candle wicks with a pair of tongs and lit another bundle of incense stick.

"Nothing doing! Just sharing the land and the property without touching the antiques and pictures isn't a thorough division!" The voice of Juehui's uncle Keding suddenly declaimed loudly from the old man's room.

"They were the things he loved best. He spent his whole life collecting them. As his sons we shouldn't simply parcel them out among ourselves!" This was Keming speaking. He was panting angrily.

"Antiques and pictures mean nothing to me. But if we don't divide them, someone will grab them all." Ke'an laughed coldly. "I say anything that belonged to the old man, we ought to share equally."

"All right. If that's what you all want, we'll make a division tomorrow!" Keming gave a fretful cough. "But, honestly, I never intended to keep them for myself."

There was a stir in the room, followed by the sound of the voices of several women. Then Keding came stalking out. "Testamentary order, testamentary bequest — they're all trumped up!" he was muttering. "That kind of division isn't fair!" He walked outside.

A little later Juexin, looking very downcast, also emerged.

"Dividing up the family property, eh?" Juehui greeted him mockingly. "Not wasting much time, are you?"

"Stepmother and I are being moved around like puppets. *Ye-ye* left me three thousand shares of West Sichuan Mercantile Corporation stock, but our uncles don't want to recognize the bequest," said Juexin bitterly.

"What about Mrs. Zhang?" asked Juemin, who had just then returned home. He of course was concerned about the woman who was both their aunt and Qin's mother.

"She only got five hundred dollars' worth of stock, and a few other things — and these only because it was in the will. But Mistress Chen got a residence and compound. Our household is the only one that cares anything about Mrs. Zhang. None of the others would say a word for her," Juexin sighed.

"Why didn't you speak up?" asked Juemin reproachfully.

"Here comes Uncle Keming," warned Juehui in a low voice.

Coughing irritably, Keming strode slowly from the apartment of the Venerable Master Gao.

34

It was almost time for Ruijue to give birth, and Mistress Chen and other women of the family were deeply disturbed. At first they only discussed the matter privately. Then, one day, with stern visage, Mistress Chen talked to Keming and his brothers about "the curse of the blood-glow."

There was a superstition that if, while the body of one of the elder generation was still in the house, a birth should take place at home, the glow of the blood emitted by the mother would attack the corpse and cause it to spurt large quantities of blood. The only means by which this could be prevented was for the pregnant woman to leave the compound and move outside the city.

Nor was that enough. The big city gates weren't strong enough to keep the blood-glow from returning — she had to move across a bridge.

Even that was not necessarily fool-proof. The coffin had to be covered with a layer of bricks and earth. Only thus could it be protected from "the curse of the blood-glow."

Madam Shen of the Fifth Household was the first to approve of these preventive measures; Madam Wang of the Fourth Household quickly seconded her. Ke'an and Keding agreed next, followed finally by Keming and Madam Zhou. Of the elder generation only Madam Zhang of the Third Household expressed no opinion. In any event, it was decided to act according to Mistress Chen's recommendation, and the elders wanted Juexin to move his wife out immediately. They said the interests of the Venerable Master Gao should transcend all.

Although the decision struck Juexin like a bolt from the blue, he accepted it meekly. He had never disagreed with anyone in his life, no matter how unfairly they may have treated him. He preferred to swallow his tears, suppress his anger and bitterness; he would bear anything — rather than oppose a person directly. Nor did it ever occur to him to wonder whether this forbearance might not be harmful to others.

Ruijue made no complaint when he informed her. She expressed her unwillingness in tears. But it was no use. She hadn't the strength to protect herself. Juexin hadn't the strength to protect her either. She could only submit.

"You know I don't believe in this, but what can I do?" Juexin helplessly spread his hands. "They all say it's better to be on the safe side."

"I'm not blaming you. I blame only my unhappy destiny," Ruijue sobbed. "My mother isn't even in town to look after me. But I can't let you get the reputation of being unfilial. Even if you were willing, I wouldn't agree."

"Rui, forgive me, I'm too weak. I can't even protect my own wife. These years we've been together . . . you know what I've been suffering."

"You shouldn't . . . talk like that," Ruijue said, wiping her eyes with her handkerchief. "I know . . . what you've been through. You've . . . suffered enough. You're so good to me. I'm very grateful. . . ."

"Grateful? You're going to give birth any day now, and I'm sending you to a lonely place outside the city where there are no conveniences and you'll be all alone. I'm letting you down. What other man would let his wife be treated so badly? And you still say you're grateful!" Juexin wept miserably.

Ruijue stilled her crying, rose quietly and walked out. Soon she returned, holding little Haichen by the hand and followed by the nursemaid.

Leading the child to the softly weeping Juexin, she instructed him to call his "*Die-die*," to take his father's hand and tell him not to cry.

Juexin embraced the little boy and gazed at him with loving eyes. He kissed the child's cheek several times, then put him down and returned him to Ruijue. "There's no hope for me," he said hoarsely. "But rear Haichen well. I don't want him to be like me when he grows up!" Juexin left the room, wiping his eyes with his hand.

"Where are you going?" Ruijue called after him in concern.

"Outside the city to look for a house." He turned around to face her, and his eyes again were blinded by tears. After wrenching these words out, he hastily walked away.

That day Juexin returned very late. Finding a house was not easy, but in the end he had succeeded. It was a little place in a small compound, ill-lighted, with damp walls and an earthen floor. The rent was cheap enough, but that wasn't the reason Juexin took it. He had been concerned with only two things — "outside the city" and "across a bridge." Such matters as comfort and convenience were secondary.

Before Ruijue moved, Mistress Chen and a few other ladies of the family went to inspect the house. They could find no objections.

Juexin insisted on doing all the packing for Ruijue. He made her sit in a chair and supervise. Before putting anything in the suitcase, he would hold it up and say, "What about this?" and she would smile and nod her head, whether she really wanted it or not. When the packing was done Juexin declared proudly, "You see, I know exactly what you like."

Ruijue smiled. "You do indeed. The next time I go on a trip I'll be sure to ask you to pack for me again." She hadn't intended to make the last remark, but it slipped out.

"Next time? Of course I'll go with you next time. Where will you be going?"

"I was thinking of visiting my mother. But we'll go together, naturally. I won't leave you again."

Juexin changed colour, and he hastily dropped his head. Then he raised it again and said with a forced laugh, "Yes, we'll go together."

They were fooling each other and they knew it. Though they smiled, they wanted to cry. But they masked their true feelings behind a cheerful countenance. Neither was willing to give way to tears in the presence of the other.

The girls, Shuhua and Shuying, came in, then Juemin and Juehui. They could see only the pleasant expressions on the faces of Juexin and Ruijue, and could not guess the turmoil that was in their hearts.

Juehui couldn't keep silent. "Big Brother, are you really going to let Sister-in-law go?" he demanded. Although he had heard something about this, at first, he had thought people were joking. But when he had come home, a few minutes before, he had met Yuan Cheng, Juexin's middle-aged servant, at the gate to the inner courtyard. The man had greeted him affectionately, and Juehui stopped to chat with him.

"Third Young Master, do you think it's a good idea for Mistress Ruijue to move outside the city?" Yuan Cheng had asked with a frown, his thin face darker than usual.

Juehui was startled. "Of course not. But I don't believe she'll really go."

"Third Young Master, you don't know. First Young Master has ordered me and Sister Zhang to look after her. They've already called in a mason to make a false tomb for the old man's coffin. I don't think she ought to go, Third Young Master. Even if she must, it ought to be to some place decent. Only rich people have all these rules and customs. Why doesn't First Young Master speak up? We servants don't understand much, but we think her life is more important than all these rules. Why don't you talk to First Young Master, and Madam Zhou?"

There were tears in Yuan Cheng's eyes. "We ought to think of the Young Mistress. Everyone in the compound wishes her well! If anything should go wrong. . . ." Yuan Cheng couldn't continue.

"All right. I'll speak to First Young Master immediately. Don't worry. Nothing's going to happen to the Young Mistress," Juehui had said, agitated, but determined.

"Thank you, Third Young Master. But please don't let anyone know I told you," Yuan Cheng said in a low voice. He turned and went into the gate house.

Juehui had immediately sought out Juexin. Although the appearance of the room already proved the truth of Yuan

Cheng's words, Juehui demanded to know whether Big Brother was sending Ruijue away.

Juexin looked at him vaguely, then silently nodded his head.

"Are you crazy? Surely you don't believe in all this superstitious rot!"

"What difference does it make what I believe?" cried Juexin, wringing his hands. "That's what they all want. . . ."

"I say you should fight back," said Juehui angrily, his eyes gleaming with hatred. He didn't look at Juexin. "This is the last act of their farce." His gaze was fixed outside the window.

"Third Brother is right," said Juemin. "Don't send Sister-in-law away. Go and explain your reasons in detail. They'll understand. They're reasonable people."

"Reasonable?" echoed Juexin fretfully. "Even Third Uncle who studied law in a Japanese university was forced to agree. What chance have I? I couldn't bear it if I became known as unfilial. I have to do what they want. It's just hard on your Sister-in-law. . . ."

"What's hard about it? It will be much quieter outside the city. . . . I'll have people to look after me and keep me company," said Ruijue with a forced smile. "I'm sure it'll be very comfortable."

"You've given in again, Big Brother! Why do you always give in? Don't you realize how much harm you do?" Juehui demanded hotly. "Your weakness nearly wrecked the happiness of Juemin and Qin. Luckily, Second Brother had the courage to resist. That's why he won."

Juemin couldn't repress a smile of satisfaction. He agreed with Juehui. His happiness had been won through victory in battle.

"Certainly, you've triumphed." Juexin suppressed his anger. He seemed to be ridiculing himself. "You resist everything, you have contempt for everything, and you've won. But your victory has deepened my defeat. They heap upon me all their resentment against you. They hate me, curse me behind my back. You can resist, go away. But can I run away from home like Second Brother? There are many things you don't know. How much abuse I had to put up with on account of Second Brother. The trouble I had over Third Brother working on that magazine and mixing with those new friends. I took it all, without a word. I kept my bitterness inside me. No one knew. It's all very well for you to talk about resistance, struggle. But who can I say those fine-sounding words to?"

Gradually his anger abated. An unbearable oppression seemed to be crushing him. He hurried to his bed and lay down, hiding his face with his hands.

This crumpled Ruijue's last line of defence. Dropping her false smile, she buried her head on the table and wept. Shuhua and Shuying, their own voices tearful, tried to comfort her. Juemin regretted he had spoken so hastily. He had been too harsh with Big Brother. He tried to think of something to say to make amends.

Juehui was different. There was too much hatred in his heart for him to find room for sympathy for his Big Brother. He could see a lake before him, and a coffin . . . Mingfeng and Mei. . . . And now . . . this . . . and what it would bring. These thoughts made him burn with rage.

Like his two older brothers, Juehui had enjoyed the loving care of a devoted mother. After she died, he tried to carry out her teachings — love and help others, respect your elders, be good to your inferiors. But what a spectacle his elder generation was making of itself today! How the dark forces in the family that destroyed love were growing! The life of the girl he had adored had been uselessly snuffed out. Another girl had been driven to her grave. And he had not been able to save them. Sympathy, he was bereft of sympathy — even for his brother. In his heart there were only curses.

"One girl has already died because of you," he said to Juexin coldly. "I should think that would be enough." He strode from the room.

Outside, he met the nursemaid bringing in little Haichen.

The child hailed him, laughing, and he returned the salutation. He was miserable.

Back in his own room, Juehui was overcome with a loneliness, the like of which he had never felt before. His eyes grew damp. The world was such a tragic place. So many tears. So much suffering. People lived only to destroy themselves, or to destroy others. Destruction was inevitable, no matter how they struggled. Juehui could see plainly the fate that lay ahead for his Big Brother, but he was helpless to save him. And this fate was not only Big Brother's, but the desting of many, many others.

"Why is there so much misery in the world?" he asked himself. His mind was filled with pictures of innumerable unhappy events.

No matter what happens, I must go my own road, even if it means trampling over their dead bodies. Juehui seemed to be hemmed in by bitterness, with no way out, and he encouraged himself with these words.

Then he left the compound. He went to the magazine office, to join his new friends.

35

Temporarily suppressing his unhappiness, Juexin accompanied Ruijue to her new abode. Madam Zhou, Shuhua and Shuying went with them. There were also the man servant, Yuan Cheng and Sister Zhang, the stout maid, who would stay with Ruijue. Juemin and Qin came out a bit later in the day.

Ruijue didn't like the place. It was the first time she and Juexin would be separated since their marriage. She would have to live without him in this damp gloomy house for over a month. She tried to think of something to console herself, but she could not. Everyone was busy arranging furniture, and she wept behind their backs. But when anyone spoke to her she managed to look cheerful. This somewhat reassured those who were concerned about her.

It was soon time for the others to return to the city.

"Must you all go? Can't Qin and Shuhua stay a little longer?" Ruijue pleaded.

"It's getting late. They'll be closing the city gates. I'll come and see you again tomorrow," said Qin with a smile.

"City gates." Ruijue repeated the phrase as if she had not understood it. Actually she knew very well that tonight she would be separated from Juexin not only by distance but by a series of ponderous gates. Between dusk tonight and dawn tomorrow even if she died out here, he wouldn't know, he wouldn't be able to reach her. She was like a criminal, exiled in a distant land. This time she couldn't control her tears; they welled from her eyes.

"It's so lonely here. I'm afraid. . . ."

"Don't worry, Sister-in-law," said Shuhua. "I'll move out tomorrow."

"I will too. I'll speak to Ma about it," added Shuying emotionally.

"Be patient, Rui. You'll get used to it in a day or so," said Juexin. "The two servants staying with you are very reliable. There's nothing to be afraid of. Tomorrow the girls will move out to keep you company. I'll try and find time too. Be patient. The month will pass quickly." Though he tried hard to appear confident, Juexin felt more like embracing Ruijue and weeping with her.

Madam Zhou gave some final instructions, the others added a few words, then they all departed. Ruijue saw them to the compound gate and watched them get into their sedan-chairs.

Juexin had already entered his conveyance. Suddenly he got out again to ask whether she wanted him to bring her anything from home. Ruijue said she had everything she needed.

"Bring Haichen out tomorrow. I miss him terribly," she said. "Take good care of him," she directed, and she added,

"Whatever you do, don't let my mother hear about this. She'll worry."

"I wrote to her two days ago. I didn't tell you. I knew you wouldn't let me write her," replied Juexin.

"Why did you do it? If my mother knew I was —" Ruijue stopped herself abruptly. She was afraid of hurting him.

"I had to let her know. If she can come to Chengdu, she'll be able to help look after you." Juexin swallowed his pain. He didn't dare think of Ruijue's unfinished sentence.

The two looked at each other as if they had nothing to say. But their hearts were filled with unspoken words.

"I'm going now. You get some rest." Again Juexin walked to his sedan-chair. He turned his head to gaze at her several times.

"Come early tomorrow," Ruijue called from the gate. She waved her hand until his sedan-chair disappeared around a bend in the road. Then, supporting her heavy abdomen, she went into the house.

She wanted to take some things out of her luggage, but her limbs were powerless. Her nerves were tense too. Wearily making an effort, she walkd over and sat down on the edge of the bed. Suddenly, she thought she felt the child move in her womb; she seemed to hear it cry. In hysterical anger, she beat her abdomen with her hand weakly. "You've ruined me!" she exclaimed. She wept softly until Sister Zhang, the maid, hearing her, came hurrying in to soothe her.

The following morning, Juexin indeed came early, and he brought Haichen with him. Shuhua moved out, as promised. Shuying came too, but she had not been able to obtain her mother's consent to live outside the city. Later, Qin also arrived. For a while, the little compound was very gay, with chatter and happy laughter.

The hours passed quickly. Again it was time to part. Haichen burst into tears; he wanted to remain with his mother. Of course, this was not possible. After much persuasion, Ruijue managed to cajole a smile from him again. He agreed to go home with his father.

Once more Ruijue saw Juexin to the gate. "Come again early tomorrow," she said. Tears glistened in her eyes.

"I'm afraid I can't come tomorrow. Masons are coming to build a simulated tomb for *Ye-ye*. The family wants me to supervise," Juexin said morosely. Noticing her tears, he said quickly, "But I'll definitely find time to come out. You mustn't get upset so easily, Rui. Take care of your health. If you should get sick. . . ." Juexin swallowed the rest. He was afraid of weeping himself.

"I don't know what's wrong with me," said Ruijue slowly with a mournful smile, her eyes fixed upon his face. She patted Haichen's cheek. "Each time you leave, I'm afraid I'm never going to see you again. I'm scared. I don't know why." She rubbed her eyes.

"You shouldn't be. We live so near each other, and I come to see you every day. And now Shuhua is staying with you." Juexin forced a smile. He didn't dare let himself think.

"Isn't that the temple?" Ruijue suddenly pointed at a tile-roofed building far off to the right. "I hear that's where Cousin Mei's coffin is. I must go and see her one of these days."

Juexin turned pale. He hastily looked away. A terrifying thought possessed him. He took her warm soft hand and pressed it, as if afraid that someone would snatch her from him. "You mustn't go, Rui!" he exhorted. Ruijue was impressed with the gravity of his tone, though she couldn't understand why he should be so set against her going.

But he said no more. Dropping her hand abruptly, after Haichen again said goodbye to "Mama," Juexin strode to his sedan-chair. As the two carriers raised the conveyance to their shoulders, Haichen leaned out of the window and called, "Mama! Mama!"

On returning home, Juexin went to the family hall, where

the old man's body was lying in its coffin.   He met Mistress
Chen, who was coming out.

"How is Ruijue? Well, I hope," she greeted him, smiling.

"Not bad, thank you." Juexin forced an answering smile.

"Will she be giving birth soon?"

"It will still be a couple of days, I'm afraid."

"Don't forget, Young Master.   You mustn't enter the delivery room!"   Mistress Chen's voice suddenly became hard.   She
walked away.

Juexin had been given this warning several times before.
But today, hearing a person like Mistress Chen issue it in such
a tone made him speechless with rage.   He stared after her retreating figure.   When little Haichen, whom he was holding by
the hand, raised his head and called *"Die-die,"* Juexin didn't
hear him.

36

Four days later, Juexin paid his usual visit to Ruijue. Because
he had been delayed by some business at home, he didn't arrive
until past three in the afternoon.

Calling Ruijue by name as he entered the courtyard, he
hurried to her room.   But before he could set foot across the
threshold, he was stopped by the stout maid, Sister Zhang.

"You can't go in, First Young Master," she said severely.

He understood, and meekly withdrew to the little garden outside Ruijue's window.   The door closed.   Inside, he heard
footsteps and the voice of a woman he didn't know.

Juexin gazed abstractedly at the grass and flowers in the
small garden.   He couldn't tell whether he was happy or sad,
angry or satisfied.   It seemed to him he felt all these emotions
at the same time.   It seemed to him that he had been in a similar state of mind several years before, though only to a very
slight extent.   Actually it had been quite different.

How he had suffered through her struggles then, how happy and grateful he had been when she presented him with the precious gift of their first child. He had been by her side when she won through to victory; his tension had relaxed, his worry had turned to joy. When the midwife handed him the infant, he had kissed its adorable little red face. He had vowed in his heart that he would love the child and make every sacrifice for him; his whole life was deposited in the body of that infant. He had gone to the bedside of his wife and looked at her pale weary face with a love and gratitude beyond words. She had gazed back at him, triumphant, loving; then she had looked at the baby.

"I feel fine now," she had said to Juexin, happily. "Isn't he a darling? You must decide on a name for him, quickly!" Her face shone with the radiance of a mother's bliss.

Today, she was again lying in bed. She had begun to moan. There were hurrying footsteps in the room and low serious voices. All that was the same. But now she was in this rustic place. They were separated by a door. He couldn't see her, encourage her, comfort her, share her pain. Today, again he waited. But there was no joy or satisfaction — only fear, shame and regret. In his mind there was just one thought — I have injured her.

"Young Mistress, how are you feeling?" he heard Sister Zhang ask.

There was a long silence. Then an agonized cry pierced his ears. He trembled, gritted his teeth, clenched his fists. Can that be her? he wondered. She had never uttered a sound like that before. But who else could it be? It must be her. It must be my Rui.

Again those terrible screams. Cries hardly human. Footsteps, voices. The rattle of crockery and cries blended together. Juexin covered his ears with his hands. It can't be her. It can't be my Rui. She could never scream like that. Nearly frantic with worry, he tried to look through the window, but the blinds were closed. He could only hear things; he couldn't see. Disappointed, he turned away.

"Be patient, Young Mistress. You'll be all right in a little while," said the unknown woman.

"It won't be long now," urged Shuhua. "Just be patient."

Gradually, the cries subsided into low moans.

The door suddenly opened and Sister Zhang hurried out. She went into another room, then hastened back to Rui's room. Juexin stared in through the half-opened door. He hesitated, wondering whether to go in. By the time he made up his mind, the door was closed in his face. He pushed it a few times, but inside there was no response. As he dejectedly turned to leave, from the room came a terrible cry. He pushed the door hard and pounded it with his fists.

"Who's there?" shouted Sister Zhang.

"Let me in!" There was fear in his voice, and pain and anger.

No one answered. The door remained shut. His wife continued to scream.

"Let me in, I say!" He furiously pounded the door.

"You can't come in, First Young Master. Madam Zhou, Elder Master Keming, Mistress Chen — they all left strict instructions...." Sister Zhang shouted through the door.

Juexin's courage ebbed away. He remembered what they had told him. Silently, he stood before the door. He had nothing more to say.

"Is that you, Juexin?" It was Ruijue's agonized voice. "Why don't you come in? Sister Zhang, let the First Young Master in! Oh, the pain ... the pain...."

A chill ran up Juexin's spine. "I'm coming, Rui, I'm coming! Open this door immediately! She needs me! Let me in!" he yelled, beating a wild tattoo on the door with his fists.

"Xin, it hurts! ... Where are you? Why don't you let him in? Oh!"

"I'll protect you, Rui! I'll never leave you! Let me in! Can't you see how she's suffering? Have you no pity!" He heard a violent thrashing about.

Then the cries in the room stopped. A dead silence followed. That awful stillness was suddenly pierced by the bright clear wail of a new-born babe.

A stone seemed to drop from Juexin's heart. "Thank Heaven, thank Earth!" he breathed. Her pain was probably over now. Fear and suffering left him. Again he felt an indescribable joy; his eyes filled with tears. "I'll love and cherish her more than ever," he said to himself. "And I'll love our second child." He smiled with tears running down his cheeks.

"Sister-in-law!" Shuhua's terrified exclamation smashed him like a blow. "Her hands are cold!"

"Young Mistress!" cried Sister Zhang.

Their cries were a mournful dirge. Besides the midwife, they were the only other persons in the room.

Juexin knew that disaster had struck. He didn't dare to think. He went on beating against the door and yelling. No one paid any attention. The door stood implacable. It wouldn't let him rescue her, or even see her for the last time. It cut off all hope. In the room, women wept.

"Rui, I'm calling you. Can you hear me?" An insane shout, embodying all his love, was wrenched from the depths of his heart. A cry to bring her back from another world, to restore life not only to her but himself. For he knew what sort of an existence he would lead without her.

But death had come.

Footsteps approached the door. He thought it was going to be opened. But no, the midwife stood with the baby in her arms and spoke to him through a crack. "Congratulations, First Young Master. It's a boy."

He heard her start to walk away, and then the dreadful words, "Unfortunately, the baby has no mother."

The announcement went through Juexin's heart like a knife. He had none of the father's love for his infant. The child was his enemy, an enemy who had stolen Ruijue's life.

Gripped by hatred and grief, he pounded savagely on the door. He had wanted to kneel at his wife's bedside and beg forgiveness for his wrongs. But it was too late. The stubborn door barred their final love, their last farewell. It would not even let him weep before her.

Suddenly it dawned upon him. The door had no power. What had taken his wife away was something else. It was the entire social system, with its moral code, its superstitions. He had borne them for years while they stole his youth, his happiness, his future, the two women he had loved most in the world. They were too heavy a burden; he wanted to shake them off; he struggled. Then, all at once, he knew it was impossible. He was powerless, a weakling. Slumping to his knees before the door, he burst into bitter tears. He wept for her; he wept for himself. His weeping mingled with the sobs inside the room. But how different the two sounds were!

Two sedan-chairs halted outside the compound gate and Juexin's stepmother Madam Zhou and another woman entered. Madam Zhou heard the weeping as she came in the gate. Her expression changed. She said to the other woman agitatedly, "We're too late!" They hurried into the house.

"What are you doing?" Madam Zhou, surprised, asked Juexin when she saw him still kneeling outside the door.

Juexin quickly rose. Spreading wide his hands, he sobbed, "Rui, Rui!" He recognized the other woman and greeted her shamefacedly, then again began to cry aloud. At the same time, wails came from the infant inside.

Not speaking, the woman dabbed her eyes with her handkerchief.

The door finally opened. Madam Zhou said, "Please go in, Mrs. Li. Our family is not allowed in the confinement chamber."

Mrs. Li entered, and her penetrating voice was added to the other sounds of grief.

"Rui, why couldn't you wait? Ma came from so far to see you. If you have anything to tell me, speak! Come back, Rui. Couldn't you have waited one more day? You died a cruel death, my poor little girl! Deserted in this lonely place.

They drove you out and left you all alone. If I had only come back earlier, you'd still be alive. My poor child. Why did I let you marry into that family? Your Ma destroyed you."

Madam Zhou and Juexin heard it all clearly. Every word was like a needle, piercing deep into their hearts.

37

"Big Brother, I can't live in this family any longer! I'm leaving!" Juexin had been sitting alone in his room at dusk, when Juehui burst in on him. He had been gazing at the photograph he and Ruijue had taken when they got married. Although he couldn't see very plainly in the dim light, her every feature was etched upon his heart. Her full pretty face, her lovely big eyes, her shy smile, the faint dimples in her cheeks — they all seemed to come alive in the photograph. He had been staring at it tearfully when Juehui's exclamation brought him back to reality. He turned to see his Third Brother looking at him with flashing eyes.

"You're leaving?" Juexin asked, startled. "Where are you going?"

"Shanghai, Beijing — any place, as long as it's away from here!"

Juexin made no reply. His heart ached. He massaged his chest.

"I'm leaving. I don't care what they say, I'm leaving!" Juehui jammed his hands into his pockets and heatedly paced the floor. He didn't know that each step fell like a heavy tread on Juexin's heart.

"Second Brother?" Juexin wrenched out the question.

"Sometimes he says he's going, sometimes he says he's not. I don't think he'd give up Sister Qin and go off by himself," Juehui replied irritably. Then he added with determination, "Anyhow, I intend to leave."

"Yes, you can leave if you want to. You can go to Shanghai, to Beijing any place you like!" Juexin said almost sobbing.

Juehui remained silent. He understood what his Big Brother meant.

"But what about me? Where can I go?" Juexin suddenly buried his head and wept.

Juehui continued to pace the floor, from time to time shooting unhappy glances at his brother.

"You mustn't go," Juexin pleaded. He stopped crying and removed his hands from his face. "No matter what happens, you mustn't go."

Juehui halted and stood looking at his Big Brother with a distressed expression.

"They won't allow you to leave. They'll never let you go!" Juexin said in a loud argumentative tone.

"I know they don't want me to go." Juehui laughed contemptuously. "But I'm going to leave just to show them!"

"How can you? They have many arguments you won't be able to deny. *Ye-ye's* body is still in the house; there hasn't been any memorial service yet; he still hasn't been buried...." Juexin seemed to be speaking for "them" at this point.

"What's all that got to do with me? How can they stop me? They won't dare to kill me — like they killed Sister-in-law!" Juehui furiously uttered this cruel remark, regardless of how it might injure his brother.

"Don't talk about her. Please don't talk about her," Juexin begged. "Nothing will bring her back to life."

"Why get so upset? After the mourning period for *Ye-ye* is over, you can marry again," said Juehui, smiling coldly. "At most you'll only have to wait three years!"

"I'll never take another wife, never. It's for that reason I've given the new baby to Rui's mother," Juexin explained weakly. His voice sounded like an old man's.

"Then why did you let her take Haichen too?"

"It's only for two or three months. What sort of atmosphere is this for a motherless child? He cries for his 'Mama' all day, but there's no one here to look after him. I'll bring him back after *Ye-ye* is buried. I'm going to concentrate on educating him. He's my sole hope; I can't let him go. I can't turn him over to another woman."

"That's what you say now. After a while you'll change your mind. You're all the same. I've seen it happen time and again. Our own father is a good example. You say you don't want to remarry. They'll tell you you're still young, that Haichen needs a mother. You'll agree. Even if you don't want to, they'll make you." Juehui still wore his chill smile.

"Other things they can force me to do, but this is one thing they can't," retorted Juexin miserably. "Not even for Haichen's sake."

"I feel the same way about leaving. They can't force me to stay!" Juehui couldn't repress a chuckle.

Juexin didn't speak for several moments. Then he said in annoyance, "I'm not going to help you. We'll see whether you can leave!"

"Whether you help or not is up to you. But I'm telling you this — the next time you look around, I'll be gone!"

"You have no money."

"That's no problem. If the family won't give me any, I can borrow some elsewhere. Anyhow, I'm leaving. I have lots of friends who can help me!"

"Won't you wait a bit?"

"How long?"

"Two years. By then you'll have graduated from the Foreign Languages School. . . ." Juexin lowered his tone. He thought Juehui was wavering. "Then you can find work outside, or you can continue studying. You'll be in a much better position than you are now."

"Two years?" Juehui cried excitedly. "I don't even want to wait fifteen minutes! I'd like nothing better than to clear out of this city immediately!"

"Two years isn't very long. You're too impetuous. You ought to give things more thought. Don't be so impatient.

What's the harm in waiting two years? You've lived here eighteen years already. Surely you can stay only two years more?"

"My eyes weren't fully opened before; I had no courage. And there used to be a few people I loved in this family. Now I have nothing but enemies!"

For a long time Juexin did not speak. Then he asked in a sorrowful voice, "Do you consider me your enemy too?"

Juehui's heart softened. He pitied his Big Brother. "Naturally, love you," he said quietly. "We nearly came close to understanding each other once in the past, but today we're miles apart. You loved Sister-in-law and Cousin Mei much more than I did, of course. Yet you let people move them about just as they liked; you even helped. If you had been a bit more courageous, you could have saved Sister-in-law. Now it's too late. How can you talk to me of obedience? Do you really want me to be like you — destroying others and destroying myself? Big Brother, although I love you, that's something I simply cannot comprehend. Please don't give me that kind of advice any more. Otherwise you'll make me hate you."

Juehui turned to leave, but Juexin stopped him with a tearful cry.

"Wait! We'll understand each other yet. I have my problems — but I don't want to talk about them now. I won't stand in your way. I'll help you. I'll speak to them. If they don't agree, you and I will find some other way. I definitely want to help you."

Just then the electric lights came on, and they saw the tears in each other's eyes. The young men exchanged a forgiving glance. They were still fond brothers, after all. But although they thought they understood each other, that was not the case. Juehui was happy as he left his brother's room, because he would soon be able to get away from the family. Juexin, after Juehui departed, wept bitterly. He knew that before long he would be losing another person he loved. Although he would be surrounded by many people, he would be isolated and lonely.

Juexin kept his word. Two days later he had another private talk with Juehui in the younger boy's room.

"I couldn't convince them. I failed," he said in a low voice. They sat facing each other across a square table. "I spoke to our stepmother. While she doesn't approve of your going, she isn't altogether against it. She's always wished us well. She's very unhappy and regretful over your Sister-in-law's death. She and Rui's mother have been looking after all the funeral arrangements; I haven't had to do a thing. I was better to Mei than I was to your Sister-in-law. At least I saw Mei before she was placed in the coffin; at least I arranged for her funeral." Juexin began to sob. "Poor Rui. She's been dead for three weeks already and not one member of the older generation has gone to see her. Fifth Aunt won't even let Shuzhen go to the temple where Rui's body is resting. They're avoiding her as if she were some sort of evil spirit. I never thought a girl like Rui would come to this. Every time I meet Rui's mother, it's like a knife through my heart. Mrs. Li doesn't say anything openly, but her words are weighted with reproach, and they're all directed at me. You don't know how badly I feel!"

Gnawing his lips and clenching his fists, Juehui listened. He forgot about his own affairs. He could see the full, pretty face of his Sister-in-law, Rui, and a coffin. Gradually the coffin became two, then three. The faces of three girls appeared — one full and pretty; one mournful and sad; the third innocent and lively. The faces multiplied. Four, five — he knew them all — more and more and more. . . . Suddenly they all disappeared, and he was confronted with only the tear-stained visage of his Big Brother.

"I won't cry any more," said Juexin, pressing his fists down on the table-top. Indeed, he halted the flow of his tears.

There was an uncomfortable silence. The brothers could hear the monks chanting prayers and beating gongs and cymbals in the large hall.

Finally Juexin sighed and wiped his eyes with his handkerchief. "I started to talk about your problem. I'm afraid I've wandered from the subject." He tried to laugh but did not succeed. "Stepmother said she couldn't decide. She told me to talk with Uncle Keming. I did, and he gave me a strong reprimand for not understanding ceremonial custom. He said you would have to wait at least until Ye-ye is buried before you could go. The others there with him all agreed. Mistress Chen made some sneering remarks. She even insinuated that your interference with the devil-chasing had something to do with Ye-ye's death. Of course she didn't dare to come right out with it, and no one agrees with her —"

"They probably will, in time. It would make a nice new scandal in the family. They all dislike me anyhow. Well, I'm waiting for their next attack!" Juehui said angrily.

"Oh, I don't think they'll do anything against you. They're preventing you from leaving as a means of striking another blow at me." Juexin bitterly rumpled his hair. "They say Shanghai is a big wicked city, that you'll go bad if you go to school there. They say that Ye-ye was opposed to us attending regular schools anyway. They say Shanghai schools produce only troublemakers, not gentlemen. We talked and talked . This uncle said this, that aunt said that. . . .

"The substance of it is they don't want you to go. Not only do they want you to wait till after Ye-ye is buried — they hope you'll never go."

Juehui rose abruptly to his feet and banged his fist on the table. "Well, I *am* going! I'll show them what I am — a rebel!" He paced the floor muttering "rebel" as if he didn't fully understand the term. Suddenly he faced Big Brother and demanded, "What's your idea?"

Juexin raised his head. His eyes lit up. With a determination that was rare in him, he said, "I promised to help you, and I will. We must act secretly. Didn't you say you had friends who could lend you money? Well, I can give you some too. It's better to take some extra money along. As to what happens afterwards, we'll face that when it comes. Once you leave I don't think there'll be any trouble."

"Are you really going to help me?" Juehui cried joyfully, grasping his brother's arm.

"Not so loud. We don't want them to hear. Whatever you do, don't tell anyone. I can pretend I don't know anything about it. Or you can leave a note, berating me. Then they won't be able to suspect me. We can work out the details later. We'd better meet in the garden. It's not very convenient to talk here." Juexin's manner was almost gay, but there were tears in his eyes.

"You're right," said a clear voice. "This isn't the place for conversation!" Juemin entered, smiling, together with Qin. "Your plan isn't bad," he laughed.

"Why were you standing outside, listening?" scolded Juexin. "Why didn't you come in?"

"We knew you were discussing something private, so we stood sentry at your door. That was Qin's idea. Isn't she clever?" Juemin grinned at Qin and she smiled back at him faintly.

"We hope you'll help us too, Big Brother," Juemin continued. "Qin's mother has already agreed to our marriage, and I don't expect any opposition from Stepmother. We're just waiting for the mourning period for Ye-ye to end and then we'll set a date. But we want to have a modern, new-style ceremony."

Juexin frowned. Another problem, he thought. "It's still early yet. We'll talk about it when the time comes. We can probably manage." Juexin said this last to comfort Juemin. Actually, he was not in the least confident.

"You must come down to Shanghai," cried Juehui exuberantly. "I'll be there to welcome you."

"It's not very likely. If Qin's mother doesn't want to go, we can't just leave her here. In any event, we have to wait two or three years before both of us can go together."

"What about Qin's school?" asked Juehui.

"She'll be graduating next year. Maybe the Foreign

Languages School will admit girls by that time. If not, she can study at home for a year or two. Then, when we go down river, she'll be able to apply directly for entrance to a university." Juemin turned to Qin. "How does that strike you?"

Qin smiled but she did not speak. She trusted Juemin. She knew he was trying to work things out for her.

Juehui silently regarded the young couple. He envied Juemin his happiness, yet he was glad he had no strings to prevent him from leaving this family he so despised. A new life was waiting for him in Shanghai. Shanghai, with its masses of people and its new cultural movement. In Shanghai were also the two or three young friends with whom he had been corresponding but whom he had never seen.

"We'd better continue this talk in the garden. Second Brother, you and Qin go ahead first." A servant outside began calling, "First Young Master!" Juexin seemed to remember something he had to do. He hastily said to Juehui, "You go along too, Third Brother. Wait for me at the 'Fragrance at Eventide' building. I'll join you soon." And he hurried from the room.

A few minutes later, Juemin and Qin followed. Juehui left shortly after. As he came out of the house, Juehui saw Big Brother examining a pair of eulogistic scrolls which had just been delivered. A servant was holding one end of them. Juehui walked over to Juexin and read:

The whole family weeps, bidding farewell to the loved one. The husband suffers added bitterness because his new-born babe cannot receive a mother's care and affection and has to be raised by his in-laws.

The scrolls were signed by Ruijue's brother, who lived out of town. Juehui mournfully went into the garden to find Juemin and Qin.

Juexin remained, staring at the inscription. Then, abruptly, he rolled up the scrolls and told the servant to take them into the house. He himself walked towards the garden. The family

needs a rebel, he thought. I must help Third Brother. Through
him I can hit back a bit. We'll show them. Not everyone in
this family is as docile as I!

38

It was quite dark by the time Juehui and his friends left the
magazine office. An autumn breeze cooled their flushed faces.
They stood beneath the eaves of a building, reluctant to
separate, watching the hurrying crowds on the street.

"We'll part here," one of the boys said at last. "I won't see
you off tomorrow. Have a good trip."

"Thank you," said Juehui. They shook hands.

Several others also wished him luck, and departed.

"We'll see you home," said Huiru, his small eyes shining in
his ruddy triangular face.

Juehui nodded. He and his three remaining companions
entered the crowded street. A couple of blocks further on,
another boy bade Juehui farewell.

They entered a quiet lane where dim street lights were paled
by the moonlight. The entrance-ways to the compounds lining
the thoroughfare were like dark caves. Locust trees rising up
within the walls cast sharply etched shadows on the silvery
flagstones. The outline of every twig and leaf stood out dark
and motionless, like a drawing by some master hand.

How can the city be so still? Juehui wondered. He could
almost forget how much turbulence and trouble the city contained. He looked up at the full moon riding silently through
the limitless night sky.

"A beautiful moon!" Huiru sighed admiringly. He asked
Juehui, "After you leave here aren't you going to miss this place
even a little?"

Juehui didn't answer.

"What's so special about this city?" Cunren demanded.
"When he goes down river he'll find much nicer places."

"All of my dearest friends are here. Of course I'll miss Chengdu," Juehui said awkwardly.

He bade goodbye to his companions at his gate and walked through the compound directly to Juexin's room. He found Big Brother and Juemin engaged in conversation. After hesitating a moment, Juehui announced:

"I'm leaving tomorrow morning, Big Brother."

"Tomorrow? But I thought you said three days from now. . . ." Juexin paled and rose from his chair.

Juemin, startled, also stood up. He stared at Juehui.

"The ship has been chartered by a relative of Cunren, and he's decided to sail tomorrow. I only found out this evening, myself," said Juehui morosely.

"So soon!" said Juexin, disappointed, supporting himself with one hand on his desk. "You only have one more night at home."

"Big Brother," Juehui said sadly. Juexin turned to look at him with tears in his eyes. "I wanted to come home early and have dinner with you both. But the boys insisted on giving me a send-off. That's why I'm so late. . . ." Juehui swallowed the rest of his words.

"I'll get Qin. She'll want to speak to you. Tomorrow, there'll probably be no time," said Juemin.

Juehui held him back. "Don't you know what time it is? You'll have to knock at her gate and get everybody up. It will attract too much attention."

"Then she won't be able to see you before you leave. She'll be very disappointed. She told me several times to let her know when you were going."

"We'll call on her first thing in the morning. I'm sure there'll still be time," said Juehui, observing Juemin's distraught countenance. Actually he wasn't at all sure whether he would be able to see Qin or not.

"Is your luggage packed?" Juexin asked hoarsely.

"I've already sent it down to the pier. There isn't much. Just a roll of bedding, a basket hamper and a small trunk."

"You're not taking enough to eat. I have a few cans of ham someone sent me. I'll get them for you." Without waiting for a reply, Juexin went into the next room and brought out four cans.

"I don't need that many. "I'll be able to buy things along the way," Juehui said when he saw his Big Brother wrapping up the cans.

"It's always better to take a little extra. Anyhow, I don't need them." Juexin placed the bundle in front of Juehui. "I'm sending you money by the method we agreed upon last time. It will be waiting for you in the Chongqing, Hankou and Shanghai post offices. Just take your postal money orders in and cash them. If the money I gave you yesterday isn't enough, you can have some more."

"Plenty. It's not a good idea to carry too many silver dollars. Luckily, the roads are fairly safe now."

"Yes. The roads are fairly safe now," Juexin echoed mechanically.

Juemin and Juehui exchanged a few words.

"You ought to go to bed, Third Brother," Juexin urged. "You have to get up early tomorrow. You'll be living on a crude, wooden ship for several days. You'd better rest."

Juehui murmured an assent.

"You'll be on your own after this. Dress warmly and eat properly. You're often neglectful about such things. It's not like being at home. If you get sick, there'll be no one to look after you."

Juehui nodded.

"Don't forget to write along the way. I'll send you your books when you reach Shanghai. You needn't stint too much on money. Whatever school you enter, I'll pay your expenses. Don't worry about the family. As long as I'm here, I won't let any of them interfere." Juexin was almost weeping.

With an effort, Juehui controlled his own emotions.

"You're lucky. You've been able to climb out of this sea of bitterness. But we. . . ." Juexin could not go on. His legs gave way and he sat down heavily on his chair. Burying his head, he wept quietly.

"Big Brother," Juehui called unhappily. Juexin did not reply. Juehui walked up to him and again spoke his name. Removing his hands from his face, Juexin looked at Juehui and shook his head.

"I'm all right. It's nothing. You go to sleep."

The two younger brothers left him.

"I want to see Stepmother," Juehui said, when the boys got outside. He had observed the light burning in Madam Zhou's window.

"You're going to tell her you're leaving?" Juemin asked, surprised.

"No," Juehui smiled. "I just want to see her. It may be for the last time."

"All right, go ahead," said Juemin in a low voice. "But be careful. Don't give yourself away." He returned to his own room, while Juehui went to their stepmother's apartment.

Madam Zhou was seated on a reclining chair, talking with Shuhua. She smiled reproachfully when she saw Juehui enter. "You didn't come home for dinner tonight."

Juehui only smiled and said, "That's right." He stood quite a distance from Madam Zhou.

"You're always running around outside. What do you do, anyhow? You should be careful of your health," she said solicitously.

"My health is fine. And running around outside is much better than sitting at home being sniped at!" Juehui laughed.

"How you love to argue!" Madam Zhou criticized him with a smile. "No wonder your aunts and uncles were complaining about you today. To be honest, you are *too* aggressive. You fear no one. Even I can't control you. Strange, you and your Big Brother were born of the same mother, but your characters are completely different. Neither of you is like her. Big Brother is too docile, and you're too stubborn!" Madam

Zhou laughed. Shuhua, beside her, looked at Juehui and smiled.

Juehui wanted to defend himself, but then he thought better of it. Suddenly he longed to give his stepmother some hint of farewell. Later on, she would know what he meant. He came a step closer.

Madam Zhou could see that there was something on his mind. "What is it, Juehui?" she asked kindly. "Do you want to talk to me about going to Shanghai to study?"

This remark reminded Juehui of Juemin's warning. He decided to be careful. "There's nothing special," he replied with a forced laugh. "I'm going to bed." He looked at Madam Zhou's round face, gazed at Shuhua, then turned and walked out. As he was leaving the room, he thought he heard Shuhua make some comment about his queerness.

We may not see each other again, he thought miserably. Once I leave I'll be like a bird released from a cage. I'll fly away and never come back.

39

Juehui slept only a few hours that night. Although he awakened before dawn, he remained in bed, thinking, until at last it was daylight.

It was time to start. He still had to go with Juemin to see Qin. He had to leave home immediately. Juexin saw him and Juemin to the compound gate.

The streets were cool and quiet in the early morning. Abroad were only cooks carrying their shopping baskets to the market, a peasant in from the countryside to collect night-soil, one or two pedlars of breakfast snacks. The sky was very clear; warm sunlight shone on the walls of the compound opposite the Gao family residence. Sparrows twittered noisily in the locust trees, welcoming the new-born day.

"I'm going, Big Brother." Juehui's voice rang brightly in the fresh morning air. He tightly grasped Juexin's hand.

"I'm sorry I can't accompany you any farther," sighed Juexin unhappily. "Take good care of yourself. Be sure to write often."

"I'm going," Juehui repeated. Again he pressed his brother's hand. "Don't feel too badly. We'll certainly see each other again." He dropped Juexin's hand, almost casting from him, then turned and walked quickly away, carrying the cans of ham Big Brother had wrapped for him.

Several times, he looked back. Juexin was waving to him from the gate. Even after Juehui was out of sight, Big Brother still stood dazedly, waving goodbye.

When the boys reached Qin's house, Juemin rapped lightly on her window. They heard her cough, and the patter of her feet. Then the curtain was pulled aside, and Qin's sleepy face appeared behind the windowpane, her hair tousled and uncombed.

Qin smiled at them. Suddenly she noticed the expression on Juehui's face. Startled, she asked in a low voice, "Today?"

Juemin nodded. "Right now."

Qin turned colour. "So soon?"

Juehui stepped closer to the window. "Sister Qin," he hailed her softly, in an affectionate tone. He could see only her face, and he was separated from that by a pane of glass.

Her gentle eyes scanned his face. "You won't forget me, will you?" she asked with a sad smile.

Juehui shook his head slightly. "Never. You know I'll always remember you."

"Wait a minute. Don't go yet." She disappeared from the window.

She soon returned. "Here's something I once promised to give you," she smiled. Opening the window a crack, she slipped him a recent photograph of herself.

Delighted and grateful, Juehui raised his eyes to look at her, but she had already drawn the curtain. "Sister Qin," he called softly. He didn't hear any answer, and his brother was urging him to make haste. Reluctantly, he followed Jeumin out of the compound.

The brothers hurried along the street, talking as they walked. When they reached the pier, Cunren and Huiru were there waiting for them.

Huiru cheerfully pumped Juehui's hand. "We've been here for ages. Why are you so late? The boat's liable to go off without you."

"Not at all. Of course we'd wait for Mr. Gao," a middle-aged merchant who had been standing off to one side interjected, smiling. He was Cunren's relative, Mr. Wang. Juehui had already met him. He now introduced him to Juemin.

"Juehui, come and see your luggage," said Cunren. He led Juehui aboard the boat and showed him his cabin. Juemin followed.

"I've opened your bedroll and laid it out for you. . . . This package is some pastries and cookies to eat on the way. It's from Huiru and me," said Cunren.

Juehui could only nod.

"Mr. Wang will take care of everything; you don't have to bother about a thing. He'll deliver you to Chongqing. From there on, it will be easy. Don't forget to look up my cousin when you get there. He can help you," Cunren chattered.

The boat at the next pier had been chartered by some wealthy official. There were armed guards on the boat; on the pier were many people seeing the official off. Now from the pier came the popping of firecrackers. The boat was about to sail.

"Don't forget to write, Juehui; write lots of letters!" Huiru had just entered the cabin. He slapped Juehui on the shoulder.

"You fellows are the ones who have to write," Juehui laughed.

"We're ready to sail," Mr. Wang came in and announced.

"Would you three visitors please go ashore?" The friends seeing Mr. Wang off had already left.

Juehui walked with his brother and his two classmates to the gangplank. They all shook hands.

"Take good care of yourself," Juemin urged. He walked down the gangplank with the other two boys.

They stood on the shore. Juehui stood in the prow. They waved and he waved.

Slowly the boat slipped away. It began to turn. The figures on the shore grew smaller and smaller; soon they were gone. Standing in the prow, Juehui gazed in their direction. He thought he could still see them, waving. He raised his hand to brush something out of his eye. When he lowered his hand again, even his mental image of them had disappeared.

The past seemed like a dream. All that met his eye now was an expanse of deep green water, reflecting trees and hills. On the boat a few sailors plied long sculling oars, singing as they worked.

A new emotion gradually possessed Juehui. He didn't know whether it was joy or sorrow, but one thing was clear — he was leaving his family. Before him was an endless stretch of water sweeping steadily forward, bearing him to an unfamiliar city. There, all that was new was developing — new activities, new people, new friends.

This river, this blessed river, was taking him away from the home he had lived in for eighteen years to a city and people he had never seen. The prospect dazzled him; he had no time to regret the life he had cast behind. For the last time, he looked back. "Goodbye," Juehui said softly. He turned to watch the on-rushing river, the green water that never for an instant halted its rapidly advancing flow.

AUTUMN IN SPRING
(1932)

Translated by
WANG MINGJIE

PREFACE

Spring. The bare brown fields turned green. New emerald leaves burgeoned on the barren branches. A warm sun smiled benignly at everybody. Birds were singing as they flitted through the air. Flowers were in bloom, red, white and purple. Stars sparkled, red, yellow and white. Azure skies, winds blowing freely, and love beautiful as a dream.

Everybody has his spring. You and I, each and all of us can know the laughter, love and intoxication of spring.

However, autumn was crying in spring.

That spring, in an enchanted old town, in the south, I bid farewell to a period of my life.

The autumn rain fell, only to be swept away by the spring breeze.

One fine day after a rain, I went with two friends along a muddy road, over a stone bridge and down a path through some fields to visit a southerner whom I had never met, a girl who had lost her mind.

We stopped at the gate of a fairly large courtyard. A little girl, whose dialect was incomprehensible to me, came and opened the black barred gate, quite different from the one described in my story, which indicated that this was the house of a well-to-do family.

In an ill-lit room, we met our hostess and saw a large bed, a large mat and thin quilts. When she sat up I saw that she was a girl in the springtime of life.

The three of us sat opposite her on a bench. A friend explained why we had come. She only smiled in silence, smile more like crying. Having shot a few silent glances at her, I came to understand all my friends had told me. During

299

our half-an-hour stay, we exchanged barely ten sentences, and I noticed a dozen autumn smiles on her face.

My heart ached after leaving her. Remembering that I had gone hoping to help her, I was close to tears.

A girl, a girl in the springtime of life. . . . For the first time I realized the meaning of madness.

All my efforts of the past years, the books I had written with my blood and tears, had been aimed at helping everyone to enjoy spring, every heart to be bathed in light, everyone to lead a happy life, freed to develop themselves. I aroused their longing for brightness. I placed before them a cause to which they should devote their lives. But all my efforts were frustrated by a force of a different kind. A young soul, when aroused, would only suffer more torment.

So that girl went mad. The irrational social system, no freedom of choice in marriage, the fetters of traditional ethics and clan despotism have destroyed innumerable young lives. In my twenty-eight years of life I have seen so many, many tragedies. In that autumn smile, more like crying, I saw the corpse of a whole young generation. I seem to hear an agonizing voice: "An end should be put to this!"

Autumn in Spring is not only a sad story but the cry of the whole young generation. I will take up my pen as a weapon and charge for them. To this moribund society, I call out resolutely: "I accuse!"

Ba Jin
May 1932

I

My younger sister sent me a telegram from home announcing the death of my elder brother.

I had no idea how he had died. So far as I knew he had been physically sound and planning to get engaged soon.

"Is it a dream? How could anyone die so easily? Especially just before his engagement?" I wondered.

I thought no more of the matter, for nothing around me had changed. There was nothing to remind me of his death.

The following day I received another telegram consisting of thirty-four ciphers, giving more details: My brother had committed suicide by cutting his own throat.

His hands slightly trembling, Xu, a friend of mine, helped me to decipher it.

"What's to be done?" he asked.

I did not know what to say: Gripping my own arm, I muttered to myself: "So it's not a dream after all."

Xu looked at me with compassion. To him, I must have seemed the most unlucky man in the world.

"Why are you looking at me like that?" Before I could ask he had slipped out of the room.

Sitting on a sofa, I gazed at the portrait of Janet Gaynor hanging on the wall. She smiled down at me. The silly girl had not smiled for a long time, so why smile at me today all of a sudden? Laughing at my bad luck? She was a blond with a healthy complexion, wearing a pale blue blouse. But what had all this to do with me? She was just a pin-up girl, and now my brother was dead.

My eyes turned from Janet Gaynor to the whitewashed wall,

301

white and spotless. But gradually there emerged from it a dark gaunt face.

There was nothing special about this face. It could have been yours, mine or anyone's. But no, it turned out to be my brother's.

It was truly his face, an ordinary young man's face which reflected his ordinary life.

"I'm dead." He suddenly opened his mouth. "I cut my throat with my own hands."

"You couldn't have," I countered. "It can't be true since you're here talking to me."

"That knife, that agony, those final death throes! Nobody knows my feelings. No one will ever miss me! That's how my life ended," he said sadly, big tears falling from his deep-set eyes.

"If a dead man can still talk and shed tears, death is nothing dreadful. Besides, everyone has to die," I said dubiously to myself, my voice too low for anyone else to hear.

"I don't want to die!" He pursed his lips, his face livid, his mouth a straight line, and his eyes two slits. I stared wide-eyed as his face kept sinking in until it looked as ludicrous as a bun.

The wall was white again, with no sign of my brother's face on it.

"Damn it!" I cursed myself. "You're dreaming with your eyes open!"

The telegram still lay on the table, that telegram of thirty-four ciphers.

2

"How would Rong console me if I told her the news? Girls are soft-hearted, she'd be sure to cry and feel distressed for me. Better not tell her." I thought my decision was right.

Just then she came in, already informed by Xu of what had happened.

"If you make me cross again, I'll follow your brother's example," she warned, pursing her little mouth. So she too could purse her lips!

Reminded of my brother's pursed mouth I was seized with terror.

"Don't talk like that!" I reached out to cover her mouth but my hand was warded off.

"Let's go for a walk," she suggested picking up the telegram to fan herself.

"Shall we go to the garden under Rock Hill?" I proposed rather wearily.

"No! I don't like it. I can't stand that Malay gateman!" She turned her head away in exasperation dropping the telegram on the ground.

"Have a heart," I murmured, picking it up and putting it into my pocket. "Better go to the garden where the jasmine is so fragrant." I straightened up.

"O.K." she agreed with a smile. "Whatever you say."

So I closed the gate and followed her. Thus we set off.

A neighbour's dog trotted over barking at me but soon ran away wagging its tail.

We walked side by side, but she kept me at arm's length. I couldn't make her out. What was she up to?

The sky, trees, houses and street were bathed in sunshine. A winding road carried her slim figure uphill. Under her short skirt, her legs in black silk stockings danced nimbly on the soft tarmac.

When we came to the cemetery she stopped abruptly. Leaning against the fence, she gazed in silence at the rows of crosses and the tombstones beneath them.

How strange that a young girl should be interested in graves!

"Let's go!" I said impatiently. "What is there to look at?"

She did not move, but suddenly exclaimed with her ringing voice: "How peaceful to lie here!"

"You! . . . You envy. . . ." Shocked by my own ejaculation, I broke off before I might blurt out something ill-omened.

"Don't disturb me," she said reproachfully though not harshly. She took my hand in her soft one and held it tightly.

I looked at her with surprise and said no more.

What was in her mind? How could I ever guess?

Near by, there on two separate tombs were two wreaths, one already withered, the other still fresh.

"This is yours," she said, pointing at the fresh one. "That's mine." She indicated the withered one.

"I don't understand," I said frankly, sensing that something was preying on her mind.

"You don't understand?" She turned to me with a wan smile. I had never seen her smile like that before, and felt it uncalled-for; for it was the smile of an invalid, yet she wasn't ill. It made me feel like crying.

"You must be kidding!" She chuckled. "An intelligent man like you surely understands. . . . My future's gloomy and so I'm like these flowers." Again she pointed to that withered wreath. "You are like those others because your future is bright. The two wreaths are so close but they're not together — just like the two of us."

My future was bright, so I had been told perhaps a hundred times. But no one saying that before had made me feel like weeping.

"That's not an apt comparison! You can't compare men to flowers," I retorted with a forced smile, not trying to comfort her for fear of being reduced to tears myself.

"But I'm very fond of flowers." She had such a ready tongue that I couldn't refute her.

It was true that she loved flowers. Every time I went to her room I would see a big vase of fresh flowers of all colours on the table. On the wall of the room there hung a portrait of her mother, a middle-aged woman.

"A young girl shouldn't linger in a cemetery, let alone peep in surreptitiously from outside." To cover up my depression, I gave a hollow laugh.

"All right, let's go." She abruptly let go of my hand and turned to leave.

At the gate of the garden we were assailed by the fragrance of jasmine.

"Well? I didn't deceive you, did I?" I was pleased.

"I knew all along!" She smiled.

We climbed the steps into the garden. The Malay gateman riveted his beady eyes on her while wiping his hands with his red-checkered apron. He was dark brown, with a bewhiskered mouth.

"Disgusting creature! His eyes are boring into my face!" she whispered as we passed him. "It's the same every time."

"That's because you're so beautiful," I said with a smile.

"Don't talk rot! Are you mocking me too? In that case you'd better leave me alone." She pretended to be angry and hurried away.

I stayed where I was, gazing after her slim figure and slightly ruffled bobbed hair, thinking over her recent behaviour. I began to have misgivings.

I found her finally sitting on a stone bench under a jasmine tree. Her head in her hands, she seemed to be deep in thought. Her hair was sprinkled with little white jasmine blossoms.

She deliberately ignored me.

I sat down beside her and reached out to hold her right hand, but she wrenched it away. When I clasped it a second time, instead of resisting she nestled up to me.

I inhaled the scent of jasmine in her hair, held her soft hand. I did not speak, hoping to sound her out without words.

The plaintive strains of a violin drifted over from a brown building partially covered by the trees on the left. The Malay with his nasal voice began to sing a native love song.

I could not tell where her thoughts — or mine — had wandered.

"Lin," she suddenly asked, looking into my eyes, "is it true that your brother committed suicide?"

"Of course. You saw that telegram, didn't you?"

"Why did he kill himself?" she probed.

"I don't know," I replied frankly. Why did she keep dwelling on unhappy things about which a young girl should know nothing? I asked myself sadly.

"I'm wondering if it's really possible to kill oneself with one's own hands," she said with an effort, her hand quivering in mine.

"That's not something you need know." I tried to change the subject.

"But I must know," she insisted.

"Then listen to me. It is possible, of course. My brother killed himself. It's a fact," I said reluctantly, hoping my blunt answer might forestall further questions.

"To live or to die, which is happier?" she said as though to herself.

"Rong, don't you love me any more?" I asked with dismay.

"Why?" She was surprised. "What gives you that idea? When have I said I don't love you?"

"Your face shows it."

"My face? Aren't you used to my face?" She thrust her cheek against my lips and I kissed her. Her face was so cold that it did tell me something. . . .

"On a fine day like this and in such lovely surroundings, don't you think it's ridiculous for two young lovers to keep talking about life and death and suicide?"

After a pause she replied, "Don't start imagining things. I'm here beside you, how can you think I don't love you?" She was certainly adept at hiding her true feelings.

Yes, she was beside me but our hearts were far apart. How far I did not know.

"Love is a wonderful thing," she said in a low voice as if to herself. "Too wonderful to come my way." Her voice was as plaintive as that violin.

I looked at the shadows on her face which — like a bridal veil — made her seem even lovelier. But this bride would never be mine.

I clasped her to me as my dearest treasure. My tears fell like pearls on her hair.

"You're crying," said she, looking up with a smile which I thought more moving than tears. She laid one finger on my lips then kissed them, quick as a flash of lightning.

But when I tried to kiss her she turned away.

"Rong, you're not your normal self today. You've changed." I was very depressed. "What's the matter?"

"I don't know myself."

"Is there anything I can do to help? Lovers should have no secrets from each other."

"I just don't know," was her naive, frank reply.

I wondered if a rift had come between us.

The sun quietly set. We were enveloped in the fragrant dusk. The Malay, bare-footed, strolled to and fro before us.

"Shall we go back?" She got to her feet and took my arm. We went back down that winding road.

"See me home, will you?" she said as if issuing an order.

"Fine."

"I cooked some dishes this morning, specially for you."

"Really?"

"There's wine too."

"I don't feel like drinking."

"It's good wine a friend of mine gave me. I've been keeping it to share it with you."

Instead of speaking, I eyed her gratefully. She smiled like a flower in bloom. The clouds had dispersed.

After rounding a few bends we walked up a slope. I recognized her house fenced off with green palings. Inside the court-yard there were red and white blossoms.

We opened the gate, climbed the steps and entered her room, a young girl's bed-sitting-room.

"You sit here." She pointed to a sofa.

Then she went to the table from which she took a vase of flowers which she placed on the stool beside me. She pressed her face to the flowers and then disappeared behind a screen.

They were white lilies, purple violets and yellow canna.

I bent over them to smell the fragrance of the lilies and her perfume.

She reappeared with two dishes.

"Shall I give you a hand?" I asked as usual.

"No, thanks. You don't know how. Just sit here quietly," she said with her usual smile.

Dinner was ready now. Two dishes on a little round table across which we faced each other.

"How does that taste?" she asked as usual.

"Delicious. Just to my liking," I gave my usual reply.

She took a bottle of wine from the sideboard.

"Look! It's as red as blood, so bright!" She poured me a full glass then filled her own.

She raised her glass and I mine.

After one glass my face began to burn.

"That's enough," I said, setting it down.

In silence she refilled my glass, her eyes flashing at me as if to say, "Come on! Drink as much as you can."

I downed another glass.

By then she had already drunk four.

Her glowing face was lovely, her eyes gleamed bewitchingly.

"I'm not drunk! I'm not drunk!" she defended herself hurriedly, her voice like a bird singing.

"Feel my cheeks and temples. They are cold." She pressed my hand to her face.

Her hand was hot! Her cheeks were burning! Yet she said they were cold.

"Yes, they are cold." I lied to her and myself, in the hope of caressing her face a little longer.

"Have some more." She raised the bottle to refill my glass.

"I've had enough. Any more would make me tipsy. And

you'd better go easy yourself. You used not to like drink." I covered my glass with my hand and smiled at her.

"It's fine to get drunk. Warms the cockles of my heart, stops me worrying and gives me a little peace. So why should we have any scruples? When we're together the world belongs to us." She pulled my hand away from the glass and filled it.

Then she began to sing softly.

"Rong, don't drink any more," I pleaded.

A smile flashed over her rosy cheeks. She picked up some food with her chopsticks and thrust it into my mouth. "Have some more," she urged, her voice as sweet as honey.

I ate and was pleased. I looked into her eyes. We both smiled.

"My head's swimming," she suddenly put down the chopsticks and said.

"You must be drunk. Who told you to drink so much?"

"Drunk? Impossible. I want to take a boat out to sea to watch the stars!" Her large eyes were wide open.

"Do I smell of wine?" She came over to me and blew at my face. Her breath certainly smelt of wine.

I could not help laughing.

"If you puff at me again I may bring up my dinner. And you say you don't smell of wine?"

"How mean you are!" She patted my head before going back to her seat.

"In what way am I mean?" I asked teasingly.

"Anyway you're mean," she pouted. She kept moving her chair towards me.

"My mind's in a turmoil, Lin." She leant against my shoulder. "I don't want to drink any more. I don't feel like eating either."

"You're drunk. I warned you, didn't I?" I challenged jokingly. "Are you still going to go out boating and watch the stars?"

"Why not?" She rose sulkily to her feet, but then plumped down again.

"Well, I give up," she admitted, shaking her head. "I'm just not up to it, I feel so limp."

3

I found it hard to get up the next morning.

Outside the window, white and red flowers were smiling in the sunshine. There came the ring of a bicycle bell from the gate.

Her landlady's little boy brought me a letter. It read:

Lin, sorry we couldn't go and watch the stars at sea last night because the wine went to my head. It should be more mysterious, more fun too, star-gazing while you're drunk. You should have taken me there. We must go tonight to watch the star clusters and listen to the whispering of the sea. I feel so pent up, I'm longing to roam the seas.

We'll set the boat adrift. You can sit there cradling my head in your arms while I watch the stars and listen to your breathing. That way I shall feel safe in your arms for ever. No one will see us, the stars won't disclose our secret. The whole world will be ours at sea!

You can tell me the names of the stars, those red and green ones, and all the lovely stories there are about them.

Oh, I remember:

I wept last night; why, I don't know. The tear-stains on the sofa and pillow-case remind me of how I quarrelled with you, or rather sobbed out all my troubles to you.

I can't remember the details. Did I annoy you? If so, have you forgiven me?

I never used to drink, but that wine was such a brilliant colour! Besides, it was as thick as blood, so how could I help drinking it? I've got another bottle here to drink next time you come. Lin, if drinking is wicked, let's be wicked for once. Young people often are, aren't they? Please don't refuse me, Lin. Don't put on that serious look like a moral preacher.

There was another note:

This bunch of lilies is from my vase. I know you love flowers and so I specially picked these for you. Let them keep you company for me, and let their fragrance dispel your pedantry.

> With love,
> Rong

"Where are the flowers? The lilies?" I asked the boy in surprise.

"I've no idea. What lilies?" The boy was puzzled and stared at me wide-eyed.

"She says in her letter that she's sending me a bunch of lilies. Where are they?"

"The young lady just asked me to give you this letter, she didn't give me any flowers."

I sent him away rather crossly.

What strange creatures girls are! What was she thinking of? Was she trying to make a fool of me? I'm not a man to be trifled with!

"Hey there!" I jumped out of bed to run after the boy. "Come back!"

It was too late. The child was nowhere to be seen. There was only a dog barking at the gate.

The ground felt warm to my feet. Only then did I realize that I had no shoes on.

It was a fine day. Red and white flowers were blooming in my garden, but no lilies.

I caught the faint sound of a hymn sung to an organ accompaniment in the church and realized that it was Sunday.

Where should I go? ... To find Rong.

The dog barked when I was knotting my tie. The gate creaked open and in came Xu.

"Any other telegram from home?" he asked.

"No."

"Any letter? The letter should've arrived by now."

"Yes, I should think so too."

"So no more news?"

"None."

"Why did your brother commit suicide? Do you have any idea?"

"No. I don't know."

Xu sat facing me. I was on the sofa, my collar unbuttoned and without a tie.

Neither of us spoke for a moment. His sallow face and rather sunken eyes revealed the wretchedness of life as a newspaper editor.

We stared at each other. His face was overcast like a cloudy sky.

"Lin," he broke the silence in a dispirited voice. I looked out of the window fancying that I heard a crow cawing.

"Lin, you shouldn't. . . ." He hesitated.

I looked back at him, pretending to be listening intently.

"I haven't seen you cry over your brother's death."

"No," I said coldly.

He was right. I hadn't shed a single tear. I couldn't force it, could I?

"You aren't in the least upset. All you think of is Rong," he said slowly.

"It's not right. Your brother was very good to you." His solemnity couldn't conceal the weariness in his eyes.

"You don't go to your office today, do you?" I asked abruptly.

I knew that he never went to work on Sunday because there was no Monday paper. I just didn't want him to go on about my brother.

"Of course not," he replied listlessly. Sure enough, he stopped lecturing me.

"Shall we go to see Rong?" I came to the point.

"No, I don't feel like it," he answered glumly.

I paid no attention but knotted my tie and put on my suit, then made him go out with me.

He still pulled a long face which amused me. He was a good man who put up with everything. He often complained about his life, his fate and all that struck him as unreasonable. But it was no use. So in the end he gave up and went along with them. What a pitiful man, a pitiful good man!

The sun stealthily climbed down from treetops to roofs and then to the ground. In many little gardens flowers were in bloom. Along the winding street, shaded here and there by foliage, people came and went. Children laughed inside their gates. A fat Western woman appeared round a corner and soon vanished down a small lane.

"I'm sick and tired of life in a newspaper office," Xu complained again. "Such a beautiful town, yet I can't enjoy any freedom." He looked up at the blue sky through the tree leaves and let the warm sun caress his sallow face. He seldom saw the sun, having worked indoors in the press for several years.

"You're luckier than I am. Everything is so dull in my place: electric light, scissors and typesetters' gaunt faces. It's so monotonous, always seeing the same few people, the same tired faces," he almost moaned.

"Why don't you resign then?" I said automatically, having heard complaints like this so many times.

"What am I to live on then?" he snapped back as if stung.

His logic was simple: A man lived on his pay and so must spend his life earning money. In other words, to keep alive you must sell your life bit by bit. Xu did not want to sell it but he had no choice.

"And there's my mother, she's the most important person in my life. I remit money to her every month. If I didn't work, what would she have to live on?"

It was true that he had a mother of whom he was always speaking. He had asked her to join him here, but the old lady was afraid of the trip by sea. Every month he sent her twenty yuan without fail. I knew all this. Besides, I could tell it from his face — each time he sent money his face became more bloodless. His mother lived on her son's blood, actually!

"A friend of mine recommended me for a post overseas," he once told me. "I might have found a better job there. But my mother wouldn't let me go, and I was reluctant to be too far from her. That would have made it difficult to raise the money to go back to see her. Besides, the manager of our newspaper was unwilling to let me go."

He was the only friend I had, who loved his mother so deeply. Once he had cried for a whole day after seeing a film called *A Kind Mother*.

"I've only one person who's dear to me, and that's my mother," he said. "I'm ready to sacrifice everything for her."

He had his mother whom he loved and often talked about. My mother had long been lying in her grave, and I was not even sure where it was. I never talked about her. Perhaps I had never loved her.

We entered the green gate and saw Rong standing on the steps, in a pink blouse and short black skirt.

"How early you are!" She greeted us with a smile, a spring-like smile, her face glowing like a petal in the sun.

"This is your day off, isn't it?" she said to Xu.

"I only slept for three hours early this morning," he answered, his voice like rain on an autumn night.

"I got drunk last night and quarrelled with Lin," she laughed, her laughter like the chime of a silver bell.

"She was drunk, yes. But we didn't quarrel. She was laughing and crying by turns," I defended myself with a grin.

Why should she harp on our quarrel? We'd never had one. She had been tipsy and wept for no reason at all, refusing to let me go and asking me to keep her company. I hadn't understood a word of her tearful outburst.

"Why don't you have lunch here, Xu? I've still got a bottle of good wine. Really, it's as bright as blood, as rich as blood." A radiant smile appeared on her rosy face.

Her smile enabled me to forget yesterday's happenings. It was impossible that a girl who was smiling so radiantly today could have wept so bitterly only the previous night.

"I've given up drinking. My mother wrote asking me to," said Xu without any hesitation. He took his mother's words for gospel.

Rong knit her brows as if needled. The radiant smile vanished. Her face clouded over. "Mother ... mother...." she murmured blankly. I knew her mother was bedridden, suffering from paralysis.

"Rong!" I called a couple of times to wake her up.

Then we went into her room.

As usual on the table there was a vase of flowers: yellow canna, purple violets and red roses. There were no lilies in it.

"Where are the lilies?" I remembered her letter. "The ones you meant to give me."

She pointed to the round table on which there stood a green vase with the lilies I had seen the previous day.

She took the bunch out, revealing a yellow ribbon tied round the stems. There was no water in the vase.

"I decided you'd have to come to fetch the gift yourself. I think you know what I mean."

Only today however, have I come to understand.

She and Xu sat down to a game of chess while I went behind the screen to her bed.

On it I saw a thin green silk quilt, a sheet printed with blue flowers and a pillow-case embroidered with the words: Everlasting friendship. This pillow-case was one of a pair, and the other was on my bed.

I smelt a scent like that of lilies.

"What are you doing in there?" her ringing voice asked.

"Looking at your pillow-case."

"What's there to look at? You've got the other one, haven't you? Come out and watch us play chess."

"I'm trying to find the tear-stains you mentioned in your letter."

I heard nothing except a giggle. Then she became engrossed in the game again.

I lay down on her bed and buried my face in her slightly damp pillow which cooled my burning cheeks. A sweet scent pervaded my nostrils. This girl was driving me crazy.

She called me several times and I pretended to be asleep.

In fact I was recalling how we had met and how we had fallen
in love.   I was day-dreaming.

4

"Zheng Peirong!"

I first noticed the name on a register in the middle school
of C town, where I had just gone to teach English.

Holding the register, I called the names one by one, pausing
each time to familiarize myself with each new face.

And then I came to "Zheng Peirong."

The reply rang out like a silver bell.   A pair of big eyes
surveyed me.   She had an oval face, and her red lips were
curved in a curious smile.   But very soon she lowered her
head and all I could see was her glossy bobbed hair.

That was how we became acquainted.

Though she was not a boarder, she arrived early and left late.
She often came to my room with a number of questions, and
later some of her questions had nothing to do with our class
work.   When she reappeared after the summer holidays we
had opportunities to talk together.

Behind our school there was a stream on the banks of which
grew longan trees.   In that little wood I spent many happy
hours.   The trees were in blossom when I got to know her.
By the time they bore fruit we had become close friends.

We both loved the green leaves and yellow fruit of those
trees.

Among the green foliage of the largest trees hung clusters of
small, round, olive-green fruit.   We had only to reach up to
pick a handful, which we ate either in the wood or beside the
stream.

White fruit, brown pips and olive-green rind; two pairs of
eyes; talk of everything under the sun.   We were in love.

I left C town because of her.   And recently she had come
here because of me.

Both of us lived with friends.

5

I was day-dreaming, and there was no end to my dream.

I couldn't understand this girl's psychology. Lately she had been behaving rather oddly.

It was she who had taken the offensive against me, breaking through my defences, so that I became her captive. But then she had begun to hesitate.

What should I do?

Girls were really perverse. She often provoked me till I felt quite frantic, yet she herself pretended to be indifferent and aloof.

She was not as affectionate as she had been. She kept things secret from me.

What should I do?

— These problems were preying on my mind.

The sun was shining brightly outside the window. The wind carried in a Russian song which always sounded melancholy.

All of a sudden Rong started to sing softly *You're Always in My Arms*.

I was still lying on her bed, my face buried in her pillow. I had hoped to moisten my cheeks with her tear-stains, but they had already dried.

"You spineless weakling!" I said to myself.

"What are this bed and pillow to me if I finally fail to win her?"

"Finally fail to win her? Out of the question! I can't conceive of life without her."

"You spineless weakling! Why didn't you settle the matter long ago? Why didn't you propose marriage?"

"What if she stops loving me? If she jilts me and falls in love with someone else?"

"Everything is possible, of course. There are no end of men who are better than me. Even more devoted lovers could split up."

— I put forward these questions and supplied the answers.

Rong and Xu were fighting over a "chariot." "Lin, come out and help me!" she called laughingly. "Are you sleeping? Get up quickly."

I stood up and was leaving the bed when I caught sight of a letter under the pillow.

How funny that I hadn't seen it before!

I picked it up to examine the envelope, and recognized her father's handwriting. The letter had been franked four or five days before. Her father, I knew, disliked people from other provinces.

I was very curious to know what he had written. However, instead of taking the letter out I slipped the envelope under her pillow again.

I stepped out from the screen regretting not having read it.

When I reached the table, the fight for the "chariot" was over.

"Did you really fall asleep? Why didn't you answer me?" she scolded. Her face was not overcast, her eyes were dancing. Obviously she had got the upper hand of Xu.

Xu had a "horse" in one hand and was hesitating, I found his look of intense concentration amusing.

In vain did she urge him to hurry. She started humming *Ramona*, beating time with one of the chessmen.

"Why take it so seriously? It's so dull playing chess!" I lifted the chessboard, scattering all the pieces, a few of which fell off and rolled on the ground.

"What do you think you're doing? I'd have won in another minute." She stamped her foot, threatening to hit me, but she was still smiling.

I ran and intentionally went behind the screen. When she dashed after me I lay down on her bed. She cuffed me twice on the head and told me to beg for mercy.

I quickly fished out the letter from under the pillow, waved it in front of her, then made as if to take it out to read.

Her face darkening, she snatched the letter away, thrust it into her blouse and left me without a word.

"Rong, Rong," I called, taken aback by her displeasure. Regretting my gaffe, I wanted to console her.

She looked over her shoulder quietly, but unfortunately I could not understand the expression in her eyes.

6

Xu proposed a trip to South Putuo Monastery. Rong agreed after a little thought. I said nothing. Whether we went or not was the same to me.

The three of us walked along a tarmac street. Sunlight danced on our bare heads.

Her face was clouded. Xu's was beaded with sweat. My own I could not see.

My mind was preoccupied with the lilies she had promised to give me. I feared they might have withered by our return because there was no water in the vase.

Other passers-by were chattering, but none of us spoke. Xu took out a handkerchief to wipe his perspiring face.

The litchi trees were in blossom. Bees circled their branches, humming. The shadows of the lush foliage kept shifting on the road gilded by the sunshine.

On our way we passed the garden and were virtually immersed in the fragrance of jasmine. The Malay was singing his nostalgic love songs.

"How lovely spring is!" a voice cried in my heart.

I turned to look at her. The cloud on her face had disappeared. She reached up from time to time to tidy her abundant black hair, revealing her lotus-white arm.

A girl with a local accent, gaily dressed, strolled past in high-heeled shoes, holding a small red parasol. Xu pointed her out to me as a typical southern beauty.

The busy street was flanked with red and green fruit stalls, and cafés with signboards inscribed "ICE." There were British sailors in white uniforms, Chinese police patrolling with measured steps, and a host of ungrammatical Chinese advertisements.

So many things caught my eye, I had no time to take in the scene as a whole.

In the shade of a huge banyan tree was a small temple, with smoke rising from an iron incense burner before its gate. Little colourful pennants were pinned on the gates of some Western-style buildings, spirit-pennants bearing requests for divine protection.

We came to a dock from which we could see a white expanse of sea. A number of brightly painted sampans were moored there.

We hired a sampan and rowed out to sea.

I remembered her longing to watch the stars from the sea, and looked up. There were no clouds. We were surrounded by blue skies, glorious sun and milky water.

We made slow progress: The wind brought us coolness. As there were no big waves it was almost like boating on the West Lake in Hangzhou. But the West Lake couldn't compare with this vast sea!

Sunshine skimming the water made it gleam like satin. Then a junk sailed over, cutting through the calm water. Our sampan rocked up and down, water splashed her hair.

I dried her hair with my handkerchief. She turned to me with a smile.

"Why are you so quiet today, Rong?" I felt emboldened to ask.

"I don't know. Perhaps because of my hangover." Her voice was still clear as a bell, but I feared the bell would soon crack.

She was so close, I'd only to reach out to take her in my arms.

I loved her as never before, and would gladly have given my life for her yet I couldn't reach out to touch her.

Looking at my hands, I thought, "Come on! Come on!" Then I stared at her as if I would devour her. The next moment, however, I calmly averted my eyes to watch a three-funnelled British warship.

As we landed at the opposite shore, I secretly cursed myself: "You spineless weakling!" I smiled — a wry, cryptic smile.

We took a bus to South Putuo.

On the bus, she and I said little. She kept looking out to enjoy the scenery.

Xu was in a talkative mood and had a great deal to tell me, as he had been here many times before, whereas it was my first visit.

Having got off the bus, I saw a half-Chinese, half-Western-style temple. Two fashionably dressed women in green satin gowns emerged from the temple, their faces very heavily made up. Tailing them were three students, all in Western suits.

Rong turned her head away. The students burst out laughing and, after a pause, followed the two prostitutes.

"You men are really disgusting!" Rong whispered to me through gritted teeth.

Both Xu and I laughed. I wanted to say, "That's because you're so beautiful!" But this time I thought better of it.

The first things we saw in the temple were four giant statues flanking both sides of the hall. When we came to the central hall, some prostitutes were consulting the oracle there.

"Look, how piously they're kneeling!" Xu sneered softly. "What do they want to find out? How good their business will be?"

I felt amused too. But Rong looked very grave.

"Do you think street girls have no souls?"

Why did she ask that? I had never given the question any thought, and never would in future either. I just found their behaviour amusing.

"Probably," Xu said, "to them, money is everything."

"Pooh! You know nothing about women's feelings." She was put out.

Who then understood women's feelings? They were such hypersensitive, complex creatures.

"All right, we don't know," I said, to make her speak. "So let us listen to you. Since you are a woman, you'll know what you're talking about."

She looked me in the eyes, and her face was clouded with an autumn cloud. Gone was the radiant sunshine. It was autumn already for her.

Why had autumn come so fast? Where was spring? Had spring gone for good?

"It's a long story," she began. "It would take days to finish, but even then you wouldn't understand. I'll just tell you one thing: A close friend of mine in our primary-school days is now a prostitute. I know she's a very good woman."

"How do you know? People change. Good people may go to the bad," Xu challenged her.

I suddenly remembered that Xu, like Schopenhauer and Strindberg, was a misogynist. It was said that a woman had jilted him, though he himself would not admit this.

"That friend of mine is really a good person, but she's the victim of her parents' prejudice," Rong continued. "She wrote to me only recently."

This was news to me. She had never told me about it.

Her friend might be a good woman, but what had that to do with me? Rong still kept many secrets from me. I had thought I had won her heart and soul. Evidently I had been wrong.

I followed Rong and Xu, filled with jealousy. I was jealous of those secrets she kept from me.

We encountered a group of students and some women. The men smiled at the sight of the women. But my heart was so gnawed by jealousy that I could not force a smile.

We came to a brook and Xu refused to go any further. He sat down on a rock.

"Let's climb that hill," said Rong to me. It sounded like an order.

We went through a tunnel and climbed up some steps, Rong taking the lead. She climbed so fast I could hardly catch up with her.

Halfway up the hill the path came to an end. Under a newly-built cement pavilion we stood for a while, then I sat down on a rock.

Slowly I mopped my perspiring forehead with my handkerchief.

"You look exhausted, but I feel fine!" Her voice rang out like a silver bell in spring. A happy childish smile appeared on her face.

So it was spring after all!

I lifted my hot face towards the blue sky, the free wind. But I had a vision of a pair of big eyes and two slender eyebrows. The big eyes gleamed with love, love of spring and love of the south.

"Lin!" she called.

Our eyes met again. I was enchanted by her big eyes and slender eyebrows. But her expression kept changing rapidly, spring and autumn alternating in a flash.

"Lin, do you still love me? As much as before?" she asked abruptly, her voice like the strains of a flute on a spring night. Her eyes were misted over, threatening rain.

Whether this would be a spring shower or autumn rain, I had no idea. My heart was quivering.

That was the question I had wanted to ask, yet she had forestalled me. So we thought alike though neither of us knew the other's mind. But now we had the chance to confide in each other. However, I hesitated for fear another mist might rise to hide our true feelings.

"Rong, you know me, know my heart. I never tell lies. I love you, love you more than ever before!"

My voice trembled. In my anxiety and fear, I did not speak fast lest she might misunderstand me.

All my blood had rushed to my face. I looked into her eyes, waiting. . . .

"Don't wait! Take her in your arms and kiss her!" my heart urged me. "Tell her your doubts and anxiety. Tell her you want to know all her secrets. Tell her how she's made you feel these last few days!"

My hands were shaking but they did not reach out.

She looked at me without a word.

"She knows now! Hurry up!" I urged myself.

Then I saw the rain in her big eyes which gleamed darkly. Rain, autumn rain! My heart was drenched.

"Rong, I love you, shall always love you! I can't live without you. I wish I could cut out my heart to show you what a place you have in it." I spoke as if declaiming a poem, and felt I had said all there was to say. In fact, I had left out the most important thing.

My eyes brimmed over with tears — a summer downpour. I seemed to hear thunder.

"Don't hesitate, Rong. I've given you my whole self. For you, I'll gladly sacrifice everything."

I could see nothing except her face, hear nothing except her voice.

"Are you sure you wouldn't regret it if you sacrificed everything for me?" This was not the sound of a silver bell but fluting on a rainy autumn night.

My heart trembled again at the thought that autumn had come back.

"No, I'll never regret it. True love knows no regrets."

What I wanted to ask her, but didn't, was: "Why are you still hesitating? Have you had a change of heart?"

"I believe you," she said, then broke off.

I was saved, I thought.

She had faith in me and loved me, so that was that. But why had she broken off short there?

I stood up, looking at her face which was in the sunshine. The tears in her big eyes were gleaming. The clouds had dispersed and spring had reappeared.

How fast a girl's feelings and expression could change!

"I believe you. But if you have a change of heart later, I'll cut my throat like your brother."

She rose to her feet too and smiled at me. The silver bell had sounded again, but I was not sure whether it was spring or autumn.

So she still remembered my brother whom I had long since forgotten.

"Let's go down and not keep Xu waiting too long," she said.

I followed her down to rejoin Xu by the brook. By then there was no sign of tears in her eyes.

7

We had dinner in her room.

Afterwards she saw Xu and me off, then closed the gate.

We walked in the dark, I with the bunch of lilies in my hand.

Stars, white, green and red, were bright against the black sky.

There were few people about in this quiet district under the pallid street lamps.

I pressed the flowers to my face. Their fragrance made me forget my fatigue.

"What did you say to her at South Putuo, Lin?" Xu suddenly asked. "Both of you seemed to have cried."

"It was just lovers' talk." I raised my head from the flowers.

"Why cry then?"

"We didn't really, only shed a few tears. Lovers' talk often leads to tears."

"Perhaps I shouldn't say this . . . but if you shed tears at this stage, your love affair won't have a happy ending. I've sensed that for a long time."

I felt put out and retorted: "I didn't expect to hear anything good from a misogynist like you. Don't you admire Rong too? You know nothing about love! There's no love without tears."

"No. I've felt something wrong about this affair of yours. Felt it instinctively. I can't put my finger on it, but I'm quite sure of it."

This was like a basin of cold water poured on my head. Although I did not believe him, I lacked proof that he had no experience of love.

"You don't understand at all. You're too biased. I love her and she loves me. No problem!"

"Look!" Xu said, suddenly pointing to the sky.

A light shot down from the sky and disappeared in a flash. I seemed to have heard a faint whistle.

"A shooting star," Xu said to himself, still searching for it in the darkness. "A lost star," he added tenderly as if calling his sweetheart's name. But then he repeated firmly: "I'm sure of it."

To me, his last words sounded like the toll of a funeral bell. I was suddenly afraid.

I covered my face with the lilies. Their cool fragrance reminded me of the scent of her pillow.

She belonged to me. I must on no account lose her.

Having said good-bye to Xu, I hurried back home.

My neighbour's dog barked at the gate at the sound of my footsteps. When I drew nearer it recognized me and ran away, wagging its tail.

I carried the flowers into my room, changed the water in the vase and put in the lilies, then I placed the vase on a little table beside my bed.

I lay on my bed gazing at the flowers.

They looked limp though not withered. The fresh water, I thought, would revive them.

I would take good care of them because they symbolized our love.

8

The spring time of our love returned! I had a few happy days
in which, although there fell some autumn rain, the sky soon
cleared again.

She sent me an enlarged photograph of herself. I took down
the picture frame from the wall and covered Janet Gaynor with
her portrait.

Now it was she who looked down instead of Janet Gaynor
and smiled at me. It was a spring-like smile.

Luxuriant black hair, slender eyebrows, shining big eyes,
sweet lips curved in a smile.

"I love you," — a bell-like sound from those parted lips. Her
two bright eyes illuminated my whole being.

Was I in a dream?

"Rong, I love you, shall love you for ever, more than anything
in the world," I said to myself as if declaiming a poem.

When she was before me I would say: "I love you." When
alone in my room, I would still say: "I love you." I had got
to know her when the longan trees blossomed. I had fallen in
love with her when they had borne fruit. Now the trees were
in blossom again and I was still murmuring "I love you" to her
picture.

You spineless weakling! — I covered my face and sank down
on the sofa.

Xu's criticism came back to my mind: "You're a prisoner
of emotion."

I wished I had been. I dreamed of becoming the prisoner of
emotion. If I had, Rong would long ago have been mine.

How could I become a prisoner of emotion? Lucky prisoner!

I felt I was losing my mind.

9

The telegram, lying on a corner of my desk, was creased. I
spotted it again when I was sorting out my books.

I had received it more than a week ago, but had still not written a letter home to ask for details.

Because of Rong, I had forgotten my only brother. All my love was for her and there was none left for him. He had loved me so much and we had spent most of our childhood together. He was only two years older than me.

Now I began to think of him — more than a week after his death.

I sat down to write to my younger sister, asking why and how he had committed suicide and how things were at home since his death.

The sun crept into the room through the open window. Outside, butterflies fluttered about the flowers. Bees and flies danced in the room.

My heart faltered as I wrote.

The melancholy strains of a violin sounded not far away. I knew the violinist was that girl who often dressed in white. I frequently saw her sitting in her balcony when I passed by. She seemed to be a chronic invalid. Otherwise, in such fine weather, wouldn't a young girl go out for a stroll or to smell the jasmine in the garden or watch the stars at sea?

I put all this down in my letter.

The dog barked, the gate creaked, and I heard the sound of leather shoes. I knew who was coming.

"Lin!" How clear the silver bell sounded this fine spring day.

She came in wearing her pink blouse and short black skirt, her eyes shining, a charming smile on her oval face.

I put down my pen and folded up the letter.

"I knew you must be at home," she said smilingly. "Why didn't you come to see me?"

"I was writing a letter." I rose to my feet.

"Whom to?"

"My younger sister."

"I don't believe you. Show me." She pursed her lips.

"Here you are." I unfolded the letter and gave it to her. She sat down by the table.

While she was intent on reading I watched her face. It clouded over once or twice, then cleared again.

"Well written. It reads like a story."

I smiled, my heart was singing.

"Why don't you carry on writing? Am I interrupting you?"

How could I write a letter while she was beside me?

"Interrupting me? Not at all! I knew you would come so I wrote it while waiting for you. I'll finish it tonight, as anyway I'm not posting it till tomorrow."

"Any letter from home? Any news?"

"No."

She sighed softly and then turned her eyes to my books.

Why should she sigh? Hadn't she just been smiling radiantly?

I looked at her face. The shadow on it was beginning to disperse. It was still redolent of spring.

"May she only feel the way she looks!" I prayed.

"Shall we go to a film, Lin?" she suddenly suggested after we had exchanged a few words.

"What film? Isn't it too late?" I fished out my watch. The spring sun caressed my head, bees were humming around me.

"Greta Garbo's *Romance*. People say it's excellent."

"Garbo's film? Why do you like her films? They're not the kind a girl ought to see."

"She's the only real artist among film stars. Her acting is so profound."

"A girl like you should go to see Norma Shearer or Janet Gaynor. As for Garbo, better leave her to middle-aged women to enjoy."

"You don't understand! Do you think Norma Shearer is typical of us girls? That's as ridiculous as some girls regarding Ramon Novarro as the ideal man."

I stopped arguing with her and we set off at once.

While talking to her on the way, I thought to myself: What a strange girl she is fond of drinking blood-red wine and seeing Greta Garbo's films.

1 0

The stuffy, ill-lit cinema was crowded and humming with the local nasal accent, the laughter of women and the cries of children.

Then the lights went out and everyone quieted down.

On the screen appeared people and action, newsreels, comedies, and romances.

The world around us vanished, we were dreaming with our eyes open. I leaned against her and she against me.

Youth, passion, a moonlit night, deep love, a young couple, another young man, the eternal triangle, an unforgiving father, money, reputation, career, sacrifice, betrayal, a business in Egypt, long years in a tropical country.

An orphaned girl, an alcoholic brother, first love, a trusted lover, solemn vows, sudden separation, a downpour one moonlit night, a deeply wounded heart, a loveless marriage, the husband's fraud and crime, suicide and honour, social misunderstandings, the brother's blame and hatred, a widow's life, a permanent secret, wandering abroad, indulgence, the brother's illness, returning home, the brother's death, life-long regret.

Reunion after a long separation, another woman, a new wife, rekindled ardour, a hurried farewell, illness, roses, meeting in hospital, avowal of love, the eternal triangle, elopement, determination to die, death in a traffic accident.

. . . People sighed softly and the lights came on. The blue curtain fell. Nothing happened. We were still in China, and had only dreamed a European dream.

After drying my eyes, I looked at hers which were drenched with tears.

Holding my arm, she pressed closely against me as we squeezed our way out.

She lowered her head, silent for a long time.

"This society oppresses us women," she said bitterly.

I was struck by this statement.

A few film shots flashed back into my mind: The woman awaking in her sick bed to find that the roses have disappeared. With a great effort, she staggers out of the ward to find them. My eyes were blurred with tears when I saw these moving scenes. Rong, close beside me, put her head on my shoulder. I heard her twice repeat the heroine's words:

"My flowers! Where are you hiding my flowers? . . . I want only you!"

I felt I understood Rong now. My heart bled for her.

Women's lives always make us shed tears. Rong was right to say that Garbo was a great artist.

But why had Rong asked: "Where are you hiding my flowers?" Her flowers were right beside her.

"Rong, this was a film, not something that really happened. Such a thing could never happen in real life." I forced a smile but it was very constrained because I wanted not to smile but to sigh.

"Don't you know there are many such cases? A woman's life is always sad," she answered dolefully.

How could I know that? I was not a woman.

"Rong, shall we have a Western meal?"

"No. I don't feel like eating. I want to go home to cry."

She was already on the verge of tears.

I wanted to ask: "Rong, don't you love me any more? Why do you want to go home and cry while I'm madly in love with you?"

However, I did not say a word but quietly dabbed my eyes. My heart ached for her and also for myself.

"I'll see you home," I said at last.

"No. I don't want you to. Let me go back alone."

It was the first time she had refused my escort. I could not help thinking of the silver bell, but now it was muted.

"She's beginning to be tired of you!" I said to myself. "You wait. The time will come when you'll be abandoned."

I corrected myself immediately: "No. She won't. She's not that type."

But these words could not stop my heart aching. I wanted to ask again: "Do you still love me?"

I gazed at her pink blouse, short black skirt and lowered head.

I loved her, more than anything else in the world. I couldn't live without her.

I said no more to her. But my eyes followed her receding figure. My eyes expressed what I dared not say — but not in speech that she could hear.

I escorted her home, so close behind her that she must have seen me.

"I've seen her home anyway," I told myself. But I hadn't the courage to call her name or to say something to soothe her.

At the green gate, I said in relief: "She'll be all right now." I went up to her.

"Don't be upset, Rong. You'll feel better after a short rest in your room. . . . You were happy when we left for the cinema, but now you've come home so depressed. Have I offended you? Just tell me frankly."

I held my breath, waiting for an answer.

"Let me have some peace!" she said with her back towards me.

She stood at the gate and I had to stand there too, looking at her while she looked at the ground.

"Go on home now."

Having said that she opened the gate and went in.

She closed the gate and leaned her back against it.

"Rong," I called from outside.

She neither replied nor moved.

She would stand there as long as I did, I guessed. But what she needed was rest.

"Let me in, Rong. I want to tell you something."

"Come tomorrow. Let me have some peace today. I don't want to see anyone."

She did not turn her head and I knew there was no hope.

"I'm leaving then," I said emotionally.

I walked away, my steps deliberately loud.

"She'll turn to look at me," I thought.

"She'll open the gate and come out."

"She'll call me back."

"Slow down a bit!" I told myself.

"Turn round and have a look!"

"Go and plead with her again!"

I slowed down and looked over my shoulder from time to time. But it was no use.

The gate was closed. The courtyard was empty. The pink blouse and the short black skirt had disappeared. No one came out to call me back.

I turned to go back to her but after a few steps continued homewards.

"What if a friend saw me? Wouldn't I look a fool?"

"Better go home. There's always tomorrow."

I walked all the way home and she didn't come after me.

The evening breeze playing round my head wafted me the sweet scents of the dusk. The girl in white sat on her balcony. My neighbour's dog stood on its hind legs against the gate barking.

I looked up and saw a silvery crescent moon in the sky as well as a few stars, some bright some dim.

I entered my room, forgetting my hunger, took out the film synopsis and tore it to pieces.

I fumed, "The Garbo woman is a menace!"

The lilies in the vase were dropping, already withered.

Those lilies were the symbol of our love.

I wanted to weep, to weep over the lilies.

I I

"Can it be true that she no longer loves me?"

"No. She's never said such a thing."

"Does she still love me as she used to?"

"If so, why did she behave like that today?"

"Was it a sign of love or not?"

Lying on my bed, asking myself these questions and answering them, I came to the conclusion:

"You don't understand women's psychology."

"She wanted you to go in."

"When a girl says she doesn't love you she means just the opposite. When she shut you out she meant you to go in. When she said she wanted to cry alone, she wanted to cry on your shoulder."

"What is a woman if not shy, inscrutable and devious?"

"You spineless weakling!"

When I was bored with lying there I got up.

"I'll buy a portrait of Greta Garbo tomorrow and hang it on the wall," I decided at last. "If I keep looking at it, I may come to understand women."

I switched the light on to look at Rong's picture.

There was no smile on the face.

I turned my back on her.

"I'd better go on with that letter," I thought. "Write to my younger sister and talk about my dead brother."

"It's after being cold-shouldered by my sweetheart that I miss him," I reflected ruefully, then got out that unfinished letter.

But my mind didn't seem to be working, and I couldn't remember all I had planned to say.

I shed tears as I was writing. I don't know why I was so prone to tears that day.

I felt I had an inkling of why my brother had taken his own life.

12

Early the next morning I went to her home, thinking the events of the previous day past and done with.

I saw her come out from the green gate, wearing a blue checked dress.

She smiled to me at a distance.

"Lin!" The silver bell rang out.

Her face was as beautiful as a spring morning.

"I thought you wouldn't come."

"Why not? Tell me why you ignored me all of a sudden?"

"Well, that was yesterday." She smiled.

"And today? Will you do the same thing?"

"Forget it! Anyway, it was my fault."

"Where are you going now?"

"I was going to apologize to you."

Her affectionate voice was like music to me.

It warmed my heart, and my spirits rose again.

"She's all along loved you. You're too suspicious-minded!" I told myself.

"Shall we go to your room or somewhere else?"

"Will you come and do some shopping with me? A spring morning like this is perfect for a stroll."

Our way wound through golden sunshine, verdant trees, the fragrance of flowers, bird-song and huge boulders.

It was very busy downtown among the fruit stalls, cafés and fish shops. There were no trees or flowers here, only throngs of working-class people.

In a narrow lane I found a small bookshop selling a few second-hand books.

We walked for quite a long time.

"How irritating! Such a big place, and you can't even buy a portrait of Garbo."

So she wanted to buy one too.

"Shall we ferry over to the other end? There must be some there."

Sure enough there were. She bought two and gave me one.

So this was the picture of Garbo, starring in *Romance,* who had reduced so many audiences to tears.

It was the same Garbo with a wealth of long hair, a melancholy expression and high lined forehead, whose apathetic speech reduced people to tears and whose own eyes seemed washed by autumn rain. She looked exactly as she had when leaving the ward with an armful of roses.

"Looking at Garbo's portrait will help you to understand the greatness of women. Despised and oppressed by the whole society, we women struggle, suffer and are destroyed. This is the fate of women who regard love as their lives."

This was what she said when she gave me the portrait.

The portrait of this Swedish film star reminded me of the young lady in *Romance*. "It's impossible," I answered.

Were there really such women, I wondered.

She and I dined in a restaurant afterwards.

We spent the whole day together.

When I left her that evening, I had the portrait of Garbo in one hand, in the other some roses she had given me.

It was a tranquil night. The air was soft. The street was silvery white under the moon. Trees moved in the wind. The sad tremolo of a violin was carried far, far away. A soprano sang *Dream Lover*.

Bathed in soft moonlight on that island pervaded by the scent of roses, I felt intoxicated.

Arriving home I congratulated myself.

You are lucky to be loved by a woman.

13

My younger sister's letter arrived at last. Though a bit late, it was a long one.

It said that my brother had committed suicide because of love.

He had fallen in love with a relative's daughter. It was their first love like that in the film.

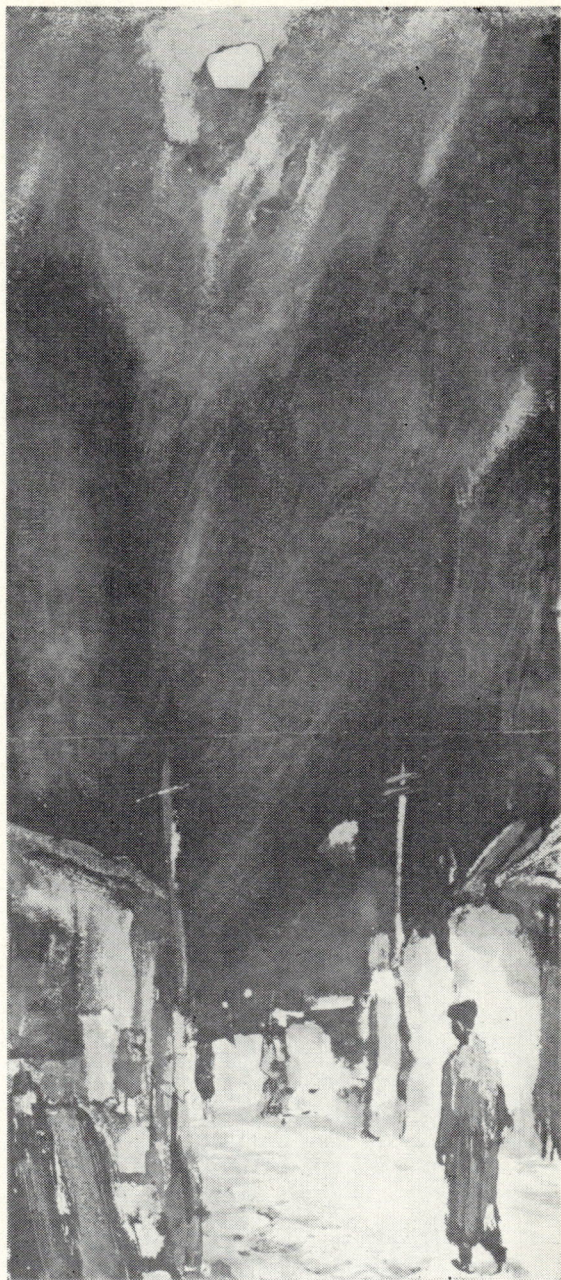

When I left her that evening, I had the portrait of Garbo in one hand, in the other some roses she had given me.

At the same time, another young man also loved this girl.

But money, social status and honours . . . had prevented my brother from winning her. His proposal had been turned down by the girl's parents.

This poetic first love had left a deep wound on his soul.

The girl had married someone else while he himself had been ordered by my grandfather to marry another girl for whom he had no love.

Pleas and resistance were of no avail and he had been driven to desperation.

Eventually he had cut his own throat.

This was how he had ended his short life.

His death had caused more terror than tears and sympathy.

He had been buried beside my parents' tomb, circled by many cypress trees. A few small peach trees had been planted in front of his grave. But they would never bear fruit, though in spring their pink blossom would be as lovely as his sweetheart's cheeks.

My sister also told me that he had left a last testament and she would later send me a copy.

I was anxious to read it for, I was certain, there must be things I ought to know.

But my eyes were already brimming over with tears.

I wept not only because he was my brother and he had once loved me but also because he had been jilted.

In the time of Garbo, there were still men like my brother who were abandoned by women and driven to commit suicide! I had never expected this.

This ran counter to what Rong had said. In this society, it was not women alone who had a miserable fate. My brother, for one, had also been deprived of his spring.

Spring! Why couldn't everybody enjoy spring?

Garbo looked down at me with sorrow instead of a smile.

Had she anything to tell me? Would she say that women's fate was more miserable than men's?

"Rong, Rong, give me an answer!"

14

Rong was not in when I went to see her in the morning.

Her door was ajar and there was a note on the table:

Don't wait for me! I'm going out to see a friend and don't know what time I'll be back. I've left two packages of sweets on the table for you. They come from my home-town. Think of me while you enjoy them. Go back and stay at home. I'll come to you this evening and we can take a sampan out to sea to watch the stars. — Rong

I kissed the note before putting it carefully into my pocket.

While eating the sweets I wished I could kiss her lips because they were just as sweet. But she would not let me kiss her lips every day.

I did not do as I was told. I went to her room again after lunch and had a nap on her bed. But even then she did not turn up.

Thinking she might go straight to my place, I went back home. Then I had another nap on my own bed.

Though it was dusk, there was no sign of her. I guessed that she might not come.

It was a starry night. How delightful it would have been watching the stars at sea together with her.

I tried to find her again.

She was in this time.

I heard a sob from her lightless room.

It must be her sobbing.

I switched on the light.

The screen had been moved aside. She was lying on the bed weeping.

I halted in amazement.

"Why are you crying, Rong? Didn't you invite me to go to see the stars?"

She did not reply.

"What's the matter? What has made you so depressed? Who has upset you?"

She was still silent.

"What on earth is it? Tell me! If I've offended you, you'd better tell me, and I can apologize. Better give vent to your anger instead of ruining your health by crying."

"Not you," she sobbed.

"What is it then? Why need we keep any secrets from each other? Couldn't our love warm your heart? Tell me what you want me to do. I'm willing to do anything and everything for you, even to lay down my life. Please, speak up!"

"You'll know in future." Her voice sounded like the strains of a flute in the autumn rain.

In future? But you're worrying me to death now!

I knew she was keeping something secret. Since I would know in future, why couldn't she tell me now?

Despite all this, I loved her and cared for her. I took her sorrow as my own. When she cried I felt sad.

I bent closer to her, whispering consoling words.

At first I tried to soothe her but soon I too was weeping bitterly over all my grievances.

We stopped finally and regarded each other with tearful eyes, then smiled. I did not know why I had cried or why I smiled.

Love was like a game.

But I felt I loved her more than ever before and she seemed to feel the same.

We brewed some tea.

When I left her it was already late at night. She attentively saw me off.

It was really a beautiful night with all those stars in the dark sky.

I found Orion. Three stars in the middle made a short sloping line, and outside each of the four corners shone a bright star, one of them a brilliant red. These seven stars were my old friends. I could always find them whatever their place in the firmament among all the other stars sparkling overhead.

Oh, the everlasting stars!

I hoped that our love would prove as everlasting.

15

Before I got up in the morning she had sent somebody to me
with a slip of paper:

> Don't come to see me! I'm going to do some shopping with a
> girl friend. Here's a bunch of lilies for you. Put them near your
> pillow and have a nice dream with them beside you. When you
> awake you'll see me already beside you. — Rong.

I took the lilies and pressed them against my face. Their
fragrance reminded me of the scent of her hair.

"Rong," I murmured her name again and again till I fell
asleep.

When I woke up, not knowing the time, I smelt the flowers.

The lilies were still close to my pillow. But she had not
come.

On a sudden impulse I decided to go and see her.

I hurriedly put on my clothes and went out.

I walked lightly through the soft breeze, fresh air, bright
sunshine, shade of verdant trees, scent of flowers and songs
of birds.

How beautiful spring was! Especially this spring that had
brought me love.

I leapt and laughed on the street. I smelt the scent of
lilies and though I hadn't much of a voice I hummed *Where
Is My Song of All Songs*.

Very soon I saw her gate.

"Slow down a bit," I thought. "She is not expecting me.
What shall I say first?"

"Perhaps she is out, in which case the door will be locked."

"Who did she go out with? Who is this girl friend?"

"She's probably stayed at home to pull my leg. Lovers get
up to all sorts of games."

However, my speculations were cut short.

The gate opened and out came two figures. Two faces
flashed past me. They were a man and a girl.

The girl was Rong. The man was in his thirties, with fat cheeks and a sparse moustache. A stranger!

They walked away from me.

"Who is that man?"

All my blood rushed to my face.

"She has cheated you. Catch up with them and unmask her!" I said to myself and set off in pursuit.

"Who is that man? What's their relationship?" I hesitated.

"Must be her lover. No wonder she's been behaving so oddly recently."

"Stop making a fool of yourself," I warned myself.

I stood there at a loss. The blue checked blouse and the blue serge suit disappeared round a corner.

I let them go quietly, standing there without making a sound for fear they might turn and see me.

Slowly, I approached the green gate.

The gate looked very attractive in the sunshine with red and white flowers behind it.

Her window was open, but screened by green wire gauze and a white lace curtain.

Leaning against the gate I scrutinized all before me.

My heart ached, gnawed by jealousy, disappointment and loneliness.

I stared intently at the house.

What made me do that? Would I never see it again? I did not know the answer.

"I'll stay here all day if need be till she comes back," I said to myself.

"When I get home I must have a good cry," I thought.

I wanted to cry then and there. I could not wait any longer.

Cry, poor man! You have been cheated by a woman.

I dragged myself away.

There was no sunshine in the street, no fragrant flowers, no shady trees. I could not see them because my eyes were filled with tears of sorrow.

The way home seemed extremely long today.

As soon as I got back I sank down on the sofa as if I had had a long journey.

"It's not worth crying for a girl. I'm not a man to be trifled with."

However, tears, blinding tears, were running down my face. I had so many tears to shed!

Suddenly the word "suicide" loomed large in my mind. I thought of my dead brother.

"Suicide is the best revenge for a man who has been jilted.

"But will she know why I commit suicide?

"Probably not.

"Even if she does, what good will that do me? I shan't have any consciousness by then, besides, she won't grieve for me.

"I'll write a last testament as my brother did.

"But people may not believe me. She's alive and able to defend herself, but I couldn't come back from the grave to answer her.

"What good would it do me if people did believe me? Some would curse me as a fool, others might write a play about me and stage it to earn money. So many men kill themselves because they are jilted, but not a single woman is punished for it.

"Better kill her and be the first man to punish a jilt.

"But she is so lovely. It would be a pity to kill her!

"Better kill that fat-faced fellow. See if she still cheats me after her lover's dead.

"But he may not be her lover. I've never seen him before. If she loves him why should she cheat me? She could simply ignore me.

"Perhaps she's only got to know him recently.

"But why should she love a man in his thirties? I'm not necessarily inferior to him. How can she abandon me for him?

"She must be trying to get hold of us both.

"No, she is not that type. The girl I love would never do such a thing.

"Besides, they weren't walking in the way lovers do.

"That man is not her lover.

"They didn't deliberately avoid me. Why didn't I catch up and have it out with them?

"Yes, that's what I should have done. Then things would have been cleared up.

"It's my fault. Didn't she tell me not to call? Why didn't I listen to her?

"You spineless, suspicious weakling!"

That was my conclusion.

The lilies beside my bed looked limp.

I had forgotten to put them in the vase, had not taken good care of what she had given me.

I went to pick up the flowers and sniffed at them. Already they were losing their scent.

"She would shed bitter tears if she knew this," I thought.

I changed the water in the vase and put the lilies in it, hoping the clean water would revive them.

"You must live on," I prayed, "to symbolize our everlasting love."

Xu came in unexpectedly.

He was puzzled by my expression.

"Have you been crying, Lin?"

Instead of replying, I turned to look at the portrait of Garbo.

"What did you cry for?"

I was still silent, my eyes now on the portrait of Rong.

"Must be because of love, because of Rong." He sat down on the sofa.

"Lin, I said your love would not have a happy ending," he went on gloomily.

"Nonsense," I retorted with anger.

"I'd like to advise you not to take love too seriously. Men do not live only on love."

I wanted to break in: "Live on money, eh?" But I thought better of it.

"Because of love you forget friendship. Because of Rong you forget your brother. It's not right, is it? Besides, a man of your age should get down to work. Instead, you're fooling about with a girl day in and day out or lying on your bed weeping. Do you still call yourself a man?"

He seemed to be reciting a text.

"Can he have seen Rong and that fellow too?" This question flashed into my mind.

But I thought immediately: "You know the way he talks. Never mind about it!"

I stepped to the desk suddenly and took out my sister's letter from a drawer. "Have a look," I said, passing a few pages to him. "Some details about my brother's death." I thought: "This should shut you up."

He sighed while reading it. Afterwards he said: "Look, this should be a lesson to you."

"But what would you do about those who are willing to be cheated by women without ever complaining?" I was stubborn.

"You can do nothing about them. Say there's a well in front of you, and I ask you not to jump in, but you insist. What can I do?"

"Well then, you'd better shut up!" I said with a grin not of amusement but anger, though I was not angry with him.

16

She came to me soon after I had got up in the morning.

"An early visitor!" I said, tongue in cheek.

"You're being sarcastic. Is it because of yesterday?" She smiled an autumn smile.

"Yesterday?" I asked, my voice trembling.

"I said I'd come but I didn't."

So it was that.

"Ask her! Who was that man?" I urged myself.

"Who's that. . . ." I faltered.

"Who's what?" She blushed faintly, her eyes sparkled.

". . . That girl friend of yours — the one you went out with in the morning."

I found it difficult to speak, my face had turned red too.

"You're lying! She'll correct you," I warned and consoled myself.

"Oh! That girl. Yes, she is from my home-town and I have to show her round for a couple of days. We went to South Putuo for the day, going early in the morning and not coming back till the evening. Then we went boating and watched the stars, those beautiful stars at sea."

"A likely story!" I thought with indignation.

Her unnatural way of talking convinced me that she was lying. Besides, I had seen that man with my own eyes.

"I knew you'd make a day of it, so I went to bed early instead of waiting for you."

I was able to tell a lie too. There was nothing wrong in paying her back in kind.

But I had got up quite late. How to explain that?

"She's leaving tomorrow. No one will ever disturb us in future."

She said that as if telling the truth.

"What's her name?"

"Lin Xiujuan."

"Lin Xiujuan," I repeated, in my mind a picture of the man in his thirties with fat cheeks and a sparse moustache. His name was Lin Xiujuan? I almost laughed.

"How lovely those lilies are!" she said looking at them on the desk. "I sent the boy to buy some, but he came back with such poor ones that I almost cried. I had to go and buy these myself."

This time she had told the truth. I should be grateful and forgive her despite her lies.

The lilies were indeed lovely. They had revived overnight I was delighted to see.

Those lilies were the symbol of our love. It would revive too, wouldn't it?

We began talking in our usual way, talking of love.

At first, I could distinguish lies from truth. But soon I took all she said, even lies, as truth. I was sure that it was the same with her.

Love was a strange thing, sort of game. But instead of our playing it, it played with us. If in a good mood it would give us wine; other times it would give us tears.

Never mind whether she lied to me or did not love me, so long as she often came to me with smiles and flowers. I loved her anyway. I would take her lies as truth. If she kissed me too, so much the better.

17

I received my brother's last testament. It was not long, less than ten thousand words altogether.

Judging by the contents, it had not been written all on one day, but had probably taken him more than a week from beginning to end. In fact, the dots at the end indicated that he still had more to write.

> I am killing myself of my own accord, because I want to die. No one has forced me to do this. No one else is responsible for my death.

This was the beginning of his testament.

> I want to die because, to me, death is preferable to life. I don't hanker after life. What I hanker after....
> I love her, shall love her until death and still wish her happy....
> I am killing myself not because of love, but because life is unbearable. An unbearable life should be ended, as others have said before.

So up to his death my brother had talked in this high-sounding way. But on another occasion he wrote:

Why should she marry into the Wang family? Didn't she often assure me that she did not love that man, loved only me?

Another day he wrote:

She's married! My sister says though it was her mother's idea she herself was willing.

So all her vows were lies. What a fool I've been! She's cheated me for so long, yet I believed her implicitly.

Another day he wrote:

It's too bad that you men who are cheated by women will never wake up to the fact! The best thing for you is to commit suicide!

He wrote later:

Will my suicide haunt her and make her remember me for ever? Probably not. Women have poor memories.

One day he wrote:

I'm not killing myself because of her. She's not worth it.

Later:

Actually I am killing myself because of her. I can't live on without her. Can a loveless life be called a life?

Another day:

There was so much in the past worth dwelling on! Moonlit nights, windy wet evenings, spring gardens and autumn suburbs, all the world seemed ours. There were only flowers, light, love and warmth in my life. But now? All these have become bitter memories.

She who stole my heart away had a voice like music and a smile like an angel's, so innocent and pure. How could she bear to leave me for another? Will she forget all her sacred vows? Will she make up her face, dress gaudily and fool away her time with that man on theatre-going, shopping and gambling?

No, I'm sure she won't. I'd rather die than see her behave that way. But that's what she's doing now.

He wrote on another page:

An arranged marriage, a match without love, the old traditional concept ... have ruined my happiness. Can I tolerate all these and live on?

My ruthless grandfather, her ruthless parents, have robbed us of our youth. Do you know the bitterness of a life without youth? ...

On another page:

You refuse me what I want and force on me waht I don't want. You don't understand my feelings yet judge me by your own.

To give yourselves temporary satisfaction you're ruining my life. Don't you realize that, if you had your way, I should have to play a tragic role all my life?

Such a life would be piecemeal murder. It would be better....

Another day:

I have ready a knife — my salvation. It will relieve me of this unbearable life.

I've downed a glass of rose wine by way of a farewell drink. The world is saying goodbye to me. The wine is as red as blood. I've gulped my own blood.

Later:

The moon is beautiful. I can't die on such a fine moonlit night. If only I could see her once more under the moon in her pale blue blouse, smiling an innocent smile. All I want is to say one word to her or to kneel down before her to be kissed, then I would sink happily into the nether world.

But this is only an unattainable dream.

Another day:

Take action! Take up the knife! Is there anything you cannot part with in this life?

Everyone has to die. That goes for me too. Better take up the knife rather than be killed bit by bit.

I'm willing to die. Let others live while I die. She will live on, but the girl I loved is as good as dead already.

I'm drinking the last glass of rose wine. I'm tipsy.

Tomorrow somebody else will drink wine made of my blood.

Wait till tomorrow....

This testament was in my sister's keeping. Apart from her, I was the only one to read it.

18

Rong came to see me that same evening after I had received my brother's testament. While reading the testament I had forgotten Rong, but when I saw her I forgot my brother.

My girl had not betrayed or jilted me. She never made up her face heavily, never wore gaudy clothes. She never fooled about with other men in theatres, stores or at gambling tables. Her voice was like the chime of a silver bell, her smile as warm as sunshine. She had won my heart. Because of her, I forgot my brother. Still, that was justified.

"Lin," she called, her voice warmer than ever before. But I sensed there was something wrong.

I guessed that she was upset because I hadn't been to see her that day. I felt that I had wronged her.

"I received my brother's testament today. So...." I said as if to excuse myself.

"Lin, I've decided to go home." She spoke firmly yet, to me, her voice sounded once more like fluting one autumn evening.

"Go home?" Forgetting myself, I cried out in a voice which shook the house. Her going home would be the end of our affair.

"Yes, I'm leaving tomorrow morning. My mother's ill.... Besides, I've something to discuss with my father."

"Tomorrow? So urgent? I thought you would never go home!" Sinking despairingly down on the sofa, I felt like crying.

"Lin," her voice was more tender than ever, "don't worry. I'll be back in three or four days."

"Impossible. You won't, you'll never come back." Forgetting everything else, I fought to hold back my fast vanishing hope.

"She will leave you for good." These words were engraved on my mind. I buried my face in my hands.

She began to sigh. The sound made my heart ache.

She came over and sat down beside me. Nestling against me, she stroked my hair with her soft hand.

I remembered: When I was a small boy and cried for something, an equally soft hand had stroked my head. That was my mother's hand which had already rotted in her grave.

Now this hand had taken its place. But only for such a short time. This hand was going to leave me for ever too.

"Lin, believe me. I love you, love you with all my heart.

"I love you more than anything else, even myself.

"I shall always be true to you.

"What makes you think that I won't come back?

"Who else deserves my love except you?

"I love you and will never leave you.

"You're the only one in the world whom I love.

"Believe me, I'll be back in three or four days.

"No pressure can diminish my love for you.

"My love for you is as everlasting as the stars. . . ."

There were tears in what she said. It was like autumn rain soaking my heart.

My heart was bleeding.

"Please, don't go home. Promise me not to go home."

I held her hand and caressed it as if grasping at my last hope.

"Lin, I understand how you feel. But I won't be long. Just wait for three or four days.

"I'll be back before those roses in your vase wither."

My heart was drenched again by autumn rain.

"Are you sure? They may keep you at home for a long time. They won't let you go."

The middle-aged man with the fat face appeared in my mind's eye again. Her decision must have something to do with him.

"They'll let me go. My heart is here, so they can't keep me there."

She seemed quite certain.

"They may be tricking you into going back. Your mother's probably all right, or they're using her paralysis as an excuse."

"They wouldn't do a thing like that. Even if my mother is all right, I ought to go back to see her. She often cries because she misses me. As her daughter, I should go and comfort her."

Her tender, melancholy voice reminded me suddenly of what Xu had once said.

Everybody except me had a mother. While she looked after her mother, I would lose my happiness....

"Besides, I have something to talk over with my father, something important."

What was it? Our affair? If she told her father about me that would be disastrous.

"Doesn't your father dislike people from other provinces?" I asked in surprise.

"It doesn't matter. I love you, so nothing can stop us." Her voice quivered slightly as if she was not really sure.

So she made it clear that she was going to talk to her father about our love affair. Why should she go? It was obvious that something had happened.

"Rong, don't go. Asking your father's consent would be running your head against a wall. Why not go on as we are?"

She smiled an autumn smile which made me feel like crying.

"What a suspicious man you are! Don't I know my own father's nature? Besides, I'm going to see how my mother is and convince her that I'm doing nicely here, to set her mind at rest."

Mother, mother, she kept harping on her mother! But I was motherless.

"Why insist on this? Wouldn't it be better if the two of us went together one day?"

"Lin, why don't you believe me? I love you. Isn't that a good guarantee? If I really wanted to cheat you, I'd leave without telling you.

"Don't keep on about it. If you do, I shall get really cross and refuse to talk to you.

"You still don't understand how I love my mother. I won't feel easy unless I go back to see her."

"Your mother again!" I thought with irritation.

Suddenly Xu's gaunt face appeared before me. He seemed to be carping at me in his usual way: "Don't let selfish considerations blind you to what's right. Don't stop her from going to see her mother."

Xu wasn't in the room but in my mind.

What could I say to this? My happiness would be taken away by her mother.

"Go then. Let hope and happiness fly away. My love will keep me company for ever. She won't cheat me. I believe her, believe in her love."

I tried to console myself despite my despair.

19

The night was still young as we went out.

Against the dark sky clustered stars, everlasting stars.

It was quiet and still, the air soft and cool. What a beautiful night!

"Let's take a boat to watch the stars," she suggested. "It's such a beautiful night!"

"Fine," I replied, too moved to utter another word.

"Let's hurry then."

We came to a ferry and got on a sampan.

The boatman rowed us out to sea.

She nestled against me, her head on my arms. I inhaled the perfume on her hair and caressed her.

The only sound we could hear was the plash of oars in the sea.

Both of us lifted our faces to see those sparkling white, red and green stars.

There were lights on the bank. We were virtually surrounded by the night and the stars in the sky.

"There are only the two of us left in this world.

"Nobody can come between us or separate us.

"I love you and you love me. We shall love each other for ever, our love as eternal as those stars."

She murmured softly as if in a dream.

In ecstasy I bent to kiss her abundant hair.

My heart was filled with love. I forgot myself, forgot everything but her.

She was the only one in my world.

"Oh, look at the Milky Way. Like a hazy white belt. Why is it so pale?"

She pointed to the sky while still murmuring.

"It's not autumn now!"

As I answered I gazed up at where she was pointing.

"Lin, see that row of three stars to the west of the Milky Way? Isn't that big yellow one in the middle the Cowherd?

"Oh, there are three others on the opposite bank. Isn't that big pale blue star his sweetheart the Weaving Maid?*

"Poor lovers! Only able to meet once a year.

"Why is there no ferry boat in the Milky Way? Why is there no bridge except on the Double Seventh?"

She kept on murmuring.

I held her close to me, feeling we were in a dream.

"Why are they allowed to meet only once a year?

"Why should they be punished so severely?

"Is it the same in heaven as on earth with no free choice in love? Has a lady star no right to choose her own lover?

"The Milky Way isn't all that wide or deep. Why doesn't somebody build a permanent bridge so the Cowherd can go across to keep the Weaving Maid company?"

We were still in a dream.

"I'd like to build a bridge across so that the lovers can meet every day."

She spoke dreamily, glancing up at me, her eyes misted over.

"Rong, how will you show your compassion for your Cowherd? I'll soon be losing my Weaving Maid."

I suddenly remembered the river separating us. I woke with a start, my heart aching.

---

* In Chinese mythology the Cowherd and the Weaving Maid are lovers, only allowed to meet once a year on the seventh day of the seventh moon.

"I shall come back, back to your side if not tomorrow, then the day after or the day after that."

"I won't be able to see you this time tomorrow. I'm not as lucky as the Cowherd who can at least see his Weaving Maid."

"I shall see you because I've captured your reflection in my eyes."

"Rong, don't watch the stars now. Come closer and let me have a good look at you to imprint your face on my eyes."

"Lin, can you see me clearly? I'm afraid it's not bright enough."

"I can see you all right by the light of the stars and your eyes. Now don't move, I. . . ."

"I feel I'm melting, Lin. Hold me tight. Don't let me go."

"I feel the same, Rong. I think this is the last time we'll be together. After today everything will be gone."

"All will be gloomy tomorrow. Will the stars and the moon over our heads be still as bright as today?"

"Rong, there won't be any stars tomorrow. There'll be rain, autumn rain. It'll be autumn tomorrow."

"So soon! Spring nights are so short! Look, another shooting star has fallen."

"A shooting star! One more shooting star in my life."

"Lin, will it come back?"

"No. Once it falls it leaves the sky for good."

"Oh, tomorrow. . . ."

"Rong, do you still remember that gypsy girl's song in *Immensee*?* You often used to sing it. Will you sing it for me again?"

"My heart is melting away. I can't sing. Hold me tight and don't let me go! Oh, today, only today am I still. . . ."

I could no longer see her eyes.

I cradled her face and kissed it madly.

---

* A novel by the German novelist T. Storm.

I could not bear to lose her.   She was more precious to me than my life.

It seemed like the night of the Double Seventh when the Cowherd and Weaving Maid meet.

But tomorrow, early in the morning. . . .

> Today, only today,
> Am I still so fair.
> But tomorrow, oh, tomorrow,
> All will be gone with the wind. . . .*

20

The next morning I escorted her aboard a little steamer.

Having exchanged a few words with her, I was forced to leave by the hooting of the siren.

Before leaving, holding her hands, I noticed that her eyes were brimming with tears.

"Please wait for me. . . ." She broke off there.

"You must come back!" I at least managed to complete a sentence.

"Come back as soon as possible!" I smiled at her despite the tears coursing down from my eyes.

Sitting on the sampan, I waved to her. But unfortunately she was hidden by a fat woman.

"Is this a dream or is it true?" I asked myself again and again, gazing at the receding steamer.

When I got home I sank down on my bed, exhausted. But I could not fall asleep. I wanted to cry yet had no tears. I was too tired to pull myself to my feet. All I could do was gaze blankly at the ceiling.

---

* Lines from a song in *Immensee*.

2 1

There was no news from her for three days. I felt aged.

I roamed the streets from early morning till evening. When hungry, I ate in a Western restaurant. When thirsty, I had an ice in a café. My heart was burning with anxiety.

Xu had not put in an appearance for several days. I wanted to see him but feared his moralizing.

On my own, I felt very lonely.

At night, I went to bed, exhausted, but my mind was racing.

"She's bound to return tomorrow."

"What shall I say to her?"

"Once she comes back she will never leave me again. She'll be mine for ever."

"Will her father keep her from coming back?"

"Will anything detain her?"

"If so, she won't come back."

"She's sure to come back. She promised."

"She's sure to come back. She won't cheat me."

"Just wait. After tonight, everything will be fine."

"Oh, why are spring nights so long?"

22

Sunlight came shining into my room the next morning.

Rubbing my tired eyes, I yawned at the sun.

I had dreamed that she had come back and said many sweet things to me.

I dressed myself smartly and went to the dock to meet her.

I waited a long time for that little steamer. How late it was today. But the other day it had cast off so quickly.

At last it arrived and its siren made my heart leap with joy.

The next morning I escorted her aboard a little steamer.

I took a sampan out to meet it.

The steamer began to discharge passengers and luggage.

I searched everywhere for my Rong.

There were men and women, old and young, but no sign of a girl with big eyes and slender eyebrows.

I hurried on to the deck and called her name. No reply.

I rushed to the upper deck.

Some passengers were jostling one another on their way down. I examined each face carefully.

By the time I reached the upper deck there were not many passengers there.

"Rong!" I called, making people stare.

I searched the steamer twice and still could not find her.

"She must have disembarked," I told myself sagely.

"Yes, that's it," I convinced myself.

I went back on the sampan, climbed ashore and ran towards my home.

When it came in sight, I put on a spurt. Ignoring the barking dog, I pushed open the gate and shouted: "Rong!"

No reply. Everything in the room remained the same. No one had come.

"What a fool you are! She must have gone to her own place first!" I told myself even more sagely.

"She must be waiting for you in her room now!"

I set off at once.

The green gate was closed and would not budge though I pushed hard. I pressed the bell but nobody answered. I knocked at the gate, still no response.

The red and white flowers in the courtyard were beginning to wither and this reminded me of my roses at home.

The green wire gauze and the white lace curtain screened everything inside.

The sun caressed my back, a violin sighed.

I passed the next house and a child smiled at me.

"She may come back tomorrow." Yet a third bright idea occurred to me.

But tomorrow seemed far away.

I must write to her demanding the reason.

"The roses will soon have withered, why don't you come back?"

23

Her letter arrived. It had been sent express.

It was short but the meaning was clear. She addressed me as Mr. Lin.

> Dear Mr. Lin, I realize that our relationship in the past was altogether childish. Now I'm taking my father's advice, studying at home and looking after my mother. So from now on we shall have nothing to do with each other, and please don't write to me or the letters will be sent back unopened.
>
> With my best regards and wishing you good health,
>
> > Yours sincerely,
> > Zheng Peirong

It was her handwriting!

"It's too bad that you men who are cheated by women will never wake up!"

"The best thing for you is to commit suicide!"

These sentences in my brother's testament came back to my mind.

"Cry! One can't help crying over the misery in this world!"

I wept bitterly, my eyes full of tears, my heart bleeding.

I gazed through my tears at the portraits of her and Garbo on the wall.

"What on earth are women's hearts made of?"

I pulled the roses she'd given me out of the vase. Pointing at them she had promised to come back before they withered.

But now they had withered.

I pressed the flowers to my heart and wept. I longed to revive them with my tears, tears that came from my heart.

24

I no longer went out for walks because spring had gone. I no longer went into the garden because the flowers there would never again be as beautiful as before. The sunshine no longer smiled at me, the stars had lost their sparkle.

There was no fragrance, no sunshine in my room. There were only pictures of Rong and Garbo, my brother's testament and my own sighs.

I dreamed all day long, either of killing myself or of her being murdered.

"It's too bad that you men who are cheated by women will never wake up!"

"The best thing for you is to commit suicide!"

But I lacked the courage to take up a knife.

Xu came. Having heard what had happened, he carped at me as usual:

"I told you that your love affair would not have a happy ending."

"But I love her, love her with all my heart," I argued angrily with him. I knew he was about to start moralizing.

"People don't live just on love.

"It's nothing to be jilted. Women are only an insignificant part of the vast world before us.

"There's nothing more foolish than committing suicide like your brother.

"I don't want to see you jump into a well.

"There are plenty of good girls. Why eat your heart out for Rong?

"Life in the newspaper office is so disgusting!"

His moralizing ended with his standing complaint.

"Mother, my mother! . . ."

The only thing he could never forget was his mother.

I had no mother. My mother had died long ago.

25

"I am ill, sick at heart.

"I don't feel like eating or doing anything. I just want to lie down and weep.

"I have begun to pine away. Every day I look at myself in the mirror and sigh.

"Has the peach blossom before my brother's grave withered? Please pick a few petals and send them to me! Those pink petals are just the colour of my sweetheart's cheeks.

"Autumn is already here. This autumn will not bring me flowers but rain, drop after drop of rain to drive me demented!

"It's autumn in my heart, the autumn in spring which is the only season in my life.

"I think of my old home, my mother's grave, the peach blossoms before my brother's grave and your face.

"Who could ever forget the scenery in the Yangzi Valley? I shall be coming back.

"If I'm to die, I prefer to die in my old home.

"When real autumn arrives, I will drag my weak body home."

This was what I wrote to my sister.

26

When autumn approached its end, I decided to go home. The ticket had already been booked.

Before setting out I received two letters forwarded to me by Xu.

Lin, come and see me! I'm already on my death-bed. But I must see you before I die to beg you to forgive me. Come what may, I must see you.

I have been ill for more than a month. Death holds no terrors for one who has lost everything. But the loneliness, the loneliness of my heart, dying a lonely death, lying in a lonely grave with

wind soughing through the trees around, like so many mourners —
how can I stand all this!

There is no autumn sunshine shining on me. I can no longer bite
through the rind of longans. The herbal brew is so bitter, always
so bitter. And my father, like the statue of some god, holds forth
as if reciting from the classics.

I often throw away the bitter brew when no one is around. Why
should I drink it? To me, death is preferable to life.

It'll soon be the Double Seventh. The stars in the sky must
be sparkling! Unfortunately, I can't get up to watch the Cowherd
and Weaving Maid's annual reunion.

When will my Cowherd come to see his Weaving Maid? The
sea, sky and stars ... how I miss them!

I refuse to marry into the Chen family. I assure you, they can't
drag me there by force. I've given myself to you, heart and soul.
I'm dying.

I love you, shall love you for ever!

Do you still hate me? Will you forgive me for writing that
short letter?

Come! Come to me! I shall be happy even if you reproach
me, because then I shall be sure that you are safe, not shot through
the head by my father's pistol.

Come! Come while my cheeks are still rosy.

With love,
Rong

That was the first letter.

Mr. Lin, my elder cousin died at half-past nine in the morning
on the twenty-fifth this month. Before her death, she often called
your name. She asked me to cut off a lock of her hair and send
it to you. That's what I have done.

She died peacefully, her cheeks still rosy, her eyes closing slowly,
her lips curved in a faint smile. The autumn sun lit up her face
and we thought she was sound asleep.

The last words we heard her say were: "Love ... everlasting
stars ... as everlasting as the stars...."

With my best regards, wishing you good health,

Yours sincerely,
Zheng Peiyu

The second letter had been written by her cousin three weeks
after the first — more than ten days ago.

"When did the letters arrive?" I almost shouted at Xu.

"You can tell from the postmark. I kept them away from
you for fear you might cancel your visit home and go crazy

again. That's why I've only delivered them today. I meant
well."

Xu's lean face was flushed and he was stuttering so that it
took him some time to complete this speech. Obviously he was
in earnest, awkwardly trying to justify himself.

This was the first time I had seen this moralist flustered. But
I myself was almost weeping with anger.

"Have a look." I gave the letters to him, cursing inwardly:
"Your morals have ruined me and killed her!" I did not say
this however. It was true that he meant well.

Now this was really the end of everything.

I sank down on my sofa, drew the lock of hair out of the
second envelope and examined it on the palm of my hand.

Pink blouse, short black skirt, shining eyes, slender
eyebrows . . . a figure appeared before me.

But in a flash it disappeared.

I fixed my eyes on the hair and lowered my head until my
face almost touched it. I seemed to smell the scent of lilies.

I kissed it as if kissing a beautiful memory.

How soft the hair was!

It had the fragrance of flowers.

It reminded me of the spring in the south.

But would there ever be a spring in my life again?

About the Author

Ba Jin, the pen-name of Li Feigan, was born in Chengdu, Sichuan in 1904. The son of a county magistrate, he was taught by a private tutor at home. In his youth, he was greatly influenced by the then prevailing ideas of socialism, especially those of social utopianism.

In 1920, he entered a provincial foreign languages school and began studying English. Three years later, he went to Shanghai for further education. There, at the same time, he did editing work for the magazine *Half-Monthly*, engaged in the propagation of new ideas. At the end of 1926, he left for Paris, where he studied French and wrote his first novel, *Destruction*. He returned to Shanghai at the end of 1928 and later wrote the trilogy entitled *Love* consisting of the novels *Fog, Rain* and *Lightning*. He also published, among others, *Family*, the first novel of another trilogy entitled *Current*. In autumn 1933, he went to Beijing and worked on the editorial board of the *Literary Quarterly*. The following year he was in Japan. In 1935, he was back in Shanghai and served as the Chief Editor of the Cultural Life Press. Three years later, he published *Spring*, the second novel of his trilogy *Current*.

In 1937, after the outbreak of the War of Resistance Against Japan, he edited, with Mao Dun and others, magazines such as *Outcry* and *Flames*. Later, he was in different parts of southwest China, engaged in various literary activities. Works of this period included *Autumn*, the third novel of the trilogy *Current*, the novel *Fire* and the novelettes *Garden of Repose* and *Bitter Cold Nights*. He also translated Turgenev's *Fathers and Sons* and *Virgin Soil*. In 1946, he was once again back in Shanghai, where he resumed editorial work for the Cultural Life Press.

After the liberation of Shanghai in 1949, he attended the First National Conference of Literary and Art Circles held in Beijing and was elected member of the Chinese People's Political Consultative Conference. In September of the same year, he attended its first conference. In 1950 he attended the Second World Peace Conference held in Warsaw, Poland. He visited Korea twice, in 1952 and 1953, and wrote feature articles with the war as their main theme. They were collected in two books and he also published a collection of short stories related to the war.

After 1954 he was elected deputy to the First, Second and Third National People's Congresses. After the fall of the "gang of four", he was again elected deputy to the Fifth National People's Congress. At present, he is deputy to the Sixth National People's Congress and Deputy-President of the Sixth Chinese People's Political Consultative Conference, as well as President of the Union of Chinese Writers.

巴 金 选 集

第一卷

*

外文出版社出版

（中国北京百万庄路24号）

外文印刷厂印刷

中国国际图书贸易总公司

（中国国际书店）发行

北京399信箱

1988年（28开）第一版

（英）

ISBN 7-119-00574-X/I·67（外）

01130

10—E—1842S A